TEENAGE DIRTBAGS

**Books by James Acker
available from Inkyard Press**

The Long Run
Teenage Dirtbags

TEENAGE DIRTBAGS

JAMES ACKER

inkyard PRESS

Recycling programs
for this product may
not exist in your area.

ISBN-13: 978-1-335-00996-8

Teenage Dirtbags

Inkyard Press
22 Adelaide St. West, 41st Floor
Toronto, Ontario M5H 4E3, Canada
www.InkyardPress.com

Printed in U.S.A.

To anyone reading this book in detention.

JACKSON

———

PRELUDE
EIGHT MONTHS BACK

The first time we decided to have a sleepover, seven years ago, Phil told me he thought we had nothing in common. I wasn't so sure. We would both turn ten that September. Both of us liked the snow. We didn't like hot dogs, we loved *Mortal Kombat*, and we were both exactly four feet, four inches. There was a lot when I actually sat down to list it out that first time. Phil didn't like living in New Jersey either. Phil didn't like how people talked to him either. Phil wanted to move away from Moorestown the second he was allowed and Phil had never had a best friend either.

The last time we decided to have a sleepover, two years ago, I gave Phil one of my Hanukkah presents and he gave me a slap across the face. After five years of sleepovers. And bagel bites. And forts under beds and falling in love with his family and teaching my sister the drums. Five years of finding each other. Finding all those things in common. All gone. Because our differences just wouldn't stop. We couldn't stop them from mattering. We couldn't make it to high school.

Phil Reyno couldn't stop himself from hating his best friend and Jackson Pasternak couldn't convince him any better. We just couldn't find enough in common.

Tonight needed to be different.

I was sitting in the dark, alone on the edge of the empty theater stage, trying to place the muffled lyrics bleeding in from the party in the gym next door. I thought theaters were supposed to be soundproof, but I could still feel the bass from the winter dance across the hall. The faint pops of music could've been anything from Bruno Mars to the "Cha Cha Slide" and I was starting to regret hiring the cheapest DJ I could find off Craigslist. Budget cuts. Sue me.

The sophomores of Moorestown High could survive a few minutes without their class president. That was what I kept telling myself, sitting on the edge of that stage. The world would be fine without Jackson Pasternak. It was alright to take some time to myself.

"You get two minutes."

His voice filled the dark room, the acoustics placing him all around me. I didn't know where to look when I stood. His shape blocked out the red glow of an exit sign and, in its edges, I could just make out his face.

I nodded. "Hi, Phil."

I couldn't make out his scowl but, if I knew his face like I used to, I was sure it was locked and loaded right at me.

"I didn't come to talk, Jackson."

I swallowed. "Okay. But…but you came?"

"You said you needed to talk. So, talk."

"Okay. Right. I'm just… I'm surprised you came. Thank you."

Nothing. Just his breath. And my breath. And some distant "Uptown Funk."

Phil's voice was all grit. *"Talk."*

I nodded for nothing and took a step closer. "I just... I know it's been...a while. It's been a long time. You were clear. I got that, I did. But..."

I took my time. Tried to say it right. "I'm really not trying to intrude or overstep. Really. Phil, I'm really... I'm really not. But... But what I *saw*..."

There was no use trying to make his face out so I just closed my eyes. I did my best thinking in the dark anyway. "I swear, I didn't mean to walk in on you, Phil. I didn't mean to walk into anything, really. Just with the party and all the people and the noise, I was just looking to find a space to be alone and I thought I was alone and—"

"—Jesus Christ, Jackson—"

"—and I'm not gonna tell anyone. I swear, I'm not. I would never do that, I wouldn't do that to you. Or him. I would never do that to anyone, you know that. I just... I just thought you might want someone to..."

I opened my eyes. I couldn't help it. "I just wanted to check in."

I didn't need to look for the scowl that time. The scoff was enough. "...*Check in?* Eat shit, Jackson. Bye."

The red glow was back. He was leaving. Those were the wrong words.

I followed his footsteps. "Wait. Wait, Phil, wait. Please."

"You don't need to *check in* on me, asshole, you're not my fucking mom."

"I thought you might want to talk about that. About him or about—"

"Not my fucking therapist either."

"Phil, he has a girlfriend."

"Everyone has a girlfriend, who gives a—"

"Philip, he was *kissing you!*"

That stopped him. Right in his tracks. And my face wasted no time smacking right into his back.

Half out of surprise, mostly out of politeness, I jolted away. "Sorry! Sorry, I'm sorry, I didn't—"

But Phil wasn't giving back the space. He had no trouble seeing in the dark and got right in my face. He was smiling. Big and mean. Not an inch of humor to it.

"OH?! He was KISSING me?! Wow! Super! And just what the FUCK does that have to do with you, Jackson? Who the FUCK do you think you are, talking to me about him? What gives you the fucking RIGHT to ask me about that? About ANYTHING?"

"Phil—"

He shoved a black fingernail into my chest. "You might have half this school up your ass now, Mr. President, but you don't get to *summon* me to some dark-ass theater in the middle of a dance to talk to me about me. Got it? I don't need you to *check in*, pal—"

"Philip. Stop."

"I am not your damn project anymore."

He took a step back. Done. A smarter part of me expected him to leave. But no. Phil just waited on that dark stage. Maybe he was waiting for another olive branch to whack me with. Or maybe he was just waiting for me to say the right words. Maybe he was hoping I'd finally found them. The words that could make us okay again. The perfect apology. Maybe he thought that was why I'd pulled him out of the gym so insistently. Why I'd finally broken two years of silence in the hallways and avoiding eyes in class. Maybe stumbling onto Philip in the school woodshop, after hours and half-dressed, smiling and laughing with some boy's tongue in his mouth, maybe that sight finally knocked something loose for me. Made it all click. That feeling that started limping through my chest, clogging up my throat, the second I saw my old best friend's hands on somebody new. Somebody else. Maybe I finally found our way back.

"We don't…we don't even know him, Phil."

He didn't need to slap me. The silence stung enough.

"…*We?*"

Phil had nothing left to say. I had no more words to try. He might have been an inch from me, but I couldn't see his face in the dark. So I built one from memory. I knew his mouth would be tight. A shotgun I'd spent years watching him aim at anyone who might hurt him. Us. The kids who'd call him poor. The boys who'd call me a freak. His mouth always kept us safe and I don't know if I ever really thanked him for that.

"There is no *we*, Jackson. You don't get to say that."

And I couldn't build Phil's face without his hair in the way. Long and messy, shielding the world from his glares. Maybe he'd dyed it again. Something punk. Whatever the style, I knew a bit would be tucked behind his ears. The ears I'd pierced at a sleepover in the sixth grade. When I'd stuck the needle in his lobe, it went straight through his ear, right into my thumb. Stuck me like a pink, fleshy bullseye. He called us blood brothers and we made so many promises to each other.

"You don't tell me who I know. You don't tell me how to be. I've been doing just fine without you, Jackson, you…you fucking *don't*."

And I knew exactly which look would be on his face. I knew his eyes. I knew them better than I knew mine, I'd simply logged more hours on them. His brows would be stern and I knew his eyes would be daggers. Fixed on me. Ready to cut. And under his brows, behind the daggers: disappointment. Another broken promise. Another person he thought he could trust. Another night where Jackson couldn't say the right words.

"The only reason I even *considered* hearing you out tonight was because of him. 'Cause he doesn't know about you and me. 'Cause he... Because he is so fucking scared of who you're gonna tell, Jackson."

It hurt. Like I was someone Phil needed to protect his people from now. Like I was ever so careless with his secrets. With his biggest secret.

"Phil. I'd never tell anyone about that. How... I would never do that to you. How could you say that?"

I heard Phil sniff. "You got a lot of new friends now, Jacks. I don't know how you talk anymore."

"You can't—"

"I don't know you anymore."

My hand found his arm in the dark, but I lost it in seconds. His boots were loud across the stage.

"Just stay away from us, Jackson. I've got something good and it's no one else's business. Not the school's, not yours. Don't you fuck this up for me."

"Don't leave. *Phil.*"

He stomped down the stairs. Walked up the aisles and hollered back to me. "Enjoy your dance, enjoy your life, and keep your fucking mouth shut."

I walked to the edge of the stage. I was almost angry. I was almost crying.

"PHILIP."

Then the darkness was gone. Phil stood in the open double doors, just his silhouette in the hallway light.

I didn't know what to say. What might keep him. I didn't know what else to do. So, I just shook my head. It was all I could do.

"You don't miss it?"

My eyes were stinging. Adjusting to the light. My voice had less of an excuse to sound so weak.

"You don't... You don't miss me at all?"

The wrong words. The wrong question. A pathetic thing to say. But Phil turned. Phil turned around in that door and I could finally see him. Philip Joseph Reyno. From Mrs. Bachman's third grade class. 511 South Duquesne Street, Browning Apartments, 4A. Born way too early September 23, hates tea, loves to whittle, and smiles in his sleep. A fan of Alanis Morissette and my dad's cassette tapes and doesn't like talking about his parents. A great drummer. A better arguer. A really, truly, confusingly sweet boy. My first best friend. My last. I could finally see his face. But it wasn't the one I'd built in the dark. It wasn't the one I've tried to remember. It was a face he'd never shown me until the very end. Until the night he ended it. Cold. It was mean. It was sure. Phil shrugged. So simply.

"I don't miss my baby teeth."

The double doors latched behind him and it was all dark again. I was in the dark again and I didn't understand it. Any of it. I didn't understand Phil. Maybe he was right. Maybe I never did.

After a responsible amount of pacing in the lobby, I slipped back into the gym, dodged a few rogue classmates on the dance floor, and noticed the giant **SNOW GLOBE BALL** banner I'd spent five study halls painting by hand was drooping sadly off a wall of bleachers. Always something. I groaned and searched for one of the many rolls of masking tape I'd hidden around the dance for such an inconvenience. I'd retaped three of the four corners when I noticed Phil had reclaimed his position at the snack table. He was lingering by the same bowl of guac I had so unceremoniously ripped him from twenty minutes prior, stacking his plate high with all the free food he could grab.

"And just where did you sneak off to?"

A woman I was eighty percent confident was an art teacher stared at Philip from across the snack table. I couldn't place her name for the life of me, but she certainly knew who Phil was. His reputation. The woman looked Phil up and down, like he might be smuggling stolen iPads under his one clean dress shirt.

"The rest of the school is off-limits after hours, Mr. Reyno. After-school events are a privilege, the party rules were very clear."

I was a ways away, but I could still pick up the tone. It was the tone any veteran teacher at Moorestown High whipped out solely for Phil and it rarely ended well. But Phil just stared deep into Mrs. Whoever's eyes. Didn't blink once.

"I'm sorry, ma'am. I had a cyst on my inner thigh and it burst. You understand."

"Excuse me?"

He raised his voice over the pounding Black Eyed Peas medley.

"I had a CYST, ma'am. On my THIGH. I had to go CLEAN UP THE JUICES."

The possible art teacher looked more disgusted than concerned and abandoned the conversation entirely. Phil started to smirk at his victory but noticed me watching him, hands full of tape. The smirk turned to spite in record time and Phil found a farther punch bowl to loiter by. But this time, I couldn't blame him. Because, wouldn't you know it, not a single chaperone paid my reentry to the Snow Globe Ball a second look. Nobody asked Jackson Pasternak where he *snuck off to*. Phil Reyno, now he must've been setting a fire or spray-painting a locker or doing whip-its in the principal's office. But Jackson? Never. He couldn't possibly have stuck his nose where it didn't belong, or ambushed Phil on the theater stage, or broken up Phil's very tongue-forward hookup in the school woodshop.

Oh, right. Phil's new secret woodshop tongue-friend. Where the hell was he?

"Hello."

The microphone feedback made a few kids wince and, as if a hundred heads all turned at once, the room was suddenly focused on the makeshift stage by the gym bleachers. The discount DJ had been helping himself to the snack table so it wasn't exactly hard for someone else to grab the mic. And there he was. A boy with a mic.

"Hi, everyone. Hello."

The dance floor was quiet. No one knew what was going on. Because no one really knew Cameron Ellis. I let the last corner of the banner droop.

Cameron teetered on stage and swallowed back a nerve. "My name is Cameron. Cameron Ellis. You might know me but…maybe not. Not a lot of people notice me, really. Honestly, this might be the most people who've ever heard me speak. So…sorry if I sound nervous."

Phones were starting to pop up in the crowd, but Cameron just shrugged, getting a bit more comfortable on stage.

"I'm sort of a loser, I don't know. I like baseball. I like to sing. I like superhero movies and big dogs and vanilla caramel lattes from Brewster's. I'm a lot like you."

I stomached a quick instinct to roll my eyes, but I found I was on my own. The room was rapt. I heard that art teacher *aww*. She actually took the time to audibly *aww* and she wasn't alone. Everyone in the gym seemed fully on board with the impromptu purse-emptying. Cameron pushed his swoopy hair out of his blue-green eyes and chuckled, in awe of all the awws.

"But, you know, even with all these eyes on me, I still feel sort of invisible. Sometimes I feel like I could just disappear. I never felt like anyone saw me."

A pause and a breath for dramatic effect.

"Until him. Until *he* saw me."

The awws turned to GASPS. Scandalized whispers rippled

through the gym but Cameron just nodded. Very ready. *Yup. It's gonna be one of those speeches.* I saw debate girls covering their mouths. I saw track bros pulling out their phones. I saw Cameron smiling on stage and I saw myself cutting across the crowd. Trying to get through. Before I could exhale, I was at the snack table again. Grabbing his wrist again.

"PHIL."

It was like my touch shook him out of something. Phil looked up and forgot to be angry with me. He was sweating. Shaking.

"Oh, shit."

He knew what was about to happen. I guess I did too. And neither of us knew how to stop it. Neither of us knew what to do. Over the whispers and gasps and shock and phones, Cameron nodded defiantly.

"I'm not going to be a secret anymore. I deserve to be seen. I deserve to be loved. You deserve to be loved. You deserve to be seen, baby."

Cameron pointed across the crowded dance floor.

"I love you, Phil Reyno."

I dropped Philip's wrist. Before everyone could turn. Before every single eye and camera in that goddamn gymnasium was on Phil Reyno. Frozen by the punch. In his only clean button-up. Just as shocked and stunned as everyone else at the Snow Globe Ball. I heard his voice. Just a whisper.

"Jackson."

He managed to look at me for four seconds. But I didn't know what to do. How to help. How to put Phil's biggest secret back in the bottle. And for a moment, Phil almost smiled. Despite the glass in his throat and the sweat on his back, Phil actually almost laughed. Because he didn't either. My old best friend had finally found something we had in common again.

TAPE ONE, SIDE A

———

THE INCOMPATIBLE MIXTAPE OF PHILIP AND JACKS

PHIL

TRACK ONE
Welcome to the Black Parade

I was melting into our usual booth, the leather guy toward the back of Brewster's, just listening to them go on and on. The Skwad was discussing queer representation in popular fiction while I finger-tested which butter knife might chop off my head fastest. I'd gone an entire summer without spending any one-on-one time with the Skwad and I had cherished every quiet moment. But Cameron Ellis was minutes away from his grand return to Moorestown after three months of baseball camp. And when one plans a *Welcome Home* dinner for one's boyfriend, traditionally one is required to invite his closest, dearest friends. Even if they are intolerable. Even if they're the fucking *Skwad*.

Augie waved a forkful of apple pie around our booth, trying to conduct the debate. "It's not about the quantity of representation. It's about the *quality* of representation. The queer community doesn't need rep for rep's sake. We can be past that now. Like, how does it behoove me to see two twinks buying fabric softener in a Super Bowl commercial? I'm supposed to settle for that? No. I don't want *any* representation. I want *quality* representation. *Good* representation."

Then Brynn was there, trying to find her dog in this fight. "Valid. But wouldn't you argue that seeing two…*t-words* buying Tide PODS is actually helpful toward normalizing the gay community for a wider audience? Especially in an ad block like the Super Bowl? I'd argue that is good rep."

Doug stopped mindlessly staring out the window and blinked for the first time all evening. "Wait. Which one's the *t-word*?"

Augie groaned and poked at his pie. "*Twink* isn't a slur. Brynn is just being overly sensitive."

"Well, it's not my word to say."

"Say it. I give you permission, say *twink*."

"Augie."

"You're not gonna get in trouble, baby girl. Give it a whirl."

"No. You're not going to bait me."

Doug sipped his milkshake and smiled. *"Twink."*

"Doug, NO."

Brynn slapped his hand. Augie finished his slice and wiped his mouth. "All I'm saying is a town like Moorestown *needs* good representation. This isn't New York. It's not even Philly. We're in butt-fuck New Jersey, our school *needs* good rep. Agreed?"

Brynn nodded back. "Agreed."

In a pointedly empty silence, I realized the Skwad was waiting on me. "Wait. How is this about me?"

Brynn folded her hands together and smiled. "Philly. You know I love you. You and Cameron… I mean, you're *CamRye*, you're my soft boys. But… Phil, you promised. Right here, in this booth, you promised us junior year was going to be different."

I was completely lost and looked at Augie for a clue. I even resorted to Doug. But Doug was no help, far too busy chewing on his hoodie drawstring. "...What the hell are we talking about here?"

Augie scoffed over his Oreo milkshake. "We heard about Dani T's pool party."

I groaned up at the ceiling. *"Oooooooookay."*

"Okay and you can't be calling the straight boys *faggots* when we get back to school, Philip. It's not cute."

Brynn jolted in her seat like she'd been shot. *"AUGIE."*

Augie rolled his eyes and ate his cherry. "Phil's the one hollering it across pool parties. I am literally quoting the man, Brynn."

"Well, you don't have to *say* it. I told you, that word makes me uncomfortable."

I snorted. "Oh. It makes *you* uncomfortable?"

Brynn threw up her hands. "OKAY. I'm SORRY hearing literal SLURS makes me uncomfortable, Phil. I'm sorry I'm SOOOOO sensitive, I'm such a MONSTER."

"You're not a monster, Brynn, you're just straight."

"And I apologized for that!"

Brynn huffed and sank in the booth. Augie leveled with me. "Look. I get it. You're reclaiming it, it's your word now, kudos on making your very nuanced post-modern point. But Cameron's got a lot of eyes on him now. I'm still seeing the video of his little speech every other day, people are paying attention to him. To all of us. And you acting up like this is a bad look, Phil. For *all* of us. We just want Cameron to have a great junior year. He deserves that. *We* deserve that."

The Skwad nodded as a group. I stomached my laugh. *"Good rep.* So, you wanna make sure the shittier half of *Moorestown's Golden Gays* doesn't make the Skwad look bad. Alright."

Brynn leaned close. Considerate. Maybe a little too considerate for my liking. "Philly. You could have a *really* special junior year. It's a brave new world. Boys like you and Cammy are living out and proud. Like, things are SO much better now. Y'know, my cousin couldn't come out of the closet until he was twenty-five. Did I tell you my cousin's gay?"

"Everyone's cousin is gay, what's your point?"

Brynn skipped past five stages in our relationship and held my hand from across the booth. "Philip. It's your time. You can be out now. You can be easy now. You can *breathe*."

I just nodded back. Let Brynn pet my hand. Let her caring, shining smile go stale on her careful, shiny face. "Mmm. Brave new world."

"Exactly."

I looked over to the front of Brewster's. The clock above the door told me my boyfriend was twelve minutes late. He hadn't texted a reason. To me, at least. But the Skwad didn't seem worried. Maybe he'd texted them instead. His inner circle. His *found family*. The third, fourth, and fifth Cameron Ellis had brought into our relationship. *The Skwad*.

"I hear you, Brynn. I really do. But, and I do mean this respectfully, but until one person in this town can give me a solid logical reason why I shouldn't, I believe it's my right to call a classmate a faggot anytime I want."

Doug snorted. Augie sighed. Brynn flinched again. I was reaching the bottom of her well-meant patience. That was what I loved most about this game of mine. Watching people sweat. Watching all their good intentions crash and burn when presented with someone not so easy.

Brynn took her hand back and shook her head. At a loss. "You're not going to get anyone on your side this way, Philly. We just wanna be your friends. You know that. Right?"

That look in her eyes. That honest care. Brynn Forester was

making a genuine effort to reach me. It made me want to shit blood. I felt a boil in my stomach. It always tasted different when it started cooking up in me, but the result was always the same. That mean thing inside of me that made me say things I regretted. That made me call people names I didn't mean. That made me *me*. Tonight, my disdain tasted like spoiled milkshake.

Very slowly, very calmly, I sat back in my seat. "Look. Last poll I took, I am *one* out of four out kids in this school. One out of four out of one thousand, six hundred, and fifty-three kids. Last poll I took."

Augie rolled his eyes. Doug was at rare rapt attention. I powered forward. "Out of that thousand and change, maybe ten or so cared to know my name before the night of the big coming out video. Maybe five of them would say it correctly. But ever since that speech, people who used to cross the street to avoid talking to me are inviting me to their Sweet Sixteens. My DMs are full of kids either calling me their personal hero or an ugly faggot. My mom is a very fun alcoholic who had my sister when she was my age and my deadbeat dad hasn't called me back in nine and a half months. That's *my* brave new world, Brynn. And you want me to make friends here?"

Brynn stared back at me, completely out of her depth. I leaned in close, letting that hateful taste fill my mouth. "None of you cared about me before that video. Nobody cared when those kids were calling *me* a faggot so why do you care if *I* say it? Anthony Lewis doesn't have half as many in-school suspensions as I do and that's been his catchphrase since the second grade. All of my potential *friends* out there have been calling me a faggot before I even CONSIDERED I might be gay, Brynn, so if I think it's *funny*, if I think it is truly HILARIOUS to call straight assholes like Ant Lewis and Amanda Allen and the entire varsity cheerleading squad a bunch of plastic, bubbly,

pom-pommed faggots at some bullshit pool party, I personally
believe I have **EARNED THAT FUCKING RIGHT**."

The booths around us were starting to pay attention. A
waitress stopped in the middle of the dining room to eavesdrop. Half of Brewster's was tuning in to the apparent scene
I'd created and Brynn looked like she wanted to hide under
the table.

But Augie didn't seem to care. If anything, he just looked
tired. A bored condescension. "Alrighty. Glad you got that
out. And if Cameron has a problem with it?"

I squinted at him. Then Brynn. Even Doug. The question
wasn't a hypothetical. I could hear it in his voice. The absence
of eye contact around the booth. Once again, the Skwad heard
from Cameron before I did.

"Has… Did he say something?" Augie looked to Brynn.
Brynn to Doug. Doug to Augie. Silent conversations I wasn't
invited into. At a booth I'd reserved. An event I had planned.
For a boy I'd gone an entire summer without. "Did you tell
Cameron about the pool party thing?"

Augie shrugged and ate the remaining bits of pie off his
plate. "You're dating the Twink Prince of South Jersey, Phil-
bert. He hears about everything."

"Augie."

"You just said there was nothing wrong with saying it,
babes. What? You don't think Cammy will find it so funny?"

I pushed out of the booth and stood. "You people are the
FUCKING worst. Stay out of my relationship. BYE."

Brynn pouted. "Philly, let's talk this out."

Doug spit out his hoodie drawstring. "Yo, check if they
got more pumpkin crumble?"

I flipped off the Skwad and left them to their bullshit. I
dodged waiters and customers in my stomp across the dining

room and found a nice stool by the pie displays to try and cool
down. Rain was blocking out the windows, but I just needed
a breather. Ridiculous. I hadn't heard a peep from the Skwad
all summer because, wouldn't you know, the loveable group
of assholes weren't so interested in me without Cameron at my
side. Though most of town had been the same. Through one
summer of my boyfriend's absence, I realized that the merry
people of Moorestown would tolerate talking to me if it meant
they'd eventually get to talk about my "better half." A realization that shot off angry fireworks in my colon. Cameron was
all people wanted me for. All summer long. Because of that
video and that speech and everything that'd happened since,
my boyfriend had gone from my favorite subject to my biggest pet peeve before June could wrap and now even his name
was enough to get my gut bubbling. I don't know. Maybe I
have IBS, I don't know.

"No, you don't understand, we LOVE you! Oh my GOD!"
I heard the familiar sound of gay screeching. At the doorway of Brewster's, two near-thirty, near-balding men were
taking selfie after selfie with a tall, tanned boy. The boy was
slim but toned and his cardigan was a little wet from the rain.
His auburn hair was damp but still swoopy and even though
his eyes were half a room away, I could still see just as much
green as blue. He smiled for each photo, click after click, always knowing exactly where to look. Easy smiles and white
teeth. Dimpled cheeks and just enough freckles. The men
never stopped their compliments and the boy never stopped
his bashful blush.

"…Such an inspiration…"
"…If I could've at your age…"
"…Great representation…"
"…Absolutely zero pores…"

Customers were taking notice. More pictures and questions and warmth. Like the entire town was taking a moment to welcome their boy back. I stood but then hesitated. I didn't want to interrupt. I didn't know my place. I knew how much he loved those moments and he knew how much I didn't. The eyes were for him. The compliments and attention. The stops in the street and the tears on the cheeks. I didn't need all that.

"Cam?"

I just needed him.

Cameron noticed me. And he smiled. He excused himself from the men and the pictures and all that love and walked right for me. He was so tan. He didn't look that tan in his pictures, but things were different face-to-face. His hair was all sandy from the sun and he looked stronger. Taller.

"You're… You got taller—"

Cameron brought my face close and kissed me. The room cheered for us, but I tried not to notice and made sure to kiss him back. At first it was like I'd forgotten how, but I remembered pretty quick. He kissed my forehead then brought me in for a hug.

"*I missed you, Philip Reyno. I missed you so much.*"

I ignored being called Philip, something I only did for Cam, and hugged him back. "Missed you too, dude."

Cameron laughed into my neck. "Don't *dude* me. I just spent a whole summer with dudes."

"Okay. What's better than *dude*?"

He rubbed my back, still holding me close. I swear his hands got bigger. "Tell me you missed me, baby."

I felt something warm melt something cold inside me and

I just smiled. I smiled like a sappy, desperate fool. I nodded. "I missed you, baby."

And I realized how much I meant it. Cam kissed my cheek and squeezed me tight. The air ran out of me and, for a moment, I held off on breathing again. For a moment, I just let myself be held. Airless. I let that kind boy with his easy smile and good tan take me over, breathe for me, just for a moment. And for that moment, I forgot about Brynn and Augie and the boiling in my stomach. I forgot about pool parties and school dances and the points I needed to make. I forgot that I was a mean son of a bitch and I forgot that I was furious with myself. Furious with the Skwad.

Furious with Cameron Ellis.

For one, singular moment, I let myself forget that I was hugging the boy who ruined my life. Who told the world my secret. Who made the world fall in love with us but never asked my permission. Never apologized. Never considered his consequences.

For a moment, it was just easier to hug him. Because Cameron made it easy. Cameron could make me easy.

"I missed you so much, Cameron."

And for one moment, the world felt acceptable. A brave, new world.

JACKSON

TRACK TWO
Come to My Window

As the incumbent junior class president and an overall "great guy," I've always prided myself on giving teachers and students my full attention whenever they spoke to me. Really looked them in the eye, engaged and enthusiastic. But that was before I heard the name *Cameron Ellis*. See, ever since January, since making his very viral speech and winning the hearts of thousands, Cameron Ellis has, as my peers might say, "got me fucked up." The night of that dance and every night since, I just couldn't seem to think clearly when it came to Moorestown's crowning gay gem.

Like, at the moment, I was sitting in the teachers' lounge, smack-dab in the middle of a conversation, and I could not pay attention. I couldn't stop peeking at my phone. I just nodded along, pretending to listen, and tried my best to be subtle about it.

THE LAST BLOG IN THE WORLD
Post #193

~On the Topic of Milkshakes~
by Cameron Ellis!

Okay, Cam Army. I have a secret. Ready? I'm trusting you. Seriously, you can't tell anyone. Okay…

I LOVE milkshakes.

Obvious, I know. Of course, you love milkshakes, you goofus, who doesn't like milkshakes? I guess what I'm really getting at here is that I love *getting* milkshakes. The impromptu trips to Brewster's to try the newest flavor. The Toffee Coffee Crunch? Seriously next to GOD.

It's, honestly, become a ritual for me. Like, sometimes I'll be sitting at home, watching some particularly trash TV with my mom or maybe rereading *Perks* for the ZILLIONTH time, and I'll get the text. An alert from the **Skwad**. Three little milkshake emojis in our infamous group chat and I know.

It's on.

When I get that text, I drop everything I'm doing, no matter what, and run to the curb, waiting for Augie or Brynn (or Doug on the rare occasion his dad lets him drive the Tahoe) to pick me up, basically drooling knowing I'm six to eight minutes away from frothy, creamy goodness.

But alas, baseball camp didn't have milkshakes. A real drag, I know. Baseball camp also didn't have the Skwad. A realer drag, to be sure. But the thing I missed most this summer? The realest drag about these last three months? Yeah. You guessed it.

Baseball camp didn't have *Philip J. Reyno*.

<3 <3 <3

I can't believe I've gone ALL SUMMER without touching that face. Listening to his drums. Looking at those eyes. That jawline! That HAIR?!

I missed him. I missed my guy. My sweet, funny, complicated, talks-too-much-during-movies boyfriend. Because I don't know if you heard but… I *love* Phil Reyno.

God, it feels so good to get to say that now. I've been saying it all summer (shut up if you're tired of me yet) but SORRY I CAN'T HELP IT!! Cuz I'm not talking puppy love, besties. I'm talking that red-in-the-face, sweat-behind-the-ears, crap-in-your-good-jeans kind of LOVE.

ON THAT NOTE! You guys gotta see what my Phil is planning. It's so sweet, I can't even tell you. But I will. So, if you follow me on the socials, you know that I've taken a page out of my good sis Brynn's book (**@TheBrynnShow** if you are *tragically* out of the loop) and I've been trying to branch out into video content. Apparently, blogs AREN'T the forefront of social media and none of y'all told me?! I'm not doing anything huge, just some check-ins, some tutorials, standard vlog stuff, you get it. I'm honestly so nervous for you guys to see—I look like such a loser on camera :p.

ANYWAY, my eventual point is that I realized I had nowhere in my room to record these hotly anticipated videos and you know what my man did? Do you know what one Philip J. Reyno decided to do for me?

He is making me a **table**.

You heard me. And make sure you register the verbiage here. He's *making* me a table. Phil is BUILDING me a table. **FROM SCRATCH.** I know I've gushed over my lil craftsman's side projects in the past, but Phil is not joking when it comes to the carpentry. He's like if Jesus Christ had gauges and a deep respect for Courtney Love.

We stan.

I'll include some progress pictures of my future favorite furniture with this post. Or, for more CamRye content, you can follow me on Instagram **@CameronEllis** or on Twitter **@Cameron_Ellis** or on TikTok **@Cameron_Ellis2**. I'll be posting my three favorite options for Back-to-School fits there if you have any thoughts, opinions, suggestions, concerns, what have you. I'm also on Facebook if you want to follow me there. Or maybe not. Should I delete Facebook? I only have it to talk to my aunts and grandparents, but lately I've been thinking it would be a good idea to delete. Are we deleting? I don't know.

ANYWHOODLES! A special thanks to *Advouch* for sponsoring this post and a specialer thanks to my stomach for enduring all the Brewster's shakes I'm about to consume. *Lord. Help. Me.*

Well! That's it for me today. I'll leave you with my Cam Quest of the week:

Try talking to someone twice your age. You might be surprised what they have to say.

Later days!

—Cameron Ellis

What a little asshole.

"Jackson? Am I keeping you?"

I looked up from my phone. "Apologies, I'm listening. My VP is just confirming the conference room for our first UNICEF informational after school."

My thumb tapped blindly at my phone to sell my bold-faced lie.

J: sihfuehfpaih12e

I fired off the text to some poor soul and pocketed my phone. "Please. Continue."

The school's new guidance counselor just beamed with pride over her big cup of tea. "The teachers were right about you. So industrious. Colleges must be knocking down your door."

I found a comfortable smile to throw on and settled back into our dead-end conversation. Mrs. Stapler mixed a fifth Splenda packet into her mug with her finger. "Well, I was just saying how happy I was you could find the time to meet with me right out the gate like this, Mr. Pasternak. Day one, I stepped foot into this teacher's lounge, I asked anyone I could find, *Okay, what's the real scoop? How's this school work, what's the 411, what do I need to know?* And God's honest, just about every teacher on the property, every adult in this darn zip code, they all had the same answer. It's not *what* I need to know, it's *who* and that *who*, Mr. Pasternak, is *you*."

Phil's making Cameron a *table*? That must've taken up all his summer. Phil really spent three months making something for *him*? For Cameron Ellis? That walking cardigan? That boring, flavorless drip?

"And y'know, Mrs. McHale even added in her little orientation packet, *If you have any questions about the students or the school, find Mr. Class President, Jackson Pasternak. He will help you. He knows what needs knowing.*"

A table was a commitment. That was a very serious project. Phil only ever made me a spoon. It was a quality spoon, I'm not knocking the spoon, but it wasn't a table. How could he make something that big in his workshop? What woods was he using, where would Cameron put it? Why a table?

"So, truly, I'm just so honored you agreed to share your

knowledge and your lunch period with me. It's just a huge help!"

Mrs. Stapler patted my hand and brought me back to myself. Up until that point, I'd been justifying my endurance of this cloyingly complimentary interaction by enjoying the less cloyingly complimentary coffee bar the teachers keep stocked in the lounge. But with thoughts of a table ruining my mood and my third cup winding down, I was starting to feel overly caffeinated behind my eyeballs.

I stood and donned a respectful voice I usually saved for grandparents or heads of state. "You flatter me. I'm happy to help you however you need me, Mrs. Stapler. I love to be of use."

"Oh, it's *Stah-pler*. Like *Poplar*. It's a family name."

"And that is so unique and interesting. But if there's nothing else you need me for, I do have a debate class to get to."

"Of course! Heavens, no, don't let me keep you."

She stood too, all agreeable, but didn't move out of my way. I waited for her to finally ask about whatever real problem she'd stolen my lunch period for. She lowered her mug and voice to match. *"Listen."*

There we are. I tilted my head, all co-conspiratorially. Yes, Mrs. Stapler was a bore and already too familiar for my liking, but Jackson Pasternak never turned down the opportunity to gossip with an adult.

Mrs. Stapler looked around, the coast apparently clear. "So. I saw the video."

Eh. My interest lessened by twenty percent. You would've thought we as a town would've moved on to new gossip in the new school year but evidently, **Brave Kid Comes Out at Winter Dance** still needed to be relitigated. "Mmm. The administration is still talking about the dance, huh?"

"It was national news."

"I wouldn't say *nation*—"

"An NBC affiliate in Dallas–Fort Worth aired the clip during a segment on the effects of social media in schools. It's certainly national news, Mr. Pasternak."

The buzzing of my three Guatemalan blends was quickly chipping away at my politeness. I needed to wrap this up. "Alrighty. What about the video?"

"Do you know Cameron Ellis?"

My eyes searched the ceiling and I tried to sound convincing. "Ummm…not really. Different circles, you know?"

"Alright, well, do you *like* Cameron Ellis?"

"I don't have an opinion. Don't really think about him all that much. Never, honestly."

Mrs. Stapler leaned against the fridge, stirring what remained of her tea around in the mug. "Well, we're all very proud of Cameron, Mr. Pasternak. And his little boyfriend. We're proud Cameron is finding such success from his speech, we're proud he found love in our humble school, we're proud to have fostered an environment a kid like that could feel comfortable coming out in. We are very, *undeniably* proud."

She took a sip and I buried a compulsion to remind the good counselor she only just started that week. She was new to all this, she had no part in *We*.

"To be frank, the administration has a keen investment in helping Cameron Ellis have a great junior year. A lot of people are looking at our school right now, and we want to put our best foot forward."

"Best foot?"

"High school isn't an episode of *Glee*, Mr. Pasternak. There are still some very scary people out there. People who look at a boy like that and think…" She shook the thought away. "I don't even want to say it. A boy like that needs friends. Allies."

I'd been slowly inching my way toward the door through her spiel, hoping to pave a clean exit, but Mrs. Stapler got right back between us. "Can I trust you to be an ally, Jackson Pasternak?"

"Pardon?"

"Can I trust you to look out for Cameron? Be my man on the inside? Everyone adores you, Jackson. I mean, I've asked around and everyone in your grade agrees that their class president is one righteous dude!" Mrs. Stapler gave me a little punch on the shoulder and I thought about elbowing her in the throat in self-defense. Her hand stayed on my shoulder, very chummy. "If your classmates see Jackson Pasternak having a laugh with Cameron, walking to class with him, eating lunch together, they'll get on board."

I stood a little straighter. *"...Get on board?"*

Cameron Ellis did not need an administration-approved bodyguard to get the school "on board" with him. Our school, our town, the entire internet adored Cameron. His coming out was met with a gymnasium full of applause and a mountain of likes and retweets. Maybe other schools or other towns, even other grades might be different, but the guy has little to worry about in our junior class. Everybody loved Cameron Ellis. Everybody.

"The administration would be very grateful, Mr. Pasternak. Looking out for the little guy. Quite the *presidential* thing to do."

I felt a crick in my back. Like a splinter in the spine. I saw Cameron Ellis's tongue fishing around someone's mouth in that dark, dusty woodshop and my shoulders felt like splitting open. Because I'd been so aggravated by what Mrs. Stapler was saying, I hadn't heard the quiet thing she wasn't.

"...What about Phil Reyno?"

She looked confused. "Phil Reyno? How do you mean, dear?"

"You want me to look out for Cameron. Fine. What about Phil Reyno? You aren't worried about him?"

Mrs. Stapler chuckled for a second. A quick little pop that she wouldn't have let escape around other kids. But I am not other kids. Then she gave me the look. Usually, I love the look. It was a look teachers would give me after class when it was just the two of us. A look that made me feel like I was one of them. Like I was special. Better than my classmates. This knowing smile and a wink in the eye that said, *I can't say it out loud, I know I'm the adult here, but between you and me: Fuck. That. Kid.*

"We're ready to help Mr. Reyno however he chooses to let us. But the administration is worried about Cameron. He's a good kid."

I was usually better at keeping my face presentable. A face for posters and pep rallies, a very unflappable face. And yet? Mrs. Stapler managed to make me flinch.

"Good kid." I just nodded through it. "You talk to Phil yet?"

"I did, actually. First thing this morning. Mr. Reyno has a...*unique* communication style."

"Mmm. Kind of a dick, huh?"

Mrs. Stapler's eyes darted around the teacher's lounge. My response had surprised her and I think she wanted to make sure I wasn't setting her up. Then she gave me a little shrug and a smile, a classic variation on *The Look*, and shook her head. "High school is a difficult time for everybody, Mr. Pasternak. Some kids handle it differently than others. You understand."

I had nothing left to say to this woman. So, I just kept nodding. Face back on. "I do. I do understand you."

"Good. I knew you would."

It was all Mrs. Stapler could do to not scream, *Phil Reyno isn't worth this school's time or effort*, and it was all I could do not to pour a hot pot of coffee on her.

She smiled and started packing up her messenger bag. "Y'know, I actually have some rounds to make over by the gymnasium. Wanna walk and talk before your next class? Coach Bianco told me you were this school's unofficial tour guide!"

More quality time with my new best friend? No thank you. I stepped back into the lounge and pointed at the bathroom door. "Actually… Dang, yeah, I need to take a pill. Do you mind if I use the teachers' restroom? I prefer not taking them around my classmates, no need to wait for me."

Mrs. Stapler smiled, so very sympathetic. "Aww. Of course, superstar! Go, go, go. I'll catch you on the battlefield."

I grunted out something of a smile and scurried into the teachers' private bathroom. The pill lie would afford me maybe fifty seconds of stalling but prove pointless if I just bumped right back into Mrs. Stapler the minute I left the lounge. Could I wait her out? The logical move, sure, but I did need to get to Debate early. It was the first day back, seats are first come, and I refused to spend another year sitting so far from the lectern.

A predicament to be sure. I ran through my parachutes. Trusted moves to get me out of stickier social situations. Force a nosebleed? It was a straight shot to the nurses and I had to assume Mrs. Stapler wouldn't want to tag along. No. My sinuses weren't dry enough and I was wearing my second-favorite polo. I could make myself throw up? But I'd skipped breakfast this morning and, again, polo.

I looked at the window above the toilet and committed to an old favorite.

Now. How do you jump out of a second-story bathroom

window without breaking your legs or alerting your nice new guidance counselor who's most certainly lurking nearby?

STEP 1: *Get the window open*

But Jackson, you might ask, what if the faculty recently installed some tasteful privacy blinds above the toilet that are technically detachable but not without unwelcomed sounds? Well, don't fret, my curious friend. I thought of that very possibility not seconds ago.

STEP 2: *Turn on the sink*

Well done! Now with the sink blocking out your noise and the privacy blinds detached, we can circle back to completing **STEP 1**. Lift that window up and get your nondominant leg out first. Whichever leg you power from, and this is important, you want to keep that foot firmly planted on the toilet. This will come into play shortly.

STEP 3: *Aim for the bigger bush*

This step is a doozy so, please, give yourself a minute to enjoy the crisp, calming summer breeze.

"What the fuck are you doing?"

I stopped aggressively inhaling and opened my eyes to the girl looking up at me from the bushes. There are two bushes under the teachers' lounge second-floor bathroom window. One big, one small. They're alright as far as bushes go, I didn't pick them out. But there she was, standing by the smaller bush, dressed for gym class and clearly bored out of her skull. Veronica DiSario. *Ronny* to her friends, but we are not friends. More like colleagues. Or maybe peers? Acquaintances? I'll go with the provable one and settle on *neighbors*.

"Oh. Um. Hello, Veronica."

The lacrosse captain grunted something like *Hello* back up at me, sipping a Red Bull and miles from what must have been her gym class. I did not know how to proceed. I'd only ever jumped out of this particular window before because it faces the parking lot, off-limits to students during school hours, and I wasn't prepared to explain myself. But if anyone was going to catch me in the act, I suppose Veronica had seen worse from me. Our mothers were each other's oldest friends in town, Janey was a first-round invite to all of my parents' fancy parent parties, and Veronica was almost always dragged along kicking and screaming. In a sea of overstuffed college professors and whatever interesting drifter my parents pulled off the street that week, Veronica and I were often the only attendees anywhere close to our age range which might be our strongest if not sole connection. Between the dark makeup, ripped skirts, and general "cautionary tale" vibe, Veronica was what some could call *unapproachable*. The demon queen of the country club scene. Personally, I found her simply fascinating.

The punk princess took a picture of me hanging halfway out the bathroom window. "So. What's the goal here, Pasternak?"

"Well. I was thinking about jumping out this window. What are you doing out of gym class?"

"No, no. Let's stay on you."

She took more pictures, finding my increasingly embarrassing escape attempt very amusing. I tried to retreat from my window-straddle but my nondominant leg was cramping and I guess I was a little stuck.

"What was the plan after you broke your foot, Mr. Class President?"

"See, the plan was to avoid that, actually."

"That's smart. Was it a big plan? Lotta steps?"

"Just three."

Veronica smiled up at me. "Ah. Keeping it simple. You're usually more thorough."

I shrugged down at her. "Well. It's been a long first day."

"It's fourth period."

I tried making myself small in an attempt to unstick myself from the window frame but my shoulders would not cooperate. If I had to blame anything for the failure of my faultless escape plan it would be my upper body. The last time I'd ejected myself through this window, I was scrawny freshman Jackson with no muscle mass and nothing to lose. But that was before I ever picked up an oar. Before I ever sat at a rowing machine and before my upper body decided to expand. The last time I looked at myself naked, something I nearly never do, I realized that my years in the Moorestown High Rowing Club had reshaped my body into something of a triangle. My scrawniness still remained in some of my lower areas, my calves could use some work, but my top half had nearly doubled in size. To put a name to it, I looked like a lollipop. A yield sign on the side of a highway. An oddly distributed, top-heavy object built to speed across local rivers and get stuck in unsuspecting windows.

Veronica had gotten into the grass below me and was tearing strips off her Moorestown-brand gym shirt. "That's the teachers' lounge, right? Schmancy. How'd you snag that invite?"

"New guidance lady wanted to get to know me. It got, uh…tiring."

"So, you're jumping out a window? It's not like you to bail on a fan, Pasty. I thought you loved impressing old people."

"What do you mean?"

"What I said." She uncapped a Sharpie and started giving her newly torn yellow top some black accents. "C'mon, dude. I got dragged to enough Pasternak dinner parties this summer. You're an impressive guy. Class president. God of rowing. Ivy League or Bust. You *looooove* talking about yourself."

I didn't know if I liked Veronica's assessment of me. She

wasn't wildly off base but Jackson Pasternak had more going
on than social clubs and college prep. That summer, I'd been
actively trying to brainstorm new things I might bring to the
table junior year to help change that narrative. Maybe I'd start
wearing hats. Or grow a mustache. Rob a bank, I don't know.

"I'm a lot more than that, Veronica."

"Why bother though? You're a parent's wet dream, Mr.
President. Like a little Jewish JFK."

"You sound bitter."

"You sound like you're avoiding the question."

With a quick inhale, I managed to fold myself into a pret-
zel and get my other leg out of the window. I let the blood
rush back into my extremities and caught my breath on the
sill, both my feet free and dangling. All set to jump and looking to stall, I decided I'd just level with Veronica. Because I
was avoiding her question. Because I do usually love these
invites. Special privileges and trips to the teachers' lounge.
To every adult inside Moorestown limits, Jackson Pasternak
was a kind, respectable boy with his head on his shoulders
and an eye on his future. A credit to his community and his
temple and an asset to his school council. The perfect college
applicant. The kind of friend every parent wants their child
to have. The kind of child every parent secretly wishes was
theirs. A hustler. A hard worker. A good kid.

"The guidance counselor started talking about Cameron
Ellis."

Veronica stopped drawing on her shirt. It might have been
the first time she'd really considered me all conversation. That
name meant just as much to her. "Oh."

"Yeah."

"…The dance?"

"Yes."

She stood up and wiped the grass off her knees. In the short time it took her to knock the last blade off, I watched her defenses fully rise. "Some middle-aged child therapist's got nothing better to talk about than some bullshit from January? Kill me if I ever get that boring."

"The school wants me to look out for him. Cameron. Keep him...safe."

"Oh, sure. Won't somebody protect the internet's favorite *widdle cinnamon roll*?" She killed her Red Bull and chucked it into a bush. "Have fun with that. I'm sure you'll hit it off, you're basically the same person."

"That's...very inaccurate."

Veronica shrugged up at me. "I dunno. Preppy rich assholes, nice parents, good hair."

"You're a preppy rich asshole, Veronica."

"Yeah, but my hair sucks. Cameron Ellis is basically your twin. Just gay."

I tensed up. My fingertips were scratching into the window ledge. "I'm... I'm not like Cameron. At all."

"Eh. Just eyeballing it? My assessment says otherwise."

I swallowed. "I don't like Cameron. At all."

Veronica's eyebrows popped up. She touched her chest, pretending to be shocked. "*Jackson.* You can't say that. We all *love* Cameron Ellis. I believe it's a federal law."

"Yeah, well... I don't."

Summer sun in her eyes, Veronica DiSario reconsidered me. Maybe in our first time knowing each other. I think she was impressed. "Well, damn. What did Cameron do to you?"

I just stared down at her. I had an answer. Answers. I had an Excel sheet of reasons not to like Cameron Ellis. Research. A summer of inane blog posts full of quality motivation. But I didn't have an answer that wouldn't call for more questions.

Questions I couldn't find ways out of. Backstory this town seems to have forgotten. My silence was getting too telling so I stalled with a shrug.

"He didn't do anything to me."

With the five seconds that lie gained me, I did some quick math in my head. What were the risks in being honest? I was at school. People could hear. Teachers, students, God, etc. But Veronica and I were alone. Alone enough, at least. And, sure, she was an overall risky person, but she could be a safe risk. We had shared history. Mothers and dinner parties and semidecent crudités. Maybe it would be safe to be honest with her. Maybe she could relate. Maybe we both hated Cameron for similar reasons.

"This summer, I just… I was thinking a lot. About a lot. That video. And the speech. Cameron. And… I don't know. I guess it all just gets me…"

Or.

Or maybe Veronica would make fun of me. Tell everyone in school about me. Tell my parents. My teammates or my bubbie or my college scouts. My world.

"Cameron just makes me…"

Maybe Veronica would change my world. Like Cameron Ellis changed Phil's.

"I just used to be really…"

I wanted to go back inside. I wanted another problem to solve. Another thing to keep me busy.

"Phil Reyno used to be my—"

I heard a knock on the bathroom door. Some teacher asking if I was feeling alright. With a gasp, the cool summer air came quicker and my face broke my fall.

PHIL

—

TRACK THREE
Misery Business

Like, the messed up thing is I didn't even say *faggot* this time.
We were maybe sixteen seconds into the first day back to
school when the new guidance lady pulls me out of first period Woodshop just to "get on the same page." I suppose the
lovely Mrs. Stapler had caught wind of my rep and wanted to
make sure we were all "working toward the same outcomes."
Because according to the permanent records, somewhere between cutting off Dave Sim's rattail and keying a dick into
Mr. McBride's Nissan Ultima, the criminal Philip J. Reyno
had been written up thirty-seven times last year for calling
kids "the f-slur." All in the wake of the Snow Globe Ball,
interestingly enough. But Lady Stapler told me the school
wouldn't be accepting that kind of behavior in the new year.
No, no. Not under her watch. She told me I ought to follow
the lead of a Cameron Ellis. An Augie Horton. Brynn Forester
or Doug Parson or *that lovely class president I've heard so much
about.* Sweet, likeable kids who knew how to make friends.
Be easy. Not call their classmates such "ugly names." Which,

to her credit, was a fair point. And it was what I promised to Cameron after all. A clean slate. A new score. An easy junior year. Yet there I sat. Outside the principal's office. On the first day back to school.

Principal Kowalczyk and I were frequent collaborators and I'd basically started paying rent to her waiting bench by the end of sophomore year. It sat in the hallway outside her office and she made a habit of letting me dry out on it for whole class periods. I was going on minute forty sprawled out on the stiff cedar thing, hoodie up and eyes on the ceiling, while my classmates passed me by. It was easy enough to ignore their looks and whispers once I got used to them. I believed that was Principal K's larger point, making me wait so long, so publicly. The administration thought some shame might do me good. But I was well trained in letting the voices and laughter of my classmates slip on by and I did my best to just disappear into the wood.

The river of kids passed, discussions of locker assignments and summer bodies rolling across my ears. Giggles about the school play and new book bags and promises to save seats at lunch. All these kids I know, bouncing and shiny, not a care in the world. Happy. Easy. Like bubbles in the air. Cute, pretty, and easy to break. Always floating above me, one prick from exploding. It was no way to go about life. It was like they were begging me to be the prick.

Then a new noise. Something harder. Not so bubbly.

"Oh, joy."

The door to the nurse's office across from me slammed shut and I heard a pair of boots clomp down nearby.

"I'll admit. You've got a great look, Phil. Anyone ever tell you that?"

I dropped my hoodie and looked at the opposing bench in

front of me. There, with a ripped-up PE uniform and grass stains on her knees, sat Ronny DiSario. We just glared at each other for a hot second. Like two pissed-off alley cats waiting to pounce on a fishbone.

"What's a *look*?"

Ronny snorted. "You know. The piercings. The gauges. All very punk. Very '90s. Very Jane Lane."

I didn't get the reference, but I didn't think I'd like it.

Ronny nodded at the sleeveless Passy's Pizzeria employee tee under my sleeveless hoodie. "Dress code okay with you tearing off those sleeves, pizza boy?"

My biceps, bare and bony, felt particularly exposed under her stare, but I'd gotten used to these sorts of comments. I sort of have a bad habit of tearing up my clothes. Come to think of it, I don't think there's a single sleeve remaining in my wardrobe. Even my Passy's delivery uniform couldn't survive the knife. Still, I hated when people referred to "my look." Like it was something put-on or intentional. It wasn't. It was just how I looked. I don't get why it's such a thing for people if I paint a nail black here or there or stick a paperclip through my earlobe.

"Dress code okay with you padding your bra, pizza face?"

Ronny giggled which was not my intent. I meant for the digs at her cup size and complexion to get her to leave me to my bench but, no. Ronny just laughed.

Now, I'd given half the town some pretty solid reasons to not like me through the years. I'd admit it, I hadn't been the most likeable guy and that was before my face was plastered over everyone's devices for a weekend back in January. But Ronny? Veronica DiSario? The third-richest kid in our town with the second-worst reputation? Ronny DiSario didn't dislike me. Ronny DiSario *despised* me. Ronny DiSario wanted to bury me under the golf course in her backyard. Ronny DiSario hated my fucking guts.

Ron kicked her boots up on her bench. "Principal's on the first day back. Ambitious. Who'd you make cry this morning, Philbo?"

The sensible side of me knew ignoring Ronny would probably piss her off worse than anything I could come up with. But my morning already got kicked in the dick by my new guidance counselor so how much could a little dart throwing hurt?

"Why you need the nurse? Mix up your Vikes and Xannies? Gotta label them better, Ron, separate baggies."

"Cute. You showering between classes again or did y'all pay your water bill on time?"

I sat up on my bench. "Heard you jerked off three dudes at Silva's Beer Olympics. Nurse helping you with the carpal tunnel?"

So did Ronny. "Wait, did the principal call your mom? Bit early in the morning for her, no?"

I scoffed. "At least my mom talks to me."

"At least my mom can drive me to school."

"At least my dad's not a Republican."

"At least my dad lives in my time zone."

"At least I'm not FUCKING HALF THE LACROSSE TEAM."

"At least I'm not FUCKING THE GUY WHO OUTED ME."

The hate in my stomach found me quick then. The game wasn't fun anymore and I was on my feet. So was she.

"FUCK YOU, DISARIO."

"GET THE FUCK OUT OF MY FACE, REYNO."

We were barking in each other's faces and people were

starting to watch. Let 'em. If Ronny wanted to settle the
score, who was I to refuse her? Maybe that was my new leaf
for junior year. The year Phil Reyno fights a girl in front of
thirty strangers, two benches, and his principal.

"*HEY!*"

Then there was Cameron. Suddenly, between us.

"WHOA! Whoa, whoa, whoa, guys. That's a lot of language for fifth period. Easy."

I don't know when he turned into the hallway. I don't know
how much he heard. But Cameron Ellis had come to save the
day, breaking out his famous, winning smile.

"Sorry, Veronica. You gotta excuse him. Phil isn't a morning person." Then Cameron turned that shine on me and I felt
the tight thing in my stomach begin to let go of me. "Phil.
Tell Veronica you're sorry, yeah?"

Cameron walked over to me and patted me on the shoulder. Ronny watched us together, not moving a muscle. I
couldn't do much better. Cameron smiled softer and whispered. "*C'mon, baby. Be nice.*"

I did what my boyfriend told me. I stood up, looked at Ronny,
and gave her a nod. Slight. "Sorry. Rough… Rough start."

Cameron scratched my back. A little rub he liked to give
me when I made him proud. "There you go."

Cam was smiling at me but my eyes weren't leaving Ronny's.
Hers wouldn't leave mine. But she blinked. "Cameron. Looking healthy. How's your mom?"

Cameron nodded. A little surprised by the pleasantry in
her voice. "Um… She's, uh…great. Good. How's…you?"

Ronny smiled, all teeth. "I good. I so good, Cameron,
thank you for asking me that."

Ronny looked behind us. Right at the principal's office
door. She smiled. "Phil, y'know, you never did tell me why

you got sent to the principal's office. Bet it was just some innocent misunderstanding. *Right?*"

Cameron's smile dropped, like he only just realized where we were standing. My jaw clenched. Fucking Ronny DiSario.

"*Phil.*"

"Cam, it's not a problem. Really, Cameron. The new guidance lady just…"

"Phil. You *promised*. You said this year would be—"

"She has it fucking out for me, Cameron, I didn't even do anything this—"

Cameron sighed. "Did you call another kid a…*that*?"

"No. Really, Cam, it was nothing, the guidance counselor just—"

"Did you call the guidance counselor *that*?!"

"No! I never called anyone fucking anything, Cameron. Mrs. Stapler just asked me to promise I wouldn't say it anymore. And…"

I waited a beat. Because I realized how little leg I had left to stand on.

"And you said *yes*, right? Phil? You promised?"

I didn't have an answer. Not one that would make Cameron happy. He just sighed and rubbed his face. Tired. And I wondered how many more times I had left. How many times I could let him down. Make things harder for him with my bullshit. Make things worse for everyone by being me.

Cameron shook his head. Finally looked at me. "I just don't know what you're trying to prove, Phil."

"Cam."

I reached for his hand. He didn't take mine back.

Ronny watched us try to untangle the mess she'd dropped us in, that smile never leaving her face. "Golly. I sure hope I didn't complicate things for you boys. Should I go? I'll go." She grabbed her backpack off the bench and gave us both a little salute. "Have a great first day, Philliam. Sorry for talking your ear off."

That satisfied look on her face. Another point for the rich girl. Another slap on my name. Ronny thought she'd won the round. But this was a game I hated to lose.

"SORRY FOR STEALING YOUR BOYFRIEND."

I said it loud. Kids stopped in the hallway. Eavesdroppers stopped trying to hide it. But Ronny was frozen. A rage bubbling under her skin. All eyes were on her again and her jaw looked like it could cut me in two.

Cameron was just as still. Just as angry. Just as stunned as his ex-girlfriend, Veronica. *"Phil."*

I expected Ronny's knee in my balls. Her nails in my face. I thought God Almighty might smite me then and there but my mother beat the Big Man to it.

"Philip?"

I turned to find Mom standing outside the admin office. Still sleeping off last night. All dressed up in her best *Meeting with the Principal* sweatshirt.

"What's going—"

"FUCK YOU!" Ronny DiSario sucker punched me square in the throat. I dropped to my knees, holding on to my trachea for dear life.

"GWAH!"

It was kind of a blur after that. Once Ronny stormed off and the hallway crowd found better things to gossip over, Cameron didn't have much to say to me. The school nurse brought me ice for my throat and, after about an hour of trying to extract my Adam's apple out of my colon, Mom drove me home in silence.

She lit a cigarette at a red light so I rolled down my window too. "So. Who was the girl?"

I pressed the nurse's ice pack close to my windpipe. "New fiancée. She was just nervous to meet you."

"Sure. In-laws can be tough."

I sank down deep in the passenger seat. "Ronny. She used to sort of date Cameron. Ronny DiSario."

"Oh. Wait, like the rich DiSarios? The *big ol' mansion in the Orchard* DiSarios?"

"Like the *loaded out the ass* DiSarios. Yeah."

"Wowee. Drama." She ashed out the window, thinking something over. Maybe doing the math. Comparing the time-lines. "Wait. How long did they *used to sort of date*?"

"A year or two. There might have been some, uh…overlap."

"Oh. *Ooooh.* Stealing boyfriends from the rich and powerful, huh?"

"I don't really wanna talk about it, Mom."

"You dog. Like a gay little Robin Hood."

I tried to groan through my smile and she mussed up my hair. She turned off Main and flew down Duquesne. I watched the homes pass by and wondered why Ronny DiSario was even at the nurse's office in the first place. Maybe she was hiding. Couldn't blame her for wanting to wait out the world. In the fallout of the Snow Globe Ball, Ronny DiSario had become our school's favorite punch line. The ex-girlfriend of Moorestown's Golden Gay. The patchy beard who should have known better. The butt of the joke of the talk of the town. It was a satisfy-ing decline to most. Because Ronny used to be pretty popular. Once upon a time, she was our school's own Great Gatsby. Her house parties were the stuff of Moorestown legend and because her parents were never in town, Chateau DiSario hosted more blackouts than Brooklyn in a heat wave. But Gatsby Ronny was always so sure to stay one step ahead. Always quick with a comeback or a teardown or some withering glare. Cameron

once told me that his childhood girlfriend was incredibly careful about what she let the world know about her. But after the
Snow Globe Ball, Cameron became a legend and Ronny became a joke. Poor Ronny DiSario. Poor little rich girl. How
could she not know? How could she be so stupid?

My guilt was getting me hot and the ice against my throat
was melting quick so I chucked it out the window and checked
my developing bruise in the rearview. Mom watched my in-
spection. "Your principal caught me up, you know. About
your...*vocabulary*."

I nodded. "I, uh... Yeah, I figured."

"I thought we were leaving that stunt behind, kid." I sat
back in my seat. Looked at my lap. She patted my hand. "You
wanna talk about it?"

I shook my head. Her voice was softer then. She was trying to talk seriously. Something my classically fun mom had
very little practice in.

"You can. If you want to. We could talk about it."

I looked out the open window. The clouds were collect-
ing over the Sticks and I could smell it would rain soon.
"You wouldn't understand, Mom. It's not your fault. But you
wouldn't... You won't get it."

"Is it a boy thing? We could call Dad."

"Can we not do this now. I had a really long—"

"Is it a gay thing? Are there any gay teachers at school you
could talk to? Maybe you could explain it to them, huh? They
might get it."

I closed my eyes and let the air keep me cool. I couldn't
keep telling her no. She was trying to help and asking all
the wrong questions. Dead ends I'd already walked down.
Helping hands I'd already slapped away. There were no gay
adults in my school. There were no gay friends I could trust.

Every safe space this town had built for kids like me had politely asked me to leave. Because I couldn't be easy for them.
I couldn't make promises to them. I couldn't be like him.

"Maybe Cameron could—"

It came out of me quick. "Cameron doesn't understand.
Augie doesn't understand, my guidance counselor doesn't understand, you won't understand. Stop."

"Philip—"

"Mom, **STOP**!"

She slammed on the brakes at the four-way intersection before we could get T-boned by a Honda Civic. We sat there,
right outside our apartment building, just catching our breath.
Mom flicked her cigarette and squinted out the back window.
"Jesus! Some punk took the fucking stop sign off the post!"

I looked back at the empty post and kept my mouth quiet.
She didn't know. I guess she hadn't been in my room the last
few weeks. Hadn't seen the most recent art installation above
my bed. What was supposed to be my new motto going into
junior year. A nice, red, reflective reminder hanging above
my mattress telling me to just fucking **STOP**.

I shrugged. "Three out of four signs ain't bad."

I retired early and paced around my room for an hour or
two. It had begun to rain or I would've burned off my energy
over at my workshop. I peeked through the blinds and tried
to spot my unit through the streaks and rain. On a clear day, I
could see the row of old storage units down the street by my
apartment. About twelve metal containers, all neatly lined up
in the middle of this overgrown field by the edge of the Sticks.
It honestly looked like someone dropped a dozen random ship-
ping containers out of the sky and never thought to pick them
up. Originally, I used the space for drumming, but the acoustics were shit and I always hated playing in public. The last two

summers though, I've gotten pretty lucky at filling my shop
with all the rejected carpentry equipment and rust-pocked tools
I could scavenge from flea markets and yard sales in the area.
I got a lot of my more serious jobs done in the school's wood-
shop but did my personal projects there. Skateboards. Tables.
Replacing our coatrack after my mom went through her White
Russian phase. I've logged my ten thousand hours there in my
metal oasis. My lonely spaceship out in orbit. My workshop.

I threw myself onto my bed, hanging halfway off and staring up at my stolen stop sign. My contraband. My reminder.
STOP. I wondered if Mom would understand why I had to
steal it. Would Mrs. Stapler? Would Cameron? It was harmless bullshit, it wasn't hurting anyone. Like the faggot thing.
Harmless. I was harmless, I was bullshit, why couldn't they
understand that? I shouldn't be that hard to get. But they
didn't. No one understood me. No one knew how to handle
me. How to help.

I was too tired to play my drums, but I needed new noise.
I dug out the mixtape hidden under my mattress and slipped
it into the boom box on my nightstand. I'd found it used
at the swap meet last month and liked to bring it out to the
workshop with me. It came with a crate of old tapes and I'd
torn through each one a dozen times, but my mattress cassette was only brought out when I really needed it. An old
favorite. My first favorite. The first track off *Jagged Little Pill*
crackled through the boom box speakers and I closed my eyes.
The tape quality was garbage, but I'd learned to appreciate
the flaws. Let them be a part of the experience. The warmth
of a tape cassette. That worn-in love.

Jackson would know. He'd know why I stole the stop sign.
Jackson would know why I couldn't help but use that word.
Jackson would know why I'm so fucking mad, every day, all

the time. Because I knew something no one else did. I knew the big secret. What our class president was so afraid of his school and his town and his people figuring out. Jackson was mad too. Jackson was difficult too. Jackson was like me. He just knew how to hide better. He knew how to seem easy. Maybe he should be dating Cameron. Maybe he'd know what to do with all the attention. All the speeches. All the love I never asked for. But that would be silly. Because Jackson wasn't gay. He was absolutely sure of it. When real life came calling, we were just too different.

My phone buzzed and my eyes opened. The rain had stopped and the sun was setting in my window. My tape was rewinding in the boom box, played all the way through. Damn. I must've fallen asleep at some point and missed the whole mix. But I had an unread text. From Cameron. Huh. I tapped it open.

C: We need to talk

JACKSON

TRACK FOUR
Constant Craving

If I still went to therapy, I think they'd tell me I was obsessed with Cameron Ellis. I wasn't, I've checked. At my most clinical, I was *fixated* on Cameron Ellis, but it had not become something unhealthy. My mother is a psych professor, I learned the basics of unhealthy behavioral patterns before I learned cursive. I was simply doing research. And Jackson Pasternak was very good at doing research.

"Today's vlog post is sponsored in part by 3Vee.com's In All Their Glory, *the new 3Vee streaming series starring indie darling Hilary Swank as groundbreaking journalist Gloria Steinem, scene-stealing Annette Bening as trailblazing civil rights attorney Gloria Allred, and* Firefly's *Gina Torres as world-shaking pop sensation Gloria Estefan. Um…just a heads up?* **EXPLOSIVE TV ALERT!!"**

I was halfway through my standard morning round of one hundred sit-ups on my bedroom floor, listening to last night's video post. Cameron had upgraded to vlog content since returning from baseball camp and I'd begun incorporating it into my morning workouts. That way, keeping up with his banal goings-on didn't feel like wasted time. I was multitasking. I was keeping my breathing steady and my core engaged. Sixty-one. Sixty-two.

"*An addictively bingeable peek at pop culture's most famous (and infamous) Glorias? Yes, please! Should we just start handing out the awards now? YES, PLEASE!! Am I tuning in every Friday night to see these three iconic queens give me ABSOLUTE LIFE?? Uh, I think you know my answer.*"

My back slapped against my yoga mat every three seconds and I could tell from the sound that I was sweating more than usual. Odd. I'd have to Google what that could mean. Seventy-seven. Seventy-eight.

"In All Their Glory *is streaming now only on 3Vee.com. Use the offer code* **CANDIDCAMERON** *to receive a free thirty-day trial to 3Vee.* **3VEE.** *Very, Very, Very.*"

A short chime played and Cameron switched out of his ad-reader voice.

"*Oh, hello. Sorry, you caught me with my business pants on. Bills to pay and all that. Apologies for the long intro but it costs a lot of money to look this cheap! Now that I've got that out of the way, I want to start off by apologizing to anyone who was worried about my appearance on* The Brynn Show *last night. It…wasn't my best moment.*"

Eighty-five. Eighty-six.

"*I just want to let everyone out there know:* **I. AM. OKAY.** *Seriously! Back to school was just a little tougher than I anticipated. I guess that's just a thing with me. I always build up these big moments in my big watermelon of a head and I'm starting to learn that I can't be disappointed when some big moments don't live up to the fantasy.*"

I rolled my eyes but kept my focus. Ninety-two. Ninety-three. Ninety-four.

"*Sometimes I think of my life like a movie. This big romantic adventure where everything happens in order and for a reason. But I'm not in a movie. I'm not some cute, six-foot something leading man with perfect skin and perfect hair. I'm not that guy. I'm Cameron. Just Cameron. So, yeah, I might've cried a little bit on Brynn's live show yesterday but believe me, it's simply the back to school blues."*

One hundred. I stared up at my ceiling, flat on the floor, and caught my breath. Let my abs scream at me. Listened to that sweet, syrupy voice.

"So, I guess the point of this post (other than telling y'all to do yourselves a favor and watch Annette Bening deliver the best supporting actress work of the decade) is to thank you for reaching out. And, most importantly, to thank my friends. The Skwad. Holy crap, do I love the f-ing Skwad."

My hand ran up and down my stomach, feeling the little hairs. I wondered for three seconds if I had time to masturbate. No. I needed to stop conflating being naked with jerking off. I probably also needed to stop working out in the nude. I ignored my unnecessary erection and grabbed the sweat towel off my desk.

"Really, if you take anything from my posts, noble reader, it's that. This year, I hope you all go out there and meet the people you were always meant to find. Because you deserve nice people in your life. You deserve to be happy. And easy. And you deserve offer code **CANDIDCAMERON** *to catch the first three episodes of* In All Their Glory, *streaming now on 3Vee.com. Available now on all iOS and Android devices."*

I picked up my portable speaker to turn off the video but Cameron cut me off.

"One last thing."

I looked at my phone and watched Cameron sitting in bed. Dressed for sleep and smiling at the webcam. Well. Almost smiling. Something sadder was sitting behind it. His nose twitched a little and I could see that his eyes were getting glassy.

"I really appreciate all your messages asking for updates on Phil's table. I think he's almost done, I know he loved all of your comments. But I don't, uh… He's gonna be holding on to it, I think. I'll make a post about that soon. This one's… This has gone on long enough."

One last, sad smile.

"Later days."

And it ended. I just stood in the middle of my room. Naked and confused.

"…The hell was that?"

Before I could think too hard, my mother knocked on my door and asked if I was awake. *"Jackson? Tu es reveille?"*

I wiped the sweat off my bare chest and rubbed it into my bedspread. "Oui, Maman. Je suis juste en train de me preparer."

My mother didn't need to know that by "getting ready," I meant "working out obsessively so I don't think about my life too deeply." I heard Maman coo and drift away, presumably to roust my baby sister out of bed for the third time that morning. I always loved when she was home in the mornings. The way she woke up the house, wafting through the halls like the smell of breakfast and coffee. She'd be leaving for her morning lectures at Penn soon then flying out for another week-long visit with her sisters in France. If I wanted to see her before the world took her away again, I'd need to move it along and I only had one last check left on my pre-breakfast to-do list.

I plopped a squat at my writing desk and clicked on a hidden folder on my desktop labelled *TAXES*. Then I searched for the even more hidden folder labelled ***LLC #197*** and finally located the hidden Excel file labelled ***NOVEMBER EXPENSES #317***. All these hidden folders and fake labels were a necessary subterfuge to ensure nobody in my house or school or town or planet ever found my journal. It wasn't really a journal but that's the closest word I could conjure to

describe it. I think *journal* humanizes it. Or maybe normalizes
it. Because, admittedly, my Excel isn't exactly very normal.
Or very human. But logging my life was part of the morning routine.

I scrolled down the alphabetical list of every person I had
ever met and stopped at *Nora Stavish*. Mrs. Stavish was the re-
ceptionist at the Jewish Community Center my dad used to
do free lectures for and I believe we only spoke three times.
In the box next to her name, I'd written everything I remembered about our brief interactions.

NORA STAVISH
- Went to Ryder College to study chemistry
- Has carpal tunnel, blames her husband's love of tennis
- Thinks her son hates her and doesn't know how to talk to him anymore
- Son is fourteen and not good-looking (I think named Matthew?)

I added a new row above Mrs. Stavish and typed in the
newest name on my list.

BOBBI STAPLER (READ: POPLAR)
- Got the job from a recruiter, previously counseled in Newark
- Smells like she has a cat and Febreezes her clothes often
- Wants me to look out for C.E. (probably school mandate)
- Will not help P if he needs it
- Very warm to me but not a kind person (opinion)

There was more to log, but I had to get my day started. Once I saved the file and hid my paper trail, my phone started to ring. I answered without thinking. "Morning."

"Hello. This is Amber from the Philadelphia Jewish Community Center. Please listen to this important message about your donation, JACKSON PASTER—"

"Goddammit."

I ended the call with my newest best friend, **SCAM LIKELY**. I met my pal SCAM off a mailing list for this fundraiser my parents threw last spring and he's been checking in once or twice a week ever since. I set a mental reminder to learn how to block that number, closed my laptop, and finally headed downstairs.

My little sister was splicing together some old home movies on her laptop when I joined her at the kitchen counter. Molly Pasternak expressed a passing interest in the filmic arts one single time in the fifth grade and, in the latest of a string of artistic indulgences, my parents have been encouraging her to bring French New Wave cinema to a new generation ever since.

She shoved a mini microphone in my face. "Morning. Say Happy Birthday to Nan."

Maman was blending a smoothie by the fridge and it looked big enough for both of us. Molly glared at the noisy Nutribullet so Maman killed it. I sighed and held the mic to my mouth. "Bon anniversaire, Mamie. Je te souhaite une belle journée. Hope you stay tan this winter. Good?"

"Passable." Molly snatched the mic back and sank into her project. Maman poured the purple health soup into a cup and slid it to me. "Nan will love that. You know, we were talking some more and your father thought it might be smarter to audition with a classic. Bobby Darin. Perry Como. Something old-school."

I accepted my acai-and-whatever breakfast. "Student council is just running the Drama Club's fundraiser, I never said I wanted to actually, like, *audition*."

I watched Molly splice together some clips from the first and only Yom Kippur we spent with the French fam. I was maybe nine and my giant bobblehead skull looked like it was about to snap off my neck and into my nan's lap.

Maman cleaned up around the kitchen. "But you have such a pretty voice, Jackson, you and your father. I think you could use more fun in your life."

"There must be more dignified ways to have fun, Maman. Musicals are silly."

"You could use silly. You've acted like you were forty since you were fourteen, my love, something silly could be incredibly enriching. Not for the résumé or the colleges, something silly and simple."

"Mmm. I've told you free therapy spoils my breakfast, haven't I?"

The home movies transitioned from Yom Kippur to a summer afternoon on our lake dock. I still had braces and Dad still had hair so I must've been young and Nan was tanning with Molly by the water.

Maman smiled and joined us by the laptop. *"Beautiful."*

Mol had done a great job. Toned down some glare, stabilized the old footage. It was like I was right back on that dock. Sitting with my feet in the water and laughing with a boy.

I watched his hand slap my knee. The popsicle stains on his tiny chest. He had that big pink Band-Aid over his ear. It must've been the week after I pierced it for him. Twelve. We must've just turned twelve. But I couldn't remember why Phil was laughing so much. What I must've said to make him laugh that hard. I couldn't remember being so funny.

Maman's laugh was soft. "God. So silly."

After breakfast, we got Maman packed up for her travels and walked her to her car. Before she could drive off, she dropped the window of the Benz and poked her head back out.

"Jackson?"

I turned around in the driveway. "Mother?"

She looked around and nodded me back to her. "Viens ici. Cone of silence?"

"Oh. Sure."

I approached the door and she leaned out to me. Close. Like anyone in the Orchard could be listening. "I left some trays in the freezer. Bring some dinners over to Veronica soon, alright? She's alone this week and... I worry."

I straightened. "Oh. What... Why?"

"Janey called last night. She's out of town for the month but apparently Veronica got in some sort of scrape at school yesterday. Something about a boy, I don't know. Janey's not worried but...you know them."

I nodded. The DiSarios, Paul and Janey, they were never worried. Characteristically. Never worried about money. Not about coming off well. Never worried about Ronny. The whole clan was simply above the act.

"Right. Do you think it's about the divorce?"

Maman slapped my hand and gave me her look. The DiSario divorce was privileged information. The rule was I was allowed a seat at the adult table, allowed to hear the adult talk, but I needed to be safe with their secrets. In my years of research, I'd found adults were just as gossipy as high schoolers, they just did it in nicer cafeterias.

She dropped her voice. "The DiSarios have been getting divorced for the better part of this decade. Don't tell your friends this, but I don't know if Paul and Janey have even seen each other this year."

"What? Don't they live together?"

"Janey's been traveling for her book and Paul is… Well. We spoke of Paul."

Maman gave me that sorry sort of look she gives me whenever she dips a toe into the "breach of confidentiality" tide pool. Veronica's father was not light gossip. At least, not before noon.

I nodded and backed away from the window. "Alright. All good. Drive safe."

Maman put her seat belt on and pointed at me. "You look out for her. It would mortify her if any of this got out. Proud girl. Proud, angry girl."

I gave her a thumbs-up, my list of people I needed to "look out for" only increasing, and I watched her car disappear along the lake and out of the Orchard.

I got to school feeling a little gross about skipping my postworkout shower, but my schedule started with a double-period gym class which would finally prove useful. After an hour of pretending to care about volleyball, I snuck into the locker room and treated myself to a twelve-minute steam. I usually despised showering at school, but I had all the hot water to myself and got my body squeaky-clean. I threw my towel on and walked through the empty lockers. To my great chagrin, I spotted a pair of Jordans sticking out from an aisle and braced myself to be annoyed.

"Who's here?"

I tightened my towel and turned the corner to find Bolu Olowe napping (or attempting to) on a changing bench. He was flat on his back and had his PE shirt folded neatly on his face, blocking out the light.

I laughed and walked a little easier. "Vice President."

Bolu grunted under his shirt mask. "Mr. President."

"Keep your eyes covered, my butt's out."

"Duly noted."

I cracked open my locker and switched back into my gym clothes. My vice president and most trusted coworker, Bolu Olowe, was maybe the most serious kid I knew. I'd known him since grade school soccer and even then, he was a no-nonsense Little Leaguer. Very quick to pause a game and explain the rule book to our grown referees. Though his father was one of the Moorestown Police Department's less lenient ticketers so maybe all the strict rule-abiding was genetic. Nevertheless, I always found Bolu's whole self-serious deal incredibly charming.

"I forgot to shower this morning. Thought I'd grab a good one while I could."

"Logical. We don't need to talk."

"Okay, thank you."

Another great thing about my veep. Bolu was my favorite kind of conversationalist. I threw on my gym shorts and headed out, strolling casually like I hadn't just snuck out to shower. When I turned into the Moorestown Athletic Center, I had to duck a few coaches hanging around the lobby. I could usually banter my way out of trouble with teachers, but coaches were a different beast. The world of the jock was another universe and my social capital didn't always transfer over. But the gym teachers all seemed too preoccupied fighting for prime placements in our school's new trophy case to notice me tarnishing my spotless attendance record. I would need to find another way back into the gym. Annoying.

I slipped past the arguing coaches and caught a glimpse of the trophy case. The enlarged yearbook photo of our town's current sports prodigy was all blown up and framed, his med-als encircling it. Made the trophy case look more like a funeral display. A candlelight vigil to New Jersey's first-ranked sprinter and our grade's second-ranked bro. *Here Lies Bash Villeda. He Was Kind of Fast.*

The men were distracted enough to let me slip right through to the science hall. If my sense of geography was correct, I could do a full loop around the school, cut through the cafeteria, and pop out right by the gym's side entrance. A bit out of the way, but I wasn't exactly raring to get sweaty all over again. I took my time clearing the first few halls but hit a pothole crossing the library. I would've felt caught wearing my PE clothes outside of the gym, but the school librarian could only see so much of me behind his stack of banker boxes.

"Jackson Pasternak! A perfect coincidence. Would you mind?"

I looked around the empty hallway. If I bolted, no one would know. But the elderly Mr. Cho was kind enough and always reminded me of a sad old turtle. It would be rude to leave him hanging.

"Sure thing, Mr. C."

I relieved him of half of his boxes, revealing a smile behind his stack.

"Y'know, Mr. Pasternak, you always seem to appear just where you're needed. Isn't that funny?"

"Not so hard when everyone needs you."

"Ah! Very funny."

Not a joke. Mr. C put his remaining half of boxes on top of my stack, fully loading me up, and stretched his back. "Be a friend and drop these off in the admin office? I'm one trip away from pulling something."

"Oh. Well, I actually have a gym—"

"They'll name libraries after you one day, Mr. Pasternak."

Mr. Cho floated back into the library before I could object. But the admin office was technically on my route back to the

gym. And it was a nice thing to do. I readjusted my grip on
the banker boxes, took a deep breath, and got to my new er-
rand. I'd already lost five of my allotted fifteen minutes left
to get back to Gym and the new weight was only going to
make me slower. I picked up the pace and turned a corner.

"Wowee. What's with the stacks, Jacks?"

Goddammit. I poked my face around my tower to find
Augie Horton texting at his locker.

"August. Just...back to school errands. You know."

"Mmm. I don't. Love the uniform. Those gym shorts make
your ass look boxy."

"Thank you. And screw you."

Augie chuckled and put his phone away. He offered a hand.
"Allow me to lighten the load, Mr. President."

Normally, I would've done the polite thing and made some
excuse, but I could feel my bandages wearing down and the
extra weight on my shoulders was setting an old rowing in-
jury on fire. Augie took the top box and walked with me
down the hall. I felt a need to match his slower pace, but the
lighter weight made our strolling worth it.

Augie smirked at me. "So. How did Moorestown's King
of the Preppies spend his summer? Remodel a country club?
Yacht across the Atlantic?"

"I sat in my basement a lot. Got good at Ping-Pong. Oh,
I finally finished *The Wire*. Yeah. Really made the most of
my time."

"Lord. Heterosexuality sounds so boring."

"Ah, but I'm so good at it."

Augie gave me a look and we both laughed. I've lived across
the street from August Horton since we were maybe ten
and we've always been perfectly pleasant toward each other.
That's *The Orchard Way*. Everyone and everything is perfectly
pleasant. Our neighborhood wasn't exactly the most modest

place to grow up and the Hortons weren't exactly the most modest people, but our sisters were inseparable and our dads golfed together. There were a couple other Orchard kids in our grade, but Augie and I were the only Lakers.

For anyone outside of the know, the Orchard is sandwiched between Plum Lake and the Moorestown Country Club's golf course. Kids who live near the country club are labelled *Clubbers* and their families are by and large the richest of the rich. That's Anthony Lewis. Brynn Forester. Veronica Di-Sario. Kids born with silver spoons big enough to choke on. Augie and I are *Lakers*. Even though we got to grow up by the water, Plum Lake homes are considered the cheap seats of the rich side of town. They're all about a fifth the size of your standard Orchard mansion and they, heaven forbid, only have *two*-car garages. That said, the Clubbers vs. Lakers distinction is only visible in the Orchard. Anyone else in town can, has, and will simply refer to us as "rich dicks" and I can't, haven't, and won't blame them. The Orchard infighting has never bothered me or Augie. Sure, our houses are smaller, but we've got the lake. What do those country club drips have? Grass? Cool.

I nodded at a passing Theater Club flyer. "Are you auditioning for the musical?"

"That question's homophobic, Jackson."

"C'mon. You don't like *Hairspray*?"

"That question's racist, Jackson."

We laughed and Augie shook his head. "The whole Skwad's auditioning. Barring Doug. Brynn and Cameron can't shut the fuck up about it. It's Cam's favorite musical."

I just looked ahead and nodded. Augie sighed. "So, yes. I am going to do *Hairspray*."

"Wow. Don't sound so devastated about it, man."

"You know, Mr. McBride emailed me personally this summer to make sure I was planning on auditioning. Really wanted to *get his ducks in a row.*"

"That's promising though, right? He wants you involved?"

"It isn't. It's numbers. Because Augie Horton does musicals. And Augie Horton must loooove *Hairspray*. And it would be a very bad look for the one Black guy in Moorestown Theater to sit out of their little white savior dance recital and—Jesus Christ, what the fuck is in this box?"

Augie readjusted his grip on his banker box. It was clear he was diverting my line of questioning away from the musical and onto a less sensitive topic. That's a thing about Augie. The guy's got masterful defense. You don't grow up fat, Black, and gay in a neighborhood like ours without a keen understanding of how to build your shields and exactly where to place them. And maybe it's our Laker connection or his parents always coming over for dinner parties, but I took it as a badge of honor that Augie never saw me as someone he needed to be shielded from.

I could tell that Augie was in no mood to go much deeper in that hallway so I didn't push. Rule number one about getting people to share their dirt with you: never push. A bit of patience, a bit of support, they'll always come to you. I'd have to wait for some late-night bonfire or cast party porch chat to get the real reasons Augie didn't want to audition for *Hairspray*. Or the real reasons why his face seemed to scrunch like that when he said his friends' names.

"QUEEEEEEEEEN!"

Or why his face quickly and decidedly unscrunched once we saw them by the lobby doors. *The Skwad.* Brynn Forester was jumping around the school lobby, waving her arms like she was trying to put herself out. Doug Parson was far tamer in his wave, but I could still hear it. Maybe I imagined it, but

I could've sworn I heard a small sigh rattle out of Augie before he waved back to his "bestie-in-crime," Brynn.

"Hey, girl!"

Interesting. I logged that for later. The face scrunches and silent sighs. Augie tossed his box back on my stack without a second look and let himself be sucked into the well-meaning whirlpool that was his *Skwad*. I suppose our time was over. The group was congregated outside of a sign-up sheet on the lobby bulletin. There was a big arts-and-crafts banner above the list reading ***HAIRSP AY AUDITIONS!*** Thing couldn't have been up for three hours and some super hilarious asshole still managed to make off with the cardboard ***R***. Great. That was the obnoxious sort of completely ignorable problem that was bound to be overdiscussed in the first fifteen minutes of my next student council meeting.

"Hey. You signing up?"

I put down my mental list of every kid in my grade sorted by most-to-least likely to vandalize a Theater Club sign and reentered the real world to find Cameron Ellis ten inches away from my face. Christ, he had good skin.

"Um… Huh?"

Cameron nodded at the bulletin board. "We're doing *Hairspray* this fall. It's a musical. Real inspiring, really tackles some big issues head-on. They made a movie about it actually, Zac Efron—"

"I know the movie. I'm not… I don't really do that."

"Oh? Do what?"

"Musicals."

Cameron laughed and moved his trademark auburn swoop back into his hair. "Of course you don't. You've got cities to build, Mr. President."

"I'm just busy. I stay busy. In the fall."

"I bet you do. Guy like you."

He was looking at me sort of strange. And close. It felt like he could sense every inch I tried to put between us. I looked up the hall for an exit strategy and tried thinking of a good defense. A stall. Anything.

"Hey, yeah, so how's Philip doing? *Phil*."

I tried to say it innocuously. Cameron had to have been asked about Phil a thousand times a day. It was just meant to buy time. Tread water. But it was like just Phil's name was enough to shake Cameron out of something. Like I'd insulted him, almost. Or at least offended him. With the reminder of his boyfriend, I watched Cameron's chemistry change.

"He's fine. Got detention thirty minutes into the school year, standard Phil shtick. Why? Do you know him?"

I just blinked. Interesting. Interesting Cameron didn't know our history. Not many people in this school remembered us like that, but I guess I was surprised Phil never talked about me. Maybe a little stung.

I shrugged. "I know everyone. Class president. Gotta know the constituents and all that."

Cameron squinted a little. Like he was trying to tell if I was bullshitting him. Then a smile stretched across his frustratingly smooth skin. "Precious voter data, I'm sure."

I didn't like how he was looking at me. I didn't understand how he was looking at me. Didn't he know? Didn't he know I found him insufferable?

I pulled the parachute and pointed my stack of boxes up the hallway. "Yeah, I've actually got to run. Some, uh…things to drop off at—"

Without my noticing, Doug Parson had appeared by our side. Cameron's oldest friend/straight security blanket. Wearing the same Rutgers basketball hoodie I'd seen him wearing since freshman year. "Sup, Pasty. Looking swole."

Then Brynn Forester was there, blocking my next move

like a knight on a chessboard. "President Pasternak! Welcome back! Did you have an amah-zing summer?"

As if following a group mind, Augie took his place in my remaining exit path from this sudden *Skwad* siege. I was boxed in. They had me.

Brynn cocked her head to the side, all smiles. She pointed at Cameron and me, side by side. "Wowzers! You and Cammy got so tan this summer. All that time outside, I bet. Baseball camp, Rowing Club. You do rowing, right? I saw you post about it."

If inching away wasn't going to work, I settled for some simple centimeters. "I, uh… Yes. Well, I *row*. You do *crew* or you *row*, you don't *do rowing*."

Brynn guffawed. A word I rarely used, but it was apt there. It echoed through the lobby and, somehow, I didn't believe a second of it. "Uh, DUH! Ugh, ignore me. I'm hopeless with anything jock-adjacent. Sportsball, amirite?"

She gave Doug a nudge but he was busy chewing on his hoodie drawstring. My precious few centimeters were regained by Brynn. "I wanted to ask you, actually. Would you ever want to guest on my show? We're live-streaming the first ep of the new season after school, I'm sure people would LOVE to hear from their favorite class president."

The Brynn Show. The semi–school-approved interview series Brynn's been doing online since the eighth grade. An invitation I'd been artfully dodging for the last three years. My brain went into bullshitting mode. "Oh, amazing. I'm actually super underwater this week with back to school and everything, but we should totally circle back sometime soon and get something on the books. I love the show, you do really important work."

Brynn gushed but Augie smirked to himself, well aware I'd never watched a second. God, why did I tell him that? Brynn shook Cameron's arm. "Awesome sauce! Cammy will send you some possible times. You two follow each other, right?"

My brain buffered on its bullshit. Something in her voice. Their looks. The real reason the Skwad had encircled me so suddenly. I was being led somewhere. "Oh. I think so. I never really… Y'know, I don't have a lot of time for—"

"You follow me." Cameron smiled. Very sure. "*@Jackson-JacobPasternak*. You use your full name. I thought that was funny, stood out."

"Oh. Did it?"

"It did. You liked a lot of my pics this summer, actually. Me at baseball camp. Me at the pool. It…stood out."

I stopped trying to inch. Centimeter. Whatever unit of measure, that stopped me. I clenched the banker boxes in my arms tighter and tried not sounding as caught as I felt. "Oh. Yeah. You… It looked like a fun summer. Solid compositions. Photographically."

It was like the Skwad was nodding in unison and I realized where I was being led. Why they were there. Why I was put there. I looked at Augie's soft smirk and wondered if he actually wanted to help with my boxes or if he just wanted to put me in front of Cameron goddamn Ellis.

Cameron smiled at the sign-up sheet. "Anyway. Mr. McBride's always looking for more guys in theater. Could be fun, us hanging out. Singing some songs. Running some lines."

I tried to match Cameron's smile, sweat just about fusing my polo to my back. "Maybe. I don't know. I think I'm pretty stacked up at this point."

I caught Cameron's eyes take a quick tour along the boxes in my arms. Down to my tight grip. Up my aching triceps. Finally landing on my chest.

"*Stacked up.* Sure."

I barked. I would like to say I laughed but, in the name

of full transparency, the sound that came out of me in that school lobby was far closer to a bark. What the hell was that? I have never, not once in my seventeen years, made a sound like that. I gave the group a big thumbs-up.

"Well. Bye!"

I just about Red Rovered my way through Augie and Doug. It felt like a claw from above had grabbed me by the neck and was guiding me out of the lobby. Away from the Skwad. Away from Cameron Ellis and his nice skin. Because Cameron wasn't being coy. He wasn't hiding it. He was flirting. Cameron Ellis was flirting with me, why the fuck would Cameron Ellis be flirting with me? Why the fuck would Cameron Ellis think I was someone he should flirt at? What did I do? Like a few photos? The guy posted every other hour, it was compulsive, of course I ended up liking a few. Of course I read a few of his blogs, I was just doing research. I was just keeping tabs on Philip, no one was supposed to know. Cameron wasn't supposed to know. Because what was there to even know? I wasn't like him. I've done that research and I knew, I was not like that. I was nothing like him. Veronica was wrong, I was nothing like Cameron fucking Ellis. The bell rang.

"Christ."

For the first time in my life, I'd officially cut class.

PHIL

TRACK FIVE
Sugar, We're Goin Down

I kicked my way through the overgrown weeds and noticed the storage unit next to mine was open. I shouldn't have been surprised that its owner was also cutting class on the second day of school. I also wasn't surprised that he'd been hot-boxing in the middle of the day.

"Mateo?"

"I'M BUSY."

I poked my head into his unit. In true Matty Silva fashion, the guy was smoking a joint in his kiddie pool and watching *Judge Judy*. He had this little portable TV he liked to balance on his lap while he soaked and smoked.

"Sup, shit-stick. You got food?"

"Good afternoon to you too." I left him to unlock my unit. "Why aren't you at school, Matty?"

"First week back don't count. Why aren't you at school?"

"My boyfriend wanted to have a serious talk with me."

"Coward."

"Yup."

The Silvas lived down the hall from us and were the closest thing our storage units had to managers. I didn't know if that title was self-imposed or not, but I never missed our monthly rent and the Silvas never asked questions. Plus, our moms are each other's favorite drinking buddies so the arrangement works out well for everyone.

I threw up my unit's grate and looked at my table. Finally ready. Finally perfect. Sitting legs-up on my work bench like a turtle on its back.

Matty's cough rattled through our shared wall. "The table's looking sick, dude. Stain job pulled it all together."

"You been spying in my box again?"

"I was here late. Got curious."

I folded that observation into my building theory that Matty might be sleeping out here. But that was his business. I didn't ask questions either.

I looked out onto the field and saw that the unit across the way was wide open. That unit had been empty for as long as I could remember, but now it was filled to the brim with antiques. Actual antiques, not the dusty lawnmowers and mildewy boxes that overstuff the other units. There was this ornate globe. A dark wood bookshelf lined with picture frames and old bindings. A rolled-up rug that probably cost twice our apartment's rent. All the fixings for an old rich man's study. I half expected to see a stuffed elephant head.

"Matty."

"Fucko."

"Who's renting Box Seven?"

I popped over to Matty's unit and he turned his TV volume down. "Shocking development, huh? I didn't know the guy, but he paid out the year. Nice shit."

"Some asshole just dumped the set of *Jumanji* in a unit and left the door wide open?"

"Seems like a trap, no?"

I shook my head. "Fucking Moorestown."

"Fucking rich people."

Matty lit up his joint then offered me a go. I declined. "I don't smoke before lunch. Ruins my dinner."

"Pussy. Y'know, if you wanna make another table, I could use a TV stand. Save me from my eventual electrocution."

"Yeah? You wanna buy one off me?"

"Why not? Shit looks like it's from a catalogue. A good one. You do good work." I shrugged. He doubled down. "Don't shrug it off, you leaking asshole, I'm complimenting your craft."

I rolled my eyes and fought the urge to shrug again. "Fine." But I nodded. "I'm… Yeah. I'm happy with it."

"Good. Bitch."

It was probably the weed talking, but the unexpected compliment made me want to vomit. It was like my nervous system was rejecting the foreign body that was direct praise so I made myself busy around my table. Matty moseyed over to my unit and dripped on the floor. Squinted across the lot, back over toward our apartments.

"You see someone stole the stop sign? On the four-way?"

I could never work comfortably in my unit with an audience so I just aimlessly cleaned up my workbench, waiting for Matty to leave. "Three outta four ain't bad."

"Shit's dangerous as hell. Saw three cars almost butt-fuck each other before breakfast."

"Someone will replace it, man. I think the super called."

"Garbage. Who steals a stop sign?"

I shrugged. "Maybe someone who needs to stop?"

Matty chuckled his way back to his unit. "Gay."

I felt some bubbles burst in my stomach. If it was a slipup, the asshole didn't bother catching himself. That was Matty though. Mateo Silva was a grade-A, gold-star dirtbag. What my good neighbor considers "just talking shit" is light-years worse than anything I would ever think to say on school grounds, and yet? The guy is arguably one of the most popular kids in Moorestown High. Boy's Teflon. Nothing sticks to him, no one calls him out, and he never says he's sorry.

If I had to try and solve the equation, what keeps Matty so clean where I can only seem to get dirtier, I'd have to blame his circle. The basketball team. His track bros. That bulletproof vest you receive the day you're deemed a *Star Athlete*. Must be nice.

He doused his joint in the kiddie pool and threw on his shirt. "Aight. My ride's here."

I looked across the field. On the other side of the chainlink, a stray dog was peeing on the tire of this beat-to-shit blue pickup at the curb. Matty switched off his TV and closed his unit's grate. "Go lock up that rich dick's unit, wouldya? Don't need some white dude bitching me out 'cause rats ate up his stuffed tiger."

But I was stuck on the pickup. Its empty bed. A solution to a problem that had been eating at me since I got the text last night. Cameron's text. ***We need to talk.***

"Yo. Do me a favor?"

Matty stopped in the grass. Surprised. He was accustomed to our limited neighborly interactions sticking to the usual *He talks shit about someone we know, I shrug or grunt my half-assed recognition* back and forth.

But he shrugged. "I don't sell drugs."

"Not remotely what I was gonna ask."

"People always think 'cause my brother used to, I can just—"

"I'm not looking to buy drugs, Silva. Chill."

Matty rolled his eyes, ready to end the chitchat. "Then spit it out. My ride's waiting."

I cleared some tools off my workbench and unclamped my table from the grips. "I gotta get this across town. Today. You think I could throw it on that pickup? It'll be quick, I swear."

Matty chuckled and coifed his hair. "Interesting. What's in it for me?"

"The satisfaction of helping your fellow man?"

He rolled his eyes. Then smirked. "You still delivering Passy's?"

"Yeah, why?"

Matty threw on his backpack and walked into my unit. Inspected my table. "Leftover slices. End of your shift, whatever they're looking to throw out, you hook your boy up."

"C'mon. Raph hates when we do that, man. If I lose that job, I'm fucked."

"Oh, you wanna drag this big bitch across town?"

Matty slapped on the table. I sighed. "Fine. Just for a week though."

"A month."

"Fucking...*fine*. A month. Deal?"

Matty snorted and we shook on it. We stretched out a little then got on opposite sides of the table. He eyed my stance with amusement. "Don't lift with your back. My boy's not making extra trips to the hospital."

I think the majority of Moorestown High would be very confused to catch a basketball bro helping some gay kid carry a gift for his boyfriend across a field of weeds. But that majority wouldn't know the whole story. Because Matty and I didn't just share a block or a homeroom or a bad reputation. It was that other thing that kept an apex predator away from easy prey. That kept the meanest kid in town from calling me a cock-sucking faggot and kept me feeling safe to ask for these little favors. It was an unwritten truce between us. Because I'd found Mrs. Silva sleeping one off in her car too many times to fuck with Matty. He'd mopped my mom's puke off his kitchen tiles too many times to fuck with me. Maybe all boys who take care of their fun, cool, alcoholic moms had this understanding with each other. I didn't know. It wasn't a conversation we'd ever had out loud.

I wasn't exactly in a place to make requests so I didn't complain when Matty made us stop at Wawa to pick up some coffee. Or at B-Town to pick up a late lunch. Or at the Rte. 130 Diner to pick up his paycheck. The sun was nearly setting by the time the pickup rolled into the Orchard and I don't think I said a single thing the entire excursion. Neither did the owner of the pickup. Our silent chauffeur for this day of errands and Matty Silva's primary "boy." All afternoon, Bash Villeda's eyes stayed stuck on the road, face frozen in the rearview mirror. Like I was looking at his picture in that new gym trophy case. Stone-still and intimidating. Luckily for both of us, Matty never shut the fuck up.

When we finally parked, Matty hopped out of Bash's truck and squinted around the fancy homes. Every McMansion looked like it was in direct competition with another, all vying to be the biggest waste of millions on the block. His eyes landed on Cameron's. "Yo. Who the fuck do you know in the Orchard?"

I closed the truck door and opened the pickup bed. "I can get it from here. Y'all can head out."

I stopped caring about sounding polite two unplanned errands ago but, moreover, couldn't think of a pair of guys I wanted to talk about my boyfriend with less.

"You made Cameron a table?"

Bash had hopped into the bed and was staring down at me. He looked about eight feet tall and every nerve ending in my spine decided to lock up at the sound of Bash the Flash's low, steady voice.

It was an innocent enough question, but I still felt stuck. Call me a queer cliché, but nothing could freeze me up quicker than "innocent questions" from jock assholes. I guess I just didn't trust them. Where the questions could lead. What might be bait.

Still, I nodded. "Yeah. Yeah, I made it for him. Took me all summer but…yeah."

Bash nodded back. Gave the table another look over. And even with the sun getting darker, I thought I almost saw something on Bash's face then. Maybe interest. Maybe respect. Something small behind all the stone. "You're a good boyfriend."

Then Matty slapped my back. "Fuck yeah, you are! Cameron Ellis better suck the skin off your dick for this, dude, goddamn."

I closed my eyes and sighed. The three of us got the table out of the bed and they helped me carry it up to Cameron's garage door. It was easy enough with six hands and I really don't know what I would've done all on my own. Matty made me swear again to follow through on my pizza promise and I thanked Bash for his help. I must've hit the guy's quota for effort this month because he was back to stone-faced grunts. Good enough for me. The boys packed back into the truck and then they were gone.

When I found him in his room, he was sitting at a new

desk. It was one of those generic pieces of hard cardboard you get on sale with free delivery. Every inch of the shitty little thing was cramped with his recent purchases. A ring light. The fancy camera all the influencers recommended. All the fixings for *Candid Cameron* to take over the world.

"I said I wanted space, Mom."

Cameron turned around in his swivel chair and saw me in his doorway. He looked like he'd been crying.

"Sorry. I should've texted."

"Phil."

"Is that… You bought a desk?"

Cameron eyed his new piece of decor. Guilty. "I needed something for my videos. You were taking a long time."

"I… A table takes a long time, Cameron."

"Fine."

"Fine?"

"Fine. Alright."

He wouldn't look at me. I took a step closer. Tried a smile. "I finished. It's downstairs, in the driveway. I didn't… I didn't want to bring it up before you made room. Or…if you wanted to maybe…"

His chair was facing me. He was facing me. I'd put myself right in front of him, but he couldn't look at me. Wouldn't.

"Baby?"

Cameron wouldn't fucking look at me.

"We… We need to talk, Phil."

I saw his eyes begin to move for mine, but I turned away. Something took over and it was my turn not to look.

"It's in the driveway. I think you're gonna really like it, Cam. I stayed up all night staining—"

"Phil."

"It's walnut which looks amazing in the sun, but it's way heavier than I thought—"

Cameron stood up and grabbed my arm. *"Philip."*

It was like his touch made me shiver. Little shakes, pulling me away from him.

"Just come look at it? Please?" I turned around. Kept the space. "Cam, c'mon. It looks great. I spent all... Come on." I swallowed. "You gotta see it, Cam. Because I made it for you. You've gotta at least see it, Cameron. Please."

Cameron wiped his eye. "I just... I had a lot of time this summer, Phil. To think. To try and think of a good time or way or... *Phil.*"

He reached for my hand again. I backed away. Stunned. "Are... Are you fucking kidding me?"

Cameron closed the space I put between us. "Listen. Please. I thought I'd feel differently when I got home and saw you but—"

"Cameron, we've seen each other TWICE. You JUST got back, we haven't even—"

"I just think we need... I think we just need some air, y'know? We rushed into a lot of this, Phil."

Funny thing? I don't know if I've ever actually, truly *gasped* before.

"...*We?*"

But I did. I actually gasped.

"WE?! *WE* rushed into this?!"

Cameron's eyes were on his rug. He couldn't do me the basic courtesy of looking at me while he ruined my life. Again. In the same damn year. "You're still so important to me, Phil. Please. I need you to believe that. But Augie thinks we might need some time to—"

I just about screamed my laugh up at the bedroom ceiling.

"OOOH! Okay. Okay, this is them? It's their idea, you're picking the *SKWAD* over me?!"

"It's not like that, Phil. I just think… I mean, they have a point."

"No. No, no, no. The Skwad never has a point. They're a collection of trends and catchphrases, there is no fucking point."

Cameron scoffed. "Oh my god! You can't even TRY to like them! They're my friends, Phil, they're a part of me. They just want me to have a great junior year. And they love you!"

"FUCK. OFF. They do not love me."

"Yes, they do! They just think you can get a little…"

Cameron searched for the word. Because he didn't know either. Watching him try to explain himself and his choices and his garbage, manipulative friends pissed me off. Made me angry. Made me scream.

"A LITTLE *WHAT*?!"

Cameron flinched. My scream bounced around his room. We stood in the echo, my rage answering for him. I tried to swallow, but it had gotten tight. I tried to speak, but it had gotten hard.

"I…" I felt tears in my eyes and hated myself for being such a fucking pussy. "I can be better, Cam."

I wanted to slap the whine out of my voice. I wanted to drag my weak ass out of that room and leave it dead in a creek somewhere. I wanted to go home. "It was just a bad day. It was just a few bad days, you just got back, we haven't… We just need more time. Yeah? We need to give it time, baby."

My legs were getting shaky so I sat down on Cameron's bed. Felt his quilt. "If we never got paired up in shop class last year, you wouldn't have known I existed. I never woulda known your name. By *a lot* of metrics, you and me never should've met."

Despite myself, despite everything wrong in me, I smiled. "I'm really glad we met, Cam. Because I didn't like a single thing about myself when I met you. And you helped me remember a couple."

I could feel them coming. It had been about three years since I let someone see. A tear ran down my cheek, but I couldn't stop smiling. "You threw me back into the world, man. And I *hate* the fucking world. But I hate it a little less when I'm with you."

I could see Cameron's coming too. He sniffed and sat with me on his bed. Held my hand. Let our tears be silent, just for a little bit.

"Did you start the fight with Veronica?"

"It wasn't my—" He looked at me. Soft. I sighed. "I'm sorry."

Cameron's hand was on mine. Almost petting it. Almost keeping me still. "I don't... Phil, I don't think you are. I don't... I don't think you care."

"I—"

"And I don't want to spend the rest of my high school life apologizing for you. I want more than that."

"I want more than that too, Cam."

"Do you? Because it really feels like a matter of time before you're screaming at me in front of the principal's office. Calling me a faggot at some pool party. Making some point out of me. When's it gonna be my turn?"

I saw Jackson's face. Hurt. Holding his cheek. Finally learning the lesson about trying to know me. Finally seeing why he never should have wanted to be my friend. Finally seeing me.

I shook my head. "I... Cameron. I wouldn't. Not you."

I couldn't look at him. I settled for my lap. "Sometimes…
Sometimes it feels like I have this never-ending argument in
my stomach. It's all I can hear sometimes. This nonstop list of
things I hate. About school. Or my parents. This town or…
or myself. I'm on it a lot."

I took his hand back. Soft. "But you're not. You're not on
the list. I can't hate you, Cameron. I can't. And I don't want
to try."

Cam watched our hands together. Like he was wondering
if they fit together. I squeezed them tight to show him they
could. "Please, Cameron. *Please* don't let your friends break this
up. I'll do whatever you want. I'll be nice. I'll be goofy and
fun, I'll do the Skwad. Our differences don't have to matter.
We don't have to let them. I'll be happy. Just…"

My tear hit our hands and I felt it slip between our fingers.
"Don't leave me out here, Cameron. Not because of them.
Don't leave me out here alone. Not you too."

With a sniff, I heard Cameron's breathing slow. He rubbed
my knuckles and I could feel the tear drying between us. I
wanted to kiss him. I wanted him to kiss me. I wanted to fall
asleep on his quilt and wake up on back to school day. Try this
terrible week out again, together. Get excited for his musical and
laugh with my guidance counselor and tell my mom I would
try to be better. Better with Cameron. Safe with my boyfriend.
I could be happy with Cameron. I could be happy.

"The Skwad told me to try and make it work. I wanted to
break up before I left for camp."

I went still. The words had come out of him cold. Like he
had decided it was time to finally say it. Pull the cord. Put
me out of my misery.

Cameron looked at me. Dead in the eye. "People are finally
paying attention to me, Phil. That's never happened before.

People know my name. They *remember* my name. You know
how many of those people have asked me what I see in you?
You know how many messages I got this summer asking me
about you? *Why him?* It's… It's exhausting, baby. It's exhausting explaining why I'm with you."

"Cameron."

His hands were still so warm on mine. His words were
cold and hard, but his hands were still soft.

"Why do you want to be with me, Phil? Why? Why are
you still with me?"

I didn't know what to say. I didn't know what to do. It
felt like I was in that booth with the Skwad again, drawing a
blank. Finding no answer to this question of *Cameron.* Why
him? Why make a table? Why did I kiss him in front of a
dance full of people? In front of the cameras and my parents
and the whole fucking world? Why was I letting myself cry
in front of a boy who outed me to the world?

I finally found my answer. I finally found the words. *"Because I'm in love with you."*

A sob lived and died in my throat and I wanted him to hold
me. I wanted him to care. I wanted nice, adorable Cameron Ellis to stop me from feeling so ashamed that I was in
love with him.

Cam returned the favor and wiped a tear off my cheek.
"Baby. That isn't my fault."

It was like someone flicked off the light switch in my brain
and everything went dark. The little light in my head went
dead and so did I. Cameron stood up and fixed his hair. Walked
across the carpet and opened the door. It was time for me to
leave. But I didn't know how to make my body move yet.

"I think we had something really beautiful, Phil. And I
hope we can both learn lessons from it. Our *beautiful something.*"

He'd said it like he'd written it. Like he knew this was always going to be the last line in our story. Our book. Some cute, easy summer read that Brynn would promote on her show. *Our Beautiful Something* by Cameron Ellis.

I finally managed to speak. "That... That doesn't mean anything."

Cameron nodded. Then he shrugged. "Well. Maybe you'll learn a lesson anyhow."

My legs moved for me and I walked out onto the white hallway carpeting. I turned back and watched Cameron from his doorway.

"You made me come out. You said you loved me. In front of the school. The whole fucking world."

Old tears were already drying on my cheek. This conversation was already over and Cameron was already over me. But I had to ask. "Was any of that real?"

Cameron had his arms crossed and he thought about it. Really thought about it. Maybe a little too long. Then he nodded. "...I'd like to think so."

The door shut in my face and suddenly I was back in the driveway. Staring at my table. Maybe I passed Mrs. Ellis on the way out. Maybe I told her goodbye or thanked her for always being so nice to me. Maybe I told her to choke, I don't know. I don't know how I got out there. Sitting on my table. Getting hit by the mist of a neighbor's sprinkler. Trying to catch my breath. It was over. And I could tell myself that was a good thing. I could tell myself that I hated that neighborhood, hated his friends and the attention and this boyfriend I never asked for. I could tell myself it was only a matter of time before I stood up for myself and broke things off with Cameron and told him to go to hell for outing me.

But it was always going to end like this. A door in my face. A shock in my system. My heart on the sidewalk.

Like before. Like with Jackson.

I felt a buzz in my pocket. An alert from the world.

@CandidCameron posted a Video

I looked back up at Cameron's window. His bedroom light was off. I opened the video. I hadn't watched anything from his new *Candid Cameron* vlog setup, but there he was. Sitting at a table I didn't make, in a room I'd just been broken in. He was wearing the same clothes. His hair was still wet from his shower. The video was recorded *right* before I knocked on his door. Cameron stared into his camera, the little white halo of his ring light giving him a second iris. He was serious.

"Hey, Cam Army. Sorry for the late post but…a lot's been going on with me. I'm sure you've noticed, a lot of you've been asking. I just wanted to hop on here and get some things off my chest. Figured I'd set the record straight. I owe that to you and I wanted you to hear it from me. Before people start talking."

Cam sniffled and stared off at nothing for a little. The ring light only made his blue-green eyes seem all the glassier and I knew he was about to cry.

"It's over. Phil broke up with me."

The light switch in my head flicked back on and I felt my body come back to me. I felt my arms and my breathing return and I felt my hate put down its bags.

"Mother. Fucker."

JACKSON

TRACK SIX
Who Will Save Your Soul?

I couldn't help but read Mrs. Stapler's frantic email like an anchor on the nine o'clock news. *The kids call it "Bushing" and it could be taking over your small town. Harmless prank or a troubling sign of things to come? More on this as the story develops, back to Todd with the weather.*

"Hey, have you heard of *bushing*?"

I showed my phone to Augie and fixed myself another plate of mini quiches. Dad only threw the impromptu dinner and drinks because he always got antsy when Maman was on long flights and I'd spent the better half of the hobnobbing glued to the appetizer table.

Augie squinted at my phone. "Why does the new guidance lady have your personal email?"

"Oh, I presume it's spray-painted in the teachers' lounge bathroom at this point."

Augie handed me back my phone. "*Bushing.* Huh. Didn't know it had a name but eighth period is making more sense now."

"How do you mean?"

Augie reloaded up his plate from the enormous platter of cocktail shrimp. "So. I'm in algebra, it's day two, we're not doing anything. Mrs. Whitaker is going around making sure we got the right graphing calculators, yada yada. Then… *Anthony Lewis.*"

He plopped a glob of cocktail sauce on his plate with a force that told me what he thought of our neighborhood's most consistent problem. Anthony Lewis was arguably the worst thing to happen to the Orchard's already iffy reputation. Maybe the richest kid in the neighborhood behind the DiSarios with a lengthy history of frat-boy bullshit and his daddy bailing him out of trouble.

"The second Mrs. Whitaker's back is to him, Ant Lewis stands up, faces Bolu Olowe, and drops his pants."

I choked on a bit of rye. "*What?* Like…like boxers too?"

"No, no. Just a peek. Just down to…"

Augie waited for it to click for me. I closed my eyes and sighed. *"The bush."*

"Simply the bush. And they call me gay."

"That… And people are just doing this? In the middle of class?"

"Guess mooning got too basic for the straight boys."

I was rereading Mrs. Stapler's plea to see her in the morning to discuss the best way to cut this trend off at the pass but paused. Some warning bell pricked my ears and it almost came out of me like an automated message.

"Yeah, we're the worst."

Augie was scraping at a bit of leftover vein in his shrimp. "Hmm?"

I shrugged, suddenly acting far more blasé than I ever naturally am. "Straight guys. Locker room bullshit, gives us a bad name. Us…heteros."

Augie looked at me, all nods and shrimps. Really letting my offering dangle limply over the app table. Then he smiled. "This is great shrimp."

The fifteen finger sandwiches I'd consumed in the last hour felt like they wanted to rejoin their friends on the table. Because the smile. The nods. They all confirmed what I already suspected. That he suspected. Nothing concrete, but Augie Horton had seen enough of me to wonder. Maybe he always had his suspicions. Maybe growing up like he did, the only gay kid in a five-mile radius for years, maybe you're trained to suspect it in every boy. Always on, always trying to sort out allies or threats. Or maybe he just knew what to look for.

Augie offered me a shrimp in my moment of silence. "Skrimp?"

I blurted out something about the sun being down and keeping kosher which made no sense because it was a Thursday and I don't keep kosher. But before I could unload the ins and outs of Judaism to him, one of my tried and true diversions, an invisible needle in my ass was guiding me to our guest bathroom. The window above that toilet was a lot easier to open though I felt a bit ridiculous pulling the same parachute twice in forty-eight hours. But I needed to escape. Whatever I did, whatever Augie must've told Cameron about me, it was my fault for not being more careful. Less suspicious. But it was Augie's fault second and that was enough to leave him to his shrimp.

I'd just gotten the window open when I was interrupted.

"Christ on sale. You're here?"

I whipped around to find Veronica DiSario groaning against the bathroom door. "This is my house. You're here?"

"Thus is my burden. Are you jumping out a window again?"

My foot was teetering on the toilet. I had no leg to stand on. "…I got bored."

I only noticed then that Veronica's boots were in her hands. "Wait. Did you come in here to jump out too?"

"Consider me inspired. Here."

She put her hands together and knelt by the window, like a cheerleader at the bottom of the pyramid.

"You're helping me?"

"If you get out, I get out faster. Move, Pasternak."

I laughed and she boosted me up. I got out on the windowsill far easier but the drop looked way rockier than the one at school.

"Just don't fall on your face this time, it'll be a breeze."

"Right. Good point. Why are you running away?"

"Same as you, presumably. Bored."

If only to stall, I looked back at Veronica by the toilet. "I'm actually running away because Augie Horton came. He never comes to these things."

"What, are you stalling?"

"A little. Yeah."

Veronica smirked, just a bit. "Fine. If we're being honest, I'm also leaving because of him."

"You don't like Augie?"

A poorly thought-out question. Of course the ex-girlfriend and infamous casualty of Cameron Ellis would have a bone to pick with the Skwad's bitchiest personality.

Veronica wiped some bathroom floor off her jeans. "No. I do not like Augie. Jump."

"Y'know, we could probably just sneak out the laundry—"

A quick shove to my sweater and I had to act fast. I made

sure my face wasn't the first thing to hit the bush and man-aged to crash on my ass pretty comfortably.

"Oh. Wow." I hopped up and plucked the stray leaf out of me. "Works better if you don't overthink it, I guess."

"Life lessons, all around us. Move."

Veronica didn't need my help to get onto the windowsill or my push to get airborne. She'd landed a little back-heavy and let out a long groan when she settled.

"There has to be a better way."

I pulled her out of the bush and chuckled. "Talk about *bushing*."

Veronica got on her feet and just stared at me. "What?"

"Oh. Earlier conversation. You had to be there."

"Then why bring it up to me?"

"I don't…know."

We'd both gotten the last of the bush viscera off our backs and, with that busy work completed, stood in an awkward silence. I tried to help it. "So, you enjoying back to schoo—"

"And you have yourself a good night."

Veronica ducked away and headed through my backyard. I don't know if she had places to be, but she certainly looked determined. I, however, hadn't planned past hitting the bush.

"Where you going?"

She looked back at me but didn't stop, like I was some gnat interrupting her solo night walk. "What's it to you?"

"You gonna walk home?"

"What's it to you?"

I caught up to her and tried to keep her pace. "Got any fun plans for the weeken—"

She huffed and stopped in the grass. "Jackson. I am not babysitting you tonight. Go find someone else to *effortlessly charm*."

I looked back at my house, the sounds of drinks and good conversation bleeding out all the way across the lawn. I didn't know if it was just Augie's attendance, the fear that my mere appearance might give him more to suspect, but the sight of my nice, charming lakeside home made my lungs feel simultaneously overfilled and empty.

"I just… I don't know where to go right now?"

Veronica sighed up at the stars, rubbing a headache out of her temples. "I'm not inviting you over."

"So, you *are* going home."

"Where else would I be going?"

"Exactly."

She shot me a look. "Hmm. And what exactly does *Exactly* mean?"

I caught myself. I guess I'd taken it for granted that Veronica would be spending the night at home. Alone. It was a fair assumption, given what Maman's relayed to me. And it was a safe bet to think she wasn't ditching my company for a friend's. Had Cameron Ellis left her with any friends?

"I just… I thought you might want to hang out?"

"Hang out?"

"You know. Hang out. Talk. Could be fun. Could be… helpful."

Veronica DiSario inspected my throat closely for the best angle to punch. I stood up straighter under her glare. "I only mean… If you had anything you wanted to talk about, you know… We've just known each other for a long time now, Veronica, and I just want you to know if you ever feel like you need somebody to talk to, I'm always free to—"

Veronica squinted up at me. "Why do you call me *Veronica*?"

I stopped babbling out whatever offer I was trying to cobble together. "I don't, uh… That's your name?"

"People who've known me since diapers call me *Veronica*. Grandparents. My doctor. Adults call me *Veronica* and I do hate breaking this to you, Jackson, but you are not a fucking adult. Stop acting like it, stop following me, and kindly fuck off."

She headed off my property and walked along the lake's edge. She hadn't put her shoes back on so her socks were getting muddy. I took off my boat shoes and followed.

"My mother told me about your parents."

Veronica stopped in the mud and cocked her head back. Certainly surprised. Certainly unamused.

"Do you…"

She shook her head, amazed at the sight of me. The gall. "Oh my God, you truly do not understand. Jackson, I do not want to talk to you right now. And I CLEARLY do not want to talk to you about THAT."

I took another step in the mud. Tried my best to explain. "I just thought you might not have somebody to—"

Veronica met me halfway, wet squishes of mud flicking up in her stomp. "How 'bout you tell me about you, huh? How about you tell me why you're so fucking upset, Jackson, maybe I'll tell you about me? What? No?"

"I'm not ups—"

"PLEASE."

She pointed a black fingernail in my face. "I watched you plaster on that fake bullshit smile through eighteen fucking dinner parties this summer, Pasternak. I've caught you jumping out of a bathroom window TWICE now. You're clearly running away from something way bigger than Augie fucking Horton. You wanna get all gushy with each other all of a sudden, you wanna bring up my shit? Why don't *you* talk about something real for once in your goddamn life, you preppy fucking puppet?"

Now I was backing away. But she stayed on me. I didn't know how long the rage had been building up in Veronica. A rage I've watched build for months at my dinner table. In the Moorestown hallways. The jokes. The whispers. The punch line. It was a rage that started brewing the night of a winter dance. But whatever switch I'd tripped, whatever pipe I'd burst with my breach of etiquette, it was all coming out. All at me.

"You think 'cause our moms are tight and I indulge your nice parents and your nice house and your cocktail shrimp, you get to ask me about me? You think I owe you an IOTA of my weeknight? Not everybody in this town wants to be your friend, Mr. President, not everybody owes you their vote."

"Veronic—"

"Not everybody FUCKING LIKES YOU."

It felt like my brain was buffering. Because I knew that. Of course, I knew that. I never needed everyone to like me. I've never needed that. And yet? Frozen by the side of our lake, my mind opened up my secret Excel sheet and was frantically searching for a rebuttal. The debater in me poured over the hidden list I'd been keeping for years that assured me I was alright. I was normal. I was a good person who people liked and liked to talk to.

"I... I apologize."

My voice squeaked out of me as my mind panicked for some defense. Something to prove Veronica wrong. It searched through the piles of evidence I'd hoarded to assure myself. Class president. Rowing captain. A shoo-in at Penn. Dinner parties and teachers' lounges and nods from the basketball team. Everybody agreed. Everybody liked Jackson Pasternak. I had the research. An endless Excel sheet. A list I'd only started keeping the night my best friend told me that he didn't. Not anymore. And Veronica had that same look. That same anger. They were always so alike. Maybe that was why I'd wanted to be her friend. Because Veronica sounded just like Phil there. The night he finally decided we were just too different. Because of how I am. How I grew up, how I think, I could never understand him and I needed to stop trying. Suddenly, by the lake, I was right back in his kitchen. Holding my cheek. Fresh from a fight that put nearly three years between us. It had been just about three years since the first person I ever truly loved told me there was something inexplicably wrong with my brain.

"Jackson…" Veronica looked almost horrified standing by that lake. I'm sure she wasn't used to people crying in front of her. "Oh, shit. What the hell, man?"

"I'm s-sorry."

I covered my face. I couldn't pull it back. But I'd bothered Veronica enough that night so I decided to just walk away.

She called after me. "That's not fair."

"It's n-not your fault, I just… Bad day. G-good night!"

"Jackson."

I kept walking, trying to stop myself from breaking down too apparently. It was an uphill battle because on the rare occasion something could push me to actual sobs, I descended into something of a malfunctioning robot. I remembered Maman's gardening shed would still be unlocked and decided that would be a safer place to ride out the wave. Reset to my factory settings.

I could hear Veronica following me in the mud but didn't look back. I didn't need to be apologized to or falsely reassured, and she was actually completely accurate in everything she'd said.

Striding for the shed, I hiccuped over my words. *"Thought you s-said you weren't babysitting me t-tonight."*

"That was before you emotionally blackmailed me, douche. Slow down."

"You don't have to st-stay. I c-can't f-fault you for being observ—" I wiped some snot off my face and calmed down a little. "Observant."

I reached the shed and closed the wooden door behind me. From the other side of the wood, I heard Veronica finally catch up and sigh. "Jackson. Get out of the shed."

"You don't have to stay. I release you."

She scoffed through the cracks in the oak. "You can absolutely fuck off, Jackson. I get honest with you for once and you go spend the night crying in a shed? You understand what emotional manipulation is, right?"

I punched on a stack of mulch bags until they were sittable and hopped up. "Well. Manipulation requires intent. Anything else is just subconscious suggestion. Ethically."

A heavily mascaraed eye squinted through a slit in the door. "*Ethically*, intent is irrelevant when judging an active party. And, *ethically*, if we're talking about intention, the terms of manipulation can only be defined by the manipulated. If you want to get *ethical*."

I leaned against the potting shelf and sighed. Veronica Di-Sario might have been kicked out of Debate Club but she was still a lawyer's daughter. I will say the back-and-forth was helping me breathe easier. Busting out SAT words always did that for me.

"Well. I'm sorry I'm manipulating you. I really didn't mean to cry. I'm sorry if I freaked you out. I just…" I wiped the rest of the crap off my face and took a long inhale. "I hate back to school."

Veronica chuckled. I heard the shed creak a little and guessed she was leaning on the door. "If it's anything…" She sighed.

"Yes. My parents are splitting. I mean, they never haven't been splitting but...this time it seems to be sticking. My dad's been moving his stuff out all summer. A lot of... A lot of empty rooms. It's...yeah."

It was quiet for a bit. I just nodded. Like she could see me. "I'm sorry, Veronica."

She laughed, sort of annoyed. "Sure. Like Maman didn't already tell you that."

"She didn't. Not all that. I'm sorry."

It was quiet for a little bit more. Then I heard a sniff. A tighter voice. "Thank you."

The shed creaked again and I guessed she'd walked away. I pulled out my phone to check the time. Maybe we'd killed enough of it and the party would be over. The clock told me I'd still have another hour or so before I could responsibly slip back into my house, but the weather app told me sleeping in the shed might not be the end of the world.

I started searching the tiny room for a passable blanket when my phone started buzzing. I picked it up without thinking. "Good evening—"

"Hello. This is Amber from the Philadelphia Jewish Community—"

"STOP CALLING ME."

I hung up on **SCAM LIKELY** because I was in no mood. I was searching the call details for a way to finally block the number when I caught an unread alert from my email. Maybe another plea from Mrs. Stapler on the encroaching pandemic of jock bro pubic hair.

One (1) New Post from CANDID CAMERON

That late? Cameron had been sticking to a pretty consistent rollout plan this summer and he'd already posted that morning. Odd. But I did have time to kill. I clicked the link and saw the headline.

CANDID CAMERON
Post #297

~Our Beautiful Something~
by Cameron Ellis

Our Beautiful Something? Ugh. I hated that sort of thing. That purposefully vague, intentionally agrammatical kind of nonspeech that romance writers and hobbyist poets like to use to "express the inexpressible." Like admitting that you "just couldn't find the words" is something romantic and not an admission that you stopped trying.

I scrolled down and found Cameron's face staring right back at me. "This better be good."

I hit Play on **Our Beautiful Something** and Cameron's face unfroze.

"Hey, Cam Army. Sorry for the late post but…a lot's been going on with me. I'm sure you've noticed, a lot of you've been asking. I just wanted to hop on here and get some things off my chest. Figured I'd set the record straight. I owe that to you and I wanted you to hear it from me. Before people start talking."

Cameron's face looked weird. Sad for sure. Undeniably sad. Actually, I think that might have been the weird part. It was like the muscles in Cameron's face were doing everything possible to make sure we all knew just how sad Cameron was.

"It's over. Phil broke up with me."

I fell off my mulch bags and hit the floor with a smack. The wind had fully knocked out of my lungs, but I scrambled across the floor to get my phone back. I wiped off a bit of dirt and held Cameron's face inches from my own.

"I met Phil Reyno in a shop class I had to take last fall. We were paired up by the teacher because no one else in class was jumping to choose us as partners. I wasn't always so talkative and not a lot of kids noticed me like that but…" Cameron laughed, very wistful. *"But they all noticed Phil. Nobody really saw me but everyone saw Phil Reyno. His reputation. We all knew the stories. We all knew he could be mean. And difficult. And angry at everything for any reason. But I liked being his partner. I liked his jokes and his complaining and his wild, punky outfits."*

Another laugh. Again, so wistful. *"I guess I thought I saw something more. I thought there was more. I thought there was more to Phil Reyno."* He looked off to pause. Then a shake in the head. *"I guess I was wrong. I thought I could help him. I thought I was helping him. But maybe you can't help everybody. Maybe some people are exactly who they say they are. Maybe some accidents are just meant to happen."*

Cameron's nose twitched. Like he had an itch he wasn't allowed to scratch. It just kept going and pretty soon tears were falling. Down his cheeks. Onto his hands. Onto his oddly cheap desk. *"I opened my heart to him. You've all seen it. You've read every chapter of this book I thought we were writing together, I've shown you every line. I tried. I tried everything I could. I loved that boy with everything I had. And he took it. Phil took everything I had."*

The nose stopped twitching and Cameron wiped his red face with a sniffle. *"God. And, before anyone asks, please, please, guys, really this is not an attack on Phil. Please. No hate, guys. I'm sure he's hurting too. I'm sure he has his side to this story. His own chapters. I hope you'll all listen to his side. Because I meant what I said at the Snow Globe Ball. Philip Reyno deserves to be seen."*

Then a silence. And another. Then Cameron looked right into his camera. *"But I deserve better."*

There was a knock on his door. Cameron sniffled one last time and turned off his camera. My phone went black and I just stayed there for a moment. In the pitch black. On the dirt floor of a gardening shed. My phone in my face and Cameron's sniffling nose in my mind. I felt numb. No. I felt numbed. I felt senseless. Something cold poured through my body, this unfeeling feeling, and it weighed me down. Kept me still.

Phil.

How could he do this? How could he be so reckless? How could he be so cruel?

Phil.

How could he do this to Phil?

The word spit out of me. Venomous. Hateful. Vengeful. I pointed my finger at the blank screen in my face.

"Liar."

PHIL

———

TRACK SEVEN

My Own Worst Enemy

I tasted blood in my mouth. I couldn't catch my breath. I was going to throw up, I just needed to catch my breath first. Why the fuck did I make such a heavy table? I finally got it onto my workbench and collapsed into the weeds. Almost two miles. Over two hours. My palms were bleeding and I felt the bottom half of my spine slipping out of my asshole.

"God… Goddammit…"

I need to shower. I needed to sleep. I didn't have the strength to hop the chain-link so I took the long way back to my apartment building. I turned onto Duquesne and nearly tripped off the curb. Then I saw the lights. Flashing. Blues and reds, illuminating the night above my block.

"What…"

Something was happening. Something had happened. Women in bathrobes and kids in their underwear were in their yards trying to catch a peek. Cop cars and firetrucks littered the intersection outside my building. It only took two hours of running and dragging and screaming but, I finally stopped moving. At the four-way stop with only three of its stop signs.

"Fuck."

After weeks of near misses and honking horns, my petty act of vandalism had finally caused an accident. Not just a fender bender. Not just a reason to exchange insurance cards. An incredible, unbelievable, entirely preventable accident.

"Oh, fuck."

I didn't know a garbage truck could tip over. I guess I never really put any thought toward the idea. But there it was. A garbage truck on its side. A mountain of trash on my own front lawn.

"Oh…fuuuuuuuck."

The front yard of Browning Apartments looked like the aftermath of a weekend-long music festival. You couldn't see a blade of grass under a neighborhood route's worth of busted-open trash bags, loose junk, and wet garbage. Mrs. Silva and my mom were standing in the middle of the street, sharing a cup of something and laughing their asses off. They couldn't see me. I don't know if Mom ever noticed the sign above my bed, but after this clusterfuck it would only be a matter of time. And seeing me would only speed up her detective work.

I found my second wind. I needed to keep moving. I slipped through my gawking neighbors, everyone asking how this could happen and who would clean it up, and ran around to the side of my building. Of course. Of course, tonight. Of course, my apartment. Of course, my fault. Of fucking course. Cameron was right. Some accidents are just meant to happen.

I hopped a railing and made it into my building's parking lot. I sprinted past the laundry room, jumped up the back stairwell, and got back to mine before I ever touched the ground. I was standing on my bed before I could lock my door and unbolting the reflective, red prison sentence off my ceiling. I don't know why I kept telling myself it would be harmless. I don't know why this town let a missing stop sign stay missing for half a fucking summer. If I lived in the Orchard, that signpost would've been restocked the second I looked away.

Soon enough, I was back outside and staying in the shadows, an Eagles towel wrapped snuggly around the evidence. I got clear of the flashing lights and hopped the chain-link back into the overgrown field. The storage units were still impossible to make out so far from streetlights, but I got to mine quick enough. The unit's grate was still open, my table still hanging halfway off the bench, and I slipped the toweled-up sign behind my tool shelf. My unit would be the first place anyone would look if tonight's mess got tied back to me, but it would have to do for now. I just needed it out of my room. Out of my apartment. Out of my fucking life.

This stop sign could ruin my life. But what life did I have left to ruin? What life had Cameron left me with? How many times can one life be over? In one fucking school year? I stared at my walnut table, sadly hanging off my workbench, and grabbed my axe off the shelf. It had to go. It all had to go.

"YOU STUPID **FUCK**!"

I let it all out. Unloaded on my table.

"YOU UGLY **FAGGOT**!"

My summer project. My proudest creation. My gift to my boyfriend.

"YOU MISERABLE! MEAN! DESPERATE! PA-THETIC—"

A boyfriend who made a fool of me. Who forced me into the ocean then left me there to drown. Who used my secret and my shame and my story to get likes and friends and followers. Who did all of this to me, who never apologized for a moment, and I still told him that I loved him.

"WEAK! LONELY! UNLIKEABLE! UNFUCKABLE! UNLOVABLE—"

I turned my beautiful something into splinters then slammed the axe into the flimsy metal wall of the storage unit.

"FUCK!"

The scream shook through my workshop. Out into the night. I stared at the axe lodged into the metal. The damage I could never stop giving the world.

I took the axe out of the wall and threw it to the ground. I hiccupped. "You… You fucking *fool*."

I wiped my face and tried to catch my breath. I heard the voice echo nearby. *"Can't get a moment's peace in this fucking town…"*

The heat on my face became boiling. I thought I was alone out there. But my meltdown had an audience. I walked out of my unit and stood in the overgrown grass. Ronny DiSario was sitting in the open unit across the way. At the fancy antique writing desk. Eating a plate of finger sandwiches and playing with her phone.

She dropped a tiny turkey club back on the pile then pulled her headphones down. "Hey, slugger. Wanna know something fun?"

She popped up from the desk and slid across the top. Waggled her phone at me. The same paused image of Cameron Ellis's teary face. She'd been watching the video too.

Ronny tapped her nose. "Cam's nose quivers. When he fakes it. Sort of sniffles around. My grandma taught him that. Old acting trick, really sells that you're crying." She left her storage unit and walked over to mine. Sort of inspected my face. "But you've been crying for real. 'Cause *Cam* dumped *you*. Right? Not whatever this was?"

I bristled at the smell of mustard on her breath. The familiarity in her closeness. "Back the fuck off."

"Aw. Or you'll axe me to pieces?"

I retreated inside my unit. "I know it might seem like a really good opportunity to *get me* right now, Ron, but… Please. Just fuckin—"

The second I turned my back to her, my face twisted. It came up on me quick. Like I thought I might be able to hide what my body needed to do if I just kept my back to her. I couldn't stop it though. I could only hide. I buried my face into my hands and choked on the sobs. *"Go away. P-please go away."*

The whine in my voice sounded like a child's and I wanted to be deleted from the world. I leaned over my workbench, over the walnut toothpicks that used to be something beautiful, and tried to keep it back. I must've looked pathetic. I know I looked ugly.

I could hear Ronny start in on a fresh sandwich. "Christ. So much crying for a Thursday." She sighed, oddly patient. "Lemme know when you're done."

I gave myself over to it. I wept on my workbench. I screamed into the toothpicks. I cursed and I punched and I got splinters in my knuckles. Ronny had the courtesy to keep her back to it all. I appreciated that. She looked up at the moon above us and just listened to me empty.

"The girls will be the first to turn on you. The ones who hear things early. Dani Touscani. Amanda Allen. The girls' girls. Brynn might act sweet, but she knows how people work. She'll tell the people who tell people."

I could feel the pain in my bloody knuckles and knew that

was a good sign. I was empty but I was feeling again. *"Leave. Me. Alone."*

"I'm just letting you know what's about to happen to you, Reyno." She took her time, scraping the lettuce and tomato off a slice of ham. "Doug won't have to say much. But his side of the school, the jocks and the bros, they don't need more than *Who* and *Why Not* to make your life hell."

I turned around and watched her back. I was starting to listen. She sighed. "But when the teachers start to look at you…" Ronny shook her head. "When grown adults start talking to you like you stole from their mothers or fucked their fathers? Like you're just fucking…*trash*? That's all Augie. And then that's everyone. The Skwad will ruin your life before sixth period."

"Why are you telling me this?"

She faced me. "Because you sat back and watched them do the exact same thing to me."

Ronny brushed past me and into my unit. Counted off the Skwad members on her hand as she went. "Sassy gay sidekick. Quirky little sweetheart. Dopey jock with a heart of gold. It's just so…*intentional*. Relatable underdogs. Kids you can root for. Kids who make it easy. We never stood a chance. We're just dicks."

She moved to my tool shelf and pulled out the wad of towel. The stop sign. It reflected a bit of moonlight. "Kids like us don't get to mess up. We aren't allowed to learn lessons. Nice kids like Cam get after-school specials. We get counselors. We get sent away."

I wiped my eyes and looked out into the distance. The lights from the accident still blinking in the night. "We get consequences."

I looked back at Ronny. Still holding my sign to stop. I

was calm. So was she. "Y'know, people always said the two of you made no sense. *CamRye?* Cameron Ellis, with his little cardigans and his swoopy hair? Why would such a nice guy go for such an absolute prick?" My scowl was met with her smile. "I thought y'all were peas in a pod. 'Cause I know Cam. I know he isn't *nice*. Cameron Ellis is calculating. He's petty and bitter and smart. He knows what it takes to *look* nice. He knows *exactly* what he's doing."

I took the stop sign back from her and put it on the shelf. "He just told ten thousand followers I took a shit on his heart. I know what Cameron is." I stopped and closed my eyes. Leaned on my bench. "I just... I really need to be alone right now, Ronny. Please. Leave me alone."

Ronny took a moment to consider. She eyed my splinters. The wound in my wall. "Okay. Just leave the axe out of it."

She watched me for one more moment then did what I asked. I heard her wade through the weeds, back to her own unit, but my eyes never left my knuckles. The little splinters stuck in my skin. That beautiful dark wood looked so perfect on my table back in June. I thought I'd overordered, but I used every inch. I took every chance and I exceeded my biggest plans. I worked magic.

"I worked really hard on it." I heard Ronny stop in the grass. I wiped my face. "I worked so hard on that table. I worked so fucking hard on it and he didn't... He didn't even look at it. He didn't even thank me. He told all his followers how excited he was for it, but he never told me. He never... He never fucking cared."

I finally met her eyes. I didn't let my guilt or my anger keep me from telling her what I'd been needing to for months. "I'm sorry, Ronny."

Her surprise was clear, even in the dark.

I walked out into the weeds. "That night ruined my life. But we were hurting you long before that. I had no right. I had no fucking right, Ronny. I'm sorry."

There were flecks of moonlight on Ronny's face, but I could only make out her eyes. Two loaded guns I was always so sure to avoid. The kind of eyes that melts steel off walls and egos out of assholes. But they weren't loaded now. They almost looked soft under all that eyeliner. I think she'd been waiting a long time to hear that.

"That night ruined my life too."

The closer I got, the more I could see of her face. The guard was still up. The threat still ready. But I knew in her eyes, we'd reached a ceasefire. Ronny DiSario and I had stopped aiming to kill.

I shook my head. "Why aren't you rubbing this in my face? I deserve it."

"It's tempting. I'm certainly tempted. But I already made one kid cry tonight and… I don't know." She crossed her arms and shrugged. "The ex-boyfriend of my ex-boyfriend is my friend. And what you're about to go through is punishment enough."

I smiled. Just a little. "Y'know… I always thought we'd get along. If we didn't waste the past year hating each other."

"Maybe. Maybe if you didn't waste the past year fucking my ex."

"Well… Cam didn't want to have sex with me."

Ronny burst out laughing. *"Oh! I thought it was just me!"*

I could feel myself warm up and, to my complete shock, I started laughing too. Our laughter echoed over the empty field and bounced around the storage units. Around the guts and gore of the busted table in mine. Across the antiques and thousand-dollar vases in hers. Our laughter probably ran all the way across my block and got the mountain of garbage on my lawn chuckling too.

Ronny settled down first and plucked out a new sandwich. I caught my breath. "Jeez. Fuck that guy."

"Fuck them all."

I opened my phone to Cameron's tearful face. The waterfall of comments under *Our Beautiful Something* was already pouring in.

Phil Rhino is CANCELED!

I never liked that punk...

I earn $1200/day working from home

I rolled my eyes and switched to Cameron's IG. A new picture of the Skwad sat at the top of his grid. Smiling at Brewster's. Maybe they were workshopping Cameron's breakup speech. Maybe they were discussing their plan to turn the world against me. Over milkshakes. At their favorite spot. The perfect picture of the perfect friends.

I counted on my hand. "Doug Parson. Brynn Forester. Augie Horton. Cameron Ellis. *The Skwad*."

Ronny talked with her mouth full. "It's a nice story. Four nice kids. Sharing milkshakes. Floating above it all."

"Floating above consequences. *Bubbles*."

The plan started to form with ease. Like it was always waiting for my call to come out of the shadows. I think Ronny had the same plan. The same shadows. "So. What are you gonna do about it?"

She gave me her tiny slider. I smiled and chewed. "I think I'm gonna cry a bit more. Prolly till sunup. When the cops clear, I'll hide the stop sign somewhere safer, maybe jerk off, and go to bed. It's been a long couple of days."

I savored the sandwich. Someone had sprung for good catering. I swallowed hard, my smile was gone. "Then I'm going to ruin their fucking lives." I wiped my mouth and looked at Ronny. "...Wanna help?"

I didn't need the moonlight to see the grin stretch across Ronny's face. She crossed her arms and looked up at the stars and I saw her hands begin to move. Tap along on her arms like a pianist at the bench. "Let's see. Speaking pragmatically, the internet's favorite puppy dog just declared you public enemy number one and we're in a dead heat for worst reputations in town. How do you plan to get within fifty feet of the Skwad?"

I considered her question. It was a fair point. "Sheer hate and good luck?"

She smiled. Then her fingers stopped. Paused the keyboard solo she was running on her arm. Like she'd figured it all out. Ronny laughed. She really fucking laughed, all the way back to her storage unit.

"What's so funny?"

Ronny shook her head and picked up the remaining sandwich. "Okay. Okay. Hear me out but..." She handed me a mini BLT. All smiles. "Do you know Jackson Pasternak?"

TAPE FLIP

PHIL

——

PRELUDE
FOUR YEARS BACK

We were sitting on my bedroom floor and I checked to make sure that the chair was wedged under my doorknob. That the earbuds we were sharing were a hundred percent plugged into my laptop. Sneaking glances at Jackson's eyes, waiting for him to get weirded out. He'd brought his Xbox over and we had the home screen of *Mortal Kombat* on high volume just in case my mom came home early. Just to cover up our experiment.

An ad blared before the video. ***"WHY JUST WATCH PORN? WHEN YOU CAN MAKE IT!"***

Jackson hit the skip ad button and grumbled. "So many ads."

I nodded. "Probably why porn is free."

"Oh. Good point."

Another ad loaded up and screamed in our ears. ***"THIS GAME WILL MAKE YOU CUM! MOST MEN CAN'T LAST FIVE SECONDS—"***

He clicked the final ad skip and a pop-up took over the screen.

ARE YOU 18+

Jackson smirked at me. "Uh-oh. How old are you?"

"Me? Thirty-one."

"Prove it."

"Billy Joel. My back hurts. TurboTax. How 'bout you?"

Jackson did some quick mental math. "Thirty-two. Aaaaaaand three-quarters."

"Wow. So mature."

Jackson had beaten me to thirteen, but I was gaining on him. It didn't stop him from always acting twice my age. My buddy Jackson has what some might call an old soul. Personally, I would specify it is an *elderly* soul. I mean, the guy's favorite soda is Diet Ginger Ale.

The porn loaded and we straightened up against my bed. Jackson finished his tenth Diet Canada Dry of the night and chucked the can. "Oh, here we go."

The first frame of *BEEFCAKE COACH FUCKS TOWEL BOY TWINK IN COLLEGE LOCKER ROOM* buffered on my family laptop. "Ugh. My internet sucks."

"S'fine. Do we have anymore Bagel Bites?"

"Yessir."

I handed him the plate of our final two, room-temp, pepperoni pizza bagels. He shoved them right in his mouth and mumbled, mouth full. *"Hey. What's a twink?"*

Jackson pointed at the title. I thought about it. My heart said "a light dessert" but the context clues were telling me I was probably off base.

"Let's see." While our porn loaded, I pulled Jackson's phone out of his crumpled-up pile of khakis. We'd decided for the experiment to work, we shouldn't be wearing pants but shirts and boxers were fine. I searched the word on Urban Dictionary and cleared my throat. *"Twink. Noun. A young/thin ho-*

mosexual who expects the world and all its inhabitants to bow down to his perfect, pink asshole. Citation needed."

"Wowee. Descriptive."

"So, like, a gay guy. But tiny."

Jackson gave me an up and down. We'd sat on my bedroom floor in nothing but boxers countless times in our friendship but lately we'd started filling out in ways we weren't expecting. Or sharing. When it started, we'd share every new update with each other. When Jacks got his first chest hair, we called it Jacques. When my voice wouldn't stop dropping, we started keeping a daily record. But the last few months, our updates have gotten sparser. The morning I discovered a patch of brown hair growing in my predominantly black crop of pubes, I had the update text all written out before deciding it might be a weird thing to text my friend over cereal. Maybe that's why his look looked so looky in my bedroom that night. There were finally things about me Jackson Pasternak didn't know.

I held my knees. "What are you looking at?"

"Are you a twink?"

"Uh… What do you mean?"

"You're small. Fun-sized." I shoved him. He laughed. "It's good! You're compact, I like it."

"Eat shit. And I think you gotta be gay to be…one of those."

"Okay. Then…are you…that?" I rolled my eyes. Jackson snorted. "Oh, what? Dani Touscani can ask you during Health but I can't?"

I shoved him away. "Uh, I don't know, asshole, are you… THAT?"

He shoved me back, just as giggly. "Uh, I don't know, bitch. Maybe if your laptop loaded we might find out."

We cracked up a little and I tried pausing and unpausing the player. It worked like a charm and the video started midway through.

"OH, FUCK, COACH! YOU LIKE THAT HOLE, DADDY?!"

We both gasped at the jump scare. The college towel boy was getting broken open on a locker room bench by a "daddy" who had to be twenty-five, tops. Jackson leaned in and squinted at the lockers and towel carts behind all the barebacking. "Huh. That's a pool locker room."

"Why does it matter?"

"The coach is wearing a baseball jersey. They wouldn't be in a pool locker room."

"I think you're missing the point. Do you like it?"

"It's distracting."

"Get over it, Pasty, do you think it's hot?"

The porn ran on and we watched in silence. Jackson and I would check in on our boxers every so often, the flaps floating in the breeze, but neither of our guys seemed all that interested. I couldn't stop sneaking peeks at his. I saw the outline there, right on his thigh. Just a bump, really. But nothing. The bump stayed a bump. I started to feel silly for suggesting we try the experiment. Our sleepovers are usually more exciting than Bagel Bites and internet porn. I just needed to know. I don't know why or when it started, but lately those secrets between us, those little things we'd stopped telling each other, they were just feeling too important. What had Jackson started keeping from me? Was it the same thing? Was I hiding the same secret from my best friend in the world?

"Nothing? You don't... You don't feel anything?"

Jackson shook his head. "A coach wouldn't even *wear* a jersey, they have their own uniforms."

"Jackson."

"Also, why the heck does a college have a towel boy?" I slapped my laptop closed and stood up. Started putting my pants back on. "What are you doing?"

"This was stupid."

"Phil, c'mon, let's just find another—"

In my frustration, I let my pants slide back down. They stuck somewhere around my shins. "You're not gay, Jackson! It's fine, we figured it out, yay for you."

"Why are you getting upset?"

"I'M NOT UPSET!"

Jackson held his knees to his chest. "Phil… I told you. I told you I didn't know. Why…" He shook his head. "Why is it so important to know? Why's that so important to you now?"

I rolled my eyes and plopped down at my desk chair. Tried to get busy with a half-whittled wooden spoon.

"Phil."

Then Jackson was behind me and his hand was on my shoulder. I considered shanking him with my whittling knife. But I was about to cry. I couldn't stop crying at that damn desk lately. I bore down. "People are starting to ask, Jacks." I dropped my spoon and put my head on my fist. Really dug it in. *"I thought I had more time. I wasn't ready for them to ask. Dani. Mom. People."*

"Philip."

"I wasn't… I wasn't ready for you to ask."

"Hey."

Jackson knelt on the floor and turned my chair around to face him. I looked at my carpet because Jackson has this thing he can turn on that gets people on board. Gets people smiling back. A quality I wasn't just born without, but one I was starting to resent.

"Phil…" I looked up and to my surprise, Jackson wasn't smiling. He was serious. He was so fucking serious with me then. "Can't you tell me? It's okay, Phil. It'll be okay. Just… can you say it?"

His hand was on my ear. Holding my piercing like he does sometimes. The ear he'd pierced for me. But the tears had come and I couldn't find the words. I didn't know who else might hear them. So, I told Jackson how I knew only he'd understand. I didn't know if my words would come. So, instead, I tried some of his.

"Je suis un…"

His eyebrow perked up. A smile. He was surprised. Maybe a little tickled. My two years and twelve D's of French couldn't touch his lifetime but I'd made a mission of trying to catch up to Jackson.

"Je suis…"

But I was always trying to catch up to Jackson. I shook my head.

"I don't… I don't know the fucking word, man."

My eyes were closed but his words were soft with me. His fingers on my ear. Soft.

"You do. You do, Phil, you got it."

I nodded. Eyes still closed. Words still whispers.

"Je suis… Je suis gay."

The second I said the word, it burst out of me. Jackson pulled me in and held my head to his. I sobbed into his polo, thrilled I'd barricaded my door.

"Please don't hate me. Please don't hate me. Please, Jackson, you're my best fucking friend, please."

He shushed me and rubbed my back. He told me to stop and he told me he knew. He always knew and it was alright.

And I guess somewhere I knew that. But it couldn't stop me from repeating myself.

"Don't hate me. Don't hate me."

Then Jackson was holding my face. Wiping away the tears. "No. Never. Never, ever. Don't say that, I could never."

He smiled. It was the winning one, the one that could make anyone smile back. Even me. Even through tears. "Why… Why are you s-smiling, you fucking cr-creep?"

Jackson was tearing up then. Something I rarely ever saw. "You told me, Phil. You fucking told me, Phil."

He hugged me tight. Really tight. I started crying all over again. *"I told you. I told you, Jacks."*

"You told me. You finally told me."

"Finally? You asshole. How long have you…"

Jackson scratched my back. Something I adored. "A long time, Phil. Since we met, maybe?"

"Since we met?!"

"I think I knew the day I met you."

My big sister used to babysit his little sister. It started out as something to save up for college but the Pasternaks fell in love with Charmaine. She used to babysit Mol and Jackson just about every Friday or Saturday and I almost always tagged along. At first, my mom felt bad dumping us on the rich side of town before her shifts, especially when only one of them was being paid to be there, but Stan and Marion were happy to host. Happier that their little prince Jackson seemed to finally make a friend. When Charmaine left for college in June, I took over as Molly's sitter/guard dog anytime Jackson gets dragged into the city with his parents. It works out great because Molly's been trying to learn the drums and the pocket money doesn't hurt. Sometimes I joke that the Pasternaks are paying me extra to be Jackson's best friend. It always gets a laugh from the parents but Jacks doesn't think it's so funny. Because friendship is a really serious thing to a guy like Jackson. And *best* friendship is just about life or death.

He pulled back and wiped a tear off my face. "That first day, my mom said it was my job to entertain you. And your mom said if we got hungry, you'd brought candy corn. And my mom said it was only August and your mom said you loved candy corn all times of year and...yeah. I knew. I saw you skulking in my lawn, not wanting to come in and meet anybody, and I thought *Oh. He's gay.*"

"Because I like candy corn?"

"Yeah. And if I wasn't sure then, you did just interrupt our *Mortal Kombat* tournament to suggest we watch gay porn together."

"It. Was. An. Experiment."

We both cracked up and Jackson picked up my little wooden spoon off the ground. He put in into my hand. "You need to work on your French, Philip."

"Why bother? Gay is just gay. Easy. What's homosexual?"

"Homosexuel."

"See?! I'm basically fluent already."

He laughed. "There are better ways to say it. Next time. If you wanted."

"I'm not gonna be saying it all that often, Jacks."

"Still. If you needed."

I nodded. "Like what?"

Jackson looked up at my ceiling and thought about it. He didn't take too long though. "You could say... 'Les garçons me plaisent.' I like boys. Or...'J'aime les garçons.' I love boys. A little more serious..."

"J'aime les garçons?"

"You got it. Yeah. Or... I don't know..."

Jackson was still holding the spoon in my hand. Like he wasn't done giving it to me just yet. Like he didn't want to let it go. "Les garçons ne me laissent pas indifférents non plus." He was quieter then. Like he'd spoken it to himself. And the ease. How familiar those words sounded on his lips. I wondered when he'd found them. How long it took him to find the right ones. How long he'd waited to say them out loud.

"What does it mean?"

Jackson blinked himself out of something. He just smiled. "Boys don't leave me indifferent."

"Oh. Wow."

"Yeah."

"It sounds better in French."

"Yeah. Most things do."

He laughed. I didn't. I couldn't take my eyes off his hands. "You… You know so many words for it, Jacks."

He stilled. And if I nodded then, if I could have just fucking smiled for him, guided him like he guides me, maybe he might have told me there. Told me that thing I also knew the second I met him. Because I saw him too. That first day, looking in from his lawn, I saw Jackson Pasternak. The little prince of the Orchard, standing in his foyer, bored with his afternoon. Wearing those big socks and sipping a Diet Ginger Ale. And I knew. I thought *Oh. He's like me.* Before I even knew it about myself, I saw something similar in Jackson. Because despite everything that was different about us, everything the world couldn't stop reminding us should matter, we'd always had stronger things in common. We had the same words. I had to believe that. I had to believe we shared enough.

"Jacks…"

He shook his head. "I'd tell you, Phil. You know I would. If I were."

"Jackson."

"Maybe one day. Maybe it's just... Maybe it takes more time for some guys. Maybe you're just quicker than me."

"You would know. If you were, you would know."

"I don't think it's that simple—"

"Are you?"

Jackson stopped shaking his head. But he looked at me. "No. Phil, I don't think I am." He wiped a tear off his face. "I'm sorry."

"It's alright."

"No. I'm letting you down."

"Never. Never, ever. Never."

"Phil, I'm always gonna—"

I leaned close and kissed Jackson. His hands went to my hair, just for a moment, then he stood up. Reached for his pants. I saw it through his boxers and looked away.

"Sorry."

"Good night."

"Stay."

"No."

Jackson put on his pants and tried to hide his erection. "That... That fucking sucks, Phil. That wasn't fucking good, man."

I covered my face. The tears had come back. "I'm sorry."

"Why did you... Dammit, Phil."

This sweaty thing had run up my spine and I was so afraid Jackson was finally done with me. "I'm sorry. I'm sorry, please don't go."

He grabbed the chair on my door then slowed down. The only sound in my room was the rain on my window. *Mortal Kombat* on his Xbox. Jackson closed his eyes. "I don't think we have a normal friendship, Phil."

His voice was too cold. "Please. *Please*. Please don't say that, Jacks."

I was too afraid to look anywhere but my hands. But I heard the rain. I heard a sigh. "That's... That's not a bad thing, Phil. I don't want a normal friendship." I finally peeked up at him. Jackson had moved my nightstand in front of the door. If only to batten down the hatches. His arms were crossed. "Aren't we bigger than that?"

He was nervous. Scared, maybe. I couldn't tell. It didn't look like my Jackson's nerves. Or his fear. That must've been someone new. Some Jackson he hadn't shared with me yet.

I nodded to him, wiping the tears away. Jackson nodded back. "Exactly. We just... We need to be straight with each other."

"Straight?"

"Honest." Jackson was back at my desk again. Back by my chair. Back on his knees. "We need to be good to each other. We can't let the differences matter. Whatever people might say. We need to stand up for each other."

His hand was back on my piercing. The hug on my ear. I hugged his too. "We need to stick together."

He nodded. "We just need to stay together. We just need to be straight with each other."

I smiled down at him, still waiting for some gag. A prank. Still waiting for some trick. And wouldn't you know it, I found my jeans around my shins again. How odd. "Straight?"

Jackson smiled up at me, still waiting for some pushback. Some red flag. Some call on the play. "Straight. Just with each other."

He took a quick breath for luck and I gasped. It felt like I'd missed a stair, walking in the dark, and I needed a moment to realize what I was feeling. That it wasn't a joke. That it was good. It was amazing.

"Holy fucking shit."

I rubbed his cheek with my thumb and covered my mouth, trying not to jinx it. Scare this new Jackson back into the brush. Wake up from the dream. Because I'd had the dream a thousand times that summer. The dream of Jackson Pasternak. In my room. That Jackson. In my hands. But the dreams had never felt so good. They'd never felt so real. Awake, I had never felt so loved.

"Philip."

Jackson would keep my secret. And sooner than later, I would keep his. When he told me. When he trusted me enough to tell me everything again. Because he's Jackson. He's my Jackson. He's my best fucking friend.

The words jumped out of me in pants. *"Just with each other, Jacks. Just with each other."*

I felt a tear hit my smile and, boy howdy, did I cum like a shotgun.

TAPE ONE,
SIDE B

———

THE TWINK MUST DIE

JACKSON

————

TRACK ONE
Stay (I Missed You)

I was sitting at my kitchen island, sipping my usual end-of-the-night Sleepytime Tea, and wondering if any class president in Moorestown High history had ever been impeached for murdering one of his constituents. I suppose I could always pardon myself. I'd have to check. It had been only hours and the comments under Cameron Ellis's latest video had already turned ugly. Like Cameron's tens of thousands of followers were just waiting for the whistle to turn on Phil.

Gaslighter

Sociopath

Emotional Abuser

The night hadn't even ended and Cam Army was already labeling Phil with whatever pop psychology term they'd learned that week. I followed the #PhilRhinoIsCanceled tag over to Twitter and froze on a screenshot. Someone had found the Yelp page of Passy's Pizzeria, the spot Phil's been delivering for all summer. Review after review, all posted within the hour.

1 STAR. If I could rate *ZERO* I WOULD.

1 STAR. DIRTY staff, RATS everywhere!

1 STAR. One of the delivery boys is a TOXIC PIECE OF SH*T

I kept scrolling but they wouldn't stop. Passy's rating was being tanked and I knew Phil would be fired before the sun came up. It was already happening. Phil's life was being ruined in front of me. Again. For the second time this year. And for what? How could Cameron do this to him?

In a pop of anger, I swatted the box of Sleepytime Tea off the counter. It crashed into the wall. Dozens of teabags exploded over my kitchen floor, but I was already heading to my front door. I wouldn't let this happen again. Not like before, not like the dance. I would not sit back and let this happen to Phil again.

I put on my jacket and opened my front door. *"Oh."*

Veronica DiSario's fist was inches from my face. Stuck mid-knock. She smiled. "Evening. Wanted to return this."

Veronica handed me one of the disposable plastic trays from the appetizer table. My brain took a second to come back, having stormed out down the lawn without me. "It's…plastic. Why are you here?"

"It's nice plastic, I thought you might—"

"Veronica."

She rolled her eyes and crossed her arms. "Look. I don't know how serious you were about helping me out earlier but…there actually is something I could use you for."

"Tonight is *really* not a good time for this."

"Oh, no, you need more time to cry in the shed?"

"Veronica, do you know what just—"

Then I saw him. I looked past the girl in my front door and saw a small shadow in my front lawn. It felt like a memory was there in my grass. A small boy. Skulking by the garden swing like a black cat. It felt like the morning I met that mean, lonely boy.

Phil looked away first.

Veronica sighed. "He's not coming in. The lawn was the compromise."

I just nodded, still watching him. Not trying to scare him off. "I'm sure it was a long negotiation."

"Oh, it was. I didn't know you used to be friends."

"Yeah. That was kind of the problem."

"What do you mean?"

I watched Phil turn away and walk around my grass. Feel the wood of my swing. Maybe he was remembering something. Maybe that day after the lake race. When we napped on the thing and woke up in the rain.

"People didn't think we'd be friends. We were just a really hard sell for some people. They thought we were too different."

"I mean...you *are* different. You're like this big, happy golden retriever and Phil's, you know...a piece of shit."

We watched Phil kick the fuzz off a dandelion. Veronica wasn't wearing the usual glare I'd seen her bust out just for him. The look was friendlier. A friendly, sad pity.

"Why are you here, Ronny?"

She sighed and pulled out her phone. "It's been a funny sort of night. A lot to cover for a Thursday but..." Her screen lit up in the night. The familiar face of Cameron Ellis. "We need your help, Mr. President."

I straightened up. For the first time since I'd pressed Play on that video, I felt my breath return to me. I nodded and pulled out my own phone. Opened to that same awful face. Veronica smirked at the fake tears on her ex-boyfriend's cheeks. We were on the same page.

Veronica did me the courtesy of hanging back as I approached Phil. The lake was calm but there was still some wind in the grass. It was quiet enough to hear each footstep. The dock knocking against water. I knew it wouldn't be my place to sit with him on the swing. Not that I could. We'd outgrown being able to share it.

I settled for a spot in the grass, cross-legged and quiet. I didn't know how to start. "...You cold?"

His nose always shivered first. Phil took a minute to shrug. "We're by the water."

"Right."

"And it's three in the morning."

"Right. Right."

I nodded. And Phil nodded. And we waited in the silent grass for a little while longer. I swallowed. "I, uh... I saw the video."

Phil almost smiled there. His voice was scratchy. Like he'd been crying all night. "Been months now and people are still opening with that. Only now we got a whole new video to bring up. Probably gonna take me through the rest of the year."

His jaw was moving. Teeth grinding. I didn't know if he was keeping anger or tears down. I didn't know if they were for Cameron or me. "Phil—"

"I'm not gonna say sorry, Jackson. I still... I still fucking hate you." It was a terrible thing to say. But he didn't look mad. Not at me at least. His heart was broken and it was all he could deal with that night. "But you just moved to number five on my list so I guess we're straight for now."

I didn't ask my questions. Why would he think an apology would be anywhere close to on the table? I was the one who messed up, what did Phil have to apologize for?

"I shoulda seen this coming. All the signs were telling me *He's gonna fuck you over* but I wouldn't fucking listen."

I sat up. "If it's any consolation, no one in town saw it either. Everyone thought the guy was friggin' gaga over you. Mostly."

"Mostly everyone?"

I remembered a dinner party, sometime last winter, when the subject of the Snow Globe Ball got brought up at the table. All the adults fawned over Cameron's bravery and his dimples and his diction. Every adult but one. "Maman was not impressed."

Phil smiled. He didn't hide it from me. Because Phil loved my mother. From the day they met, the morning after our first sleepover, Marion Pasternak understood Phil. They were both early risers and had no respect for small talk. My mother knew Phil, she knew who Phil was to her family. To me. And my mother was not a person who forgot people.

"She thought Cameron was very…presumptuous."

"Presumptuous?"

"*Rude little shit* were her words. It sounded better in French."

Phil laughed a little and rubbed his eye. He wasn't looking at me anymore. "And you?"

"Me?"

His eyes moved up for a moment, just a glance, then he was back on the grass. "What did you think about Cameron? Him and me. Us."

I didn't know what to say. I hadn't spoken to Phil directly since our moment on the theater stage, minutes before his life changed forever. I didn't know what level of honesty would be appropriate.

"I thought…" I swallowed. "I thought he'd take care of

you. I thought… I thought he must've really loved you. To do something like that." My finger was itching a hole into the dirt. I let the truth keep coming. "I thought you must've really loved him to put up with that."

"The Skwad?"

"Him." Phil was looking at me then. I found my nerve and met his eyes. "He outed you, Phil."

Phil made a face. "Wow. Okay, Jackson."

"He literally outed you. And everyone clapped. And you still—"

"Oh, like you give a—"

"Stop. Phil." I sat up straighter. Leaned in closer. "I know you didn't want to come out yet. I know you weren't ready for ANY of that."

He looked away. His eyes were getting full. His voice was getting tight. He was going to leave soon. "'Cause you know me so fucking well."

My breathing was getting heavy with his. "I did. I do. Enough. Phil, I know you enough."

He wiped his face hard, trying to stay angry. "Then you should have fucking said something."

He stood and walked through my yard. I kept his pace. "Phil, stay."

"This was a mistake."

"Philip."

"We'll handle this on our own. Go back to sleep."

I reached for his wrist. Before I could even get close, whether he knew I was about to touch him or maybe it was just two and a half years of anger, Phil turned around and shoved me back. I stumbled a little. More out of shock than anything, I'd only gotten all that much taller than him in our time apart.

"Ow."

"FUCK you."

Phil had found that in-between. He was just as pissed as he was sad and it was all coming out. Tears running down, he dug a maroon fingernail into my chest. "You had MONTHS to tell me this shit. You had YEARS to tell me you were sorry. You were—" A sob cut him off but he spit it away. Right at my feet. "You were my *best fucking friend* and you... you never asked if I was okay."

He shoved me again. I stumbled again. Shove. Stumble. Again. Then, again. I stopped giving way and just let him push at me. Fists hit my arms. Slurs echoed over the lake. The tears were taking over.

"You should have... You should've fucking asked me, Jackson."

"I know."

"You should have fucking stopped him."

"I'm sorry."

I was hugging him then. He sobbed into my chest. *"He broke my fucking heart, Jacks."*

"I know. I know, Phil."

"He broke my fucking heart."

He couldn't stop crying and I didn't try to stop him. I just rubbed his back and stopped waiting for him to calm down.

In a quiet moment, I closed my eyes. "I wanted to talk to you. I thought you'd... Phil, you fucking hated me. You hate me, you just said it. I don't... I didn't know my place."

He was trying to find his breath. It was coming to him in gasps. *"You shoulda fucking tried."*

I opened my eyes. Considered making the fair point. Considered that might be pushing my luck. Considered that might be worth it. "I did try talking to you."

"What?"

"That night. Right before it happened."

Phil pulled back and looked up at me, confused. He looked

like he'd had a reaction, his wet face all puffy and red. "On… The thing on the stage?"

"Exactly. I was trying, I said we didn't know him, Phil. I tried to warn you."

Phil just stared at me. Processing. His eyebrows furrowed. "Un-*fucking*-believable."

He peeled his arms off my back and slipped away from me. I sighed and followed his stomp through my grass.

"So, you haven't learned a fucking thing, huh? I come to you for help and you give me an *I TOLD YOU SO*? You still think you got all the fucking answers?"

"Great. And you still don't know how to have a damn conversation."

Phil stopped in his tracks and whipped back around. He was all cried out and all he had left was anger. "OH! Because you love to talk, right? Action Jackson *loooves* to solve everyone ELSE'S problems. Hey, good job on Class President, by the way. I really felt my vote counted."

I wouldn't budge. Maybe I was just ready for bed, but I'd had about enough of people dressing me down on my lawn for one night. "You don't get to ignore me all through high school then tell me this is all my fault."

"Fuck off, Jackson, you don't get to—"

I got close and cut him off. "You don't get to tell me I'm a bad person then come to me crying, Phil. You don't get to make me feel like a broken piece of shit for YEARS then come ask for help. You don't."

I was calm. I'd left my tears in the shed and would do this part calmly. "I am sorry. I am sorry for how things ended with us. But *you* ended them. I messed up but *you* stopped calling. *You* put up the space, Phil, *you* won't talk to *me*."

Phil stared right back up at me. A stalemate. Both of us furious with the other. Both of us wanting to get to the other side of our anger. Neither of us knowing exactly who was in the wrong. Not for sure. Not anymore.

Phil swallowed. "You think that was easy? Putting up that space? You think I didn't want to call you every Saturday night, you asshole?"

"Phil…"

"You haven't stopped moving since the eighth fucking grade, Jackson. When was I supposed to forgive you? Between pep rally speeches? The two seconds you stopped to breathe?"

I looked back at my house. My second-story bathroom window. The dented bushes below. A summer of me trying to escape. Months of trying to stay busy. Three years of trying to do this alone. "How was I supposed to know that, Phil?"

He laughed at the ground. "I guess I thought you *knew me enough*."

He was throwing my words back at me. A tired move Phil always used to try whenever he was losing an argument. Still. Something in my skin moved. It wasn't anger. Maybe resentment. It was something that had been moving through me since the night of that dance. Our moment on that stage. I could throw his words back too.

"I don't miss my baby teeth?"

Phil looked up. And his moment of confusion, that lost look on his face, dragged the feeling out of my skin. It made me want to scream.

"You said you didn't miss me, Philip. You called me fucking *baby teeth* and you don't even…" I laughed. "You don't even remember! Jesus Christ! That has been KILLING ME for fucking MONTHS, Phil, and you don't even remember saying that, do you?"

"Jacks—"

"Do you?!"

Phil was still. Maybe he was trying to remember. Maybe he

was restrategizing. But I wouldn't let him work himself loose of it. I took a step closer. I had nothing left to lose with him.

"I missed you. Phil, I miss you every goddamn day. Did you think I stopped? Do you think I could put that away? I *miss* you. I miss you in my house, I miss you on my lawn, I miss you at fucking lunch, Philip, I miss you in…"

I crossed my arms.

"I miss you in my life. I miss you all the time. Even if you don't. Even if I'm just *baby teeth*."

Phil couldn't look at me. But the ground could see his guilt. That shame.

"I don't remember that. I don't… I don't remember saying that, Jackson."

I nodded.

"How about *broken*? You remember that?"

"Jackson…"

"*Fucked up? Incomplete?* You remember those, Phil?" The words hit him deeply. All the things he called me. That night in his kitchen. The lights on his Christmas tree. The slap in the face. The words I'd hear him call me whenever I stopped staying so busy. Because of how I think. How I am. "You think I stopped thinking about you? Phil, I hear you *every night*."

I could feel the crash coming. I was about to break down again and I would be useless for the rest of the night. That long, awful night. But then there was Phil's hand. Right above mine. He'd taken my forearm. Like he just couldn't help it.

Phil shook his head up at me and he looked so ashamed. "Jackson. I didn't…" He looked so damn ashamed. "I never meant that. I didn't. You really hurt me that night but… Jackson, I never should have said that. Those things. I knew what that meant for you and… I just wanted to hurt you back. You know I don't think before I fucking… I am so sorry." I felt his squeeze on my forearm. An old squeeze. "I'm sorry, Jackson."

I took a moment to remember it. That squeeze. Then my fingers wrapped over his wrist and squeezed him back. Because, despite myself, I guess I had been waiting. Because Phil had hurt me too. I'd been angry too. And he apologized. He might still hate me but Phil could say he was sorry. Progress.

His voice lowered. "Of course, I missed you, asshole. I miss you all the fucking… *Goddammit*."

My eyes went wide. Because Phil was hugging me. An *Arms Around Torso, Face in My Ribs, No Sobbing or Crying or Plotting to Murder Me* hug. No tears. Just an old friend hugging his friend. A concession. A surprise. A bridge.

I laughed and hugged him back. "Okay. Was that so hard?"

"Excruciating."

We squeezed each other tight and held our breath. Like our bodies needed to check back in with each other before any more decisions would be made. It had been some time since they'd talked. I could feel my body ask his if we still felt the same. I could hear his answer that I needed to cool it on the back workouts.

"You got so damn huge, Jacks. Like hugging a triangle in a polo." I cracked up, my chin on his shoulder. He snorted. "What?"

"Nothing. I just thought you'd be thinking that."

"Calm down. It was a logical train of thought."

"Don't discount my ESP, bitch."

"Asshole."

We both laughed and kept the hug going. We were nearing minute two and I was surprised that it hadn't gotten weird yet. Maybe we were just getting it out of the way. Making up for lost time. But before either of us could question why it didn't feel strange for a single second, a groan cut us off.

"OH MY GOD, ARE YOU FUCKING DONE?!"

We turned to find Veronica sipping a glass of orange juice on my stoop. I guess sometime during my chat with Phil, she had helped herself to my home.

Phil held up a finger and screamed back. **"WE'RE WORK-ING THROUGH SOMETHING!"**

She flipped us off and sipped her juice. I whispered. "It's actually really late so if we could—"

Veronica kept hollering. **"PHIL! HEY, PHIL!"**

"WHAT?!"

"DID YOU ASK HIM YET?!"

"I'M GETTING TO IT, SHUT UP!"

"YOU SHUT UP!"

"YOU—"

I put a hand on Phil's mouth and gave Veronica a thumbs-up. Phil spat into my hand and wiped his tongue off.

"Ugh, you taste like grass."

"I've been in a lot of grass tonight. What did you need to ask me?"

Phil straightened his flannel and nodded. "Right. So…"

He pulled out his phone and opened it. Cameron's Insta-gram was up on Phil's cracked screen. A photo of him in a booth at Brewster's with the Skwad. Four full milkshakes melt-ing in their glasses, just for show by my estimation.

"You remember Cameron Ellis? Goes to Moorestown? Ruined my life?"

"Vaguely. Something about a dance, sure. What about him?"

Phil smiled, put away his phone, and stuck that dark red fingernail back in my face. "I need you to join the Skwad."

PHIL

———

TRACK TWO

Lifestyles of the Rich & Famous

When Ronny offered to give me a quick tour of her mansion after school, I thought it might kill an hour or so, but by the time we'd reached the fourth floor of Chateau DiSario, I could see the sunset in one of their countless stained glass windows. Getting smacked in the ass by all the Orchard luxury that afternoon only made me feel worse about my recent lack of employment. Raph fired me after Cam Army review-bombed Passy's and I'd been wasting the last few days trying to find a new gig. I've been fired from half the businesses on Main Street and the other half seemed to be big defenders of *That Adorable Little Gay Boy*. It had only been a week since the now-infamous breakup video went live but Cameron's influence in our town had developed past petty gossip and hate in my DMs. The bastard had reached my wallet.

Three sitting rooms and two shuttle buses later, Ronny led me into her garage. I froze in the doorway, but Ron walked through the space comfortably, like the garage might be the one room of her thousands that she felt no need to explain.

The room spoke for itself. Wall-to-wall soundproofing. A mixing table, a recording booth, an area just for stereo equipment. Guitars. At least five hung up on the wall, like hunting trophies. A keyboard. A saxophone. Drums.

"Holy shit."

Those fucking drums. A white five-piece, sitting untouched in the corner. Acrylic with a frosted finish. Nearly see-through shells with cymbals that almost looked like carved bone.

Ronny got comfy behind her keyboard and smirked at my jaw on the floor. "They're Pearl."

"I know. Crystal Beat. Ringo's preferred."

"Huh. Would've figured you were above the Beatles."

"I've picked more interesting hills to die on."

I hovered around the drum set. Like an unwelcomed breath might be enough to shatter it.

Ronny picked up a remote and turned on her stereo system. "You can sit if you'd like. They don't bite."

I didn't need to be told twice. I perched at the set and stretched out over the drums. Oriented my wingspan to them. Felt every inch of acrylic. "This is not fair. How do you have these drums, Ronny?"

Hiatus Kaiyote's "Red Room" poured out of each corner speaker and Ronny ran around the melody on her keyboard. "It's a funny story. When I was six, I asked my parents if I could have a piano. And when I was ten, I asked them if I could have a guitar. And when I was thirteen, I asked if I could have those drums and, well, here we are."

"Lucky break. Can I?"

I picked up a pair of sticks from under the stool and wagged them at Ronny. She nodded. "As long as you stay in time."

I listened for the rhythm and jumped on a natural entry point. Just a steady beat on the rack toms. Ronny smiled at my skill, maybe a little surprised. God's honest, I was a bit surprised myself. It had been some time since I'd played in front of anyone, but I seemed to be exceeding whatever bar Ronny had preset for me.

"You're good. I'm impressed."

"Drums like these do most of the work."

"You don't like compliments, huh?"

I sped up into a combo, muffling out whatever snark Ronny was gearing up to, and finished it out with one big smack to the cymbal. It was crisp. The crack was satisfying, like a shout. Nothing like my old worn-out plates.

I shrugged at her. "People usually just think it's noise."

Ronny shrugged back. "What's so wrong with noise?"

I held the cymbal quiet and smiled. I liked her point. And her noise.

"DID IT START?!"

I heard his frantic panting before registering Jackson's bike was careening through the open garage door.

"Did it start yet?!"

Ronny nearly fell over her keyboard bench at the sudden interruption. "JESUS."

Jackson was dripping sweat onto the cement floor and catching his breath, like he'd just biked a marathon. He wiped his face and parked his Schwinn.

"Sorry I'm late. Why aren't you watching it?"

I passed him a rag off the table and Ronny handed him the rest of her water. "They're running behind. Are you dying?"

Jackson downed the water in two gulps and dried his face with my rag. "Sorry. Sorry. Had to speed over from play practice, thought I was gonna—" He collapsed into the couch and finally found his breath. "*Fuck.* Thought I was gonna miss the meeting. I like to be on time for meetings."

Jackson smiled up at me, face red and sweating. "Hey."

I laughed. "Hey. When I said we were *meeting*, I didn't mean, like, *we're having a meeting*. You could have just texted."

"In-person attendance is important, Phil. Shows everyone's committed. They're running behind?"

Ronny turned off her keyboard and paused the stereo. Our jam session was over and it was time for more important business. Ron paired her phone with this overhead projector and the image of Brynn Forester's Instagram blew up onto the garage wall. *The Brynn Show.* The real reason I hauled my ass all the way to Rich Dick Village that evening.

Ronny squinted at the little Live icon above Brynn's profile picture. "Shit, I guess they started already."

Jackson groaned. "You weren't checking?"

"Don't start with me, *play practice*, doing recon was your idea."

Jackson pulled a notebook out of his backpack and sat up straight on the couch. "Research is important."

I smiled at his Boy Scout posture and plopped on the other side. Kept a respectable, professional distance. I nodded to Ronny. "Mr. President's right. Let's go."

Ronny hit the Live icon and perched on the back of the couch like a gargoyle. The garage wall took a moment to buffer before the well-decorated basement of Brynn Forester took over. Somewhere in that very neighborhood, Moorestown High School's favorite gossipmonger was sitting on her usual pink beanbag, midinterview with another familiar face.

Ronny scoffed. "It's the second week of school, how'd they already run out of guests?"

In the opposing beanbag, Doug Parson had his headphones on and was almost swallowing the microphone in front of him. Despite his trademark monotone ramble, Doug actually seemed incredibly engaged in whatever rant we'd dropped in on halfway.

"It's wild. It's nuts if we're being honest, the versatility alone. Like, you got peppermint. Wintergreen. Cinnamon. Fruits. Like, there are *a lot* of fruit flavors. Cherry. Strawberry. Watermelon. Grape. Lime. Lemon lime. Raspberry. Blue raspberry. Spearmint."

Brynn nodded along, clearly mindful that her show was live and only allowed to run so long. She returned to her cue cards. "So… Okay, so, circling back to the viewer question, you'd say your favorite food is…"

Doug smiled at the camera. "Gum."

Ronny sighed. Jackson wrote that down. I just shook my head. "A fascinating person."

Brynn wrapped up the show's opening segment of viewer questions and transitioned into her standard school news and update corner. Jackson transcribed every little thing Brynn reported, always a studious notetaker, but only cherry-picked the odd remark whenever Doug would chime in. His focus got me focused. Because Jackson was right. If I was going to ruin Cameron's life, I would need to have my head on straight. And if we were going to destroy the Skwad, we would need to have the right ammo. That's why we decided to start with Brynn.

She finished up "The Backstage Report," a new update series about her time as *Hairspray*'s spoiled rich girl villain Amber Von Tussle, and moved on to more serious business. Brynn sat up in her beanbag and looked deep into the camera, like a president giving a fireside chat. "Now. Before we get into our game for the week, I'd like to discuss something of dire import."

I rolled my eyes at the whiplash in tone. Brynn soldiered

on, checking in with her cue cards every so often. "We at *The Brynn Show* pride ourselves on accountability. Transparency. From our very first episode, all we ever set out to do here is give a voice to our community. Friends, strangers, classmates, anyone who wanted their story told. We wanted to foster that dialogue."

Ronny's brow twitched. "She keeps saying *we*. Isn't this her show? Her name's all over it."

Jackson didn't look up from his pad, basically writing Brynn's address word for word. "Delegating responsibility. Speak in the abstract long enough, you can say a whole lot without ever actually committing to a real opinion. Very political."

Ronny nodded. "Very Brynn Forester." She leaned in closer to the screen and nodded at Brynn's cue cards. The hostess never went live without her trademark stack of pink index cards, all screaming *THE BRYNN SHOW*. "So. What's on the cards?"

I chewed on my fingernail and snorted. "They're her script. Brynn writes out everything she's gonna say ahead of time. Even her *off-the-cuff* moments."

"No shit. Everything?"

"Down to the fucking *Um*'s. Cam told me once. She spends all week writing out her answers. She never goes into these things unprepared. Especially with the advice stuff."

Jackson smiled into his notepad. "Because Brynn Forester always knows *just* what to say."

I smirked at him. I could almost hear all those empowering speeches and vital life lessons that Brynn had directed at me in the booths of Brewster's. All those helpful, "spontaneous" suggestions she'd made to help me fit into the Skwad's perfect story. "Pretty easy when you give yourself a weekend to workshop all your sage advice."

Jackson smirked back. Brynn powered to whatever point her sudden serious mood was building toward. "Which is why we feel it is imperative to apologize for certain word choices on our previous episode. We've seen your comments, believe me, and we hear you. Language evolves. And there was no excuse for my or my guest's language."

Everyone on our couch just squinted. Ronny cocked her head. "Wait. Did Brynn say something fucked-up? Did anyone watch the previous episode?"

Jackson went back through his notes. "Uh… Dani Touscani guested, talked for thirty minutes about working at Brewster's, the *Hairspray* cast list, and bread bowls. Brynn barely got a word in all ep, what could she be apologizing for?"

Brynn looked like she was about to cry. And the funny thing was, I actually believed it. Brynn wasn't like Cameron. Her aggressive brand of sweetness might get toxic, but it wasn't some act. Brynn cared *a lot*. She shook her head, solemn. "When good people say nothing in the face of ignorance, they are just as complicit as the ignorant party. They are just as wrong, and they have just as much responsibility to own up to their role in systematic—"

After three straight minutes of blinkless staring, a lightbulb went off in Doug. "Oh, is this 'cause you and Dani T said the cheddar broccoli bread bowls at Panera were like crack?"

Ronny and I fell off the couch laughing. Brynn closed her eyes. "Douglas. We are live."

"What? Bread bowls are dope. Are we not saying *crackhead* anymore?"

"We never— The point is, we were speaking from a place of ignorance and it is never, *never* ever okay to make light of drug addiction."

"Right." Doug nodded and pointed a finger at the camera. "Don't do drugs."

Brynn grabbed the finger and pulled it away, trying to stick the landing of her little public service announcement. "That's not the point. Or the...you know, message."

"Oh. No?"

"Doug. No, we are in no place to judge or dictate, we are... You know, everybody here at *The Brynn Show* believes people should live their lives however they want!"

Doug seemed to misread the clear *Let's Move On* in Brynn's eyes and decided to keep helping. "Right. People should do drugs. *If* they want."

The three of us all leaned in and watched Brynn's well-meaning, well-overextended smile begin to give her a charley horse. I could see her eyes scanning over the live comments piling in and they were starting to overwhelm.

I slapped on Jackson's back. "Hey. Hey, there. That."

"I see it. I see it."

Brynn's good intentions were starting to choke her. She threw herself into her cue cards, desperate to get back into her pleasant, inoffensive chat show rhythm. No matter how much time she spent perfecting this apology no one asked for, Brynn hadn't accounted for her delightfully unpredictable cohost chiming in. Throwing her. Forcing her to say something unprepared.

Brynn beamed into the camera. "You know, everybody makes choices. And, you know, just as long as we're all being safe and legal or... I mean, not to measure morality or, you know, worth by the *legal* system, I just mean we should all... You know..."

Without looking, she shuffled through her cards. Busying her hands, trying to pull out of this spiral. "Live and let live, you know? Really, if we can take anything away from this experience, this life, we should all just… You know, we should just do our best. Do your best, that's what we're all trying to do, right? I mean, you do you. Do what makes your heart happy."

Brynn had entered the "empty platitudes" phase of her defense stratagem. A desperate exit plan I'd seen her pull many a time in the Brewster's booths. She skipped ahead a few cards and landed on one of the last in her stack. "Anyway! We're in the studio with my good buddy Doug Parson here on *Skwad Appreciation Month*. All month, all Skwad, all FUN! We've got a lot of show left and a bunch of your questions for Mr. Basketball Superstar over here, so stick around after the break, 'cause we're playing *Apples to Apples!*"

Doug pumped his fist in the air, chanting, *"APPLES, AP-PLES,"* and Brynn leaped to turn off her phone. The live stream ended and the garage wall reverted back to Brynn's Instagram page. We all sat on the couch in silence. Digesting. Jackson checked his watch and slapped his notepad closed. "Alrighty. I don't feel any particular need to stick around and hear Mr. Basketball explain his favorite flavors of Gatorade so let's talk strategy."

Jackson popped up and pointed at the projected image of Brynn's Instagram page on the wall. Specifically, the follower count. "For whatever reason, people follow Brynn Forester. Brynn understands social media. The Snow Globe Ball video never would've gone so viral without her hand. She knows what plays well. Social media likes her, it likes what she has to say."

Ronny clomped her boots onto the coffee table and sank into the couch. "Or what she *doesn't* say."

Jackson nodded and pointed at her. "Exactly. Brynn is

palatable. Inoffensive. Just enjoyable enough to keep around. That's why Cameron needs her. Brynn knows how to manage people. She knows how to package him."

Jackson paced around the garage like some young politician at a fundraiser. White button-up sleeves all rolled up. Before the pep rallies and presidential speeches, I'd watch Jackson grandstand and filibuster over Pop-Tart preferences. *Dragon Ball Z* power rankings. The "correct" order to listen to *Jagged Little Pill*. It was an intensity I'd admired. A look I'd missed.

Jackson gesticulated all around the drum set. "That's her magic. She's always around but never rocks the boat. Never says too much, never leaves a bad taste. Delightful, sure, but unnecessary. She's vanilla."

I snorted. "She's *gum*."

Jackson snapped his fingers. "Exactly. Exactly. That's how she controls gossip. She gets in people's ears without them even knowing. She's a mosquito without a buzz."

Ronny grimaced at Brynn's smiling face on her garage wall. "A butterfly that sucks blood."

I got to my feet and approached the wall. Face-to-face with the first target on our list. Always the nicest of the Skwad. Always my least favorite. Sweet, bubbly Brynn. "Cameron hides behind the Skwad. Doug has his bros, Augie has the teachers. But Brynn just has her reputation. The trust of the people. If we ruin that, the channels open way up."

Jackson stood by my side and nodded. "Brynn's been telling a pretty good story. Knock her out and we can start telling our own. Control the narrative."

Ronny joined us at the wall, biting into a Twizzler. "God. If only we knew someone who wasn't blacklisted from ever stepping foot in *The Brynn Show*'s studio..."

I smirked. "Wowzers, good question. Huh. Drawing a blank…"

We both smiled up at Jackson. He closed his eyes and groaned, resting his head against the cement wall. "You have no idea how artfully I've been dodging her invitations."

Ronny snorted, slapped his ass, and picked up her universal remote. "Well, it's either that or I burn down her house. I leave the decision to you."

The projector turned off and the garage door began to close. Ronny gave us the *wrap it up* gesture. "Now everyone get out of my house. It's dinnertime and I've schemed enough for a weeknight."

Jackson and I both jumped to it. He grabbed his bike and we both ducked under the door right in the nick of time. Alone on the driveway, we heard Ronny's voice echo from the other side of the metal door. *"See you in school!"*

The crack of light in the cat entrance went out and I guess Ronny was done with us for the night. Jackson and I stood in her driveway, still processing the quick and abrupt farewell. I huffed. *"No, Ronny, I don't wanna stay for dinner.* Fuck her."

Jackson shrugged. "Well, to be fair, you hated each other this time last week."

"You're one to talk."

We laughed and headed down the DiSarios' fancy tree-lined driveway. Jackson's bike clicked along the cobblestones and I could see him smiling in the dark.

"If you *did* want dinner, my pop's dying to see you. Maman's in France for the month, but Dad's been asking all about you lately. Molly would be over the damn—"

I hiked up my backpack straps and shook my head. "You told your family about me?"

Jackson's eyes got a little wide. "Oh. I mean…no. Not, like… I told them you came over the other—"

"I didn't *come over*, I'm not—"

"You literally came over, Phil."

"To your lawn, the lawn isn't—"

"My lawn is a part of my house, the lawn is over—"

I nearly broke my skateboard, dropping it to the pavement like that. Jackson shut up. I looked up at him, stern. "Jackson. Don't talk about me to your family. Don't invite me to your house for dinner. We're not twelve anymore, that's not what this is."

"Phil. Come on."

Jackson took a step forward. I took one back. "I'm…" I shook my head. "This is hard for me, Jackson. Please get that. Okay? Can you… Do you get that?"

Jackson took a moment. A little embarrassed. It hurt to see. He was just excited, I couldn't fault him for that. I had the same excitement. I was just being more careful with it. He knew I missed him. That had to be enough for now. Rushing ahead ruined us last time. And Cameron taught me enough lessons on being rushed.

Jackson smiled. "You'll let me know."

I hopped on my skateboard and gave him a nod. "I'll let you know."

Jackson hopped on his bike and nodded back. "Alright. Good night, Philip."

I smiled. Just a little. It was dark on that Orchard sidewalk and I knew he wouldn't see it. But I smiled. "Night, Jacks."

JACKSON

TRACK THREE
The First Cut Is the Deepest

Uh-oh, I hate theater.

We were doing this vocal warm-up/improvisation thing on the auditorium stage, all twenty or so of us standing in a circle pretending we were goldfish, when I first suspected this whole *Hairspray* gambit might have been a mistake. But Jackson Pasternak was an actor now. And if I wanted to help Phil, I needed to act the part.

After three hours of cast-bonding exercises, Mr. McBride called it and released us out into the school parking lot. The air had begun to crisp this past week and I'd need to start looking into jacket options for the autumn. My new scene partner and leader of the Drama Club, Dani Touscani, detached herself from her usual horde of theater girls and joined me at the curb. "That was torture."

"What, you don't like improv?"

"I came here to do real theater. We have literal scripts, I see no point in making shit up."

"I think they're meant to bond us as an ensemble."

"Well, Dictator McBride can bond to my assho—" Dani cut herself off. The thirteen-year-old Mr. McBride had plucked from the neighboring middle school was walking out of the theater with his mom. We both returned his little smile and wave.

"Great scene work today, *Seaweed*."

"Super-duper job, bud."

Griffin's mom held his hand as they walked across the parking lot. Dani dropped her voice. "Augie Horton must be humiliated."

"How do you mean?"

Dani smirked, happy to bestow her hard-fought theatrical wisdom. "I know you're new to the theater game, President Pasternak, but there are rules here. A hierarchy. And an upperclassman like Augie getting his role scooped out from under him? By an infant? Mortifying."

"An infant with star quality, Danielle. You can't buy that."

I looked down the street and saw a bunch of tech guys unloading a U-Haul full of building supplies. I scanned the area until I saw him bossing everyone around. Phil had been building sets for the plays since middle school and, while he would never admit to it, he'd become a crucial fixture in the theater department over the years. Personally, I thought it was good for him. Since rehearsals have begun, he's put a lot of his angry energy into running the *Hairspray* woodshop like an absolute tyrant. Phil was barking orders at the freshmen, waving around his clipboard. I smiled at his iron fist.

Dani also noticed him and tsked. "God. Didn't know he had it in him. Breaking Cameron Ellis's heart like that?"

I looked back at Dani, intrigued. Ever since joining this dastardly plot, my Excel had gotten a new tab. I'd become very interested in gathering my class's opinions on the heart-breaker, Phil Reyno. "Really? You don't think so?"

"I dunno. I've always liked Phil. He tells me to choke on colon anytime I see him building sets for us but…yeah. Matty weirdly defends him. Makes me invite him to things."

Interesting. I didn't know that. I reconsidered Dani and re-opened the mental copy of my Excel.

DANIELLE TOUSCANI
– Lead role in all our musicals (not Fiddler cuz Mono), weak falsetto
– On-again, Off-again with Mateo Silva since 7th Grade ("On" as of August)
– Nosiest person I've met outside of my father

I tried to keep personal bias out of my list but the queen of Drama Club's infamous nosiness was an undisputed fact. She was no Brynn Forester but Danielle had a similar gossipy vice. Though where Brynn liked to spread it, Dani was a collector. She just liked to know everyone's business. Sit on secrets like a dragon on a pile of gold. I could appreciate that. I could certainly relate to it.

Dani made sure we were alone. "Do you believe what people are saying about him? About Phil?"

"Oh. What have you heard?"

"That he… You know." Dani got a little closer and dropped her voice. "I heard Cameron was getting scared of him. Like, *scared* scared. I mean, Phil's a scary guy sometimes but like… like Haunted House scary. Halloween. I never thought he was the kind of guy to actually scare his boyfriend."

I nodded. I'd heard the rumor. The day after Cameron posted his breakup video, the gossip had spread through our school like a sickness. It didn't take long for me to trace back its source.

"Did Brynn Forester tell you that?"

Dani's mouth shut. Mum's the word. A person as nosy as her knew better than to rat out a reliable source. Still, I nodded. "I don't know, Dani. If you and Matty think Phil's a good guy, maybe you shouldn't let a rumor rattle your gut. Do you believe Phil is that kind of person? Scary?"

Dani thought about it. She shook her head. "No. I like Phil. I still like Phil. Even if the school thinks he should jump in the Schuylkill."

"Well. I'm sure he really appreciates your friendship, then."

Dani smiled and spotted her ride. Her on-again boyfriend's head was sticking out the passenger's window of a pulsing blue pickup. We said our goodbyes and she stomped across the lot to cut off Matty Silva's very poetic catcalling. But I lingered there in the brisk evening air. Stood on the curb and simply waited. Because I'd timed my exit intentionally. Positioned myself just so. In just a handful of rehearsals, I already knew more than enough of my target to guess his next move.

"Hey, killer."

Cameron Ellis slipped through the side auditorium exit. Five fifteen, right on schedule.

I smiled. "Hey, superstar. You following me?"

Cameron laughed and sidled up next to me on the curb, hands in his cardigan pockets. "Just doing some talk back with Mr. McBride. Sometimes I stay after and dig into character while he packs up. I think he really values creative feedback."

"I'm sure he does."

Cameron looked up at me, face all lit in the first bits of sunset. "Hey. You were really good today. I was really impressed."

I shrugged. "Look, I've always been great at pretending to

be an ice-cream cone in the desert. Just happy to finally have a place to show it off."

Cameron chuckled and nudged me. "Not the improv stuff, weirdo. The read-through. You really sold the character. You've really never acted before?"

I shrugged again. I wanted to tell Cameron I was acting right there on the curb with him. My smile was my greatest performance to date. My restraint deserved an Oscar. "Never. Never ever."

Cameron sighed and shook his head. "And you still got the lead. Lucky." His sigh got a little heavier. "Lucky, lucky *Link Larkin*."

He kept his wistful sigh going, but I knew that had to burn him up. Jackson Pasternak, the guy Cameron propositioned in the lobby, happened to swing by auditions for Cameron's favorite musical of all time, all off Cameron's suggestion, and swiped his dream role right out from under him. Jackson Pasternak, who'd never stepped foot on the school stage outside of a campaign speech, brought the house down with his audition. A quick rendition of "Your Song" (yes, the *Moulin Rouge* version, yes, in perfect French), and he secured the romantic lead and resounding applause while Cameron Ellis could barely get through his weird, self-written monologue without asking to restart twice. Jackson Pasternak was cast as teen heartthrob Link Larkin while Cameron Ellis was stuck as the comic relief bandleader, Corny Collins. Hierarchy be damned.

I smiled down at the wistful little monster. "Beginner's luck."

Cameron's eye twitched and I thought about how hard I'd make Phil laugh when I told him about that later. "Yeah. Also, you're a baritenor. Which is *amazing*. Really useful in theater.

I don't know, I guess my voice is just too deep for some of those songs. It's a curse, really, I hate it."

Cameron started across the parking lot and turned back to me. "Wait, you're coming straight to Brynn's, yeah? You want a ride?"

Jesus, about time. "Oh! Well... Sure, yeah, that would be great, actually. Good thinking."

"Awesome! And thanks again for agreeing to do the live show. I know it's silly or whatever but Brynn's been bouncing off the walls since you agreed."

"Hey, she's helping me. The student council budget got slashed this year and we've got like fifty events before October's out. This appearance will do more than a million home-made posters could've."

Technically, this was true. But promoting bake sales and Spirit Weeks wasn't my main motivation to appear on *The Brynn Show*.

We waited for some classmates' cars to pass and Cameron smiled up at me. "You really do have a million jobs in this school, huh? How do you keep it all straight?"

I shrugged. "Want to know my secret?"

Cameron seemed intrigued. I looked around to make sure the coast was clear then dropped my voice. Walked a little closer. "I'm a quadruplet."

Cameron snorted and shook his head. "Aaah. It all makes sense. Which Jackson am I talking to now?"

"Well, it's Thursday. So, Thursday Jackson."

He giggled. "You're so stupid."

I think Cameron was blushing. I know he was charmed. I wanted to push him into the passing sewer grate for calling me stupid but I was too busy being charming. The realization that I might be seen making our town's most recognizable face blush sent a spike of panic through my abdomen and made me pull back. Tone down the charm. "Yup. Very...very stupid."

We crossed the road over to Doug's waiting Tahoe and I made sure to keep some safe, preventive steps away from Cameron. Because when I agreed to join this plan, Phil was very clear with me. All I needed to do was get close to the Skwad. Be Cameron's shiny new pal, nothing more. And I was prepared for that. I was happy to be helping Phil. I was happy he trusted me again, however scant that trust might be. I was over the fucking moon that Phil Reyno wanted me around again. But the cost of this favor was already a little more than I'd budgeted for my junior year. The cost of Cameron. Being seen with him. Because Jackson Pasternak doing the musical was one thing. People could write that off as just another extracurricular for the Class President to throw on the ol' CV. But Cameron Ellis by my side had been garnering double takes. Cameron's company carried implication. Invited questions. Questions I didn't feel ready to answer just yet. Answers I didn't know if I had yet.

After an only slightly insufferable car ride with the rest of the Skwad, we arrived at Brynn's house. Despite a lifetime living minutes from each other, I'd never actually been to the Forester home before. Largely by design. Brynn was the third wealthiest person in our grade behind Ronny DiSario and Anthony Lewis and, as far as Orchard politics were concerned, was as Clubber as you can get. The Forester house might as well be sitting in the middle of the golf course and the country club stables bled right into Brynn's backyard. I'd call the proximity to hay and horse shit *rustic* but their driveway was still heated so it all evened out.

I helped Brynn out of the cramped car. "Hey, do the Pruitts still keep all those horses at the club stables?"

Brynn's eyes lit up. "Oh my god, yes. The DerHagopians and the Glenwood-Farbers now too, we're up to SIXTEEN horses. Do you ride?"

"Not as a rule. But I have. At birthday parties or whatever."

"That's AMAZING."

I nearly slipped on her drool. Before she was known far and wide as Cameron Ellis's primary hag, Brynn was better known around Moorestown as a tried and true "Horse Girl." Before gossiping and gay culture became her primary personality traits, I'd wager every other shirt Ms. Forester wore to school from grades one to eight had a picture of a horse or some pony-adjacent pun. It was a phase she had retired by high school. Phil told me Cameron would chide her if she ever veered too close back into "Neigh-Neigh territory." As far as the school was concerned, *Brynn the Horse Girl* had died. Or maybe been killed.

The basement of the charming Forester home looked like the set of a Nickelodeon show. Not one of the good ones but certainly one with budget. Two air hockey tables. A giant retro fridge with the word **COLA POP** painted across the front. An aquarium, a bright orange shag rug, and more beanbags than should ever be seen together. Three beanbags were huddled next to microphones against a familiar wall, the loud neon *THE BRYNN SHOW* sign looming above. While Augie prepared the tripod for the recording, Cameron and Doug were keeping two separate games of air hockey going across the room. I watched Augie's eyes roll with an exhaustion I was coming to know. Maybe he was annoyed by Cameron's intensity. Maybe Doug's trash talk or the noise of their games. Or maybe Augie was wondering why it always seemed to fall to him to help Brynn get ready while the other boys played their games. I couldn't tell for certain. But I didn't need to know the reason for Augie's apparent exhaustion with his nearest and dearest. Because its mere existence was enough. If I wanted to break the Skwad open, I didn't need to create the cracks. I just needed to find the ones that had always existed.

I joined Augie on set. "Hey, hey. We missed you at rehearsal today. McBride had us do this boring mirroring exercise thing for an hour, you would've hated it."

"Thrilling. Don't know how y'all went on without me."

"We only read through Act 1. Mr. McBride just had Cameron read your lines, it was a pretty low-key rehearsal overall."

"Line."

Augie moved the tripod to the center of the room, adjusting it just so. I smiled. "Huh?"

He put his own phone into the setup and oriented it around the set to find the right angle. "You said *lines*. I have a *line* in Act 1."

"Right, sure. I just meant we—"

"Cameron can have it honestly. Give it to Brynn, I don't even care. Not like anyone's leaving Act 1 of *Hairspray* thinking about *Gilbert*'s single fucking line." His phone kept drooping in the tripod so he ripped it out and busied himself around the snack table. "Anyway, you hear a cop was asking around school about that garbage truck accident?"

Augie Horton and his diversions. The guy changed subjects like a DJ in a booth, always so sure to play his preferred tracks. Something about *Hairspray* really got to Augie, I could hear it. Something personal. Something about the Skwad.

He ripped open a bag of trail mix and popped a raisin in his mouth. "They're saying someone stole a stop sign."

I joined him at craft services and helped myself to some fruit snacks. I knew full well Officer Olowe had visited the school asking about the accident. I knew because my new best friend Mrs. Stapler had pulled me out of first period the day after Garbage-Gate asking what I'd heard. Phil had told me all about his theft and its subsequent consequence and after I scolded him for the better part of an hour, he agreed to hide the stop sign in a neutral zone until we thought of a better plan. Obviously, that wasn't what I'd told Mrs. Stapler. I simply gave her some diversions of my own. "I'm sure it'll blow over. No one got hurt and the state insures government vehicles out the ass. Everyone on that block's gonna get good and taken care of."

"I bet." Augie cocked his head to the side. "Phil Reyno lives on that block. If I recall."

Walked right into that one. I was too focused on where Augie was diverting me from to clock where I was being led. I cleared my throat and shoved thirteen fruit snacks into my mouth. "So does Matty Silva. A lot of Moorestown kids on Duquesne. Needle in a haystack, really."

Augie gave me a look. He always gave me the same look when he smelled me being obtuse. Playing his game back at him. Augie seemed to be the only member of the Skwad who noticed my sudden and unquestioned proximity. Cameron and Brynn might have been drooling over the idea of Jackson Pasternak's guest appearance in their social lives but Augie was never so quick to drool. Or trust.

He threw out his half-full bag of trail mix and smiled. "Well. Glad you decided to join us. It's gonna be a good show."

"Hairspray?"

The little twitch in Augie's neck. The falter in his smile. A crack. "Brynn hasn't had a new guest in a minute. I'm sure everyone will be tuning in to see you." He left me at the table and sat on his beanbag, pulling out his phone. Something in my stomach told me to feel guilty for something, but I didn't have time to sort out what.

My phone buzzed in my pocket.

P: starting soon??

I made sure I wasn't being watched and found a corner to text in.

J: eminently

J: *imminently

Phil sent a picture from the DiSarios' garage couch. He must've wrapped up in the woodshop and skated right over to catch the show. They were sitting together and had the projector with Brynn's Instagram ready to go. Veronica was sipping a Red Bull and flipping off the camera.

P: ron says break a leg

I smiled. Ever since the night of Cameron's breakup video, those two had been spending just about every day together. Their sudden friendship made no sense given their history, but all the sense in the world given everything else. All they shared. I mean, I'd literally spent a childhood cataloguing everything I could find in common with the guy, but you didn't need a list to see it with Ronny. To the outside world, Phil Reyno and Jackson Pasternak were night and day. But Phil and Ronny are both night.

Brynn plopped down on the host beanbag and waved me over. "Jackson! We're ready!"

I gave her a thumbs-up and fired off one last text.

J: I'm on. Wish me luck.

P: dont do that thing where u ssmile with teeth u look like a serial killer

J: Thanks!

I pocketed my phone and got situated next to Augie on the bags. Brynn gave her stack of pink index cards one last review.

"So, I'll do the usual *Hi's and Hellos* then intro you both. Jackson, we'll talk with you first because you're new. Our audience has seen Augles a thousand times at this point."

I could feel Augie's micro-grunt shake my shoulder. He might have noticed too because he scooted his beanbag a few inches away from me.

Brynn smiled big at Doug manning the camera. "Alrighty! Let's pop off, y'all!"

Brynn remained frozen for seven seconds before Doug registered that *pop off* was supposed to mean *go*. He gave a thumbs-up and turned on Brynn's Live.

The host took a second to defrost, but she covered with a warm, welcoming laugh. "*Helloooooooooo, internet!* It's your number-one hostess and number-seven favorite Libra, coming at you LIVE from my beanbag basement. We are BACK for another thrilling episode of *The Brynn Show* here on Instagram, the best way to spend your seven o'clock or your money back. For those of you joining us live, hello! Thanks for coming back, we have a heck of a show on our hands. For anyone catching this later, I hope the future is as FANTASTIC as the movies make it seem."

She said it in a single breath. I had to hand it to her lung capacity. "So! Continuing *Skwad Appreciation Month*, live in the basement today we are joined again by fan favorite and *my* favorite, August Theodore Horton. Hi, Augles!"

Augie's smile had returned to him and his voice jumped maybe two pitches higher. "Hey, baby girl! Happy to be asked back."

"Of course, girlie! The fans wouldn't have it any other way."

Augie opened his mouth to continue, but Brynn's claw slapped down on my knee. "Now you all are in for a TREAT. If you go to Moorestown, have been to Moorestown, if you've stepped foot within five hundred FEET of Moorestown, you've heard of this boy."

Augie sank into his beanbag as I tried to look modest. Brynn counted off her fingers. "Class president. Captain of the Rowing Club. Debate Club. French Club, Key Club, and the National Honor Society. LEAD of the school musical, he's Link FRIGGIN Larkin, AND he has shoulder muscles like a young Mandy Patinkin. My *Yentl*-heads know what I'm talking about."

I batted away the compliment, sure to use my camera-facing shoulder, and Brynn threw up her hands. "It's JACKSON PAS-TERNAK!"

Doug hit a button on the soundboard app on his phone and prerecorded applause roared. Brynn rested back in her beanbag and I laughed. Again, very humble. "Brynn Forester. Wow. That was quite an introduction. Even Augie didn't get all that."

Augie snorted, but Brynn kept that smile going. "You're an impressive man, Mr. Class President. I'm still gooped you agreed to be on our silly little show."

I crossed one leg over my knee and sipped my water like I'd seen actors do on late-night talk shows. "Happy to make it to the basement. I so rarely get over to this side of the Orchard. More of a Laker, myself."

Brynn piped up and spoke to the camera. "Oh! Fun Moorestown lingo, y'all. In town, there's a neighborhood called the Orchard. It used to just be a bunch of apple trees but now it's got all these amazing houses and parks and this BEAUTIFUL lake, Plum Lake. Well, a *Laker* is someone who lives by Plum Lake. Like Jackson."

Augie sat straight. "And me."

Brynn perked up. Maybe remembering she had two guests. "Oh! Yes! Augies here is right on the water. He's hosted some of the fiercest cannonball-contests this side of the Ben Franklin Bridge, I'll tell ya."

Brynn gave Augie a moment to speak. But he decided to let it sit. I felt a tap on my back. Phil kicking me in the ass. *There, Jacks.* I saw the scab and chose to pick at it. "And you're a Clubber."

Brynn and Augie both looked at me. It was immediate. Right under the scab, I'd hit a nerve. Brynn smiled with teeth. "Yes. Our funny little town, so many little names and… little quirks."

She returned to her cards, ready to move on. My finger kept searching for the scab though. Because she was doing it again. Like before, what Ronny had noticed. Brynn only spoke abstractly. *Our* show, not *my* show. *We're* excited to have you, not *I'm.* Never committing herself to a point. Never tying herself to an opinion. *A neighborhood.* Not *my neighborhood.*

I looked at the camera, trying my best to sound casual and helpful. Innocent. "See, in the Orchard, there are *Lakers* and *Clubbers.* Lakers live by the water but *Clubbers,* like Brynn, they—"

"I mean, it's not really an official title—"

"Brynn lives right on the country club. A Clubber."

Augie shifted. Cameron poked his head up from his phone. It was as if I'd called Brynn a very different C-word.

She just smiled. It was getting tighter on her face. "Yeppers. Yes, yeah, my parents really... They lucked out. It's very... You know, it's rural? More by the horse farm than the country club, I don't even know if they're members, actually."

In all my research, all my hours watching the backlog of *The Brynn Show*, I could never make heads or tails on whether Brynn was avoiding the topic or if it truly just never came up. But I knew it now. Brynn's big secret. The relatable, endearing underdog didn't want her followers knowing the Foresters were filthy fucking rich.

"Dodgeball!" Brynn waved a cue card like a lifeline and regained focus. "For those of you who don't know our Jackson, the man is constantly on the move. And today, the busy bee has come on to talk about our school's most *infamous* fundraising event. All. Night. DODGEBALL. Jackson?"

She turned to me, happy to be back in her centrist flow. I'd just gotten a good lick in and did have some business to take care of so I agreeably picked up her cue. "That's right, Brynn. All-Night Dodgeball is back and better than ever. Only twenty bucks a head this year and that covers team shirts, waters, and a slice or two of pizza from Passy's on Main."

"Amazing! And fill our viewers in on the *All-Night* concept."

"I mean, it's your standard dodgeball tournament just spread over the course of an all-nighter. Get three to five of your friends together for a team, and the winners get free Passy's for the school year. It's a blast."

Augie made a face. "All night? That is my Saturday. No thank you."

Brynn laughed all cheery and patted my knee. "Ignore our resident wet blanket here, Mr. President. Augles and school spirit aren't exactly on speaking terms. The rest of the Skwad will be there, five hundred percent."

I smiled and shook Augie's shoulder, trying on Brynn's big smile for size. "Oooh. Come on, *Augles*, the whole Skwad's going! What's the Skwad without Augie Horton?"

Augie humphed. "Now that's a question."

He was screwing and unscrewing the lid on his water bottle, over and over. Brynn might have noticed but, in an effort to make peace, led us right into a minefield. "Well! Now that we've got our dodgeballs all in a row, how 'bout we give the people what they want and talk *Hairspray!*"

Augie stiffened. Brynn had thrown the segue to camera and I could feel an audience applauding in my skull. Because it was the exact wrong area to lead the broadcast, but Brynn couldn't see it. She was too busy being a host, being a good sport, she didn't see the clear struggle on her apparent best friend's face. All the signs to handle with care. Augie's clear and present frustration with this awful musical. I clapped. "You can't stop the beat! Love *Hairspray*, love everything about it."

Brynn smiled. "Apparently! Now, Jackson Pasternak joining the school musical... Kind of a plot twist, huh? I mean, we were all truly GAGGED to see you on that cast list, but you are so good in this role, Jackson. Have you always had an interest in theater?"

I leaned back in my beanbag and shrugged. "To be honest with you, Brynn? No. Not even a little. I kind of auditioned on a whim, actually. Just a bit of fun, you know? Something easy. And, yeah, it all just sort of...worked out."

Augie tripped over my bait and scoffed. I smiled. Brynn pushed on. "Wowzers! You know, it really goes to show…" She looked into the camera, suddenly serious. Really grasping for a teachable, sharable moment. "If you want something, viewer, you can't wait for it to happen for you. It pays off to try. To step forward into the future *you* want. For something *you* love. Even if you don't have the experience or the background, if the *love* is there, nothing can stop you. Remember, *you* are the writer of your book, okay? *You* are the teller of your story."

"That doesn't even mean anything."

My eyes widened. He had said it in a chuckle so, for a moment, we all considered it was just a joke. But there was nothing funny on Augie's face. Nothing angry either, more of a flatness. Like this broadcast, this basement and this Skwad, like none of us fuckers deserved another ounce of his effort today.

Brynn's face was stuck somewhere between a laugh and a plead. Augie rolled his eyes. "Sorry? Whoops?"

He shook his head and looked at me. "Jackson, you know that doesn't mean anything. You're a smart guy. And you know coming on here talking 'bout how easy it was for you to get the lead in the musical is really, deeply fucking annoying, right?"

"OOOOOOOOOOOH."

Everyone looked at Doug at his soundboard by the camera. He put it away. Not the time. Cameron had joined Doug's side. Trying to get Augie to look at him. But my Laker neighbor was stuck on me.

"I've been doing these shows for *years*. Longer than you. Longer than her. Longer than Dani or Samantha or Shelby or Dwayne or Lydia or anyone in the ensemble. McBride *called* me. He made sure I was auditioning, he told me he needed my *good energy*, and he still couldn't bother giving me a part with more than two lines. I didn't even get a fucking callback. GILBERT doesn't require a fucking callback, but hey. You got the lead. On a whim! Good job, Jackson, I'm glad it all *worked out*."

Brynn's hands were strangling her cue cards. There wasn't a chance in hell she would know the right next words. Because who would? Not me. Which is why I intentionally chose the wrong ones. "Well... I mean, *Devil's Advocate*... What role did you want? Seaweed?"

Augie shrugged. "It's not about what I wanted. Clearly. But the only Black male lead in the show? Sure. It would have been nice to get a shot at him."

"I think you're right."

"And thank God for your approval, Jackson. Can we move on?"

I turned to Brynn. She looked terrified I might pass her the speaking stick. "Brynn. Do you think Augles would have made a good Seaweed?"

Brynn immediately nodded. "*Of course.* Of course, Augie, you would've been fantastic. You would've been so good. So fantastic."

The friends took a small moment to actually look at each other. Maybe for the first real time that recording. Brynn really meant it. And Augie needed to hear it. Because despite the cracks in the air, the festering resentment that maybe always existed underneath the Skwad, those two really were close.

But.

"But..."

But Brynn just couldn't help herself. Her eyes forced themselves back to the camera, another very good friend, and left

Augie hanging. The smile fought its way back and her tone returned to sweet. "You know, to take nothing away from Griffin. We all think little Griffy is doing an *amazing* job. Truly. Such a young talent, worth your ticket alone."

If the crack had been splinters before, that was the shatter. I closed my eyes and saw shards fall from the ceiling. Augie sat up straight. "Brynn Forester. If you really think a MIDDLE SCHOOLER is doing a better job than me, just say that. If everybody would prefer an ACTUAL CHILD bopping around that stage over me, why should I even bother showing up to fucking—"

"Augie, please, the cussing—"

"I mean, be serious, Brynn. Did y'all expect me to play Mo-tormouth Maybelle? Did you want me to throw on a wig and a dress and belt some Jennifer Hudson for my audition? No! It was always Seaweed or nothing. And I got NOTHING. Which is why *Hairspray* is NOTHING to me. This show is BULLSHIT."

Augie settled into his bag with a grunt. I was worried he'd stuck his point and might be finished so I held up a finger, very unhelpful.

"But Augie. Brynn loves *Hairspray*. Cameron loves it, always has. Shouldn't people be allowed to enjoy things?"

Augie turned his glare on me. "Oh. You want to talk about *the people*, Jackson?" He counted off his fingers. "Tracy Turn-blad. Corny Collins. Edna Turnblad, Wilbur Turnblad. Amber and Velma Von Tussle. Link Larkin, Penny Pingleton, MRS. Pingleton, Mr. Pinky, the principal, the gym teacher, the ENTIRE Corny Collins cast. Brad, Tammy, Fender, Sketch, Shelley, IQ, Brenda and Lou Ann and those are the charac-ters with LINES."

He cleared his count and started again. "Seaweed. Little Inez. Motormouth Maybelle. Gilbert."

Augie chucked his water bottle away. "I could've danced Seaweed. Seaweed is a dancer, first and foremost, and I'm the best dancer in our grade. I also don't look like a fetus two-stepping with Dani Touscani on that stage, another strong plus. So why not call me back? No, really. I wanna talk about it. Why not give me a shot? Why make sure I'm auditioning then not see what I can do?"

He looked at Brynn. She was looking at the floor. She was out of cards. "Sorry, Brynn. Is this topic making you *uncomfortable*?"

But Brynn wouldn't meet his eyes. "It's not fair, Augs. You deserved the opportunity. But… Augles, no one's ever really happy with these things, you know? I mean, is anyone ever really happy in the theater? I was dying to play Penny Pingleton and I *bombed* my callback. I literally could not stop sweating."

She tried laughing for the camera. But Augie just stared holes into Brynn. Her tried and true attempt to endear herself only rang all the falser in the face of Augie's legitimate hurt. A real issue.

He sniffed. "How many people did you get called back for? Before you got Amber Von Tussle?"

Brynn blinked. "Um… I don't know—"

"Seven. You got called back for seven characters, Brynn. You don't think that's a little much? You don't think that's a little unfair?"

There was a quick flinch in Brynn's mouth that I'd never seen before. A sting. An anger. Something she couldn't smile away. "I don't… I don't think it's *unfair* that Mr. McBride wanted to see what fit me best."

"Uh-huh. And he landed on the spoiled little rich bitch. Interesting."

"Augie!" Brynn looked to Cameron and Doug at the camera. Maybe for an out.

But Augie held up a finger. "Nah. Uh-uh, keep it running. Since our hostess wants to get real all the sudden." Augie turned to me. "So sorry for this, Jackson. We usually have a better back and forth. Why do you think I didn't get Seaweed?"

Brynn grabbed my shoulder, a little harder than I loved. "Do NOT bring Jackson into this, he is our GUEST."

"I'M YOUR GUEST TOO!"

"WELL, YOU'RE BEING A JERK!"

Augie laughed and threw up his hands. "Okay! Okay, then please tell me, Brynn. Why do YOU think I didn't get Seaweed?"

Brynn unclenched my shoulder and shrugged, a little looser. She'd dropped all facade and wasn't fighting for control anymore. She was just fighting her bestie. "I don't know! Okay?! I don't know, Augie, maybe you weren't good that day. Maybe you picked the wrong audition song."

"Oh, do NOT blame my song choice. The worst song from *A Strange Loop* is LIGHTYEARS more impactful than 'You Can't Stop the *Fucking* Beat.'"

"It wasn't right for this audition! I told you that!"

Her voice got tighter and quicker and it crashed into Augie's, overlapping and careening and running around in circles. "I told you that a million times, Augie, but you insisted. You insisted, you needed to do it *your* way—"

"Brynn, I didn't want to DO this show in the first place—"

"And if Augie doesn't get it *HIS* way—"

"I only did it because you kept calling me a wet blanket, which—"

"And I just wanted to spend more time with you because—"

"And you and Cameron were SOOOO excited—"

"Because you just get so hard to talk to sometimes—"

"Because I don't like dodgeball and I don't like *Hairspray* and—"

"Because I didn't want to tell you, you were never gonna get Seaweed and—"

I felt Phil's hand. A quick tug on my ear. I piped in. "And why is that, Brynn?"

"Because he's too—"

Brynn's good sense returned to her one word too late. She covered her mouth before she could finish her sentence, but the damage was done. For once in that basement, a real thought got out. Brynn's real feelings. *Too.*

I sat back. I didn't need to say anything else in that room. Augie just stared at his friend. "*Too*...what, Brynn? What am I *too* for you now?"

Brynn shook her head. Eyebrows furrowed. Using everything in her to keep herself from crying. Because how would that look? Resorting to tears? "I didn't mean... You're not *too* anything, you're... You're my—"

Augie shrugged. "What's the issue? Too femme to play a leading man? Too big to play a romantic lead? C'mon. Don't stop now, Brynn. Commit to something."

"*Augie.*"

"Too fat or too gay? Which is it?"

Brynn started to cry. Augie walked off. Cameron turned off the recording and Doug did whatever Doug does. Me? Well, I just stared at the water bottle in my hands and wondered if I was a sociopath. No. A therapist once expressly told me that I wasn't. Sociopaths never ask if they're sociopaths and I had asked a lot.

The Skwad didn't notice me after that. I just stayed seated

on the beanbag while the friends tried to recalculate. That kind of conflict was clearly new to them and I don't know if they had the first clue on how to deal with it. I think Brynn went to her room. And I think Augie went home. Pretty soon, Doug went upstairs to check on Brynn but Cameron never left the tripod. Never put his phone down. Never gave Brynn a second look.

"What are you doing?"

Cameron's eyes were scrolling up and down his screen. His finger never stopping its hunt and peck. "People are commenting. A lot... A lot of people were watching."

"Oh. Are they mad?"

Cameron nodded. But he didn't look worried. I couldn't tell you what that look on Cameron's face was. It was almost cold. Almost detached. But there was interest too. A confused interest. Like a vulture over old roadkill.

"A lot of people are gonna watch this." The blue glow of the screen made his eyes look sunken.

I sat up in my beanbag. "Maybe... Maybe you should go check on Brynn, Cameron."

"Yeah." But Cameron didn't move. He wouldn't stop scrolling. Reading. The vulture wouldn't stop feeding. "Yeah..." And those cold, empty eyes were almost a comfort. Because whatever people might think, whatever I might've told myself before, I truly was not like him. Because I was already feeling indescribably guilty for the hurt I'd facilitated in that basement. For the people I'd made cry. Brynn in her room. Augie in his way.

But their good pal Cameron felt nothing. Cameron Ellis felt nothing at all.

PHIL

TRACK FOUR

My Dad Says That's for Pussies

I thought one upside of my very public breakup would be finally leaving Brewster's in my rearview. Knowing my luck, I shouldn't have been surprised when Chuck Reyno said he found this "real fancy spot" for our annual father-son dinner. We were about a third of the way through our milkshakes and burgers when I caught Chuck staring at my plugs. Trying not to stare, at least.

"What?"

"Nothin'."

His staring got less subtle. I could feel the twin pink circles in my earlobes start to sweat. *What?*

"Nothing! Y'just… You didn't have those things before, right? Last time I saw ya?"

Something about my father's unfiltered Tennessee twang always put me off. I think it's because I have the same one when I'm not careful. I've been in Jersey long enough to sandpaper most traces of *hick* off my tongue but it still creeps out when I'm tired or high. Or pissed.

I sat back in my booth and decided to be a bitch. "Well. Let's see. These are size three gauges. You gotta wait fourteen weeks between each size up so, let's see... Fourteen times three, forty-two weeks, that's maybe nine or so months give or take so... Yeah, no. You're right, man, I didn't have these *nine and a half* months ago."

I let my point land on Chuck and returned to my burger. He chuckled. "I get it. It's been a minute. But you are quick. Y'get that from me."

"Ooooh. *That's* what I got from you. I was starting to wonder."

"Okay, cool it, chief. We're just eating. We don't gotta always be...*on*." I rolled my eyes and focused my attention on my quickly melting cherry shake. Chuck stomached a burp. "Anyhow. Didn't have time to getcha a gift. For the big One Seven. Got a couple of gigs in Philly though, figured you could come see me before I head out. Doing the Comedy Cellar in LA on Friday. Pretty exciting stuff."

He took his time wiping sauce off his mouth, waiting for me to look impressed by his C-list comedy career. But I'd tuned out long before I could care. "Okay. Right. I see what went wrong."

Chuck sighed. "Why does something always gotta be wrong, Philip?"

"My big One Seven is *next* weekend. You're leaving *on my birthday*. You'd know that if you ever bothered to call me back."

"Philip."

"You'd also know that I don't go by fucking *Philip!*"

"Hey! Now, that was your grandpap's name—"

"Well, SORRY to Grandpap."

We both found the natural lull in our shouting and got

back to our burgers. I let myself cool off a bit. Chuck grunted. "What's wrong with *Philip*?"

I rested my head back on the booth and decided it would be in my best interest to try talking like a palatable human being. There was no winning with my father so why fucking bother. "I used to work at the Sunoco by the Orchard. That's the neighborhood with all the mansions and shit."

"I remember."

"It's fine, you don't. But turns out *Philip* isn't the best name when you're pumping gas for your rich dick classmates."

Chuck had a question on his face. I spelled it out for him. *"Fill up."*

And my fucking dad burst out laughing. I closed my eyes and did what I do when Mom does this. Finds my life hilarious. Busts a gut over something that embarrasses me. How I survive having two fun parents. I pressed my eyelids shut and I tried to wait all that fun out.

Chuck calmed down a little and took a small notepad out of his shirt pocket. That goddamn notepad. He clicked his pen and found an open area to scribble something down. "I'm gonna use that. *Fill up.* In my set. Know *exactly* where to try it out. Jesus."

I watched my dad fight to cram his new material into his overfilled joke pad. He's had hundreds of these things over the course of my life. Every thought, every observation, any unique moment in a conversation with Chuck Reyno gets paused, digested, and shit back out into these pads. He never lets anything just be. It all goes in the book.

"My manager thinks it's gonna be a much better year for me, kiddo. Lot of people out there are itchy for my kind of shit, y'know? Unfiltered. Real shit. Not so fucking PC."

He slapped his notepad closed and got back to shoving

cheese fries into his mouth. I focused on a trail of oily cheddar dripping down his patchy beard, if only to block out his
rantings over cancel culture and the "woke police." And I
started to wonder if this hate in my stomach, this disgusting
taste that fills my mouth whether I want it to or not, I wondered if I got it all from Chuck Reyno.

Chuck eyeballed the cozy, coffeehouse decor around us.
"I thought Jersey was all diners and hoagie shops. What happened to the grime?"

"You brought us to the rich side of town. I would've preferred Wawa."

"Your mama said your friends come here a lot. You get
in good with another rich kid?" I made a face. Chuck tsked.
"What, you're still pissed at Jacksy? It's been years, Philly, get
over it. We loved Jackson. Only friend you ever had I didn't
wanna throttle. Lord, y'all were *obsessed* with each other."

"You realize I will leave, right? Can you fucking stop,
Dad?"

"C'mon, bud, I'm just kidding around with—"

"Stop it. Stop. Please."

I wanted to sound stern but it came out as pleading. Ugh.
I think Chuck could tell I was hitting my limit. Maybe that's
why he decided to cut to the chase. "How 'bout, uh...the
other one? The...y'know. The friend in that, uh...the video?"

I felt what could have been anything from a brain freeze
to an aneurysm over the thought of talking about my "other
friend" with my father. "You saw the video?"

A bit of me assumed as much. A lot of me assumed that was
why he hadn't called me back for so long. For ten months.
But Chuck sat back in his booth and nodded. It was the first
time all dinner that his hands weren't knuckle-deep in some
ground beef or repackaging my trauma into his joke book.

He just nodded. "That was some…yeah. A lot of views on that one, I'll, uh… I'll tell ya. Lotta likes."

Almost at once, we both looked up at the ceiling. Maybe so we wouldn't have to make eye contact. Maybe we were looking for oxygen masks. Neither of us wanted to have this conversation. Honestly, neither of us was prepared to.

"My manager. His daughter is…like that. Like your friend. But he's from Nashville so…it's a whole other world, y'know?"

Like a sign from heaven, my phone buzzed. Saved by the bell.

"Look. Philip. I—"

I smiled at the text and got out of the booth. "Would you excuse me, I have a cyst on my inner thigh and I think it just burst."

I was five steps away before Chuck could react. *"What?"*

I didn't turn around, quick on my beeline to the restroom. "CYST. INNER THIGH. DRIPPING DOWN MY LEG."

My admittedly weird go-to lie distracted a waitress and she nearly tripped over a dessert cart. I apologized, hustled along the rows of booths, and slipped into the men's room. At the bathroom sink, a very nice sweater was stretched over a very muscular back. Their owner was hunched over the counter, drowning himself under the faucet.

"What the fuck are you doing?"

Jackson pulled out of his waterboarding and patted his face with a paper towel. "Grounding exercise. Helps with anxiety."

"So, your first Skwad dinner's going well, then."

Jackson looked at me and shook his head, dire. "It's *just* us, Phil."

I stiffened. *"What?"*

"It's just Cameron and me, he didn't… He said the Skwad bailed. Last minute, 'cause of the fight, they're not coming.

No one else is coming, Phil, I think he…" Jackson's shoulders got stuck in this frantic sort of shrug. "I think he thinks it's a date?"

"Oh. Oh, Jackson."

"I think he tricked me into a goddamn date? Would he… Would Cameron do that?!"

I leaned on a bathroom stall and let out a long exhale. "Of course he fucking would."

"I hate him. Holy shit, Phil, I hate him so much." Jackson paced around every inch of the tiny bathroom. Front to back, back and forth. "We walked here from Main Street, half a mile, and he didn't ask me a single question. He just talked about the guys he met at baseball camp and the skincare sponsor he just got for his vlog and how *Hairspray* educated a whole generation of theater lovers on race relations in America and I wanted to light myself on fire. And now people are gonna see us here and see us together and… AGH."

I sighed, watching him spin out. "Cameron is literally here all the time, man, it doesn't mean this…*means* anything to him. Just keep it casual. Cut out early."

Jackson covered his face and breathed. He needed more than that. I had to admit, I was a little surprised to see him so thrown. I knew he'd been keeping Cameron at arm's length but Jackson was usually better about rolling with life's punches. The apparent ambush was really throwing him.

"Jackson. You good?"

He shook his head, face still in his hands. "I don't know what to do here, Phil. I can't… I can't think right."

"It's dinner at Brewster's, Jackson. I've blinked my way through dozens of them."

"I haven't… I never had to do this before. I've never done this."

"Yes, you have. You've bullshitted your way through millions of your parents' cocktail parties, Jackson, you're great at getting through boring dinners."

His hands dropped, but his head kept shaking. "A date. It's a *date*, Phil, I've never been on a date before." He looked like he was about to cry. "I don't know how to pretend. I don't know how to act here, I should've... I should've left. I shouldn't..." Jackson looked at the bathroom window. "I shouldn't be here."

I hopped off the stall wall and put myself between Jackson and his escape route. "NO. You are not jumping out that fucking window."

"I can't do this."

"Well, falling ass-first into a dumpster isn't the answer either, man. If you need to get out, we can get you out cleaner."

That stilled him. "But... I agreed to help you."

"I know. But if this is too much—"

"No. No, I want to help you." He started pacing again. *"I just don't know how to do this."*

I put my hands on his shoulders. Just to ground him. "Jackson. Listen."

"I don't know how to do—"

"And I'm gonna teach you, shut the fuck up and listen."

Jackson's eyes were big, but he nodded all the same. I kept my voice steady and my focus on him. Jackson was always a better student than me. I just needed to be a good teacher for him. "It's just dinner. You know how to have dinner, Jacks. He's gonna sit y'all by the front window. 'Cause he's gonna wanna be seen. That's okay, he's here every other night, you don't gotta be nervous about people seeing you there. He'll order guac for the table and he'll get real weird if you eat more than him. Prolly make some comment about not filling up too fast."

Jackson's eyes calmed down a bit. He kept nodding and I knew if he had his notebook, he'd be writing this all down. Asking me to talk slower for him.

"If he thinks it's a date, he'll ask if you wanna split a milkshake. If you're looking to win points, his favorite is the Toffee Coffee Crunch. It's actually pretty solid so get the large 'cause he's gonna finish it before you get a second sip."

I noticed my hands were still on Jackson's shoulders. I should've taken them back by then. "If he likes you... If he *really* likes you, he'll order your dinner for you. Something off menu. To impress you. If he likes you, he's gonna try and make you feel real special. Like he could make anything happen for you tonight. Whatever you ask for. But that doesn't matter. Because it's not a date. Because you never fucking agreed to that. Right?"

That time he nodded. I patted his shoulder. "Right. It doesn't matter what Cameron thinks this night is. It only matters what you think, Jacks."

Jackson swallowed. He'd come back down to earth. Grounded. "...Am I going to have to pretend to like pie?"

I smiled. Mournfully. "I'm so sorry, Jackson. I know that will be hard for you."

"It's just so much crust."

"I know. I remember."

"And even the good ones are just—"

"Are just okay, I remember. You're gonna have to be brave."

Jackson closed his eyes and prepared himself. "I'm gonna be so brave."

I laughed and took my hands off his shoulders. He double-checked himself in the mirror and dabbed at some water on his nice UPenn sweater. It was a little small on him. But I had to imagine most of his tops were now that he'd learned to funnel his anxiety into pull-ups.

"How's your dinner going? Caught a peek of you two on my way to the bathroom. Did Chuck get hair plugs?"

Jackson popped some bubble in my head and I remembered the conversation I'd abandoned not minutes ago. It was only a matter of time before Chuck came searching for me. I don't know what he would've done if he found me in here with Jackson. My old friend. My *Jacksy*. I suddenly felt my black bean burger and cherry shake going to war in my stomach.

"I don't wanna talk about my dad with you, Jackson." I'd sounded colder than I'd meant to.

Jackson looked at me in the mirror. He didn't realize he'd overstepped. I watched his apology start and end in his lips. He must've decided against it. Instead, he just looked at me. "Is this really how it's gonna be, Phil? I get to keep running into these doors? I get to be your friend again until I'm not? 'Cause if those are the terms, I can do that. If that's how it's got to be for you." Jackson turned to me and crossed his arms. I suddenly felt like I was watching one of his Debate Club practices again. "But it would be a lot easier for me to pick a side."

"A side?"

"Am I your friend again or am I just helping you? Are we trying to be friends again or did you just…miss me?"

I'd been on the receiving end of Jackson's argumentative logic before and never could win. Did I have the answer he was looking for? Had I gotten any better at debating Jackson in our time apart?

A man walked into the bathroom and headed for a urinal. Jackson's arms uncrossed and I breathed easier. Saved by the piss. Jackson smiled at the obvious relief on my face. "You'll let me know. Sure."

Jackson walked right by me and out the bathroom door. I gave it a second and followed. Across the dining room, past the busy waitresses and the kid's birthday party in the booths, I saw my dad writing in his joke pad. Looking around at the hip Brewster's clientele, sure to mine a solid tight five from it all. I probably could've left and he'd text me next week asking where I went.

Across the way, I saw Jackson sit down at the table by the front window. Away from the noise and guests. A table just for two. A bowl of guac already on the table. Cameron Ellis wearing the pale purple sweater I used to love on him. Their hands were close. Not touching, Jackson wouldn't go for that, but they were close. People would see it. Them together. How they fit together. How perfect they both looked at a table I could never sit comfortably at. Cameron and Jackson. A natural pair. A better fit.

Jackson made Cameron burst out laughing and I realized I was jealous. That was the word. *Jealous.* Cameron patted Jackson's hand and I realized I wanted to cry. I had to check and make sure that I wasn't. Because I didn't know how to win Jackson's debate. I didn't know what I missed. Because I didn't know which boy I was jealous of.

JACKSON

TRACK FIVE

Damn I Wish I Was Your Lover

Fourteen minutes. Fourteen minutes and I hadn't said a single word.

"I know everyone thinks their high school shows are special, but I legitimately believe Moorestown has put on some legitimately higher quality productions. Like, when we did *Les Mis* four years ago, people in the audience actually cried. I was there, my mom *actually* cried right next to me. And she hates amateur theater, she won't even see off Broadway. But I think Mr. McBride really has something this year. It's a very solid cast, no weak links, everybody's putting in the work. The *real* work. And we're hungry for it, you know? Like, the energy is there. Everybody just wants to put on a good show. I don't know. I just think it's a really important piece."

Our waitress returned and Cameron jumped in before she could ask a thing. "Hey, Stacey. We're thinking milkshakes. Right, Jackson? Wanna split a milkshake?"

The milkshake. Cameron's tell. Just like Phil had warned me. I swallowed, trying to rehydrate my stagnant vocal cords. "I—"

"Awesome, yeah. Stace, we'll do the Toffee Coffee Crunch. It's amazing, Jackson, you're gonna die. Seriously, next to God."

Cameron thought we were on a date. Stellar. I shut my mouth and I went back to shredding my napkin under the table. Cameron patted Stacey on the hand. "And can you tell Dani to do the caramel thing like I like? And two straws, please. Wait, how are the kids? Is Lindsey still going as Ariel for Halloween?"

I blocked out Cameron's attempt to humanize himself and watched Dani Touscani working behind the counter. She was making lattes behind the register, joking with customers and wiping down her station. Her boyfriend, Matty, was sitting at the counter and would play with her hand whenever she'd walk by. Last year, I'd watched Matty Silva knock in a kid's front tooth with his own environmental studies textbook for looking at him too long. He was one of the meanest sons of bitches I'd ever avoided but there he was. Gooning at his girlfriend, hearts fluttering out of his eyes, for all of us to see. All that mean, put on the shelf. Just for the right person.

Our waitress headed off and Cameron smiled at me. "I think you can tell a lot about a person by the way they treat waiters. I sort of have this dorky little dream of waiting tables in New York after graduation. Just a day job to help with rent while I audition. I mean, breaking into the theater scene there takes years. But I'm ready for that next step. That's what branching into video content is all about for me, preparing me for the next step. What happens in the Cameron Ellis story *after* Moorestown. But I'm planning on taking a gap year to get settled in Brooklyn first. Or maybe *Washing-tone Heights*. Then I'm applying to Juilliard."

I felt my thigh under the table. If I could just find my femoral artery, I'd only need to ask our waitress for a sharper knife.

Cameron shook out his hands. "Gaaah. But enough about

me. I feel like I've been talking forever. Tell me about you. Tell me about Jackson Pasternak. The *real* Jackson."

I wasn't sure how to respond. I wasn't really jumping to have a go in the conversation, I think I was more just annoyed I hadn't been given the option. Finally holding the mic, I was drawing a blank. What did Cameron Ellis deserve to know about the *real* Jackson?

I remembered Phil's advice. The night was no different from one of my parents' dinner parties. If I couldn't escape, I just needed to impress. "I'm, uh… You know. I'm a relatively normal guy. Love to row. Love my little sister, really don't like Brie. I'm Jewish. Pretty big on that. Oh, and my parents are fantastic. Know exactly who they are, know exactly what art looks good on our walls, they're both just really great people. *Obsessed* with each other. They're professors over at UPenn. Dad's an adjunct in philosophy and my mother basically runs the psych department."

Cameron leaned in close, maybe only then noticing my UPenn sweater. "Oh, wow. That must be so great for you. Do you think you'll go? Ivy League, that's wild."

I shrugged the shrug I shrug every time I inevitably get asked this question. "Hopefully. If I get in."

And Cameron laughed the laugh everyone laughs whenever I give that answer. "Jackson. You're a shoo-in. Your résumé? Your… I don't know, *pedigree*? You would need to set the Cherry Hill Mall on fire to get rejected. Honestly, you'd probably still get wait-listed."

I sipped my water and let my practiced modesty speak for me. It was an ugly brand of bragging but Clubbers like Cameron loved that sort of thing. A humble prince. Modest dickswinging. "You never know. I don't want to jinx it. But if my parents happen to trot me out to dinners with some old favorites in the admissions circles, I'd be a fool to say no. I love a good trot. If it means getting into Penn, I'll be the prettiest show pony at the goddamn derby."

Cameron's eyes were practically twinkling. Personally, I felt like a coat of grime had oozed out of my pores and figured that was enough *Action Jackson* for one dinner. "Hey, how's Brynn holding up? Shame she couldn't make it."

Cameron's twinkles evaporated. He took a second to blink them away. "She's, uh… She's Brynn. You know Brynn. She's always very hard on herself."

"How do you mean?"

Cameron looked around for a waitress or some other distraction. "I just think she has a tendency to overreact. But she knows that. She's conscious of it, it's a big part of why she said…you know. All that." Cameron gave up on a distraction and shrugged. "I just don't think she needed to deactivate. I know it's trendy or whatever to knock social media, but it's important to her. I don't know. I just really hope she bounces back. Starts the show again. It's a really great outlet for her, you know? The community at large. She does really important work."

Cameron was bullshitting me. I knew because it was the exact same bullshit I'd used on Brynn not weeks ago. *Really important work.* Like a talk show series from beanbags was curing polio. He didn't give a shit how many sick days Brynn took from school. He didn't care how many apology videos she sobbed through. Cameron only cared that he'd lost an outlet. His social lifeline. The safety net of fans and followers that his good bestie Brynn could provide.

"Well. I'm sure she treasures your friendship."

Cameron's eyebrows got all soft as he pouted, incredibly touched. "Awww. That is so sweet of you to say, Jackson. I am a good friend, thank you."

Cameron patted my hand. Before I could pin it to the table

with my pie fork, I caught Dani Touscani looking at us from the counter. His hand on mine. Aw, crap.

Dani was never as shameless in her gossip as Brynn Forester but Brynn was "taking some time off." We didn't know what would happen to the rumor mill without Brynn's compulsive regulation. I didn't know what Dani would do with this possible gossip.

"Would you excuse me, I need to take a pill."

"Huh?"

I stood and let about three dozen bits of napkin fall off my lap. "Pardon."

"Oh. Okay—"

I left Cameron at our table and sped for the bathroom. Once I cleared the corner, I hid behind an arcade cabinet and located Dani hanging by the kitchen door. Matty was still waiting at the counter so Dani was alone, counting a wad of tips. I could try to defuse the bomb. I'd gotten to know Danielle well enough in rehearsals, I was sure I could explain a way out of my proximity to Cameron Ellis. Or I could try to escape. That bathroom window looked mighty jumpable and falling into a dumpster would be an upgrade at that point. I was torn between strategies. Frozen by good logic and self-defenses.

Then I saw Phil. Across the dining room, in his booth. The Reyno men were in the middle of a very tense conversation. I could only see the back of Phil's head but Chuck looked stern. As if he had any right. The D-List comedian who always chose bombing a set in some casino basement over showing up for Phil. Birthdays, Christmases, the single time Phil played his drums in public. Chuck always had better gigs.

I felt myself defrost. I think Dani waved to me. I think she asked me how I was enjoying my night. I think Chuck saw me walking over and I think he didn't recognize me. It had been some time. I slipped into the booth right behind Phil and just listened. My head right behind his.

His dad sounded tired. "You know I just want you to be happy."

Phil sounded dead. He must've shut down. "Super."

"Shut the hell up and look at me, would ya?" Phil sighed. Chuck dropped his voice. "Now listen. When your mother told me you might be...*like that*? I thought to myself, I honestly said the words out loud: *Well. Well, maybe that's why he's always been such a fucking asshole. Maybe that's why he's always been so goddamn unhappy all his life.*"

I couldn't see Phil's jaw, but I knew that would clench it. Tight. Like he was daring his teeth to crack under all the pressure he was putting them through.

"So, if your *friend* makes you happy? If you are actually, truly, finally fucking happy? Suck all the dick you want, Philip. *Phil.* I just want you happy, kid." Chuck laughed. "Just... Just be happy."

It wasn't how I remembered Chuck laughing. It sounded genuine. I didn't know if I'd ever heard him laugh without some joke attached to it. At no one's expense. But Chuck was being very honest with his kid right then. Chuck truly wanted him to be happy. Even if that meant his only son might be gay.

I closed my eyes. Thought it loud. Like I might send Phil a message, my head so close to his. *Don't. You don't. Don't fucking settle for that, Philip.*

"PHIL, WHAT THE FUCK?!"

I felt Phil jump out of the booth and watched him stomp straight for the employee's exit. I'd jumped up just as quick and looked back at Chuck. He was busy frantically fishing his joke pad out of a half-drunk cherry shake. He still carried that goddamn joke pad? The glass was full enough to

soak the paper through in seconds. Chuck didn't even notice
me standing there.

"GODDAMMIT."

He wasted every napkin in the dispenser trying to salvage
what had to be months of punch lines and put-downs. All
that work, gone in a mess of ink and heavy cream. I didn't
care. I got why Phil did it.

Just be happy?

Chuck looked up at me, desperate. "Kid, hey, grab me some
more napkins, yeah? Hurry, I got a whole set in—"

"Eat shit."

I'd never cussed like that in front of an adult. Ever. I turned
and headed out the back of Brewster's. Asshole didn't even
recognize me.

Phil was standing in the alley by the recycling dumpster.
His hoodie was up and his forehead was pressed against the
brick. I thought I'd have to run to catch him but he wasn't
going anywhere.

I came in slow. "...Phil?"

He peeled his face off the brick and looked at me. He'd
been crying. I'd caught him between the waves. "Bad man-
ners. You're being real rude to your big date."

I nodded. "Ditto."

He sniffed and wiped his face. "Get back in there, man.
Cameron gets bitchy if you take too long in the bathroom."

His face was really tight. Like he was holding it all together.
Waiting for me to leave him so he could get back to his night.
I looked up at the alley wall. There was a light mist in the air.
Floating around the floodlights of the restaurant. It would
rain soon. Not too soon but it was coming.

"We covered a lot already. Shared some guac. He ordered
the Toffee Coffee whatever all on his own, I didn't have a
choice. I used the pill lie to get out of there."

Phil's laugh cracked in his throat, stuck against tears. "Classic. I used the cyst one."

I snorted and it bounced around the alley walls. I wiped away some of the early mist from my forehead. "Can…" I looked back at the Brewster's door. My table with Cameron felt like miles away. "Can I walk you home, Phil?"

Phil cocked his head. I nodded up at the sky. "I didn't drive here. I'm guessing you didn't either. And if we leave now, we can get to yours before the rain gets too bad. Yeah?"

Phil just looked at me. He couldn't argue with me there. I'd made a compelling case and Phil was always more of a screamer than a debater. But still. Phil just looked at me. Thinking over something. Whatever it was, it was calming him down. Keeping the tears back. His face was just wet with mist, then. "Can I ask you something?"

The rain was already starting to pick up. A drop here or there. Phil's hair was already clinging to his neck. The long black fingers falling out of his hood.

"Last March, I got written up at a pep rally for calling Ant Lewis and his tug-of-war partners a bunch of fags." I'd heard about the incident. And all the others. Phil's favorite word. He shrugged. "Why'd I do that?"

I didn't expect the question. I definitely didn't understand the question. But the rain was only coming quicker then. I didn't know if I had the right answer, but I had one.

"In the sixth grade, when you brought up those Moon Pies from your aunt in Chattanooga, Ant Lewis called you a cousin-fucker. And when you said all your cousins were boys, he told everyone you were a boy-cousin-fucker. Which we told him was a very clunky insult and just calling you a faggot would be easier for everybody. So, he did. A lot."

Phil nodded. Satisfied. But I wasn't done. "But that's incidental. Anthony is an asshole, that's not news."

"Oh?"

"No, no." I paced down the alley. Slipping into Debate mode and walking between the drips of the fire escape. "See, throwing a slur back at the offending parties is small potatoes. No, big picture, you're making a point about the *teachers*. The adults. The Staplers. All those helpful, well-meaning people telling you you can't. You *mustn't*. They decide it's a word you're not allowed to use, all the while they can't even say the word themselves. 'Cause there are no gay teachers at Moorestown High. No queer mentors, just platitudes and internet links. Their system is ill-equipped to handle you. So much so that they often don't bother. You've broken their careful system. Which makes you feel very special."

I stopped my pacing in front of Phil. "And it makes you feel very alone."

The sky had opened up, but Phil didn't seem to mind. He didn't move. But once his hoodie was fully soaked, black hair stuck to his neck like a tattoo, he nodded. "I'm sorry Cameron sprung that on you, Jacks. I know you aren't...ready for dates."

I appreciated that. The tact. How he put it. Phil knew how to put me. "Thank you, Philip."

He sniffed something back and nodded up the alley. "Walk me home."

My dress socks were ruined and my UPenn sweater was dry clean only. It was a long walk down Duquesne and I couldn't afford getting a cold so deep into rehearsals. I had a rock in my shoe and a milkshake I didn't finish, but I didn't care. I didn't complain. I didn't look back to see Cameron Ellis in his coffee shop window. I just walked my friend home and we talked about the weather.

PHIL

TRACK SIX
Smooth Criminal

There I was. Sitting atop a toilet. Hiding in the second-story men's room of the Moorestown Community Center, my swift and certain execution an out-of-line whimper away, and I couldn't stop smiling. If I laughed, a chaperone might catch me. If I cheered, I was sure to be thrown out onto the street. And yet? Reading Cameron Ellis's latest blog post made me want to break out into song. Because it had worked. It was working. *The Brynn Show* was on hiatus. *Taking the time to focus on herself.* The Skwad dropped out of All-Night Dodgeball last minute. *Some important family stuff just came up.* Doug had to beg his basketball friends to let Cameron on their dodgeball team and Augie had one foot out the door. *Sometimes friendship is work.* With just a sprinkle of Jackson's charm and a drop of Ronny's spite, *Operation: Ruin My Ex-Boyfriend's Life* was going off without a hitch and the moon felt like it was shining just for me.

Ronny's text knocked me out of my read.

R: Leggo

It was starting.

I hopped off the toilet, slipped out of the stall, and paused by the mirror to adjust my disguise. Moorestown Rowing hoodie. Gauges out and hair up in a bun. Sweatbands on my wrists and forehead and my school colors painted on my cheeks. I looked like any nameless jock. I looked absolutely brimming with school fucking spirit and nothing like the outlaw Philip J. Reyno. Since the Skwad torpedoed my reputation, to say nothing of my generous detention count, the lovely Mrs. Stapler had "gently advised" that I not sign up for All-Night Dodgeball. Not cause any more trouble. But the Scarlet Asshole that had been branded on my skin wouldn't stop me from my mission. Nothing could.

I was undercover. I was ready to play.

I caught Ronny in the stairwell. Even though she'd worn her Moorestown lacrosse uniform a thousand times on the field, the show of after-hour school support looked every bit as out of place on Ron as it did on me.

She spat up half of her Red Bull at the sight of my disguise. "NO MY GOD."

Ronny cackled at the ceiling, her laughter running up the stairs. I did a little strut down, shaking my butt in my Moorestown-brand gym shorts. "Who's the town that's hard to beat? Moorestown! Moorestown!"

Ronny joined my dead-eyed cheerleader bit, clapping her hands to the beat and doing a little cheerleader box step. "C'mon, Quakers, on your feet! MOORESTOWN! MOORESTOWN!"

Ronny did a skillful high kick in her lacrosse skirt and I dropped to a knee, shaking my invisible pom-poms in the air. We cheered for nobody. ***"GOOOOOO MOORESTOWN!"***

We almost collapsed to the floor laughing, but Ron remembered we were spies in enemy territory and pushed us back on track. Because while I was disguised and ready to assist, tonight's scheme was all Ronny DiSario. Phase One was Jackson's domain, the social assassination of Brynn Forester, but the second name on our list was Ronny's skull to claim. Because I knew nothing about the world of athletics. And while Jackson's shoulder muscles might have convinced the world he enjoys the gym, the guy's always been more of a team mascot than a team player. But, despite what she'd readily admit, Ronny knew sports. A childhood of country club tennis and lacrosse camp made sure of that. That was why the second Jackson drove his stake into Brynn's control of Moorestown's gossip channels, Ronny snagged us both tickets to the jock event of the autumn.

All-Night Dodgeball. The start of Phase Two. The end of Douglas Parson.

The first floor of the community center was another world from the peace and serenity of my bathroom stall hideaway. I kept my head down and Ronny kept hers on a swivel as we slipped through crowds of overcaffeinated footballers and underdressed cheerleaders. The lobby had kept some semblance of decorum during the first of this eight-hour all-nighter, but now that the front doors had been locked, the opening games had been played, and the smuggled-in energy drinks had been chugged, my student body had quickly devolved into *Lord of the Flies* territory. I saw kids in homemade jerseys and slapped-on face paint hyping themselves up for their upcoming games. I saw the wrestling team sneaking shots of something green behind a broken vending machine and Bash Villeda already asleep on the lobby floor. I saw chaperones giving the bare minimum their volunteer positions required and I saw Jackson Pasternak trying to control all the chaos. Always the school's go-to shepherd, Jackson wasn't allowed to play tonight and had been spending his entire day setting up and preparing the gym for this event. How he planned to transition from his day of event planning into a long night of refereeing without chemical assistance was Jackson's cross to bear.

Ronny and I slipped into the dimly lit rec room, far less overrun with our peers. Pizza hadn't been served yet, but there were snacks and drinks and a movie projector showing *Forrest Gump* on a wall. There were about ten or so kids relaxing, texting, or sleeping in the folding chairs around the room and I joined Ronny at one of the large water jugs in the corner.

She showed me her phone. "Hey, Dani Touscani was passing this around earlier. Is Jackson freaking out?"

I squinted at her screen. She had the end of Cameron's newest blog post up, all about Candid Cameron's new mystery man. I met a boy <3

"Gotta love that Cam would cap off an hour of throwing Brynn under the bus to gush over his *secret crush*."

I scrolled through all of Cameron's vague words about the new paramour in his life. I've sort of always known him, but let's just say I've been getting to know him in a whole new light this autumn. And readers? It's a pretty good light. Barf.

"Eh. Cameron never named names. I think Jacks is okay."

"Well, Dani and the theater girls seem determined to name the name."

"Jackson knows how to cover his ass. He's rolling with it."

That was technically true. I didn't tell Ronny that by *rolling with it*, I meant Jackson had thrown his anxiety face-first into planning this event in the name of keeping his mind occupied.

Ron slid her phone into her skirt. "Alright, my team's up next so we need to move quick."

"*Your team*. Look at you, claiming your lacrosse girls."

"The Laxatives don't fuck around, man. But I've been temperature checking people between matches. Everyone seems appropriately off-board on Miss Brynn."

I sipped my water and nodded. "I've been getting the same read. People were surprisingly quick to write her off."

"That's the thing about bubblegum. Very easy to spit out once it's lost its flavor."

"Poetic. But how can we use that to knock out Doug?"

Ronny picked around a snack table, trying to land on something to nibble. "Well, Philbo. I've come up with a plan. A simple, tidy plan." She landed on a giant bowl of mixed fruits and started loading up a plate. Watermelon, pineapple chunks, cantaloupe, the rest. "Your boy cleared the chessboard for us with his little mind games. With Brynn out of the way, no one is looking out for Doug and Augie. They're vulnerable. And with Augie still licking his wounds from that clusterfuck on the live show, Douglas is ripe for the axe. Now. My question becomes *this*."

She popped a strawberry into her mouth and looked at me. "Why the fuck is Doug Parson in the Skwad?" I laughed and shrugged. She pushed me on it. "I mean it, Phil. You were in there, you saw how they all were together. Doug's inclusion in the Skwad makes absolutely no sense. Cameron and Doug make sense together, sure. Old friends, basic white boys. Cameron and Brynn, Cameron and Augie, Brynn and Augie, that all checks out. But Doug and Brynn? Can you imagine Augie Horton and Doug Parson trying to have a conversation one-on-one?"

Ronny tossed a grape high in the air and chomped it. "Doug and the Skwad only makes sense because Cameron *needs* it to make sense. Because Cameron *needs* Doug." Ronny stabbed a chunk of honeydew with her fork and pointed it across the room. Over by a table of unopened pizzas, Ant Lewis was talking Bolu Olowe's ear off. Matty Silva was trying to sneak a slice. The leaders of the Basketbros. "I mean, look at them."

Ant's face was painted like some barbarian warrior and his regulation team shirt was intentionally ripped open. The hard muscles of his chest were exposed and he'd finger painted three fat, red letters between his nipples: **ANT.**

"You think the Basketbros would be caught dead letting a theater kid on their team without the gentle giant's letter of recommendation? You think Anthony *'Cokehead'* Lewis would be seen in the same room as Cameron without Doug constantly by his side? Absolutely the fuck not."

"Whoa, Ant does coke?"

"Very much not the point." Ronny finished her fruit and trashed the plate. "Cam's racked up a lot of points on the internet. His clout makes him a god among men with the theater department and the choir girls and the teachers. But with Matty Silva? Bolu Olowe? No. Cameron's magic doesn't work on guys like that."

"Mmm. You want to get into the boys' club, you need a cosign."

"A *bro-sign*. That's why Cameron keeps Doug around. He covers Cameron's bases. Keeps the straight dudes off his ass."

I nodded. The path was coming together in my head. "But…if the bros dropped Doug…"

"Cameron drops Doug. He'd be useless to him. Like Brynn. No more bro-sign, no more Doug Parson. Which means…"

I laughed. "All we need to do is get his team to turn on him. How the hell do we do that?"

Ronny smiled. "Well. What do jocks hate more than theater kids?"

I looked back at the pizza table. Doug Parson had joined his Basketbros. He looked a little silly in his team's dodgeball shirt. The thing was about six sizes too small on him and his Moorestown-issue gym shorts were riding up into his small intestine. He looked like a little boy who'd made a wish to get big and his buddies were slapping his pale thighs like some weird kind of tag. All in good fun. Just another game.

I grunted. "Losing."

Ronny smirked. "And if Doug happened to be the reason the Basketbros lost jockdom's biggest dick-measuring contest?"

"I mean…how could we possibly make that happen?"

"Sweet Philly, I told you. I have a plan. Simple and tidy."

I shook my head. Something wasn't adding up. "You really think Cameron would do that though? He's known Doug since they were fucking kids, Ron. You think Cameron could drop him that easily?"

Ronny looked across the room and watched Doug yuck it up with his team, a scowl running across her lips. "Cameron knew me longer." She turned and gave her makeup a once-over in a window reflection, double-checking that everything was where she left it. "I've known Cam and Doug since diapers, Phil. I knew them in Little Leagues, I knew them in summer camps, I knew them in backyard barbecues. We used to be the Orchard's very own Rugrats. Me and Doug and Cameron go way back."

Ronny hiked up her skirt another inch and looked at me. "Those two boys act like we don't have history. Because it's easier for them to forget. Cammy took Dougie and found new friends and new squads and new people to step on. Veronica D from down the street is just a joke now. They made me a fucking joke in this school, Phil. In this town. But I remember." She smiled. It was mean. "I remember a whole lot about little Dougie Parson."

Ronny looked over at the herd of assorted jocks. Matty Silva had just flashed his pubes at a very unamused Bash Villeda. The dozen or so bros hooted and hollered, Ant was rolling on the floor cackling, but Bolu looked like he found the prank beneath him. Doug was chuckling through a mouth full of pizza and Ronny cleared her throat. "YO! DOUGIE BEAR!"

My eyes bulged and I secured my hoodie. The crowd of bros paused their pube party and looked across the room. Bolu seemed intrigued. Doug seemed caught. It had to be rare that someone was calling out for only him. But for once, Cameron wasn't at his side. Ronny was only yelling at him.

Doug swallowed his wad of pizza then gave a sheepish sort of wave. "Uh… Hi, Veroni—"

As loud as she could, Ronny gagged. Instinctively, I jumped away because the girl sounded seconds from puking. *"EUUUUCK. GEUUUUUH."*

It was like a cat choking on a hairball. Acid reflux getting caught in your throat, over and over. That couldn't be her plan. That wasn't simple or tidy, that was going to blow our cover. I hissed a whisper at her. *"RONNY! What the FUCK are you—"*

Then Doug Parson covered his mouth. He looked terrified. He looked sick. "D-DON'T."

Doug started gagging. Like he'd caught something. Like Ronny was contagious. Ant jumped away from him, disgusted. "Dude, what the FUCK?!"

Ronny took a step forward and got louder. *"BLEEE-EEEEEEAGH! GEUUUUUGH!"*

The room was starting to watch. Everyone was awake again and no one was watching the movie. Doug shook his head, covering his mouth. He spoke between gags. "RONN— P-PLEA—*PLUU*—"

He started eyeing exits. Matty hid behind Ant. Bolu pushed Doug away from him. "PUKE ON ME, MAN, I WILL BEAT YOUR FUCKING—"

Ronny let out one last gag and Doug returned three slices of pepperoni back to the pizza table. Coated an entire stack of

Passy's catering and a good bit of the floor. All his good bros were screaming and laughing and trying to get away from the mess. Doug bolted for the door, trying to hold back an encore. "I'M S-SORRY! I'M SORRY! OH, SH-SHIT!"

The room was chaos and the chaperones were filing in. But Ronny just joined me back at the snack table. Plucked one more honeydew from the bowl.

"Get Brynn Forester to spin that, ya big fuck."

People were running around the room like so many headless chickens, but I just stared at Ronny. Stunned. She looked at me. "…What?"

I shook my head. "I think I'm in love with you."

We burst out cackling then noticed the chaperones were starting to ask around. I saw Mrs. Stapler grilling Matty Silva on what led to this volcanic eruption. He spotted me from across the room and squinted right through my half-baked jock disguise. He took a second to be confused then his head jerked at the doors. *Get the hell gone, fucko.*

With Matty distracting The Stapler, Ronny and I slipped out into the busy hallway. We elbowed our way through the crowds of eager dodgeballers and spotted two gym coaches blocking our exit paths. Ronny gripped my hoodie. *"Here."*

She pushed me through a nearby door and closed it behind us. The dusty, musty room was what must pass for a kitchen for the community center's rare catered events. We caught our breath and I threw down my hoodie. "How did you do that?!"

Ronny smiled and fixed her ponytail. "Lawn party at the country club, first grade. Mrs. Ellis steps in some dog shit, starts gagging over her smelly Louboutin, little Dougie pukes in the kiddie pool. He can't help it. Never could."

"Jesus Christ. You got a fucking cheat code."

"Hey, Doug's a very sympathetic guy."

"Is that enough for the team to drop him though?"

Ronny laughed. "That room was packed, Phil. Every jock who wants to take down the Basketbros saw what I did. If they don't cut Doug loose now, just wait for their first game. Half the school wants to beat those fuckers and I just gave them the perfect ammo."

I pictured it in my head. The Basketbros on the court. Cameron Ellis expecting cheers from the audience, all impressed that he's playing with the jocks, only to hear jeers and gags and the sound of puking. All because of his best bud Doug.

"You are...*really* good at this, Ronny."

She shrugged. "Hey. I'm a hateful bitch."

The kitchen door burst open. Ant Lewis barged through, eyes closed and frantic. *"IT'S ON ME! IT'S FUCKING ON ME, HOLY FUCK!"*

The richest douchebag in our grade had his arm extended as far as it would go. A smear of barf glimmered on his wrist and Ant looked like he might chop it off. Dani Touscani followed him in, barefoot and holding her sneakers like two ticking time bombs. "WHAT THE HELL IS WRONG WITH HIM?! I JUST GOT THESE!"

Ronny and I politely backed away as the pair drowned themselves in the industrial-grade sink. Ant was spraying his arm raw with the hose and Dani was fighting for room. "ANTHONY. IT'S SETTING INTO THE FABRIC."

"IT'S SETTING INTO MY SKIN!" Ant was dousing his entire arm with dish soap, his war paint dripping off him. "This is what fucking happens! I told them! I told Bolu not to let that little faggot on our team and LOOK!"

Dani hit him. "Don't be an asshole!"

I stood up straight. Immediately pissed. Because what in the ever-loving fuck did letting Cameron Ellis on their dodgeball team have to do with Doug puking on that walking lacrosse stick?

But Ronny beat me to the yell. "HEY."

Ant and Dani finally noticed we were in the room. Ant looked me up and down, confused. "Who the hell are you?"

I might've given my disguise some credit there if Ant Lewis weren't such a self-involved piece of shit. But why would someone like him recognize someone like me out of the context of school, disguised or not?

Dani didn't have as much trouble. "Phil? I thought they banned you from this."

I ignored her and stayed on Ant. "Watch your mouth, you cock. It's not Cameron's fault you got puked on."

Even with my name in the air, Ant still didn't seem to know me. The bro-hawked homophobe just eyed me with disgust. Like I was another blot of barf in his way. "Of course, it's his fucking fault. Doug Parson brings that kid everywhere he goes. Games. After-parties. It's fucking CONSTANT with them."

Dani dropped her shoes and they hit the tiles with a wet splat. She was covering her mouth, struck by some sudden realization. *"Wait."* She pulled out her phone and read something. Her jaw dropped. *"I've sort of always known him, but let's just say I've been getting to know him in a whole new light this autumn."*

Ronny and I shared a look. Oh, shit. The queen of the Drama Club had found something more pressing than barf on her shoe.

"IT'S DOUG. CAMERON ELLIS IS FUCKING DOUG PARSON, DOUG IS GAY, OH MY GOD."

Ant's eyes went wild. "WHAT THE FUCK?!"

He only scrubbed harder then. Like the idea of having a gay

guy's puke on him made it fifty times worse. I felt an urge to brain him with a spatula. Ronny made a face. "Easy, Ant."

Ron had come into the night with a simple, tidy plan and this new wrinkle wasn't something she'd planned for. A witch hunt for Cameron's secret lover could get complicated. I didn't need people pointing fingers where they shouldn't and Dani Touscani liked to talk.

Ronny gave me a look. We were on the same page. "Outing" a straight guy felt like a bridge too far.

I shook my head. "It's not Doug, man."

Ant scoffed. "How the fuck would you know?"

"I just…do. Alright? You have very heterosexual vomit on your arm, no need for amputation."

Dani was eying me then. Like a dog to a hydrant. "Wait. You know, don't you? Of course you would know, it's your rebound."

"Dani."

"Oh, come on, Phil. It's just us! Please, I won't tell a soul."

Ronny grabbed my arm. "Let's go. This is pointless."

She was right. We'd made our moves and Phase Two was running smoothly. This was just a distraction. We moved for the door but Dani wouldn't let up. The Drama Club's drama queen had the scent and refused to be the last to know.

"Is it Jackson Pasternak?"

I froze. Ronny's grip on me tightened. God fucking dammit.

Dani smirked. "You know, they've been spending a lot of time together in rehearsals. And I saw them getting dinner together. At Brewster's. At Cameron's favorite table. They looked…cute together. Kind of a perfect pair, actually."

My spine felt like an icicle. Ronny was staring at me hard. In an instant, the night's plan felt very far from me and all I could think about was steering our school's new gossip baron away from Jackson's deepest secret.

"I mean, he's literally never had a girlfriend, Phil. Not that I've seen. Like, I asked around and no one can remember him even *kind of* flirting with them."

"That's not… I don't think that means a guy is—"

"Also, c'mon, Cameron dating Jackson would make a whole lot more sense than Cameron dating you, right?"

My teeth slid against each other and I could feel it. Something that I thought I'd gotten a handle on. A low boil. A bubbling stew. The taste of hate. Never too far from my throat. "Dani. It's *not* Jackson."

She laughed. "Fine! If it's not Doug and it's not Jackson, then who?"

I felt the hate fill my mouth. Coat my tongue. I was going to say something awful. I was going to tear Dani to pieces.

But my hate didn't get out first. No. Something decidedly worse beat me to the punch. Ronny cut in. "I heard it was one of the Basketbros."

Dani's face went blank. Ant's face went red. And I just looked at her. We were only three hours into All-Night Dodgeball and Ronny DiSario had just set off her second bomb. Simple and tidy, my ass.

JACKSON

———

TRACK SEVEN
Foolish Games

**HOUR SIX OF ALL-NIGHT DODGEBALL
(HOUR TWENTY-TWO WITHOUT SLEEP)**

I am going to kill Veronica DiSario.

My hosting obligations had me glued to the recently re-cleaned pizza table, updating the tournament bracket on my laptop and trying to stay awake. Luckily sheer rage had provided me with a second wind. Our plan had been running so smoothly and now they decide to involve Ant Lewis? One of the most volatile concentrations of macho bullshit in the tristate area?

Phil hadn't answered any of my strongly worded texts since telling me what happened and I had to hope he was busy doing damage control. Veronica's incredibly shortsighted lie could be contained. Dani wasn't a gossip, she was just a nosy asshole. But who knew what Ant would do? I needed to get ahead of it. I needed to know who knew. I needed to find Phil.

"Excuse me, I need to go take a pill."

I looked to my left and realized I was alone at the pizza table. Lying to no one. *Wow. Keep it together, Pasternak.*

Across the room, Cameron was helping Mrs. Stapler look through some of the rec room's bookshelves, trying to find any other DVD than *Forrest Gump*. I'd been subtly checking in with Cameron over the break between games to see if he'd heard anything about his newest school scandal, but his focus seemed fixed on dodgeball. He'd chalked any weirdness up to Doug benching himself, posteruption. Maybe Cameron thought Ant Lewis icing him out of their last three matches was just standard jock bullshit. To be honest, his inability to read the room sort of baffled me. I guess with Brynn out of commission, Cameron's finger on this school's pulse had been amputated and he was completely unaware of the shit show his old girlfriend Veronica had thrown him into. With Mrs. Stapler and Cameron distracted, I closed my laptop, packed up my bag, and slipped out the double doors.

The hallways had become markedly low energy compared to the zoo that'd consumed them at the top of the night. No more fight songs or selfies. Kids were half-awake on the floor and I tripped over a snoring corpse. Captain of the track team and the tournament's recently disqualified Generic Team Name glared up at me, all drowsy.

"Watch your fugging step, dude."

"Sorry. You know there's a nap room, right?"

"Smells like fuggin'…ass."

Bash Villeda curled back into a ball and passed out again. The rest of his team got sent home around two for fighting. The event had a zero tolerance policy on fighting and throwing a punch was an instant bounce. But the interaction did remind me where I might find Phil. Before he went radio silent, I'd recommended Phil go hide in the nap room for the rest of the night. His "disguise" idea didn't fool a few less-sleepy teachers and he'd been trying to find somewhere to hole up ever since.

I snuck into the dark nap room and tiptoed by the sleeping Coach Bianco, a few snoring kids in sleeping bags, and eventually reached the back. Once my eyes adjusted, I could see that Phil wasn't there. Crap. But even in the pitch dark, Doug Parson was pretty noticeable all sprawled out in a corner cot. He'd taken a "medical leave" from the last few tourney rounds and he was snoring into a large trash bag, sure to catch any further barf attacks. I did my best not to wake him. But I did slide my backpack under the Snorlax for safekeeping. Shame and vomit were likely going to keep Doug on that cot all night and the event had land mines around every corner. I needed to be quick on my feet and if my laptop got smashed, my life might literally be over.

Bag secured, I tiptoed out of the room and resumed my hunt. I speed-walked through the lobby and caught a couple arguing inside the front door vestibule. It wasn't a surprising sight. Because it wasn't a real Moorestown party if on-again, off-again couple Dani Touscani and Matty Silva weren't fighting. Their spat was loud enough to be perfectly audible from the lobby. Well, Dani was. I could catch fragments of her defenses but none of whatever Matty was hissing back through clenched teeth.

"Matty! I didn't say anything about YOU!"

"MATEO!"

"I only told people it WASN'T YOU!"

"I KNOW YOU'RE NOT FUCKING CAMERON!"

I went pale. "Oh, shit."

Matty spat out what was clearly *FUCK YOU* then pushed through the doors. He spotted me instantly and I searched for a smoke bomb to throw.

His lip curled. "Keep your eyes in your fucking skull, Pasternak."

Matty threw up his hoodie and stormed out. Guess he and Dani were off-again. Again.

I got out of the lobby before Dani could spot me and headed into the empty gym. The semifinals would be starting soon, only ten games left until we could release the undead back into the wild, and coaches were resetting the courts for the first rounds.

"JACKSON."

I whipped around and wondered which bleacher might be talking to me. "Hello…"

I squinted and made out two little eyes peeking out from behind the steps. I made sure no chaperone was watching me then snuck behind the bleachers. My shoulders had to be pressed through the first crack, but once I got under the steps, there was a good amount of breathing room. Phil had made himself comfortable living in the walls and was polishing off the last slice of an entire Passy's pizza.

"You stole a whole box?! Mrs. Stapler got on the delivery dude for being short."

Phil scoffed and tossed the last crust back at the box. "Derek Velazquez took my job, he can suck my literal hole. What's up?"

I laughed, incredibly annoyed. "*What's up?* Why aren't you texting me back?"

"Phones only live so long, Jacks. What'd you text me?"

"I mean, it's a lot to recap, but I guess the main thesis would be WHY THE FUCK WOULD YOU INVOLVE THE BASKETBALL TEAM?"

Phil sighed and leaned on the wall. "Jacks…"

"Phil, that was BAD. That was a BAD idea, what the hell were you two thinking?"

"Jackson."

He looked at me. I knew that face. It took a lot for him to feel it, but Phil's shame always looked the same. "I should've stopped Ron. I know. Ant Lewis was just being such an asshole and I was getting so fucking mad and I was probably gonna say something way worse anyway so she just... She was trying to help us."

"Us?"

He closed his eyes and shook his head against the bricks. "Dani Touscani started... She was talking about you. Talking about Cameron and talking about you like...like I know you wouldn't want her to. Ronny was just trying to stop her."

"Oh."

Phil's eyes stayed shut, but he turned up at the bleachers above us. "This isn't supposed to be about you, Jacks. This is my shit, you're just trying to help me. I get that. And I know getting close to Cameron is the smart play but..." He looked at me. Still ashamed. "I don't want you to get rushed. Wherever you are or however you put it, I don't want you getting forced, man. Like me. Like what Cameron did to me. If that happened to you, if that was my fucking fault, Jacks—"

"Philip."

"If I fucked that up for you—"

I walked to the wall and hugged him. He hugged me back. He put his head into my shoulder and shook into it. *"I shouldn't have let Ronny do that."*

"It's okay. We'll handle this."

"I'm bad at executing schemes."

"It's handleable. Just gotta figure out who knows and handle it. We're okay."

Phil pulled away and rubbed his face. "I... I'm *so fucking tired*. This is a *terrible* event."

"Hey, we raised a lot of money for the school track."

"That means nothing to me."

We heard the sounds of oncoming adults and I dropped my voice. "We need to find you a better hiding place. This disguise idea was poorly thought out."

Phil scoffed and backed away from me. Struck a few athletic poses in his gym shorts and tube socks. "What? You don't like my new digs, Pasty?"

I smiled. "I don't know. I miss your gauges."

"Come on. The jock look not doing it for you?"

He hiked up his shorts, showing a good amount of thigh, and shook his mesh-coated ass at me. I laughed. "I forgot how pale your thighs were."

I applauded my tired brain for not blurting out my actual first thought. Truthfully, I'd forgotten how hairy Phil's thighs were. But remembering that fun fact reminded me of how hairy Phil's stomach was which reminded me where all that hair leads down to which made my brain force quit my stroll down memory lane. That kind of thinking was unproductive and we had bigger fish to fry. But still. That little ass in mesh. Not nothing.

Phil batted away my comment. "We don't all spend our hours rowing on lakes in spandex."

"Uh, it's a stretch-woven nylon, Philip."

"Results are still the same, moose knuckle. C'mon. Coast is clear."

Phil chuckled and slipped out from under the bleachers. I needed a moment to get back to myself. I guess I'd spent the last few weeks enduring Cameron Ellis ambushing me with flirting, but it was like my brain needed to relearn how to feel it sincerely. Was Phil flirting with me? Was that what it was supposed to feel like? Was that how I was supposed to feel after? High? Awake? Or was my deteriorating brain just running on fumes after hours of all work and no sleep? I realized my brain wasn't the only part of me needing adjustment and worked my issue up into my waistband. I shut my eyes and thought of Matty Silva bushing me in gym class. The end of *Toy Story 3*. Clams. My waistband regained some wiggle room and I breathed. Okay. All good. I left my erection under the bleachers and continued on to the next hour of my waking nightmare.

HOUR SEVEN OF ALL-NIGHT DODGEBALL (HOUR TWENTY-FUCKING-FOUR WITHOUT SLEEP)

I was in the second floor bathroom. I had my phone in my hand. Phil had stolen a charger from the nap room and I needed to text him back. My sight was getting fuzzy, trying to focus on his messages.

P: ur plan worked :0

P: just followin Bianco room to room

P: should i b offended he has no idea who i am??

J: Called it. You'll be good if you can just stick with him for the rest o

I'd gotten to the end of my response, I knew what I wanted to say, but for the life of me could not get my brain to figure out the word. O. O? *Ove?* The rest *ove* the night? No. That was clearly not the word, *ove* wasn't a goddamn word. *The* land ove the free. *Ove Mice and Men.* I could hear the word, it was arguably the most common preposition in the English language, but HOW DID YOU SPELL IT?

Suddenly, from somewhere in the bathroom, I heard a noise. A low grumble from the last stall on the left and I considered it might be a ghost. The ghost of a tranqued-up grizzly bear.

"Um…hello?"

The strange hidden animal woke with a yelp. *"FUCK OFF, RAPH!"*

A few gasps and whoever was behind the stall door realized they weren't in their bedroom. I leaned up on the sinks and waited for him to regain his senses, the giant Nikes under the door finding their footing.

He cleared some junk out of his throat. "Who's there? What time—" He scoffed. "It's FOUR?!"

He sighed and the Nikes spread out, their owner presumably sinking on the toilet. I smiled. The anonymous voice had a rasp to it that I found charming if hard to place. "Sorry, man. You been in here all night?"

"I'm not on a team. I was gonna try to slip out when everyone got busy, but I guess I fell asleep. Fuuuuuuck."

"Y'know, there's a nap room downstairs. I hear it smells fine, you could probably ride it out in there till six."

"Nah. I don't…" Another sigh. A sadder one. "I don't want people to see me."

Hmm. Interesting. I had fires to monitor and gossip to staunch, but something else was keeping me there. Maybe it was the sad sigh. Or maybe I just preferred solving other people's problems.

I got a comfortable seat on the sink's edge and put on my

President Pasternak cap. "Why don't you want people see-ing you?"

"It's, uh… It's a whole thing."

"I've got two and a half minutes."

The heavy voice cleared itself again. "So, I was supposed to be on the Mathemachickens. I was the one who suggested we even do this, the Math Club didn't even want to. Then I show up like two seconds late and they fucking bump me. But that new guidance lady said I already signed in and there was some fucking contract and I legally couldn't leave unless my parents came and got me."

"And your parents couldn't come get you?"

There was a silence then. One that didn't seem nice to push. But despite the very distinct rasp and notably clownish foot size, I couldn't for the life of me place the man behind the stall. It was killing me. Maybe in Math Club? Maybe tall? I could've just asked, but I should've known it by then. What was the point of keeping my Excel sheet if I couldn't place the human being five feet away from me?

I tried a different tactic.

"You don't want to play? Be an alternate?"

"I shouldn't have to be, dude. I made a team. I paid my money. I'm not a fucking afterthought, I don't wanna play with people who don't fucking…know me."

The Nikes sort of fell to the side. Defeated. I'd never felt bad for a pair of shoes before. I might've not known who they belonged to, but I knew enough. He was in my class. Maybe he even voted for me. Maybe he didn't, maybe he hated my guts, but I still felt a deep-set duty to help my classmates. Es-pecially the ones with names I could forget. The ones hid-ing in bathrooms.

"Listen. We're coming up on another hour break. I've got

a guy from Passy's delivering our last round of pizzas at four thirty, that's in—"

"I don't want Passy's, dude, I just wanna be left alone."

I hopped off the sink and checked my watch. "That's in twelve minutes. Chaperones rotate every thirty which means there's a shift change right before the delivery. They're posted up at all the exits, but I'm letting the pizza guy in through the back. Coach Bianco's guarding that exit at that time, but he'll need to help me carry all the food in. Leaving his post empty."

I got a little closer to the stall. "Now, I'm *supposed* to lock that door after me. But if no one's guarding the back between the slim window of four fifty and four fifty-five, and if someone *happened* to forget to lock the door until five on the dot, I mean…who could blame them?"

I leaned up on the adjoining stall and yawned. "And who could blame a guy who just wants to go home? Especially if he's polite enough to lock up after himself and save me the trouble?"

There was another silence. This one didn't seem so loud.

"It's gonna be so fucking cold outside, dude."

"Eh. It's October."

He chuckled. "Thanks, Jackson."

I smiled. I guess my voice was easier to place. But his finally clicked. "No problem, Sandro."

The bathroom door opened and Bolu Olowe nodded his way inside, interrupting our moment. "Mr. President. Hard man to find. We need to chat."

I stood up. He sounded serious. But Bolu always sounded serious. I could hear what was now so obviously field captain Sandro Miceli's chuckle from behind the stall. "Hey, Bolu!"

Bolu just squinted at the faceless greeting and motioned for the door. "Let's do this outside."

I followed him into the empty hallway, the noise of our classmates echoing up from the stairwell. I clapped and tried to sound as put together as I could. "Bolu Olowe! Hey, your team is doing great, y'all excited for semis?"

Bolu's eyebrows bunched up, a little wary of my interest. Despite being my VP, I'd spoken with the basketball captain about as much as I'd talked to anyone in my grade which is to say a fair amount but never with any substance. Truthfully, the only times we've talked with any sort of intention was debating whose club could fundraise in which hallway. He's the co-chair of Youth Life, a Christian-focused athletics org for the sportier gentiles, and I'm a rep for more clubs than I can count, yet we still never bothered much with small talk. It was actually one of Bolu's greatest qualities, never needing to bog me down with void-filling chitchat. Which made him seeking me out like that decidedly unnerving.

Bolu finally nodded. "I'm just going to cut to the chase. I think Anthony Lewis is going to do something to Cameron Ellis."

My spine hardened. "Oh." I didn't have it in me to keep the fear off my face. "Okay. Okay, I need you to tell me what, Bolu. What's going to happen?"

He stared at me for a long while. "Interesting." Then he shook his head. "You look guilty, Mr. President. Mad guilty."

I blinked. Bolu didn't. But his head sort of leaned. Like he was trying to sort through the bloodshot cobwebs around my eyes. "You've been all over tonight, Jackson. Whatever's going on with Cameron Ellis...you know whose fault it is. Don't you?"

He just stared at me. I didn't know what to say. What he knew. But Bolu nodded. "Thought so. All roads lead back to Pasternak."

Bolu leaned against the window and rolled out his neck. Stretching for his next match. "We got eight minutes till game time. You better work it out quick. Whatever it is."

He was right. I checked my phone. Seven now. Dammit.

I headed down the hall. Bolu's voice chased after me. Just as calm and level as always. "Don't make me stop them, Mr. President. This isn't my problem to solve."

I left him to his stretching and tore down the stairs. My gut was telling me they wouldn't be in the lobby or the gym and the quiet areas wouldn't be conducive. Anthony would wait for the chaperones to be occupied and glued to a room. I heard the whistles from the gym. The Mathemachickens and Three Guys Named John would be in the middle of their semifinal match. Now. It was happening now. But where?

I got to the base of the stairwell and found Ronny and Dani midargument on the steps. Dani was close to crying. "It's just a PRANK, Ronny! It doesn't fucking mean anything!"

Ronny groaned and threw her hands up, trying her best to get out of the interaction. "I DO NOT care, Danielle! I have no stake in your relationship or interest in Matty Silva's social life, you need to stop telling people about—"

"But ALL the guys are doing it though! It's funny! It doesn't mean Matty's—" Dani spotted me and redirected her desperation at me. "Jackson! Guys show each other their pubes all the time, right? It's like a fucking joke, right? It's a thing, every guy does it!"

I ducked her approach and tried deescalating. "Uh, hey, Dani. Shouldn't you be stretching with your team? The Turnpikes are playing soon."

Dani scoffed and rolled her eyes. "Stop trying to control everything, you rich prick, nobody actually fucking likes you."

"Okay, wow, never mind."

A crowd had started paying attention to Dani's ranting. The Jersey Turnpikes. Half of Dem Baddies. Most of the Laxatives. All the sporty girls of Moorestown High were laughing and recording and whispering to each other. I guess Dani had told more people than we thought.

Dani smacked the phone out of one girl's hands. "FUCK you, Sydney. This whole night is BULLSHIT, you assholes are ruining EVERYTHING!"

There were some snickers around the hallway and Dani pushed through the group. She stormed off, shouting back. "MY BOYFRIEND ISN'T GAY!"

Some Drama Club girls ran along to check on their sobbing leader and the crowd slowly dispersed. It was something to behold, watching someone's own gossip blow up in their face so quickly. Spin enough grapevine, you'll just end up hanging yourself.

Ronny cracked into what had to be her eighth Red Bull of the night and we headed down the hall. "So. Containing my wildfire has not been working."

"Yes, I see that."

"Is Phil safe? He's hiding?"

"We figured something out, he's good. Have you seen Ant or—" I spotted someone up the hall and gasped. *"Sorry."*

Before I could explain, I shoved Ronny into an open closet. "WHAT THE FUC—"

I shut it closed before Cameron could spot us together. I leaned on the door and raised my voice before Ronny could burst through. "Hey, *CAMERON*. Ready for the semis?"

Ronny's pounding ceased. She got it. Cameron walked up to me and smiled, sipping on a Gatorade. "Hey, killer. Haven't seen you all night. Missed that face."

I couldn't be sure, but I think I heard Ronny gag behind

the door. Cameron nodded down the hall. "Wish we could chat, but I'm actually meeting the team. I guess Anthony wanted to talk."

I swallowed. "Oh. The, uh, Basketbros? Where? Where, uh… Where did Ant want to…do that?"

"In the kitchen. He wants to talk strategy, you know? Coverage, ball control, sports lingo. Wait, do you play sports? Is rowing a sport? I guess I always thought it was more of an exercise but—"

I put my hand on his shoulder and dropped my voice. *"Hey."*

Cameron blinked a few times, registering my touch. He was surprised. It was the first time I'd ever touched him on purpose. And I could see how long he'd been waiting for it. My hand on him. My eyes on his. My attention, all his.

"People are saying Doug just puked all over the cots."

Cameron groaned, the spell broken. "God DAMMIT."

Without another look, Cameron bolted the other direction. Down the hall and out of sight. The lie would buy me minutes, but I could always chalk it up to bad gossip.

I opened the door and let Ronny out. She was all smiley. "Aww. You just saved Cameron's life. Hero?"

"Yeah, I feel like a really great person, come on."

Ronny and I hightailed it down the hall. We turned the corner and found the door to the kitchen. The hall was mostly empty, everyone busy watching the semis, and I could hear voices muffled through the door.

"FUCKING BULLSHIT!"

"LET HIM ON OUR TEAM!"

"DOESN'T EVEN PLAY BASKETBALL!"

Ronny had her ear to the door. "It's Ant. And Matty."

"What the fuck do we do now?"

Ronny closed her eyes. "I don't know. I don't know. I have to go play in like two minutes."

"You're seriously thinking about the tournament right now?"

Her eyes snapped back open. "The Laxatives are sweeping the bracket, man, I did not come here to lose."

"Ronny, you didn't want to come at all."

"Yeah, but that was before we started winning."

She cracked open the door and we peeked inside. Matty was pacing in circles, cussing and kicking and slapping invisible words out of the sky. All Ant's exhaustion and energy drinks (and, rumor had it, drugs) had left him looking feral. Ronny whispered. *"We could always fight them first."*

I scoffed. "How the hell would that help?"

"Immediate expulsion. No exceptions. You fight, they throw you out."

"Sure, but then we'd have to fight Anthony Lewis and Matty frigging Silva."

Ronny inspected Matty as he dug circles into the kitchen tile. "I could take Matty. Oh! Or I could punch you in the face and you tell Lady Stapler one of them did it."

"Ronny, these are terrible ideas."

She elbowed me. "You are not a team player, Jackson. You have been against every plan I've tried tonight."

I elbowed her back. "Because your plan got us here!"

"I said I was sorry!"

"No! You actually fucking didn't!"

"Who the hell is that?!"

We stood up in the doorway. Matty and Anthony were staring right at us. Ronny took a step backward to run away, but I held her there. She sighed. "Hey, y'all. Just…looking for my phone."

"Yeah. Yeah, Ronny lost her…phone."

Ant headed straight for us. But he was pointing straight at me. "Pasternak. You know everyone. You know Cameron fucking Ellis, who the fuck has he been talking to?"

"Ant, buddy, you need to calm down."

"We weren't gonna do anything to him! I just want to know. I have the right to know, Pasternak, I have the right to defend MY FUCKING NAME."

Ant was getting very red and very close to me so Ronny closed the kitchen door and slipped between us. Put a hand on Ant's shoulder. "Anthony. *Sweetie.* Hey, it's me. It's Veronica. From your neighborhood. Hello."

Ant grunted, momentarily quelled. "Hello."

Ronny smiled warmly, trying to communicate with the overstimulated ox. "Heya, hon. It's been a really long night. A lot is going on, yeah? And I assume you've taken a little *hmm hmm* tonight?"

Ant froze. Eventually he nodded. I didn't know what *hmm hmm* meant, but I didn't speak Clubber. I might live in the Orchard but Matty Silva and I were bearing witness to the two wealthiest children in our zip code trying to hold a conversation.

Ronny laughed. "Okay. So, you're tired. And wired. And maybe not thinking too clearly, huh? Like the Fourth of July? Remember? You jumped off that big tree?"

"People are saying some really messed up shit about me, Veronica. It's really messed up."

"I knoooow. But it's just talk, Anthony. I've been doing the rounds, no one thinks it's true. Believe me. No one would think that of you. Not Anthony Lewis."

Ant started blinking again. Ronny's snake charming was working. "They don't? Really?"

"No! Nobody thinks it's you. Right, Jackson?"

I perked up. "Oh. Oh! No! No, man, no fucking way. Not you. You're Ant Lewis! You're... You're a fucking stud...bro."

The red was beginning to cool off on Ant's forehead. His pupils were probably going to stay dilated until Friday, but there was no helping him there. He smiled. "Fuck. Yeah, Pasty. I just... I got worried, man. People talking and shit, I just... Fuck them."

"Exactly! Fuck those people!"

"They're fucking nothing! NONE of them!" Ant cackled and shook my shoulder. "Jackson fucking Pasternak, man! Kid's a legend!"

I gave Ronny a look. She shrugged to tell me to roll with it. I patted Ant on the back of his sweaty, torn shirt. "Yeah... Legend."

Matty watched the three of us Orchard kids pat each other on the back for longer than I thought he would. "Uh...hey? What the fuck about me?"

Ant remembered his buddy was in the kitchen with us and hooted. "Oh, damn! Matato Potahto, get in here, lil man!"

Matty backed away from Ant's claws. He gave Ronny and me a look. "People are fucking talking about me. I know they are, don't give me that shit. Whoever started that rumor made my fucking girlfriend cry, don't give me that bullshit." He squinted at me. "Danielle said you hang out with that faggot more than anyone in this building. What do you know about—"

Ant cut him off and got between us. All his paranoid, potentially drug-fueled rage had released him and he was back to the frustratingly chummy asshole I know and avoid. "*Mateo.* Let's cool it on the homophobic slurs, huh?"

"Ant, you just called him fifty different—"

Ant hugged Matty in a tight bear hug. "Ssssh. C'mon, bubba. I get it. I get it now. But all this internalized shit is beneath you, amigo. You don't gotta do it anymore."

"What the fuck?"

"If you're sucking off Cameron Ellis, I'm not gonna give you shit for it. You're my bro. That's for *life*."

"WHAT THE FUCK?!"

Matty shoved away from Ant and scrambled free. Ant hooted at the ceiling. "It all makes so much sense now! Matty! You're gay, man, that's fucking rad!"

"ANTHONY."

"C'mon! I'm chill! I mean, don't get all fucking Augie Horton on me but, dude, you'd be like the coolest fag I know!"

I heard Ronny scream before I realized Matty had socked Ant across the jaw. "MATTY!"

He had Ant on the ground and was pummeling his face. Screaming his throat raw. Ronny pulled Matty off and I held Ant to the floor. Kept him from lunging after Matty. Tried to keep him from headbutting me. The bros screamed at each other from their respective grapples.

"FUCKING FAGGOT!"

"HIJO DE PUTA!"

"I'LL FUCKING BEAT YOUR—"

Matty tore away from Ronny and ran out of the kitchen. Ant got to his feet, holding a bloody nose, and screamed after him. **"YOU'RE FUCKING DEAD, SPIC!"**

Something came over me and I slammed Anthony into the fucking wall. Before he could fight or push or speak, I shoved my forehead into his. *"Say another word and I will ruin you."*

My words came out without permission, but my brain reassured me that I had a half a foot and thirty pounds of muscle on Anthony Lewis. If I needed them.

"Jackson. Stop." Ronny had a hand on my back. I moved away and let Ant go. He stared at me, nose bleeding. I realized only then that my own nose was dripping. I don't know when he got me but I hadn't felt a thing.

Anthony spat blood on the kitchen tile. Right at my feet. "Great event tonight, Pasty. Good on you." He nodded at Ronny on his way out. "Catch you at the club, babe."

Ronny flipped him off and Anthony headed out the door. I looked down at myself. My shirt was already getting stained. Ronny handed me her Red Bull. I sighed. "I forgot the word *of* earlier."

Ronny nodded. "You should really get some sleep."

I went over to the kitchen sink and tried to stop the bleeding.

HOUR EIGHT OF ALL-NIGHT DODGEBALL
(HOUR TWENTY-FIVE WITHOUT SLEEP)

Ronny found me a less bloody hoodie to switch into and we'd gotten my nostrils adequately tamponed. We headed through the empty hallways, curious, then heard roaring cheers coming from the gym. Ronny grabbed my arm and we ran over to join the rest of our grade. All eighty or so students of Moorestown High, everyone who had managed to survive the night, had flooded the gym to see the hot ticket item.

Cameron Ellis, the internet's favorite twink, was standing on the court with his good pal, Doug Parson. Waiting for his teammates. One of whom, if rumor was to be believed, knew Cameron not only as a *Basketbro* but also in the biblical sense. Carnally. Explicitly. Bareback in the Brewster's parking lot. If rumor was to be believed. But where was his team? Where was his lover? Where were the *Basketbros*?

"Where the fuck are they?" Ronny was scanning the gym. All five of the Jersey Turnpikes were ready to play on the other side of the court. Even Dani Touscani seemed refocused and ready to kill. But facing them was just Cameron and Doug. Cameron looked at the crowd, a sort of shy smile on his face as he returned the odd waves. As if to say, *Me? All these eyes on me?*

And I could see behind it so clearly. The satisfaction behind his smile. *Me? All this for me?* He knew the rumors. He fucking loved the rumors. Cameron loved that the school thought he could bag a basketballer. He loved that they thought he was capable of a secret affair with a straight, hot jock. Not that he'd ever confirm the rumors. But he would never deny them either. Even if it meant his oldest friend's life was about to be much harder because of them.

I tapped Ronny and nodded at Doug. Sweet Doug. Always at Cameron's side. Always his best bro. Always there for his friend. But Doug's gaze wasn't aimless tonight. It was like he was trying to look at nothing. Trying not to think about what Cameron was allowing. "He knows."

"Poor fucking guy."

There was a quick clamor then a quicker hush as Bolu Olowe strode into the gym. Behind him, Ant Lewis and Matty Silva walked in silence. Ant's nose was still clearly busted. Matty was silent and stewing. Neither would look at the other, but they both followed their captain, heads forward. The trio walked past Cameron and Doug without a glance and headed straight for Mrs. Stapler and Coach Bianco at the ref's table.

I turned to Ronny and shrugged. She nudged me. "Move. Move, I wanna hear."

We cut across the bleachers, keeping our heads down. The hum over the crowd grew by the step, everyone wanting to know what had happened. Why was Ant's nose busted? Why did Matty look like he might kill someone? Why did Bolu look so calm?

We got within earshot of the ref's table right in time to hear Bolu answer Mrs. Stapler. "—for wasting everyone's time, Mrs. Stapler. I truly am sorry. But the basketball team will have to forfeit."

Mrs. Stapler looked at Ant's nose, confused. "I don't follow, Mr. Olowe. Anthony, what happened to your nose?"

Bolu stepped in front of Ant. It was his time to speak. Bolu was their captain and Ant had done enough to his team that night. "The three of us got in a fight. I don't remember who started it, but we were all involved and we all settled it." Bolu nodded. "But rules are rules. Our parents have been called and you will need to ask us to leave."

Mrs. Stapler took a moment to catch up to the administrative action Bolu had already completed. "Uh… Okay. But… what about your remaining team members?"

Bolu looked back at Cameron and Doug on the other side of the court, both very unsure of what they should be doing. "Bring in substitutes. Forfeit. It's your call, Mrs. Stapler. I respect your rules. But my team is done for the night."

Mrs. Stapler gave Bianco a tired look. He shrugged. "Rules are rules. And it is pretty close to sunup. I'll take the boys out."

Mrs. Stapler sighed and grabbed her megaphone. "And everything was going so well."

Coach Bianco escorted the trio away from the table and they headed for the door. As he passed, Bolu caught my eyes. And I couldn't decipher his expression. He'd always been sort of unreadable like that. *Good job. You dealt with it. Fuck* you. *Look what you made me do.* I didn't know. But it didn't last too long.

Ronny leaned close. "What the hell was that look?"

"I think Bolu Olowe is going to kill me."

"Oh, no."

"Or he wants to be my friend."

"Aw, that's sweet. He's so fucking hot."

"Alright, Veronica."

The three ex-Basketbros passed by their remaining two members. I didn't need to move to hear the exchange. The room wanted to hear and had gone very quiet. Matty wanted us to hear and had gone very loud. He broke off from his bros and stuck a finger into Cameron's chest. "Stay the **FUCK** away from us." He looked up at Doug. "BOTH of you."

Doug was frozen. He looked like he might cry. Cameron was also frozen. He looked like he might fake it.

The basketball team left the gym and the crowd resumed their whispers. It was almost deafening how quick it all came. The theories. New rumors. What might happen next to Moorestown's own Cameron Ellis?

The squawk of a megaphone cut through the noise and Mrs. Stapler's robotic yell filled the room. "Alrighty! We're gonna need to find some alternates for the Basketbros! But don't you fret, we're just gonna switch... We'll switch... Okay, let's go ahead and take a fifteen-minute break, just FIFTEEN and let's get the Laxatives and The Master Debaters up here after that... God, these names... FIFTEEN EVERYBODY!"

Ronny tossed off her hoodie and chucked it into the roiling crowd. "I'm up! Wish me luck."

I looked around the room as the crowd funneled into the hallway and the decorum descended back into chaos. "You really still want to play dodgeball right now?"

Ronny jumped around, hyping herself up. "Can't stop now! I've been possessed by the school spirit! Slap me!"

"No."

She slapped herself and screamed in my face. "MOORES-TOWN!"

I left Ronny to crack herself up but felt myself crashing hard. I let my exhaustion win me over for a moment. Let the crowd of students flooding into the hallway take me away. I rode the waves like a white water river and let the Joey Tans and Syd DeStefanos of the world move my body for me.

Before I knew it, I'd been dropped off on the stairwell steps and thought about curling up right then and there. I always thought I'd die in the arms of a loved one or on a poorly maintained rollercoaster but the stairwell wouldn't be the worst ending for ol' Jacky P.

I felt a buzz on my phone. But when I looked at the screen, I saw that my phone was dead. Maybe it had been for hours. I felt the imaginary buzz again and saw the imaginary texts.

P: Come find me, Jacks.

P: I miss you, asshole.

P: You did enough for one night.

P: Find me.

"Jackson?"

I looked up. I guess I'd sat at some point. But there was Cameron, standing over me. His eyes were full like he was about to cry. "Can we talk?"

I tried to blink myself awake. But I guess I already was. Okay. "Oh. Uh. About what, Cam?"

Cameron shook his head. "Did you see what just happened in there? Matty Silva just fucking… You need to do something." He sat next to me. "Jackson, please. You need to do something about him. *Please*."

Cameron started to cry. And I might have been tired and sleep-deprived and my eyes might've felt like they were about to melt out of their holes and drip onto my nice khakis, but you have to get up pretty earlier in the morning to pull one over on this guy.

I laughed. Pointed at Cameron's face. "Your nose."

Cameron stopped crying. He'd eased out of it, a sniffle here or there, but he'd completely, easily stopped. "Did you just *laugh*?"

I squinted at his face and tapped my nose. "You wiggle it. Your nose. When you fake it."

Cameron just stared at me. I pulled myself up on the stairs, grabbing the railing and finding my sea legs. "You should go find your alternates, Cammy. You've still got a tournament to win."

"Jackson."

"Gooooo Basketbros!"

I slapped my face awake and left Cameron downstairs. "*Jackson!*"

I stumbled over the last step and left Cameron's voice in the past. I made my way down the hallway and imagined myself texting on my dead phone.

J: Coming, bitch.

J: *Philip

I headed into the second-floor bathroom and threw some water on my face. I tried focusing on my reflection, but I was nearing the end of my eyesight for the day. I settled for chucking the two tampons Ronny had lent my nose and cleaned up the dried blood in the sink. I heard a snore.

"Whosat?"

I faced the wall of stalls. Maybe Sandro Miceli hadn't taken me up on my offer and spent the rest of the night snoring away in the men's room. I peeked over the snoring stall and was surprised to find Phil instead. Sitting up on the toilet tank. Presumably to avoid detection. Presumably so he could pass out in peace. His head was smushed against the stall wall, buried in his hoodie, and his legs dangled off the tank. God bless the tiny folk. I could never sit comfortably on the top of a toilet like that.

"What's up, Elf on the Shelf?"

Phil grunted. Not enough to tell me he was awake but enough to tell me his brain was on. I slipped into the stall and locked it behind me. Flipped the toilet lid down and popped a squat between his legs. He stirred. *"Mmm?"*

"It's me."

"Mmm."

His legs sort of hugged me and I rested my head back on his thigh. His voice was drowsy and far away. *"Did we get Cameron hurt?"*

I shook my head against the mesh of his shorts. "Only socially. But we did some real damage. Gonna be a lot to sort out."

He grunted. *"We'll be okay."*

I rubbed my face on his shorts a bit until I got to his bare thigh. Better. "We'll be okay."

I rested my face on his hairy skin and let myself give in to it. The tired. The comfort. Philip. I closed my eyes and felt myself drifting. Seconds away.

"Are you sleeping?"

"Are you?"

"Mmm."

I smelled his skin. Sleepytime Tea. It smelled the same. He felt the same. *"I forgot how hairy your thighs were."*

I felt his chuckle. His fingers along my cheek. Holding me against his thigh. He played my hair like strings until we were both at sleep's door.

I smiled. *"I missed you tonight, Philip."*

He said it as I finally let myself sleep. *"I miss you every night, Jacksy."*

I finally let myself stop.

PHIL

TRACK EIGHT

My Songs Know What You Did in the Dark

~DO NOT SHARE~

RSVP BELOW

*If you are receiving this message,
you are cordially invited to the home of Veronica DiSario.*

*The party starts at sundown and ends when I tell you
to leave. If you don't know where I live, take that
as a sign that you should not come.*

*The dress code is strictly enforced and cause for immediate
ejection. Anyone not dressed for the night's theme will be
bounced by event security and blacklisted from any future
DiSario-sponsored event. No exceptions. No reentry.*

Tonight's Theme:

That's a Bad Look

Wear your worst outfit. Don't be funny, don't get cute with it, but don't lie to yourself either. I want you to go into your closet, really look at your fashion sense objectively, and come wearing the ugliest clothes you own. Revel in the bad choices of your past and give that terrible outfit one last hurrah. There will be an optional bonfire at midnight if you wish to burn it but I do not supply backups.

Don't be late, don't overstay your welcome.

Later days!
Ronny <3

Oh, and can someone bring ice?

If all went as planned, we really could have just enjoyed the party. It was a celebration, after all. Jackson had drawn out Cameron and depowered Brynn. Ronny had turned the jocks and none of them missed Doug's *plus one*. I had helped them both, leaving the last member of the Skwad alone and vulnerable. We had officially entered Phase Three.

But we'd all agreed that defeating Augie Horton wouldn't require *The Brynn Show*'s traps and baits or the whisper campaigns of All-Night Dodgeball. Because Augie wasn't like Brynn or Doug. Augie had no real love for Cameron. Augie saw Cameron's value. His strategic advantage. But what value did Cameron have left? Brynn was now controversial and Doug had lost his lease on Planet Bro. If we wanted Augie to cut ties with Cameron, all we had to do was make a better offer. Show him another way. Invite him to the party.

Jackson and I were a little late to the event but Ronny said it would be better that way. Less conspicuous. We walked through the first two foyers of Chateau DiSario and quickly gave up on trying to recognize anyone. There were a good number of uninvited strangers but, moreover, the party's theme made it hard to look at anybody for too long. Cheetah print leggings. Denim dresses with too much fringe. Metallic-print rompers and so many fucking clogs. Jackson gasped at a passing Lucy Jordan, already tipsy and in a full Canadian tuxedo. Denim shirt, denim jacket, denim bucket hat. She looked like a walking pair of jeans and she was having the time of her life.

"*Lucille.*"

She toasted Jackson in response, sloshing her fruit punch mix onto the jeans without a care. "I'm burning this in twenty minutes!"

The room cheered along with her. Lucy cackled and headed down to the basement. When she opened the door, a wave of pounding bass and strobing lights poured out into the foyer. The patented DiSario basement rave. It had been a minute since Ronny let people into her house, but all the old Ronny Rager trademarks were out in full force. Speakers in every room blaring her methodically curated playlists. An entire dining room devoted to the world's biggest game of King's Cup. The entire JV football squad patrolling the rooms in their Ronny-fashioned security shirts and a kitchen's worth of enough Jell-O shots to fill the country club pool.

Ronny had pulled out all the stops. And why wouldn't she? She'd been riding off the high of her legendary dodgeball upset last month, the Laxatives dominating their bracket and beating the once great Basketbros in the final round. The long night had beaten everybody down but Ronny DiSario stepped into that cold parking lot with a renewed sense of power. After months of whispers and rumors and graffiti on her locker, Ronny had finally won.

We stopped in the kitchen to marvel at the terrible out-fits. A girl I didn't know was wearing a shit-brown jumpsuit and pulled two beers from the ice sink. She inspected the cans with disgust and waved them at us, yelling over the ear-splitting music. "I HATE YUENGLING! Y'ALL WANT?!"

I looked to Jackson. He considered it then shrugged. I could barely hear him so he leaned in close to my ear. "You still don't?"

The question had thrown me a little. Maybe because I tend to spend a good seventy-five percent of my conversations at parties having to explain myself to people. Trying to come up with new and creative excuses besides *I just don't drink* or *I just don't like it* or *Have you met my mom?*

I took a second to remember how well Jackson knew me. I shook my head. "You can. If you want."

Jackson grabbed a Sprite from the ice. He hollered over the music to Poop Suit. "WE'RE GOOD. THANK YOU."

The stranger tossed the cans back into the sink and snagged a tray of Jell-O shots on her stumble into the backyard. Jackson laughed.

"I know it's on-theme and all but—"

"But it literally looks like she painted herself with shit, I know."

"Exactly. Like she paid money for that."

"Wild."

"Wild."

Jackson sipped his Sprite and put a hand on my back. Led me out into the backyard. The chill in the night air bit my nose but the fire pit on the patio warmed me back up. Jackson's hand on my back didn't hurt. It was quieter outside, most of the partiers were smoking out in the grass, so Jackson and I were alone by the fire.

I put my hands in my pockets and noticed my breath was fogging up. "Damn. I need a better jacket."

"You cold?"

Jackson's hand left my back and his arm found my shoulders. I laughed up at him, a little happy for the new warmth. "My shit's three winters old. A light wind might unravel it."

"Hey, at least it's fitting with the party theme."

"Fuck you. Your jacket's way uglier than mine."

"Philip. This is J. Crew."

"Who's that, your uncle or whatever?"

We both burst out laughing and his arm got snugger around my neck. I was glad it was dark out on the patio because all the sudden touching was making me smile real weird. Jackson rambled on about all his potential jacket choices for the evening, but I couldn't stop thinking about waking up together. In a bathroom stall in the Moorestown Community Center in the morning after ten hours of dodgeball. How surprised I was to find Jackson Pasternak sleeping under me. My legs draped around him like his quilt. His face in my thigh like his pillow. I must have watched the guy sleep on me for an hour. Every muscle in my body was aching from the night, but I couldn't waste the sight. Jackson asleep. Holding my leg. Drooling on my thigh. After thirty minutes of watching, I rubbed his neck. I couldn't help it. Maybe I wanted to wake him up. Maybe I wanted to sneak out while we had the chance. Or maybe I just needed to touch him again too. Like I used to. And even in his sleep, I could feel him feel me. Remember what it felt like. All that exploration. Jackson's lips had just kissed my thigh when he woke up. Cleared his throat. Remembered where he was. And before he could remember me, I shut my eyes and pretended I was asleep. Pretended I wasn't melting at the sight of Jackson's lips on me. Because I'm a coward. Because it felt so fucking good.

Jackson nodded. "We should find Ron soon. Make a plan for when Augie shows."

"Sure."

I rested my head back on his arm and watched the smoke rise from the pit. "It's nice though. Just… I don't know. Being at the party. In the mix."

Jackson smiled down at me. "Phil Reyno? Enjoying being around people?"

I laughed. But I didn't feel a need to explain myself. I think Jackson understood what I meant. What I wasn't saying. He knew me that well. Because I never seemed to give the world much thought. What had the world done for me? But tonight was nice. At least for tonight. It was nice to be a part of the world that night. It was nice being in the world with Jackson.

His hand rubbed my arm. "I like it too, Phil."

We smiled at each other. Warm.

"Pasternak."

The screen door opened and Jackson pulled his arm away. Put his hands back in his pockets. We both turned to find Bolu Olowe standing in the doorway. He was wearing a powder blue suit that was two sizes too small on him. His ankles showed and he looked ridiculous but, in classic Bolu fashion, his face was all business. "Can we talk?"

Jackson gave me a look. If Bolu's lack of eye contact wasn't an indicator, his tone was clear. I was not invited to this meeting of the minds. I gave Jacks a nod. "I'll be around."

He tapped my shoulder and headed over to the grill area with Bolu. I watched Jackson put on his presidential posture and the two very serious men sat for their session. They'd been chatting more frequently since dodgeball, which truly made me happy. Jackson had gotten something from my revenge crusade outside of helping me. I guess I still felt indebted to him after that bullshit ambush date at Brewster's.

Though Jackson said Cameron hadn't been talking to him nearly as much at rehearsals lately. Not since the All-Nighter, really. Theater kids are very superstitious and with Tech Week approaching, Cameron's taken a vow of silence anytime he's not onstage. *Vocal rest*. Jackson told me he had never enjoyed rehearsals more.

I was about to start my search for the party's host when laughter from the pool area caught my attention. I saw fifteen soccer girls trying to cram into a Jacuzzi, then noticed someone by the pool. It was covered for the season, but the girl still sat alone. Like she'd have her feet in the water if it weren't mid-November. What was the point of sitting by a pool you can't touch in weather like that at a rager like Ronny's? But the answer wasn't hard to find. Brynn Forester came to a party to be alone.

"…Shit." I sighed and headed down the patio steps. Before I could talk myself out of it, I walked along the pool's edge and joined Brynn on the ground. I left a responsible two yards of distance between us and sipped my soda.

Her eyes never left the pool tarp. "Your clothes aren't ugly enough."

I nodded and looked at her outfit. She was wearing a simple enough hoodie with some text on the front I couldn't make out in the dark. "What's that say?"

Brynn sighed and faced me. The pink hoodie looked better suited for a preteen and the big bedazzled words screamed: **I'M FEELING A LITTLE HORSE.**

I crossed my arms under my flannel and tried to stay warm.

"Ronny's probably gonna bounce us both. I don't know if a cheesy hoodie or a shitty jacket is bad enough."

"Whatever. She only invited me as a joke."

"You know that for a fact?"

"Why else would she? She hates me." Brynn pulled on the drawstring of her hoodie. "Everyone hates me now." She flicked the string away and stared up at the stars. Like she could just cry. Woe is me, life's so hard, won't somebody just think of the nice, sweet, rich girl?

"You want me to feel sorry for you, then?" I was cold. I couldn't help it.

Brynn looked at me and I thought I'd see tears in her eyes. Some plea or pity. But they were clear. Maybe she was all cried out. "Did you really love Cameron?"

The question lingered. I didn't know how to answer that. She let it hang though. We had very little left to say to each other and I don't think she had other questions. But I felt no obligation to answer.

She shook her head. "Augie said... Augie used to say he never understood you. He never understood why you were with Cameron. He got why Cam was with you. *Opposites attract, taming the rebel.* We understood what Cam wanted out of you. But... Augie never understood why you gave it to him."

My eyebrows furrowed. "Gave him what?"

Brynn looked at me. "*You*, Phil. You stayed with him. You put up with us. You never fit, you always complained, but you kept coming back. You kept trying to fit. Augie didn't get that." She nodded. "But I got it."

Brynn looked at the party behind us, shaking her head. "I thought I was the luckiest person, finding Cameron. He was exactly who I hoped I'd meet when I got to high school. Before Cameron, nothing lived up to the fantasy. Kids were mean or sad or just…nothing. But Cam was so nice. And he liked me so much. He liked our friends so much. The Skwad. And now he won't even call me back."

Her face got tight. She sniffed. "I messed up one time. Once. And he tells me I need to be alone. He *makes* me be alone. After everything I meant to him. After everything he asked me to do. I love him so much and he just threw me away."

She wiped her eye with her hoodie sleeve. "I understand, Phil. Why you loved him. Why you stayed. And I'm so… I'm so sorry, Phil. Phil, I'm so fucking sorry he did this to you."

"Brynn."

"I'm so sorry I did this to you."

I stood up. Because I didn't need to be cried at. My guilt and my decency made me sit by Brynn's side. I didn't know what tears would do to me and that girl didn't deserve my guilt. Or my decency. "You don't even know what you're apologizing for. Keep it."

I started to walk away. She stood too. "I wrote his Snow Globe speech." I stopped. Brynn sniffed. "He wanted something perfect. Right out of the movies. I spent two whole weeks on it, I probably wrote ten versions."

I heard her walk closer. "I didn't want to use your name. He didn't need to, it worked without it. People would've still cheered. People would've still loved it. Cameron could've just come out and been proud and brave and…"

She was right behind me then. "He said he needed to tell the world about you two. He said he loved you that much. And I didn't… I don't think he did, Phil. He just thought it was the better story. I don't think he ever really loved you."

"*Fuck you.*"

I turned around. I wanted to shove her into the pool. I wanted to fucking cry.

"If he loved you, he would never have done that to you, Phil."

I felt my jaw shaking. I'd started shivering. But it wasn't the cold. Tears were burning my cheeks and I wanted to run away. Go home. Find Jackson.

"He outed you, Phil. We outed you. I…" Brynn took my arm. "*I* outed you. I didn't stop him. Every time I felt it was wrong, I never stopped him. And I'm gonna spend the rest of my life hating myself for that."

She was crying too then. "I'm sorry, Phil. You don't need to forgive me, I won't, but I need you to at least know. Please, Phil. I'm so sorry."

I didn't wipe my face. I wanted her to see them. But I took her hand off my arm. "You're not going to make either of us feel better about this, Brynn. There are no words."

I stood by the pool and wondered if that was true. Were there enough words I could scream at Brynn Forester to make what she'd done alright? Maybe I could find the right ones if I spent enough time on it. I knew I could find the right clever comeback or the perfect biting insult if I gave it enough thought. Or maybe I'd given Brynn enough thought. Maybe I'd given the Skwad and that speech and that boy enough of my time.

"I don't think you're a bad person, Brynn. I think you are a *deeply* careless one. I think you care about the wrong things, the wrong ways, and I think you have no fucking idea what your consequences are. The consequences of being you." I shook my head. Wiped my face. "And I think we are very similar."

I left her by the pool with that. It wasn't my decency or

guilt that made me say it though. It was just the truth. I didn't look back and saw the patio was empty on my return. Jackson must've gone inside. I checked my phone. A few texts from Ronny.

R: If you're looking for me, I'm giving a *private* piano lesson in the garage

R: Give me ten

R: 8===0~~~{I}

I squinted at the last text. "...*Oh.* It's a vagina. M'kay."
I scrolled down to my texts from Jackson.

J: Ronny interrupted us.

J: She took Bolu with her. Something about piano lessons.

J: Wait, are you talking to Brynn???

Ronny and Bolu? Good on her, guy's got a very high ass. I went to respond to Jackson but was stopped by an incoming text. A private number. Interesting.

Private: Meet me in the movie theater.

Private: Come alone.

Private: The smaller movie theater, not the main one.

Interestinger. Very spy movie. Very suspicious. I looked around the area in case I was being watched then walked back into the party and wondered who in my life might be waiting in the smaller movie theater to jump my ass. Matty Silva? Probably the most likely ass-jumper on the table, but I had his number saved in my phone in case of mom-related emergencies. I tiptoed around a few passed-out classmates on the way upstairs. Maybe it was Anthony Lewis? That racist little homophobe would have no way of knowing my hand in his nose getting broken at All-Night Dodgeball and a secret summoning didn't seem his style.

I took a left, trying to remember my way around the labyrinthine DiSario mansion, and passed by the large screening room. Could the texter be Doug Parson? That could make sense. After dodgeball, the bros cut Doug loose. He just wandered the halls like a lost dog, he barely even hung out with Cameron anymore.

I stopped outside the last door in the hall, my hand on the knob. *Cameron.* What if it was Cameron? What if he'd figured us out? Maybe something got back to him or Ronny had slipped or Jackson said too much. Had I been summoned into some final confrontation? Was I walking into the boss battle? Was this the end of the road Cameron put me on the morning we got paired together in shop class?

I took a steadying breath. "Once more unto the breach."

I turned the doorknob and went into the movie theater. Where normal families might put their TVs in living rooms, the DiSarios watched their evening news in either of their very modest, very relatable movie theaters. The large screening room was for events, stocked with a concessions stand and rows of theater-grade seating. The smaller screening room however was far homier. Recliners and couches, big pillows and mood lighting, more suited for a cozy date night or Ronny's annual *Gilmore Girls* hate watch. In the half-light, I saw the back of a head sitting in the loveseat closest to the front. He was alone, eating a bowl of popcorn and sipping a glass of red wine. Eyes glued to the silver screen.

"But, you know, even with all these eyes on me, I still feel sort of invisible. Sometimes I feel like I could just disappear. I never felt like anyone saw me. Until him. Until he saw me."

For a moment, we both watched the YouTube video projected up on the wall. A familiar boy making a familiar speech, twenty feet tall up on that screen.

"I'm not going to be a secret anymore. I deserve to be seen. I deserve to be loved. You deserve to be loved. You deserve to be seen, baby."

Augie turned around in his seat and looked at me by the door. Cameron's voice shook through the stereo speakers.

"I love you, Phil Reyno."

Augie tapped a remote and the image of Cameron on that stage froze on the wall. He smiled at the screen. "You know, for iPhone footage, the quality holds up on the big screen."

I closed the door behind me and the soundproof room was silent. None of the bass and laughter and party noise got through the door and it felt like we were alone in the world.

I walked through the couches and recliners. "I got your texts. Very dramatic, Augles. Really know how to set a mood."

"Well, I don't like anybody at this party. Gotta find my own fun."

"C'mon. Brynn's out back. You don't wanna go play flip cup with your bestie?"

I reached Augie's row. He just smiled at me. "Thanks for the invitation, Philip. It's nice to find some time."

"You invited me to pistols at dawn, Augs, I just showed up."

He looked around the theater. Grinned at the popcorn machine in the corner. "Y'know, I thought Ronny DiSario hated my fucking guts. Thought she hated yours too." He shrugged and sipped his wine. "But you've had a busy fall, huh, Phil? Covered a lot of ground, really made the most of your autumn."

Augie turned the grin to me. "So. *Again*. Thanks for the invitation. How are you two going to ruin my life?"

I nodded. If anyone was going to piece together our plan, I guess it always was going to be Augie. He was smart like that. Which was why our plotting ended at the invitation. Because I knew Augie could be talked to. And if he showed up to the party, maybe he just wanted to talk.

"We're not going to do anything to you, Augie."

"I doubt that heavily."

"I mean it. We've done enough."

Augie eyed me, trying to read my cards. "*Ronny and Phil.* The exes, united in a righteous cause. It's all very impressive. I truly don't know how you did it. Doug lost all his friends. Brynn barely leaves her room. Kudos, Philip. You really *got them*."

I sat on the edge of a couch. "We're just playing the game y'all started. I'm not going to feel bad about that."

"Mmm. How very tough of you. But to what end?"

"His."

Augie laughed. He raised his eyebrows and sipped his wine. "And I'm the last one in your way. Should I be looking out for buckets of pigs' blood?"

"Augie."

"Or are you gonna cut out the middleman and trap me in a locker room with the basketball team? Make up some bullshit to Ant Lewis and get my teeth knocked in? Take me down a fucking peg."

"I'm—"

Augie's glare shut me up. "You think that rumor train was hard to trace back, Philip? You think Dani Touscani's a tough nut to crack? Do you think I will not tell the entire fucking town what you've done if you try to fuck with me for a single second?"

"Augie."

He pointed at me. "You never should have been outed. You deserve an apology. You don't deserve what Cameron did, you don't deserve how this school handles you, and you deserve a good fucking therapist." I looked at my feet. Augie stayed on me. "But you could have gotten Cameron hurt. Phil, you two could have gotten Cameron *attacked*. You don't understand that? You don't see how that's a bridge too fucking far?"

"That wasn't in the plan, Augie, that… It was an accident."

"Oh! Which always seem to follow you, don't they? What's the common denominator?"

I saw the flashing lights. The cops. A garbage truck in my lawn. Augie leaned in. "We are gay and in Jersey, Phil. I can count on one fucking hand how many live in this town, and you're attacking *us*?! You team up with some straight girl, rile up any jock who will listen, and you put that target on *US*?!" He shook his head. "And you really think you're the hero here? You really think you're doing the right thing?"

Augie stood and finished his glass. Loomed over me. I waited for the slap. Spit in my face. But Augie just looked sad. Tired. "We hit you first. I know that. If Cameron listened to me, he would've let you down gently before we ever stepped foot in that damn dance. Because you take things too far. You both do. And I knew you two together would only make my life fucking harder. And my life is hard enough."

He laughed. Just a little. "You really think he won't hit you back? Do you really think Cameron is gonna let this go easy? He's… He's not going to make this easy, Phil. You know him. He's petty. And cold. He doesn't let shit go. And when he figures you out… And he *will* figure you out…" He crossed his arms. "He'll hit you back cruel. He'll hit you back permanent. He'll get you expelled, he'll get your mom fired, he'll take shit too far. He'll…"

Augie sighed. "He'll out Jackson."

It felt like I'd fallen. My breath had been low but it left me completely then. *"What?"*

Augie looked away. "He doesn't know for sure. That Jackson's a part of this. Or that he's…whatever Jackson is. But that doesn't matter."

"What are you talking about?"

"He'll make another speech or make another video and he will take Jackson down with you. For helping you. For embarrassing him."

I swallowed. My brain felt like it was shaking against my skull. "You… How do you know?"

"I know Cameron."

"Augie, how do you know about Jackson?"

Augie sat with me on the couch. Looked up at the frozen video on the wall. "I've known Jackson Pasternak a long time. Since I moved to the Orchard. And I always thought there was something…you know. There." He smiled. "I used to be so jealous of him as a kid. I hadn't met Brynn yet and I didn't know anybody in town and nobody wanted to be my friend. But Jackson was nice. Kind of quiet, kind of weird, but he was always nice to me. I wanted to be his friend. I wanted to be his *best* friend. But that position was already taken."

He looked at me. "I don't know how you two met or why you fell out, but… I always found it so weird that no one knew. Nobody in school knew you two were friends. They still don't. No one remembers you two. No one saw it. But I would. I'd see y'all playing on the lake or fighting in your

forts or napping in the grass. I'd be sitting in my room and…
And I used to get so sad. 'Cause I knew I'd never have that.
Normal boys having normal boy fun. That kind of fun wasn't
for boys like me. I was alone in my room. I could never have a
friend like that. The way you two talked. The way he would
look at you."

Augie's eyes moved to the floor. For a while. A really long
while. "He was so amazed by you."

I stood up. Wiped my face. "If Cameron does that, Augie…"

I didn't know what to say. What would I do? All of my
thoughts were too much. Any action would go too far. What
could I do? My breath found me again but it came back too
quickly. It filled me too far.

"Augie."

Augie stood with me and took out his phone. He put it
in my hand. "Tell him. Tell Cameron you'll stop. You were
feeling angry, he'd hurt you that much, and you didn't mean
for all of this to spin out."

"I can't—he won't believe that."

"He doesn't know about Jackson yet. He thinks Brynn
brought that on herself and Matty Silva just has it out for him.
All y'all did was say some outta pocket shit at Dodgeball and
it just got away from you."

"He won't… Augie, he won't listen to me, he doesn't—"

Augie snatched his phone back. "Then I'll tell him! Please!
I will clean up your goddamn mess, just promise me you're
going to stop, Phil. You won. Brynn is a leper and Doug is
alone. Cameron's rep is tainted and you made up with your
rich boy toy. You won. You got your revenge, you got your
Jackson—"

"Augie, he won't stop—"

He screamed it in my face. *"WHAT ELSE DO YOU FUCKING NEED?!"*

I fell back into the couch. It was the first time I'd seen Augie scream. Lose his cool. Even on *The Brynn Show*, Augie had never lost his cool. At anyone. Never in class. Never in the halls. Never at the names Ant Lewis would blast through the lunchroom. Never at the silent ways Cameron would talk about his weight. The guy had been cut a thousand times, a thousand different ways, but this was the first time I'd seen Augie Horton bleed.

I nodded up at him. "It's enough. It's enough, Augie. I'm done."

We stood there for a moment. Catching our breath. Letting it end. Augie wiped his face and nodded back. "My name is August."

He grabbed his wine glass and left me on the couch. I gave his exit some time and wondered if I'd be better off waiting out the party on that couch. Before I could think about it too hard, the lights in the room went black. It was sudden and felt like a blink. Cameron disappeared from the wall and I was alone in a soundproofed dark room. It felt like the end of my movie. I expected to see credits start to roll.

I checked my phone. I had dozens of missed texts and calls from Ronny and Jackson. Shit. I hopped up and left the theater. The sound of the party washed over me, but there was a notable lack of music. Just yelling. The hallway was dark and I could hear some guy holler from the billiards room. *"WHO TURNED OFF THE POWER?!"*

I leaned over the bannister and saw a woman in an actual wedding dress stomping downstairs. It looked very eighties and more ruffle than dress. The bride cocked her head up and hollered right back. *"IT'S AN OLD HOUSE, SHUT THE FUCK UP!"*

Ronny spotted me above her and sighed. "Phil! What in the Sam's Club took you so long?! I've been calling you for an hour—" Ronny squinted at my clothes then smiled. "Thank you for dressing for the party. That jacket is terrible."

I flipped her off and hustled down the stairs. "Is that a wedding dress?"

Ronny swooned and played with her ruffles. "It's terrible, right? My grandmamma was married in it. You like?"

"Wow, Ron. That seems...really disrespectful?"

"Ew. Don't bitch out on me now, Reyno." She scoffed and I followed her downstairs. "If it makes you feel better, Grandmother was a staunch Republican who was married four times."

"I mean, that helps. What happened to the power?"

"Breaker flipped. It happens all the time, I blame all the strobes."

"Mmm. Or maybe it's the thirty speakers blaring different house music simultaneously."

We reached the foyer and Ronny retrieved a comically large flashlight from a side closet. She handed it to me and pointed to the basement.

"The circuit panel box thing is in the wine cellar, way in the back corner. I marked it with a big ol' orange X, very hard to miss."

I handed her back the giant lightbulb. "And you're pawning off this duty to me? A guest?"

"Philip. I am trying to host a successful party, there are certain expectations. Have you never read an etiquette book?" I gave her a look. She rolled her eyes. "Okay, I was about to fuck Bolu Olowe when the lights blew. He's waiting for me in my room, please, please, please don't ruin this for me."

"Ruin what for you?"

From somewhere in the darkness, Jackson emerged with a piña colada. I smiled. Ronny did not. "None of your business, Ferris Bueller."

"She's about to smash Bolu Olowe." Ronny slapped my chest. I sighed and took the flashlight back from her. "And I'm gonna go fix the power."

Ronny cheered and hugged me. "Thank you! I'll pay you back with gory details."

"Don't be gross. Bolu is a good Christian gentleman."

Jackson toasted her with his tropical drink. "Exactly. Now go get filled with the Holy Spirit."

I snorted. Ronny gasped and looked at me. "Jackson made a joke! Jackson's having fun! I like Fun Jackson, keep her around."

"Alright, alright."

I grabbed Jackson's arm and dragged him toward the basement. I held the door open for Jackson and he offered me his piña colada. "The DiSarios have a Tiki Room. This is virgin, I just like coconut."

"Mmm. A nice tropical November drink."

"'Tis the season."

We headed downstairs, sharing sips, and felt the stairs get older and creakier with every step into the dark abyss. We excused our way through a mob of partygoers, all sweaty from their interrupted basement rave, and I followed Jackson into the cavernous wine cellar. It felt like we were walking through the stacks in an old library, searching for some ancient tome, and I held on to Jackson's sweater for guidance.

"I feel like we're in *Pirates of the Caribbean*."

"I feel like we're going to die down here."

We passed rows and rows of wine shelves and dusty bottles. Every few, we'd bump into some random classmate lost in the dark. The blackout had disoriented the already disoriented ravers and I guess some of the stragglers had wandered into the wine maze by mistake. We finally reached a wall at the end of all the nothing and our flashlight found the circuit box in the corner.

"Yahtzee." Jackson opened the panel and stared at the breakers for about a minute before looking back at me. "I don't know what I'm looking at."

I rolled my eyes and we switched places. He held the light for me and I inspected the switches. Everything I knew about electrical bullshit came from shop class or movies, but I figured my scraps of knowledge had to beat Jackson's crumbs.

"So. What did Brynn have to say for herself?"

"Oh, you know. *I'm so sorry, I'm so terrible, pwease pwease pwease forgive me.* The expected stuff."

"Mmm. Did it work?"

I flipped one switch. Nothing. "Did what work?"

"Do you forgive her?"

I unflipped the switch and shrugged. "I'm not looking to forgive Brynn. That's not why I did this." My fingers stopped on another switch. "I did... I did feel bad though. Just a little."

"Yeah?"

"She seemed really... She's really fucking sorry." I flipped it. More nothing. "But I knew she would be. That's not the point. You don't just blow up people's lives, let people suffer, then get to feel bad about it in your fucking mansion. Brynn needed consequences. We showed her consequences."

"Aha. So, you don't want an apology, you want a thank-you."

"Wouldn't be a bad place to start."

I squinted at the illegible handwritten instructions on the panel. They told me to restart the main breaker. How the fuck do I do that?

Jackson joined my side. "Did you find Augie?"

I nodded. "Augie, uh...found me."

"How'd that go?"

My fingers found the biggest switch. Maybe the main breaker. "He knows. More than we thought." Jackson looked concerned. I shook my head. "It's okay. He's on our side. I mean, he's on no one's side which is still better than... He's trying to keep things good."

"Good?"

"Keep things from going too far."

"Phil. What does that mean?"

I flipped the big switch. The lights came back on and I realized just how close we were. The room looked smaller in the light. All the endless magic of the dark was gone and the wine cellar looked disappointingly average. Ravers around the room gave sighs of relief and tried to find their exits. Pretty soon, bass pounded the ceiling above us and the rager had quickly resumed. But Jackson's eyes never left me.

I leveled with him. "Augie said we needed to stop. For everyone's sake. He said Dodgeball went too far and he made good points, Jackson. He said we'd done enough."

Jackson's eyebrows furrowed. "Do... Do you think we've done enough? Do you want to stop, Phil?"

I crossed my arms. Really thought about his question. Augie's question. His scream. What else did I fucking want? I'd already wounded Cameron. Pretty thoroughly. Pretty permanently. He wouldn't get the perfect junior year he wanted. He wouldn't get the fairy-tale high school life he thought my presence was keeping him from. He didn't get Link Larkin. He couldn't trust Brynn. Doug was useless to him and Augie had one foot out the door. And he wouldn't get Jackson. Cameron wouldn't hurt Jackson.

I turned off the flashlight and put it on the dusty floor. "I wanted to hurt him back. And I hurt him back. And I'm…" I shrugged. "I don't know if I feel any better, Jackson. I don't know if I feel…good. About what I've done. I think I'm gonna feel really fucking bad about some of this one day, Jacks. I think I'm gonna really regret it someday."

Jackson's hand was on my shoulder. "Phil."

I shook my head. "But I did it. And I got some good shit out of it too, man. I got to see Cameron sweat. Show him he couldn't knock me out. And Brynn learned to stop. Hopefully. I got Augie off my back. And I got Ron. And I… And you."

I heard a group of partiers pass by a shelf. They weren't looking at us, but they could see us through the shelf if they wanted to. Jackson watched them walk out of sight. His hand was firm on my shoulder but I could feel the nerves too. We might have been alone, but we were still in the world. Jackson still had his lines.

I held his hand to my shoulder. "There's you, man."

Jackson nodded. He let himself feel alone with me. "Yeah. There's that. There's us."

"That's pretty good. That's really fucking good, Jacksy."

He smiled back, soft. "It's good. We're good." His hand squeezed my shoulder. "And… And we get to keep the promise now. We can stick together now, Phil. We can do it right this time. Even with the differences. We can do it right."

I smiled and shook my head. "*Because* of the differences, Jacks. They're good differences." I got closer to him. He smelled like coconut and fire pit. "I like how we're different.

I like all the differences, I love how they fit together, Jackson. I love how we fit."

Jackson closed his eyes. His head leaned close to mine. "I love that too."

I felt a tear run down my cheek. I could see two run down his. "I love that you're back. I love that we're back."

"I love that too."

Our voices got tighter together, like they were braiding into one.

"I love that we're friends again, Jacks."

"I love that too."

"I love that you found me again."

"I love that too."

I held his face. "I love you, Jackson."

"I love you so fucking—"

Another group of voices passed our shelf and I saw quick fear in Jackson's eyes. My hand slammed that main breaker and the lights went out again. The world had gone dark again and the cellar was endless and Jackson's lips were on mine.

"I love you, Philip. I love you so fucking much, man."

He kissed me with all eleven years. Jackson kissed me how he'd been waiting to since the morning we met. All around the darkness, people were shouting, looking for the light, but we were alone in our corner of the world. Alone together, Jackson's lips on my cheeks. My hands in his hair. His arms lifting me high and holding me close.

"Jacks."

His tears in my neck. His pained joy. His long relief. *"Phil."*

Jackson and me. My Jackson. Mine.

NEW TAPE

JACKSON

The Christmas lights were the only things keeping the apartment from going completely dark. Their tree was in the corner, but it lit the entire space. The living room and kitchen. But Phil's apartment was almost just that one room. A living room and a kitchen. The entire place, the size of my basement. An entire home lit by one tree.

"Please. Please, don't cry."

Phil was sitting on the kitchen floor. Head in his arms. Sobbing through his sweatshirt. He'd asked me to stop trying to touch him. He told me if I got up off the couch and tried to touch him again, he'd have to ask me to go. And if he asked me to go, he didn't know if he'd ever ask me to come back.

"Phil. Please talk to me."

He coughed up a sob and shook his head into his arms. I had to tell myself to stay seated. He didn't want to throw me out, but the threat had been issued and Phil would have to hold himself to it.

He sniffled. *"You d-don't understand."* He was looking at me then. His face red and puffy. And so fucking heartbroken. *"Why don't you understand, Jackson?"*

I didn't. I didn't understand. All I did was give him a gift. It was supposed to be nice. It was supposed to make things better. Things had been getting so hard lately, we'd been getting so weird with each other, the gift was supposed to help. We just couldn't stop fighting this year. Ever since eighth grade started, all autumn long, we kept hitting the same bumps. These new problems. He'd pick a fight with me because I didn't approve of what he called some kid in the hallway. Suddenly, I must not care about him enough if I happened to blow Phil off for a student council meeting. If I asked about his mom, I was being insensitive. If I tried to help with homework, I was talking down to him. Wanting a night to myself had become an attack on Phil's character and every piece of advice had become a damning judgment. He just kept putting things on me. I couldn't do anything right anymore and I'd run out of ideas.

"What don't I understand, Phil?"

That's why I'd given him my Xbox. We'd spent the last five years lugging the thing back and forth between our houses, sleepover after sleepover, rematch after rematch. I knew I was about to get the new system for Hanukkah and it seemed like the perfect gift. One of our favorite things to do together, this object that'd been with us all this time, now all his. Phil could have an Xbox all for himself.

His head was back in his arms. *"You don't understand me, Jackson. I thought you fucking— What's wrong with you? What the fuck is wrong with you?"*

I'd gotten choked up before, watching him so angry and upset, but I hadn't let myself cry. I thought it would've been rude. But that did it for me. "There's… There isn't anything wrong with me."

Phil picked his head up and glared at me. "You don't fucking believe that. Don't fucking lie to me."

I had to look away. I had to cry at the wall. I wouldn't give him that. *"It was just a f-fucking gift."*

It was just a fucking Xbox. And he acted like I'd given him the leftovers off my plate. The crusts off my sandwich and some gum off my shoe. Hand-me-downs.

Phil stood up. He walked right past me and headed down the hall. "It's not about the FUCKING GIFT."

He slammed his bedroom door. I broke the rule and got off the couch. Walked around the pieces of my broken present along the floorboards and waited at his door. I felt the dent. Where he'd chucked the box after seeing what was inside. "Philip. Please don't tell me to go."

I could hear him crying. I wanted to go in and hug him, but that would be overstepping. If I couldn't give him the couch, I could give him his door.

"We're too different, Jackson. Everyone knows it. Everyone says it."

"Who cares what they think? Why should that matter? Why does that matter to you?"

"Because you don't see it." I could hear him get close to the door. The shadows under the crack told me he was an inch from my face. Just a dent between us then. *"You don't see. You don't see how it matters. It matters. The differences matter."*

"No. Phil, they don't have to. We don't have to—"

A fist pounded on the door. "STOP." His breathing was stuttering. "You… You aren't listening to me. You haven't been listening to me for fucking months, Jackson, you don't fucking hear me. You don't… You don't *see me*."

"I don't under—" I stopped myself. Because I clearly didn't understand.

Phil sniffed through his words. "You don't care that I'm mean. You don't care that I'm gay. You don't care that I'm… You don't care that I'm fucking poor."

"I don't, Phil, I'd never—"

"JACKSON!"

Another punch on the door. I held my mouth. His voice got quiet. "You don't care. And I thought that was a good thing. You think that's a good thing, you think the differences don't matter. So, you don't see it. You don't see how it hurts me. You don't see how you hurt me. How a gift like that…" He choked on a sob. *"That makes me feel really fucking worthless and you don't understand."*

Phil broke down behind the door. I opened it and he crumbled into me. His legs had gone weak and I held him up from falling.

"I don't want to fucking lose you, Jackson. I'm fucking losing you."

"You're not. Phil. You're wrong. Don't cry."

"We fucked it all up. We ruined it."

His panic and pain was running out of him and it felt like his words were cutting into us. Everything he was saying, all those things he didn't mean, they were putting up a wall and scaring what we had away. He was making it real. He was ruining us.

"Don't. Stop, Phil. Don't cry. Calm down, Phil."

"Why don't you get it? W-Why don't you—"

"PHIL." I held him by the shoulders and tried to sound calm. Logical. If he was going to fall apart, I could be the strong one. I could fix this. I could make it okay. "CALM DOWN. **STOP.**"

Our faces were close and his twisted at my words. Something so angry and betrayed. Phil pushed away from me and stormed down the hall. He tripped on a bit of Xbox and punted it into the wall.

"Phil!"

I joined him in the kitchen. He'd thrown open the door. "GET OUT."

"Stop—"

"GET THE FUCK OUT, JACKSON!"

I wouldn't move. I tried to be reasonable. "We need to talk this out. You're upset. I upset you. Help me understand."

"Leave me the fuck—"

"HELP ME UNDERSTAND."

We glared at each other from across his living room. Still so dark. Still lit in the Christmas lights.

He shook his head. Steaming. "Okay." He pushed the tears off his face. "Okay. I'm in class with Lucy Jordan. She asks me if she can borrow a pencil, I say I don't even have my own. I tell her I let Jackson Pasternak borrow it during History and he forgot to give it back."

"What does that—"

Phil's eyes went wide in the dark. I kept my mouth shut. "So. I'm shit out of pencils and both of us are fucked. And Lucy says that's what I get for helping strangers." He shook his head. "And I've heard that before. I don't think much of it. People don't link us together, whatever. Their loss. They don't know us. They don't… They don't know you're my best friend in the fucking…"

Phil sniffed and shrugged. "Why do you think they forget, Jackson? What do you think they see? When people look at us together, what do you think they see?" Phil shook his head. "Why do your parents not let me walk home at night?"

"What? It's… That's a long walk. It's dark out—"

"Why did your mom introduce me to every security guard in the Orchard?"

"What?"

He took a step closer. "Why did your dad get so mad at that hostess at the country club? When she asked me who I knew there? Did you ever ask him? Did you ever ask me?"

"Phil."

"Why wouldn't I let my mom drive us to the movies last Friday? Why did I make us walk all the way home? Why, Jackson? Why?"

"You didn't want to talk about her—"

"WHY DIDN'T YOU ASK?!" He was right in my face then. His spit hit my cheeks and his breath was hot. "You don't understand what makes me different from you. You don't see it and you never had to. I thought you'd learn by now, I thought you needed time, but you just don't. You just won't. Because you aren't as fucking smart as you want to be, Jackson."

"Stop it."

It felt like a slap in the face. It felt like every light on that tree was being stepped out. One by one. The light was leaving and it would be dark soon. We would be done.

He took a step back from me. "You treat me like a gift you got. You don't know how else to treat me, Jacks. You have no idea how to put yourself in my shoes. And why would you? You got born into some really great shoes. It's not your fault. You're just... It fucked you up. It's not your fault you're broken."

"Fuck you." I walked into the kitchen. Stared at the wall. I heard Phil follow me. "You're just trying to hurt me."

"Why would I want to do that, Jackson?"

"Because you're fucking mean."

He snapped a finger. "There it is."

I turned around and walked to him. "You're not going to push me away by being fucking mean to me, Philip. You're my best friend, you piece of shit, you're not going to scare me."

"Oh, I'm your best friend? This is how you treat your best friends?"

I slammed a hand on the kitchen counter. "You're my fucking FAMILY, Phil. You are the most important person in my life, you always have been. You're the first person I want to talk to in the morning and I call you every fucking night. I always pick you. I always want you. You sat with my family at my fucking bar mitzvah, Phil. That mattered to me. You matter to me, you are a part of me, and if people don't think we make *SENSE*? That's their fucking problem. That's not our fault. That's not my fucking fault."

Phil just stared at me. Like he wasn't letting it sink in. I could see it in his face that he'd already made that decision. Whatever I'd said, however I put it, Phil had made the choice not to hear me. To stay mad. To stay mean. "People thought I was sitting with your family at your bar mitzvah so I could babysit Molly. Dani Touscani asked me if I worked for your family."

I didn't understand his point. "You do work for my family."

That sank in. He'd heard that loud and clear. Phil slapped me across the face and the room went dark.

I didn't understand.

TAPE TWO, SIDE A

———

I COULDN'T HELP IT, IT'S ALL YOUR FAULT

JACKSON

———

TRACK ONE
Linger

I crept up my stairs, doing my best not to wake up the house or spill any cereal, and had to open my bedroom door with my foot. I took a moment to admire the sleepy sight. A sunbeam had cracked through my window at the perfect angle and Phil's bare ass was lit in an orange morning glow. Thanks, God. I put my breakfast tray down and ran my fingertips along the tiny sunlit hairs. My hand cupped a cheek and I shook it around a bit. Just a little jiggle.

Phil stirred into my pillow. *"Mmmm. Cameron?"*

I slapped his ass hard. Half for fun, half to discourage those kinds of jokes. And another half because I knew he'd like that. Something I'd learned last night. Around hour four, we'd made requests of each other. Asked for the things we'd gotten curious about over the years. Stuff we didn't want to tell anyone else. Phil wanted a little spank here and there. I had him put on tube socks and mesh shorts. Just something I thought I might like on him. And I was right. I was really fucking right.

"Come in."

"Hmm?"

"Come here. Come back." Phil made room on my bed and lifted up the quilt for me. But I couldn't stop watching him. Phil in my room. Phil in my quilt. Phil in my bed. "The fuck you looking at?"

Phil naked. The way his dick flopped over when he turned. The way his balls dropped down his thigh. The zigzag of dark black hair climbing up his stomach. I got to look at it all now. Phil in my life. Phil in love with me.

"You."

Phil smiled really big. Almost bashful. Almost blushing. "Come here. Now."

I did what he asked and got into bed with him. He wrapped the quilt over us and burrowed his face into my neck. I could smell his body spray recoating me all over again and I wouldn't have it any other way.

"I wanted to wake up in bed with you, Jacks."

"You woke up in bed *near* me. That's close."

"Not good enough. We're gonna have to try again."

"Okay. Tomorrow, it is."

"And the next day too."

"Philip, now, that's a school night."

"And the next and the next." His lips hopped and dragged and kissed down my chest. They landed on my nipple and he gave it a little nibble. "You made me breakfast in bed?"

"Mmm-hmm. Did the Cap'n Crunch how you like."

"You remembered?"

"Milk before cereal? It felt morally wrong. But yes. I remembered."

"Aww. You bitch."

His lips kept going down and down and I laughed when

his teeth chewed on my waistband. "Your cereal's gonna get soggy."

"Mmm, yeah, talk dirty to me."

"I got you extra pulp OJ. And a blueberry scone. And a sausage patty with ketchup."

"Oh, fuck, I'm gonna cuuuum." I cracked up and Phil buried laughs in my stomach. He pulled me out from under my undies and gave it a quick kiss. "Good morning, ma'am." He nodded at my balls. "Gentlemen."

He put my junk away and joined me back above water. I kissed him on the forehead. "Good morning. I love you."

"Yeah, let's not wear that out."

I gasped. He rolled his eyes and gave me a quick one on the cheek. "*I love you back.* Needy ass." He reached over and grabbed the sausage patty off our tray. He let me get the first bite then shoved the rest in his mouth. "So. What should we do today, lover boy?"

"Well, we could do a sauna. Or we could go to the movies. We could hang with Ronny."

"Ron specifically warned me not to contact her today. When we left, she was in the backyard with the LAX team playing beer pong with lacrosse sticks. She's probably sleeping till sunset."

"Ah. Well, it was a long night. For everyone."

"Ohoho. I'll fucking say." His hands reached back down and rubbed me. "That was really... That was *really* fucking fun, Jackson."

"Yeah?"

"That was really fucking hot. We got a lot better at that."

"C'mon. I remember us being pretty good with each other."

Phil laughed in my face. "Jackson. We were *terrible*."

"What?!"

"I mean, we should've been! We didn't know what we were doing."

"You told me you liked it!"

Phil shrugged, trying to be polite. "I mean, a blow job's a blow job. Of course, I liked it."

"Well, I feel very unappreciated, Philip. I was only doing it for your sake."

"Bullshit. You sucked my dick nine times, Jacks, I think you liked it too."

"Eight and a half."

We cracked up. Over the course of last night, we'd gotten that number well into double digits. To say nothing of where I explored in the shower together.

My hand lazily rubbed across his chest. Played with his little tuft of hair. "You think Bolu and Ronny did it?"

"I think they tried. And I think Ronny talked her way out of it."

"That does sound like her. Plus, Bolu's got his Christian Athlete thing. Don't know what his rules are with the whole virginity thing." My nail scratched around his chest hair. Felt his heart tap against my fingertip. "Are you still... Did you and Cameron ever...you know?"

Phil shook his head against my neck. "Nah. He never wanted to."

"Did you?"

"Maybe. If he wanted to. If he asked, maybe. I might've."

"Sounds very passionate."

"I mean, I blew him once. Night before he left for baseball camp. He made us do it under covers though. With the lights off and his music real loud. I didn't get that." He stared up at my ceiling. For a little bit. "I don't know if Cameron ever liked me. I know he didn't... I know he probably didn't *love* me. I know that wasn't real for him. But I don't know if he ever really *liked* me. I don't know if I was ever who he thought I was."

"What do you mean?"

Phil shrugged. "Cameron talked about me like I was this… I don't know. A *bad boy.* 'Cause of my rep, I guess. He always said *opposites attract*, but it's like he needed us to stay…opposite. He'd talk to me like I was some arsonist anarchist motorcycle guy. Piercings and tats, from the wrong side of the tracks. It was never really me."

"Sure. You don't have a motorcycle. You can barely ride a bike."

Phil giggled. He kissed my shoulder. "After the night of the dance, if I ever tried to…you know. Get close with him. Kiss him more than once. Touch him how…how we used to. It's like I was popping this bubble. Like he had to see me as a person then. Not whatever guy he'd built up in his head. 'Cause that guy wasn't the one trying to kiss him. It was just me. Cameron didn't want me."

I moved his face to mine and kissed him deep. Held his chin in place and showed him how much I wanted him. I felt him getting hard against my leg and I wondered how much of the Sunday we could spend wanting each other. He wrapped against me, hugging against my body, and covered my leg with his.

He blew an eyelash off my cheek. "Have you? With anyone?"

I shook my head. "Never found the time."

"Really? Nobody?"

I thought about Paige Something. The Model UN field trip. When my Moorestown team and her Philly friends snuck out of our hotel rooms and broke into the pool. How she got cold and I let her share my towel and we talked all night behind a stack of lounge chairs. Knowing we might never meet again and telling each other more than we should. A story about her dead brother. The panic attack I'd had in a therapist's bathroom. My hand on her breasts. My mouth on her stomach. Her thighs on my cheeks and my swim trunks staying on. I said I just wanted to focus on her and she said I wasn't like other guys. She'd meant it as a compliment. I thought about it for weeks.

"I don't think I'm ready for that."

Phil looked up at me. "No?"

"I know. It's weird."

"It's not weird, Jackson."

"Come on. We just spent the night dehydrating each other, Phil. I sucked your dick when I was fourteen, man, I've done a lot already. I just…" I shook my head. "I don't know if I'm ready for the *sex* part. I don't think I'm ready for sex." I sat up a little, trying to say it right. "I don't mean with you. I'm not saying I wouldn't with you, it's not you, I'm just saying—"

"Jacks."

"I just don't think I'm ready at all. It's just a really big step and you can't take it back and I'd need to be in a real good head—"

Phil laughed and covered my mouth. "*Jackson.* I'm not ready either. I don't want to either, you're okay. No pressure."

I smiled against his hand. "Yeah? You mean it?"

His hand moved to my cheek. "I mean it. I really mean it. We're not rushing. Not this time."

I laughed and kissed his palm. Nuzzled into it. "I think it'd be great though. I think we'd be really great."

"Hey. Look at the track record."

I looked into his eyes and nodded. "Someday. It'll be great."

"It will."

"Someday. I'd really like to lose it to you."

"Me too, Jacks. Someday."

We watched each other's eyes. Our smiles. Thinking about the day. The day we'd be ready for each other. Soft with each other. Lost in each other. I think we had the same thought at the same time and I tried to beat him to the punch.

"Dibs on—"

"Dibs on top."

"FUCK!"

We'd spent the rest of the morning in bed together. It was almost December and neither of us was excited to leave the warmth under our covers, but there was a scary movie Phil'd been dying to see. I'd suffered through a childhood watching heavy-R horror through my fingers because of that kid, but Philip had found some new, very effective ways to convince me to go along. So, after we finished off our breakfast, finished each other off in the shower, and finished some Thanksgiving leftovers in the kitchen, we bundled up for the chilly afternoon and headed out.

We got our tickets quick and the cashier told us the theater would be basically empty. Not many people wanted to see an alligator man bite the heads off unsuspecting blonde women on a Sunday afternoon. That couldn't deter Phil though. He would see *Bayou Bloodbath* if it killed him.

We stopped at concessions because, while we had thirty bucks worth of Wawa candy shoved up our asses, I'd never once gone into a movie theater without a bucket of popcorn. That was always my rule. Tween Phil could drag me to all the guts and gore he wanted, but he had to buy me popcorn first. We were waiting in the line when he leaned back onto me. I looked around at the mostly empty lobby and decided that would be okay. Not many onlookers, no one our age, plus he was just leaning. He could just be my tired, leaning cousin. When it was our turn in line, I realized we knew the concessions cashier from school, but I didn't feel a need to stop holding Phil's arm. I thought that was very brave of me and I think Phil appreciated it but Syd DeStefano didn't seem to notice. She rang us up without a hello or goodbye.

Phil upgraded us to a large popcorn and gave me a wink. "Yo, Syd. You were at Ronny's, yeah? You feeling it?"

Syd just rang up our order, snapping away at a wad of gum. "Thirty-two fifty-two."

I didn't love her tone. Neither of us knew Syd all that well. She was kind of a burnout and what a lesser person might call *Jersey Trash*. But Syd certainly seemed to know us. At least enough to want us out of her face.

Phil took our bucket, but his glare stayed on Syd. "And you have a *super* day, Sydney. Don't work too hard."

He must've picked up on the weirdness too, but we didn't need to be getting into something. We had a movie to watch and the day had been going so well. I touched his back and tried to get us going. Syd popped a bubble. "I got cousins on Duquesne, Reyno. Little ones. Love to ride bikes out there."

Phil ducked my hand and turned around. "And what the fuck does that have to do with me, DeStefano?"

She huffed. Shook her head and pushed through the Employees Only door. *"Fucking dirtbag."*

It swung shut. Phil laughed, very confused by the random stray he'd caught. "...What the hell was that?!"

"Syd's an asshole. Famously. C'mon, I like the trailers."

"I don't even know her, man."

"I know. C'mon."

I rubbed his neck. Phil gave in and let me lead him along

the theater doors. It wasn't a rarity that some classmate or teacher or stranger on the street would pick a fight with Phil in broad daylight. After Cameron's breakup video, Phil couldn't go a day without someone stopping him in the hall or on Main Street to remind him how he should feel about himself and it was even worse online.

The theater was dark, but the place was completely empty. Just us in there. Phil ran around the empty theater, loving the freedom. "Aw, fuck yeah! We can sit wherever we want!" He jumped over a seat then paused. Gasped at me. "We could do...*stuff*."

I chuckled at the concept of getting my dick sucked while watching an alligator man tear a fisherman in half and settled into a nice middle seat. Middle aisle, middle row, best seats in the house. "Mmmm. I've got a sick and sexy counteroffer."

Phil grinned and plopped down in the seat next to me. "Yeah? Wanna jerk off during the trailers? Ooooh, we can race."

I put the popcorn bucket in the next seat and unpacked our smuggled candy. "We can watch the movie. And not break the law. And we can eat our candy and heckle the screen. And..." I put our drink in the cup holder and put Phil's hand in mine. "We can hold hands the whole time."

Phil smiled. If it weren't so dark, I'd wager he even blushed. "Okay. Yeah."

"That enough?"

He squeezed my hand and cuddled into my shoulder. Found a comfortable place for his head to bury. "That's everything, man."

I kissed his hair and dropped my voice. "And if we're good, we can make out during the credits."

"That's very disrespectful to the people who made the movie, sir."

Phil kicked his boots up on the seats in front of us and got situated on my arm. We watched the pre-show trivia and thanked Maria Menounos for her service. I let the nerves of the lobby stay outside and got comfortable cuddling Phil over an armrest. After a zombie movie trailer ended, Phil huffed. "I haven't talked to Sydney DeStefano directly since the seventh fucking grade."

"Philip."

"No, it bothers me. What the hell was that? We're just minding our own business, I didn't even do anything to her."

"You shouldn't…"

I had the instinct to tell Phil he shouldn't let it bother him. But he was close to me again. We were starting something new this time. I needed to do better this time.

After Phil and I had our big Christmas blowout, I'd spent the rest of the year replaying the fight. I needed to understand what I didn't understand. If I was never going to be his friend again, the least I could do was learn the right lessons. And while I hadn't gotten my head around every way I'd messed up that night, I understood one thing very early. Phil was crying in my arms. He was begging me to listen to him. And my fifteen-year-old ears wouldn't. I wasn't hearing him. He was upset and I was telling him to calm down. He was crying and I was telling him to stop. All these supportive words, all trying to help my friend, and all the wrong moves. I wasn't listening. I was too busy trying to fix him. Tell him how he could do better. Be like me. All my smart, logical reasons not to feel.

"It's okay to be upset. Sydney was being really rude to you.

If she had a real problem, she should have articulated it. You're right to be bothered."

Phil looked up. Maybe a little surprised. "Yeah. Thank you."

"You were just buying popcorn. You should be allowed to buy popcorn without someone calling you out for something they're not even gonna talk about. Especially on the clock. It was unfair."

"Exactly!" Phil nodded. "Exactly."

He smiled up at me. Validated. Lighter. Like the frustration just needed to be talked out without my commentary or judgment. "I appreciate that, Jacks."

"Hey, whatever gets you to shut up during the trailers."

"Fuck you." He kissed my hand. "I mean it. I don't really… get that a lot. *Heard.* Thank you." Phil closed his eyes and burrowed into my arm. "I love you."

I rubbed his cheek with my non-buttery hand. "Don't wear that out." He smiled and kissed my knuckles. I nodded. "I love you back."

We settled into each other and watched our terrible movie.

Phil's phone had died sometime after Dr. Alan E. Gator fell into the radioactive bayou, but before the team of sexy bayou scientists found the entrance to his underwater laboratory. When we got home, he threw it on the kitchen charger and caught up with my dad over a game of backgammon. Phil had his old rituals with both of my parents and theirs had been just as warm a reunion. I stayed at the counter, helping Maman cook our dinner, happy to watch Stanley Pasternak remember his favorite opponent. I was useless to my father on that front as the game made no sense to me and my brain refused to absorb the rules. After a minute of silent thought, Phil picked up one of those puck circle chip things and made his moves. *Clack, clack, clack* and I watched a vein tense up on my father's bald dome.

"He thrashed me, Marion. The boy throttled me. What will become of us?"

Maman tsked and kissed his shiny head. "I'll send for my things. Farewell, my love."

Phil smiled up at them both and I could see the relief in his cheeks. I knew exactly what he was thinking at that table. He looked at me smiling and I heard his voice in my ear. *I'm back.*

Phil's phone chirped next to me. The power had returned and he had one percent. And a few email alerts. A notification from his bank app and twenty-three missed calls. Forty-three unread texts.

"Oh."

Then I heard the doorbell. It echoed through the hall, and Maman put her wine down. "It's family dinner, Jackson. Did you invite someone?"

I felt an odd tightness across my back. Like a charley horse stretching through my shoulders. Something. Something was off. Phil noticed me then. "Jacks?"

I didn't know my feeling. It felt expected though. Like some looming nerve over this perfect day. Lingering threads I'd been too happy to count.

I followed the echo down the hall and into the foyer. Maybe Augie had come to discuss treaty terms. Or Cameron had come to see my room or stab me in the ribs. Maybe Syd DeStefano wanted to explain her anger or Brynn Forester had connected some dots. Anthony Lewis was there to settle the score. Bolu Olowe wanted to finish our fire pit conversation. His warning that I might be stretching too thin. Something was coming. My guilt had come to collect.

I opened the door. I heard Maman behind me. "Oh! Ve-ronica! Welcome—"

Ronny DiSario punched me across the jaw. I saw pops of light and stumbled back. She didn't stop. She grabbed me by the hair and yanked me down to her level. *"WHAT DID YOU DO?!"*

She slapped my face hard, her grip ripping out hair. Pummeling me. Pushing me into the wall. ***"WHAT THE FUCK DID YOU DO?!"***

Then Phil was there and Ronny was sobbing. She must've been crying for hours and her face was a mess. "RON!"

Phil held her back. Maman was holding my face. Terrified but calm, checking and protecting me. She looked back at Ronny, just as concerned. "VERONICA."

I was crying too. I couldn't help it, I didn't know why. My face stung hot and Ronny just looked so fucking mad. I whispered to Maman. "I'm okay. I'm okay."

She left my side and went to Ronny. Ron pushed away her concern and wouldn't be touched. "NO. NO." She backed away from everyone. My dad had joined the room and Molly was watching from the bannister.

Ronny choked on a sob. "Who did you tell? What did you do?" Then she looked at Maman. Heartbroken. *"What did you f-fucking tell him?"*

My mother's face was stone. I didn't understand. "Ronny. Ron, I don't know what happened. What…"

Ronny held up her phone. Phil took it and read. He scrolled and scrolled. His eyes went dark. I wiped my face. "Phil?"

He just kept scrolling. Whatever it was, it wouldn't stop. Phil looked at me, confused. "Jackson…"

He looked away. Like his brain was flooding with all the

new things to fear. All the new problems the world had decided to give him. After his one nice day.

I took the phone from Phil. It was a Twitter account. New.
Following nobody. Only a few followers. Maybe a dozen
posts.

@TeenageD1rtbag

I was confused. "What's…"
I read the most recent posts.

@RonnySoSorry Love the parties, ur parents r always out of
town. R they trying to get away from each other or u?

@RonnySoSorry Is it true ur parents left you alone in that mansion for SIXTY-TWO days last year? So cool! #vibes #latch-
keyprincess

@RonnySoSorry Sorry about the divorce, girly. What finally
broke the camel's back? Ur moms new boyfriend or ur dads
pill addiction?

Ronny whimpered. *"They trusted you."* I looked up at her.
She was stuck in place, bawling in my foyer. *"W-who did you
tell? H-how do they know?"*

Maman hugged her tight and tried to calm her down.
Ronny broke down into her shoulder. I couldn't move. I just
looked at the phone. The posts.

@AntLewis buys cocaine from the caddies at the country club

@MateoWorldwide cheats on Dani T with half the soccer team

@Bolu22 cuts

My throat was disintegrating. Phil was holding my arm. "Jackson. What's happening?"

My list. My Excel. The facts I'd learned about my class. The DiSario family. The Basketbros. Leaked. Outed. Privileged information, things my classmates had confided in me, repackaged into something awful. Something mean. Secrets turned into attacks. Online for anyone to see. Out.

"I don't... I don't understand."

Who could have seen my list? When did I slip, what did I do? How could I have let this happen?

"*No.*" Phil covered his mouth. I looked at the phone. The first post. The first secret.

@MoorestownPoliceDepartment If ur looking for a Stop Sign, check the laundry room of Browning Apartments. Some dirtbag Junior's got sticky fingers...

#GarbageGate

PHIL

—

TRACK TWO

I Write Sins Not Tragedies

It might surprise one to hear, but I had actually never been inside a police station before. Got to say, I'm not impressed.

Officer Olowe looked over the printouts on his desk. All the anonymous posts. One for Ant. One for Matty. A few for Ronny. One for Bolu. People we'd involved. People we'd used in our plan. All of our consequences.

"I don't envy you kids. When we were in high school, the gossip stuck to bathroom walls. Not so public."

Mom sipped her third cup of old coffee that afternoon. "I'm sure your number got Sharpied on a couple stalls back in the day, Jed. *For a good time call.*"

Officer Olowe smirked at my mom. Mom knew Officer O from AA and they were both very apologetic that the other had to be here today. The man was just doing his job. Getting some answers. Closing the case.

He sifted through the printouts. "Tell you the truth, the department's a little more focused on your classmate buying coke at the country club. Allegedly. Honestly, we'd put the garbage

truck incident to bed. No one got hurt, the driver got a vacation, and both vehicles were nicely insured. Frankly, I hadn't
thought about it in weeks." His finger tapped on the papers.
The post. The tip. "Until we found a stop sign under a wash-
ing machine in the Browning Apartments laundry room. A
little harder to forget."

I was digging into the skin around my thumbnail. It was
a long day of waiting in that office and the lack of fresh air
was drying me out. I felt the officer's eyes on me.

"Someone put that sign there, Mr. Reyno. Someone's got
to answer for it. We're going to need a name, son."

It wasn't hard to get my cuticle to bleed. I wondered how
deep I could go if I kept focusing. Mom elbowed me. "Look
at him."

I almost listened. My eyes stopped on his desk. The printouts. "Your son's in there." I finally met Officer Olowe's eyes.
"Bolu did nothing wrong and now everyone knows something they have no business knowing. He is a good guy, he
doesn't fucking deserve—"

"Son."

I sat up. "Someone is RUINING people's lives. Why are
y'all not talking about THAT?"

Mom grabbed my wrist. *"Philip."*

I sank back into my seat. Officer O wasn't rattled. I was
just some punk kid. He must've seen a hundred of me a week.
But he picked up one printout. It wasn't rattling him. But I
knew it hurt him.

"Bolu is a strong boy. We raised him right. It'll take more
than some words on the internet to get to him." He showed
me Bolu's post. His secret. **@Bolu22 cuts.** "This isn't real.
Bolu knows that. These are pixels in your pocket. Some face
behind a keyboard. Comments on the internet are not real
life, Mr. Reyno. These words don't matter."

He put the paper down and I wanted to spit. Because adults love saying shit like that. They tell you words don't matter. Words shouldn't hurt you. When Cam Army spends all autumn filling your inbox with hate and bile and death threats, simply turn off your phone. When Anthony Lewis scribbles *FAGGOT* in your library copy of *Hatchet*, you shouldn't let it hurt you. You simply shouldn't give him the power. But when you fight back, when you call Ant that word, suddenly you're giving in to hate. You're a red flag, you're too far gone. Suddenly, that word matters again because some adult decided it should.

You couldn't win. You were never meant to.

"Baby. They need to know if you stole the sign." Mom looked at Officer Olowe. "Jed, it's going to be fine, right? Kids steal signs. I had a One Way pointing at my toilet all sophomore year. I mean, we're not talking, like, prison sentences here, right?"

He considered his answer. For a little longer than we liked. Mom's hand on me got tighter. "Jed. It was a fucking stop sign. It's harmless. He's... He's fucking harmless, Jed."

Her voice was getting just as tighter. Officer Olowe looked at me. "It caused a wreck. There are rules. It could be a fine. It could be...time away. I can't give you a concrete answer today. What happens next isn't up to me, Angela."

"Jed—"

"I didn't steal it." I couldn't make my mom cry there. I couldn't add that to the list. "There. I said it. That's all I have to say here. Right?" I sat up in my chair and pointed at the printouts. "'Cause if these are *just words*, then there's nothing else keeping me here, right? You just have to take my word today. Right? If these don't matter?"

"Philip. We found the sign in your building's laundry room."

"That's…circum-whatever. Circumstancey."

"Circumstantial?"

"That. Anyone could've put it there, anyone could've stole it."

"Anyone?" Officer Olowe nodded at us. Slow. He finally asked the question he'd been walking us toward all afternoon. "Could Mateo Silva have stolen the stop sign?"

The question sat. I let it.

Olowe pulled another printout from the stack and read. *"Some dirtbag junior has sticky fingers."* He looked back at me. "You're not the only junior in Moorestown High School who lives in Browning Apartments."

It took me a moment to realize what was being put in the air. The only post not to name names. The only one that could condemn two. Mateo Silva or Philip Reyno. Two terribly similar boys with terribly similar apartments with terribly similar mothers. Mean boys. Kids who don't make it easy. Difficult and hard to root for and just as likely to steal a stop sign.

Mom met my eyes. "Phil? Did Mateo…"

I cut her off with a look. I wouldn't let them go down that road. I wouldn't do that to Matty. Matty did nothing wrong.

I turned to Officer O. *"Circumstantial."*

I wouldn't budge. I would give him nothing. And I saw where Bolu got those serious looks. But Officer O nodded. "We'll be in contact."

It took two showers to get the police station stink off me and an hour of skating to get out my nerves. Before the sun could set, I looped back to my block and headed for my workshop. I kept my head down passing the apartments and avoided some looks from the old lesbians in 2C. They stopped liking me after I replaced Charmaine's bed with my drum set and their passing whispers used to make me feel like a pariah in the stairwell. But they weren't whispering anymore. None of my usual critics in the building were. It was just looks now. Unspoken judgment. Silent hate. Because what was left to whisper?

I hopped the fence and waded through the weeds. I didn't have any projects to work on, but I'd figure something out. My hands just needed something to do. I only got halfway to my storage unit before I smelled a familiar odor. I slowed my pace and found my neighbor's grate open. Smoke clouds wafting into the air. I zipped up my hoodie and walked over to Matty's unit. His usual kiddie pool was deflated and he was sitting in a corner. His focus was on his shoes and he blew smoke through his nose. I waited for him to notice me. He didn't.

"...It's cold out."

Matty didn't budge at my banal offer. He just hit his bowl again. "Inside's worse."

He blew the smoke and put the bowl on the ground. Just stayed on his shoes. I stepped into the unit. "They talk to you yet? My mom's good with Bolu's dad. He told her they barely care. It might not... He said it could be okay. Everything."

Matty wouldn't look at me. "There are rules."

I waited for more. He wasn't going to give me any. "Officer O said kids break rules like this all the time. Teenager bullshit's worked into their budget. No one got hurt and... They don't even know what'll happen yet."

Matty looked at me. His eyes were thick and glassy from the bowl. "There are *rules*, Reyno. I don't fuck with you. You don't fuck with me. We get through their shit, we get through this shit, and we go our separate ways. We had a fucking rule. Did you not get that?"

"Matty."

"I should kill you." He shook his head. "I...should *fucking* kill you."

His hands stayed on his knees. He was calm and he kept

his voice low. "My life might be over. I had no plans for it. I expected *nothing*. And all that might be fucking done. Because you couldn't keep your shit in line. 'Cause you couldn't leave our *home* out of it. 'Cause you don't know the rules."

"I'm sor—"

In a pop, his heel cracked into the wall of his unit. The metal dented and I saw it was littered with them. He'd been out there a while. He stared at the dents for a long time. "How's Ang?"

I swallowed and nodded. "Upset. It's hard for her to talk about for too long. She's, uh... She had a hard year. How's Dani?"

Matty lit up the bowl again. "We're off."

"Damn. Off-again?"

"No. Off."

I sighed. Shit. "Sorry, man. Your mom feeling better? She hasn't been over in a bit."

Matty finished his hit and emptied the dead junk out on the ground. "She's feeling great. We're talking a lot lately."

"Oh. I mean...that's good. Talking's good."

Matty nodded at his dents in the wall. "A lot to talk about. Where I'll go. How I'll get there. What I can't take with me." His voice was drifting. Feeling the smoke. Getting quiet. "But she said she'd help me pack. Which was very kind."

"Matty."

"Leave me alone." The quiet was getting tight. "Leave me alone, Phil."

I backed away. I'd done enough. "I'm gonna make it alright, okay?"

He didn't look at me. I'd said enough. I left Matty to himself and walked out into the weeds.

JACKSON

—

TRACK THREE

Where Have All the Cowboys Gone?

The Christmas wreath on their door was the size of a car tire so it was hard to find the right place to knock. Eventually, the door opened and a tall beanpole squinted down at me. The lanky man had on a durag, piercings up his ears, and a crop top that screamed **SURE**. I stared at his very hairy belly button for a moment then looked up. "Kenny? Ikenna? Are you Ikenna Olowe?"

He just blinked. His head poked out and he looked up and down the hallway. "Pretty lonely for a caroler. Pretty early too."

"Oh. I'm not a caroler."

"Mmm. Clearly a joke."

"Oh. Ha-ha." I wiggled the gift basket in my arms. Well, regift basket. Another end of the year plea from one of my dad's undergrad students to reconsider their failing grade. "I brought muffins. They're from the city, this place by Rittenhouse."

Ikenna looked over each and every bribe muffin with an understandable distrust. I soldiered on.

"Bolu wasn't at student council this morning. I went to his place after school and I talked to your dad and I don't know how he feels about muffins, but he did *not* want to talk to me or about Bolu but I figured you might be open to... I thought you might help me talk to him? If he's... If Bolu is trying to talk to anyone right now? I know he's gotta be real upset with everything going on, but if I could just talk—"

"Did you post that shit about him?" Ikenna stepped out of his door. Stood up straighter. I could feel all of his height then and I wasn't sure how my muffins would fare as a shield. "You tell the school about his shit?"

I shook my head. "No. No. I just... I just wanted to talk to him. He won't answer his phone. I wanted to see if he was alright." I swallowed. "If he was safe. If he had someone to talk to."

Ikenna gave me another few moments of silent staring. Then he snatched my muffins from me. He hugged the giant carb basket and nodded. "And who are you?"

"Jackson. Jackson Pasternak. I'm Bolu's class president."

"Ah. So, you're here on official business, then."

"Sure. If you like."

Ikenna reassessed me then hollered behind him. "AY, BOOBY! THE PRESIDENT'S HERE FOR YOU!"

He walked inside and left the door open for me. I politely closed it after us and followed Ikenna into his apartment. A shirtless bear of a man was on the living room couch watching the news and rubbing his stomach. He gave me a once-over. "The fuck are you wearing?"

I looked down at my costume. My sixties-era plaid suit

was feeling particularly poorly tailored. "I came straight from school. Didn't have time to… The musical opens tonight."

The bear nodded. "Mmm. *Bye Bye Birdie?*"

"*Hairspray.*"

"Ew."

Ikenna tossed the man a muffin and slapped his bald head. "He's Bolu's. Play nice."

Ikenna sat on the couch arm and the men shared a muffin over the news. I looked over Ikenna's apartment while I waited for Bolu. A lot of wall art. Very African. Photos of the two men hung around the space. Some in Philly. Some around the world. Big smiles and held hands. I turned back and Ikenna was rubbing the man's head. With love. It was their apartment. I'd never seen anything like it. Like them.

Ikenna nodded down the hall. "He'd be out by now if he wanted to. You'll have to go in. Last door on the left."

"Oh. Just…go in?"

"If you're worried he's gonna throw you out, you shouldn't have come in the first place."

"Right. Fair."

Ikenna tossed me a muffin. "Try getting him to eat. *Mr. President.*"

I nodded and headed down the hall. Last door on the left. I opened it slow but no one was slamming it back on me so I just walked in. The guest room was lived-in but still very Bolu. Tidy and professional, but still very cool. He must stay there often.

Then I noticed the Legos. The bedroom was all mood lighting and chill incense, very grown-up, but his shelves were full of Legos. Lego cars and castles. Colorful scenes of pirates and aliens, all made of little bricks. Dozens of builds. Thousands of Legos.

Bolu sat at a desk, face-deep in his newest build. His eyes were laser focused on the half-constructed cowboy saloon in front of him. "I'd rather be left alone, Jackson. Just to cut this off before you start. You can go."

I cleared my throat. "Uh…hey, Bolu." His hands never stopped moving. He just adjusted his lamp and got to work on a water tower behind the saloon. I stayed at his door. "I just… I wanted to check in. You weren't answering your phone."

"Mmm. So, you're going to still try talking. One sec." Bolu finished snapping the doors onto the saloon and sat up straight. Wheeled around. He looked odd. Like he'd both been awake for days but never left his bed. Rested but restless. An odd contradiction. He took off his glasses. "I am currently in day eleven of a major depressive episode. I know my pattern very well, this is not new to me, and I know how this conversation will go. I am not going to be helpful to talk to. I will not be able to make you feel better. I do not have anything for you."

"I don't want anything from you, Bolu, I wanted to—"

"There is not a part in this where you should speak." I nodded. Bolu continued. Very steady. Very calm. Like he'd given this spiel a thousand times. Like he was telling me how to cook a turkey. "I've had a diagnosis since I was thirteen. I had a very hard time in middle school and after one poor decision, I had to be hospitalized. I've been accepting help and figuring out medication ever since, but I can still get pushed. My father and my stepmother are not good at handling me when I get pushed so I stay with my brother and his partner, I'm assuming you met them. Three people at our school know about any of this and none of them are students so I'd like to know who of those three told you." I went still. He nodded my way. "*Now* you can speak."

I held the muffin in my hand. I didn't know what to do

with Bolu's invitation. "You talk about it really calmly. All your...your stuff."

"I used to cut myself and I almost died twice. It's not news to me, Jackson, I've been in this for years." His eyes stayed on me. "And it's not news to you. You knew. How?"

I didn't know how to answer him. Because I never liked to talk about that. The head stuff. The things that could go wrong. The things that might be broken. Never out loud. Never with my parents. Never with the therapists. Not even with Phil. I kept those conversations between me and my list. But I hadn't come there to lie to Bolu. I had come to make things right.

My voice was quiet. "Mrs. McHale. The old guidance counselor. Last March. I was returning a rolling cart to the teachers' lounge and I stopped for some coffee and she was talking to Mrs. Morgan back at the tables. You'd been missing school and Morgan was trying to get some homework sent to you and Mrs. McHale just..." I shook my head. "I didn't even need to eavesdrop. She always talked too loud. She didn't care."

Bolu's face was silent. I couldn't look at him. "I didn't write the post, Bolu. I would never do that. This is your business, it has nothing to do with us."

"Don't come here dressed like that and lie to me."

"I would never do this to you, Bolu—"

"But it's still your fault. Isn't it?" He shook his head. "You got that same look on your face, Pasternak. Same look you got that night. Dodgeball. You knew something was about to happen to Cameron Ellis. It wasn't your fault, but it was. You didn't make the post but you knew. You look just as fucking guilty."

"You're right."

"I'm aware."

I stopped trying to sound calm. I needed him to understand. "Phil Reyno." I needed to be understood. "Cameron ruined Phil's life, Bolu, and Phil is... He's my friend. He's been my best friend since the fifth grade. I know people don't get that, but he is. And Phil asked for my help and we came up with this plan. We were going to take Cameron down. Not let him get away with everything he's done. But someone..."

I took a few steps closer. "Someone found my list. I don't know how or who, but somebody found my list and they found out your secret and they posted it on that fucking account."

"Your list?"

"It's...like a journal. I don't know why I do it, I just... I like having things written down. What I know. It helps me keep the important stuff in mind. So, next time I get annoyed that Calli Padalecki's talking my ear off in the lunch line, I remember the time she opened up to me about her eating disorder. Why a school cafeteria might make her nervous. Why she might need to distract herself with small talk. It was just a way for me to remember. Be mindful. Be better."

I took a breath. "Because it's really hard for me sometimes. I don't know why. I don't understand it. It's really hard for me to remember that I'm here, sometimes. That what I do here matters. Who I meet. What I say. And I do so much to remind myself. I help so many people and I'm a part of so many things and I make such a great argument for myself. *Jackson Pasternak exists.* He must. Look at everything he does."

Bolu was sitting up. Watching me curiously. "It's a contradiction. Doing so much. Feeling so far from it."

"Yeah. A contradiction. An inconsistency."

Bolu nodded. He watched me for a very long time. He

folded up his glasses and put them with his Legos. "The night I tried to stop... The night I had to go to the hospital... I couldn't handle my contradictions." He turned back to me. "I was very curious about myself as a kid. And the more I learned, the less I made sense. Every time I'd figure something new out about myself, another fact would call it into question. I loved my parents and my brother, but they didn't love each other. I loved basketball, but the pressure made me miserable. I loved God, but I couldn't stop sinning. The things I loved were at war with themselves. And I couldn't understand them."

Bolu inspected my face. "Have you ever loved something that you don't understand?" I swallowed. And I nodded.

Bolu stayed on me for a moment. Thinking something over. He turned back to his Legos and put his glasses back on. "Was Veronica DiSario a part of your plan?"

"She was. But whatever you two had going on wasn't part of it. Honest."

Bolu stuck a little cowboy on his Lego horse. "They hit her worse. Whoever's behind it. That isn't right."

I nodded. Bolu seemed to be getting back in his workflow. It wouldn't be right of me to try pulling him out of it again. That was his process. That was how Bolu processed.

I left the muffin on his nightstand. "I'm going to fix this, Bolu. We're working on it. I won't ask you to trust me but... I just wanted you to know. And when you come back, you can talk to me. If you still... If you think you might want that."

I walked for his door. Bolu finished the roof of his saloon and clicked it into place. "So careful, it makes you careless. Inconsistencies." I stayed in his doorway. His fingers moved around the set, making sure everything was where it should be. "I guess you would have a UPenn sticker on your laptop."

"Huh?" I didn't understand his point. Or his accuracy. "I do. How...how do you know that?"

He shrugged. "I was in the rec room for most of All-Night Dodgeball. But I thought about taking a nap." Bolu clicked the gun into a bank robber figure. The finishing touch. "And Doug Parson had your laptop."

I froze. Doug. Doug was sleeping on a cot in the nap room. That night was a blur, but I'd hidden my backpack under him, I left it there for hours. *Doug?*

Bolu sat back in his chair and admired his new Western scene. A saloon full of cowboys. A bedroom full of Legos. Shelves full of episodes. He didn't turn around. "You're the only person who's come to see me."

Bolu didn't say anything more.

PHIL

———

TRACK FOUR
I'm Not Okay (I Promise)

I wiped some steam off the bathroom mirror and noticed a hickey on my neck.

"C'mon, man."

Jackson had a problem with biting. He could never just kiss my neck. Like a dog on a bone, he couldn't help it.

I got dressed for my night out then plucked a frosty coin from my freezer. The copper stung my neck and I wondered what the hickied youths of the future would do when coins become obsolete. Maybe switch to spoons.

"What are you doing?" Mom was on the living room couch, crocheting her third scarf that week. She'd been crocheting a lot this month which told me she was trying to live that sober lifestyle. I'm sure the investigation into my most recent fuck-up had only fueled her productivity.

I took the penny off my neck and showed off my hickey. "Burnt myself with a curling iron." Mom gave the joke a bare minimum grin and kept on her scarf. "Ronny's picking me up soon. Gonna get dinner in the city first."

"Good idea. Chinatown?"

"We're thinking something on South Street."

"Mmm." She shook her head. Threading and looping. "I shouldn't… I shouldn't let you go out, right? I think other moms wouldn't let you out right now, huh?"

"Mom."

"Better moms."

"Mom, c'mon."

She wiped her eye, but was determined to finish her loop. "Hey, can you take the trash out?"

The last two weeks, anytime we got close to talking about the constant problem I've been to our lives, Mom plucked an undone chore out of the air to get us away from it. To stop whatever talk I tried to start with her. Stay fun. Because Angela was a cool mom. Everyone who met her told me I should feel lucky. We didn't have much, but at least I got a cool mom. Never told me to be home on time. Never came down on us too hard. Never had the big conversations.

"Mom…"

She wiped her cheek. "Take the trash out, baby. It stinks."

I stayed by the fridge. Holding my penny. Freezing my fingers. "Can we talk about it?"

Mom's eyes stayed glued on her handiwork. "What do you want to talk about?"

"Mom."

"What, you wanna admit it? You wanna tell me you flipped a fucking garbage truck? Covered the lawn in shit for weeks, you wanna talk that out? You got us called into the police station, you got the whole block looking at us funny, and I…" She laughed. There were tears in the chuckle. "I still want you to go out tonight. I still just want you to have a fun night.

I'm… I'm doing this wrong, Philly. I'm doing this real backward. Maybe we should talk about that."

I looked away. I guess I didn't know how to have a real conversation either.

Mom sniffed. "Put on a jacket. Trash chute's still busted."

That was that. Maybe it was for the best. Ronny would be coming any minute and I didn't need her seeing my place. I threw on my jacket, ignoring the newest hole in the armpit, and pulled the trash out of the can. Something with cheese or fish had rotted a week ago and the smell made me want to hurl. I tied it off and reached for the door.

"PHIL—"

Before I could unlock the deadbolt, my boots were wet. My jeans, my socks, my shitty old jacket. Soaked. Rank. Covered in garbage. I just held up the torn, empty bag. Frozen. Like some reeking, dripping asshole.

Mom had her hands on her mouth. "Philly…"

I smelled like shit. I smelled like my front lawn. Garbage. No matter what I did. What I tried. *Garbage.* Everywhere. Every time.

I didn't want to get garbage juice on my face so I just let the sobbing go wild. *"I stole the f-fucking sign."* I fell against the wall and sat in the mess. Why not? I was already covered in it. *"I'm a fucking p-piece of shit."*

"Jesus! Phil." Mom dropped her scarf and her needles and knelt right down in front of me. *"Hey."*

"I'm sorry. I'm so sorry, M-Mom."

Her jeans were getting soaked in what I had to assume was last Tuesday's curry. She held my face and wiped the tears for me with cleaner hands.

I coughed up a sob. *"I'm s-sorry I fuck up. I'm sorry I keep fuck-*

ing up. You don't deserve that. I know shit is really hard for you and I keep making it harder and I'm so fucking sorry, Mom, I'm so—"

She held my head to hers and wiped some wet coffee grounds off my shirt. "Hey. Shut up." Mom kissed my cheek hard. "You are the best kid I know. And I hate kids. I fucking hate children, you're the only one I've ever liked. You're the list."

I wiped snot off my face, still sobbing. *"W-What about Charmaine?"*

"Fuck Charmaine, she's not crying on me."

I choked on a laugh. *"I don't w-wanna l-laugh right now, Mom, s-stop."*

She hugged me close and rubbed my back. "Come on. We'll be serious on the couch. Take your clothes off."

Mom helped me up and out of my ruined outfit. We dumped the jacket and jeans in the sink and Mom guided my sniffling, tighty-whitied ass to the cushions. She sat me down and pushed my hair back. I sniffed. "I j-just… I don't want you to think you're a bad mom. You're not a bad mom. I'm just a bad p-person."

"What? You're not a bad person, baby. Not the easiest son, but that doesn't mean shit about you as a person." She cleaned my face and held it. "I wish I was a better mom."

"No."

"No, I mean it. I wish I was harder on you, Phil. I wish I knew how to do that for you. The parent stuff. The tough stuff. My mom was tough on me and I was a perfect kid. I never stole a stop sign. I never got called into the police. I never keyed my teacher's car or set fires in chemistry. I never even got detention."

She held my hand. "And I never liked her. I never talk to her anymore. I never think about her anymore. And I want you to think about me. You and Charm. I want you to like me. I want you to have fun in the city with your friends. I mean, fuck, kid. The cops are ready to arrest my son and I just want him to have a nice night. Because I want you to have a better time than I did. And 'cause I've got no clue. I don't have a fucking clue how to be your parent."

I calmed down. Let her hands and her scarf warm me back up. "That's not true, Mom."

"Well, I'm not exactly Parent of the Year."

"No, you weren't a perfect kid."

"I was pretty close."

"You got pregnant at seventeen, Mom. And Gammy's a fucking dick."

My mom had, in her words, a "fuck-ugly" laugh. The unattractive child of a wheeze and a cackle. Charmaine said it looked like Mom was barfing up air anytime we'd caught her off guard with something. "Fuck you!"

Mom wiped her face and hugged me again. I was starting to get her shirt wet, but I hugged her back. She touched my face. "You're my little man now, Philly. You're gonna make a great one. I'm just sorry you had to get there on your own sometimes. Fuck knows your parents weren't helpful."

I shook my head. "You did help me, Mom. You do. You do enough."

"Yeah?"

"Yeah. You got in the garbage with me."

I patted her gross, stained knee and we laughed. After a quick second shower and a change of clothes, I helped Mom clean up the kitchen just in time for my ride. Mom handed me a scarf to give to Ronny and told me to say hi to my father for her. I said I would but made a rule at age twelve to never mention my mom in front of Chuck Reyno again. I didn't need to hear his feedback and had grown tired of being their voicemail.

Ronny drove this vintage lavender Mustang convertible and the top refused to stay up. I yelled over the freezing wind whipping past us on the Ben Franklin Bridge. "YOU'RE GONNA HAVE TO TALK TO JACKSON EVENTUALLY!"

Ronny rolled her eyes and our windows up. It barely helped but the glass slightly shielded our ears from the wind. If we slumped.

"Ron, you're gonna have to forgive Jacks eventually. We need to make a plan. Hit Doug and Cameron back."

"No. Forgiving Jackson Pasternak is your character flaw. I can get revenge on my own."

"*Ronny.*"

"*Phil.*"

It had only taken Ronny two minutes of elimination to realize Jackson must have had his hand in the posts. Who else could know all of that about our classmates? Who else talked about everything with his mom, the therapist? Who else could have a private knowledge about the DiSario home and who else was spared a post of his own?

Ronny merged lanes. "Doug found the list. Cameron posted the list. But Jackson MADE the list, Phil. He's the reason my very personal shit is running around school. AGAIN. I don't need to split hairs here, I am peachy keen cutting all three boys loose."

"Jackson didn't mean for any of this to happen, Ron. He's mortified, man."

"Then he shouldn't have recorded my shit! Or my mom's shit! Or my fucking…" Ronny shoved her sunglasses up. Calmed down a bit. "No one else knew about my dad. No one in school, not Cameron, no one knew. Just family. And Marion fucking Pasternak."

Ronny flipped off a passing minivan. "My dad doesn't have a *pill addiction*. Okay?"

"Okay."

"He had a problem. Once. For one part of his life. He's doing a lot better now and I'm really fucking proud of him, okay? It's been years."

"Okay, Ron."

"But because my mom's best friend can't keep her mouth shut, and your best friend can't keep his mouth shut, now all my family's worst shit is out there. For anyone."

Ronny merged into the exit lane. We were entering Philly. "You don't think it's fucked? Jackson's list? You really don't think it's wildly fucking creepy?"

I kept my eyes on the skyline. Because I guess I hadn't made up my mind. Jackson's always had his things. His quirks. They annoyed me and fascinated me and they made him who he was. I don't know if he ever would've broken through to me, all the times Jackson's broken through to me, without his unique *Jackson* approaches. But the list had been hard for me. Cataloguing secrets. Needing a cheat sheet to your life. I wasn't sure I understood that. I didn't have an answer for Ron.

After some cheesesteaks from Jim's, we bopped around the music stores and venues on South Street. Once we got close to our ticket time, we headed over to the South Street Comedy Club and showed a lady out front with a clipboard our tickets.

"And who are you here to see?"

"Chuck Reyno. He's a regular."

"I'm aware. He already started."

I pulled out my ticket. "I thought it started at eight."

"New kid bailed. Chuck wanted to test some new shit, went on early."

I groaned. It was very much like my father to sop up all the extra time he could on stage.

The lady looked us over, a little wary. "Chuck's a bit... Do you have your IDs?"

I sighed. "He's my dad."

The wary look on her face moved into something a little more pitiful. "Oh. Yes. The famous *Philip*."

I just blinked. Ronny nudged me. "Wooow. Philly, have you been famous this whole time and not told me?"

I looked up the street and wondered if I had another cheese-steak in me. Or maybe a passing police horse could trample me.

The clipboard woman laughed. "He talks about you in his set. A lot. Always something new anytime he's in town."

"Joy."

Ronny followed me inside and we found some seats toward the side. The room was half-filled, not a great showing but not his worst, and Chuck didn't see us walk in. He was too busy doing crowd work with a man in the front row.

"Okay, *Boston*. Go Sox, woot woot. I played a college up in Boston two months ago. Student show, some fundraiser or whatever. Lady who books me comes up to me before the show with a *list*. And I'm being conservative when I say *list*. And I'm being *very* conservative when I say *lady*. This blue-haired monster hands me the Dead Sea Scrolls and tells me it's a list of all the words I'm not allowed to say in my act."

Chuck looked up at the long, invisible list in front of him. Squinted his eyes at the top, all the way at the ceiling. "No *pussy*. Sounds like me in college."

Some laughs. Ronny shrugged to me. *Not terrible*.

Chuck moved down the list. "No *cunt*. What? We can't say fucking *cunt* anymore? I thought those feminist college girls loved cunt. I mean, until graduation."

I rolled my eyes. Ronny gave it a five out of ten.

Chuck kept scrolling. "No *retard*. But how's my pop supposed to find me in the airport? No *spaz*. Not even a hot spring. No *lame*, no *tone-deaf*, no *are you fucking blind?* Apparently, I was too able-bodied for those words which was ironic 'cause this college bitch was crippling me. Oh, right, no *cripple*."

Half the audience was checked out, the other half was already drunk. People were either silently nodding or drunkenly hooting. Philly on a Thursday. But my dad always had stage presence. I'd grown up watching him do a lot worse with a lot less in that very room. He knew how to sell his bullshit.

"No *faggot*."

I flinched. Someone grumbled in the audience. Chuck waved it away. "Hey, I can say *fag*, my son thinks he's gay."

I went cold. Both halves of the audience let themselves laugh. He'd won them back. But Ronny stopped smiling. Chuck settled into his foothold. "Kids these days are sunburnt. They think they want the heat and just end up fucking sensitive. I don't get it. I mean, it's not all of them. Like, I raised my kids on the right side. Ten-I-See all the way, I'll tell you what. Charmaine and Philly, my backwoods babies. You wanna burn the pussy out of two young'uns, let'm watch their favorite Dairy Queen burn to the ground 'cause Tweaker Tammy from the post office cooked herself up a meth lab in the basement. My kids know what to complain about."

Ronny held my hand. I was staring bullets into the trash onstage.

"Their mama thinks I raised them too rough. But the ol'

ex-wife's always been a bit of a princess. Even back in high school, Angie liked to pretend she didn't love running off with me to the bleachers. One of those stick-up-my-ass or a dick-up-my-ass kind of good girls. *Bubbles*, I used to call'm. Floating above it all, one prick away from popping. It's like they're begging us to be the pricks."

I tasted blood in my mouth. Hate. My stomach was filling with it. Had he stolen that from me? Or had I learned it from him?

Chuck chuckled over his beer. "My kids aren't bubbles. Nah. I raised my kids right. I raised them to know what mattered. How to fight. How to survive." He shrugged. "But Princess Angie wound up being a wine drunk so I guess they were gonna learn one way or another."

I thought my tooth had cracked. I wanted to spit its shards onto the stage. I wanted to break his bottle over his fucking head. I wanted to ruin my father for everything he put in me. All of this useless hate.

"BOO!" Ronny was standing above me, cupping her hands. **"YOU'RE A FUCKING HACK! BOOOOOOO!"**

Oh, shit. Everyone was looking at us. Drunks telling her to shut up. Staff moving to reach us. I grabbed her jeans. *"RONNY."*

Chuck squinted through his spotlight. "Sorry, folks. Must be a Bubble."

Ronny never stopped booing. Her face was back to furious. The fury I'd seen during a fight outside the principal's office. At Jackson in his foyer. At the graffiti on her locker and the teachers who'd treat her like she's trash. Everything our town had thrown at her, every adult who'd let her down, she was throwing it all back at my dad.

"YOUR KIDS FUCKING HATE YOU, YOU SAD MAN! GET OFF THE FUCKING STAGE!"

I was up and pulling her then. We moved through our aisle and Ronny flipped off the booing audience. Chuck smiled the whole time, tickled he'd gotten the desired reaction from my generation. But stopped when he noticed me.

"Wait, what the hell? Philip?" I stopped in the aisle. A bouncer was grabbing my arm, but my eyes were back on my dad's. He was very confused. "What... Guys, lay off him. Phil, what the fuck?" He smiled for the audience, finally thrown. "Sorry, ladies and gentlemen, my *son* brought a heckler with him tonight. Sort of late on the Father's Day present, kiddo."

The booing turned to amusement. The bouncer let me go and Ronny was trying to get us out of there. But I stayed. Chuck smiled.

"What's that face, Philip? Not agreeing with the set?" He looked at his audience. Thrilled with his new material. "My boy Phil here might be going to prison. Yeah. *That* kind of kid. Rumor has it, the little rascal stole a stop sign. Not too big, every kid does it, every town's got a Phil. My town had Hunter Shipley. Used to throw old roadkill off the overpass, caused a couple wrecks."

Chuck paced around the set, finding some natural flow in his ad-libbing. Or maybe this was prewritten. Like the Boston student bit. His crowd work seemed natural, like he'd gotten some random suggestion that launched him into this off-the-cuff story about cancel culture on college campuses. But the man in the front row could've said any city. That story didn't happen in Boston. That story didn't happen at all. It was invented to fit his joke format. His narrative. His excuse to say those words on stage for the sake of "topical commentary."

"Everyone always said Hunter Shipley was the kind of boy who'd end up dead. Boys like that often did our neck of the woods. But I always hoped he'd pull out of it. Hunter was fun. Had a real mouth on him, kinda like my boy. You always hope they'll grow out of it. Get with the program. Learn the right rules to break."

Chuck shrugged at me from across the half-packed room. "But Hunter drove a Hummer into a McDonalds going eighty. We call that a Double Quarter Pounder down South."

The audience laughed. Chuck grinned at his fans. And it confirmed for me that he'd written the whole thing. Nothing from the heart for Chuck Reyno. He probably heard that story or remembered that boy or made it up completely and scribbled it all down in his notepad. All bullshit. He just needed to get it down. All these stories, all these jokes, everything in his life, repackaged and catalogued. Nothing was ever for him. Or us. And I thought of Jackson's list. His Excel. A similar need to observe. A detached relationship to your life.

Chuck nodded back to my seat. "Now, how 'bout you learn a thing or two from funny, dead Hunter and enjoy the show, Phil. Take a joke. Grow out of it. Grow up."

I stayed still. Because it wasn't the same. Jackson's list was supposed to be for him. Just his. Something to help him make sense of his life, something he needed just for himself. It was never meant to be taken from him. It was never meant for the world. But Chuck's notepad was for the world. My family was just another joke to him. I was his best fucking joke.

I took a step forward. "You didn't raise us. Our mother raised us. Charmaine hasn't talked to you in years." Chuck's smile dropped. I shook my head. "I get it now."

The crowd was quiet. Uncomfortable. It wouldn't be an easy one to win back. Chuck had no comeback and I let Ronny lead me out. We walked across the street in silence. She'd been worried about street parking, but it turned out we wouldn't need to feed the meter again. We didn't even stay the full quarter.

Ronny hopped over her car door and into the seat. I opened mine and put my scarf back on. We sat in silence a little while longer. I wiped my nose. "Can we at least turn the heat on?"

"Please, don't be mad at me." Ronny looked at me, scarf also tightened. "I just… Phil, fuck your dad. Like, what the fuck was that?"

I nodded. "I know. I warned you."

"You said *racy*. You didn't say *racist*."

"Hey, he didn't get to those jokes. Yet." I crossed my arms and tried getting warm. "It's not the first time he's been booed. He takes it as a badge of honor."

"Oh. Well, whoops. Shoulda thrown my two-drink minimum at him, then."

"He'd call that a standing ovation."

Ronny turned on the car and cranked up the heat. It did nearly nothing with the top stuck down but it was nice to hold my hands on the vents. Once it was warm enough, Ronny put a hand on mine. "I'm glad I saw that though. Very illuminating."

"What, you see where I get it from now or something?"

"No. You're a lot funnier than Chuck."

I looked back at Ronny. I would never admit it, but that meant a great deal to me. Ronny smiled, her nose getting red. "It was nice seeing you stand up for yourself."

I snorted. "What? I give fuckers shit all the time."

"C'mon. We were trying to kill each other for most of

the year, Phil, and I saw you run away a hundred times. One snappy comeback then you were gone. Always one and done. You'd drop your little firecracker then run from your damage."

She leaned back in her seat. "You'd say the worst thing you could possibly think of, just so I wouldn't try and actually talk to you. Tell you how much you and Cameron hurt me. Ask you to say you're sorry. You'd rather your damage speak for itself. It's why you needed this giant revenge plot to even consider speaking to Jackson again."

I leaned back in my seat and listened. Still holding hands. Keeping warm.

"It's why you never walked into the Orchard, rang Cameron's doorbell, and just told him that he really fucking hurt you. No, you'd rather begin a criminal enterprise. Methodically plot out the demises of his friend group and ruin his life from behind a curtain. Never have to stand in the damage. Never have to have the talks."

Ronny nodded back to the comedy club. "So. It was nice seeing you do that. Stand up. Stand by it. I was proud."

"Proud?"

"I've grown quite fond of you in my old age, Philip. You are a very hard person to get to know." She kissed my hand. "But I'm glad I stuck it out."

I smiled. Squeezed Ronny's hand. Ronny DiSario. Somehow, a friend. Maybe my best. My best platonic friend, at least.

My best straight friend scoffed at my neck. "Is that a fucking *hickey*?"

"Alright, can we go?"

"Are you fucking *twelve*?"

"DRIVE YOUR CAR, VERONICA."

I didn't ask Ronny to drive me to his house. She probably wouldn't have if I did. But it was a short enough distance from her place and I'd gotten used to the cold. On my walk across the Orchard, I passed a shiny, pristine stop sign and I thought about what Ronny had said. Could it all have been avoided if I just talked to Cameron? Walked up that lawn one last time and rang his door? Caught up with his mom and little brothers and asked my ex for an apology? Some kindness? Some respect?

Maybe. Maybe I could have stopped those posts from happening if I'd learned how to stand up for myself.

I listened to the doorbell echo through the foyer. His door opened and it looked like he'd been crying. I wiped my nose in the cold. "Are we alone?"

Jackson nodded, shivering in his workout shorts. "My parents are at Molly's drum—"

My cold hands made Jackson's skin jump, but I kissed him. I warmed my lips on his. His cheeks, his nose, his neck. He held my face and kept giving them back. We spoke through them, our words fighting to get out.

"Were—were you crying?"

"Yeah, I was—I was rowing a 2K and just—just started weeping."

"That sucks. Are you—did you finish your—"

"Yeah, six forty—six forty-seven. I row faster crying."

"Go fig— Go figure."

He kissed his handiwork on my neck and giggled. "Oh, no."

"Don't pretend to be embarrassed."

"Damn, you could get dental records from that thing. Come in." He brought me inside. "So. How was Philly? You got back early."

"Standard night. Ronny got us booted for heckling, Chuck

said *faggot* for a half-full theater, I told him to go fuck himself. We had cheesesteaks."

"What? Phil."

"Jacksy, you gotta stop by Jim's."

"Philip. Be serious."

Jackson held me in place. Hands on my shoulders. I swatted them off me and did the same to him. Hands on his shoulders. "I am serious. Listen."

I looked him in the eye. They were so bloodshot. Jacks told me he couldn't stop it lately. The crying. Ever since the list got out. He felt lost. Exposed. Even though only a few people knew it was his fault, Jackson said it felt like the backside of his skull had been removed and now anyone could see his pink, bloody brain. Like the world could finally see him for what he truly was. A freak. Fucked-up. Broken. That anonymous account had taken a bone saw to his head and now we could all see our helpful, normal, friendly president had a broken brain. His beautiful brain.

"We're going to make this alright, Jacks. Somehow. I don't know how yet, but you and me can make a plan. We'll think of something. 'Cause I can get real creative when I wanna be. And you're…" My hand moved up his neck and I rubbed his cheek. "You're so fucking smart, Jackson. You've got a really great way of looking at the world. You're the first person I ever met who knew how to look at me. You knew how to talk to me. Even when I didn't make it easy." I took off my scarf. "You and me will figure something out. Because we understand each other now. I understand you, Jackson. I understand the list."

Jackson's jaw was tense. He swallowed. "You do?"

"I do."

"You don't think it's… You don't think it means I'm really fucking—"

I put the scarf around his neck and wrapped it tight. It fit him better. Like my mom hadn't made it for me in the first place. "I think the list was for you. And I don't want you to stop it or show me it and I very much don't want to see my entry."

"It's really long."

"I bet." I poked Jackson's chest. "But it's yours. It is just yours. It was never meant for anyone else and you do not have to explain yourself. Not to me. Not to Cameron fucking Ellis. Heard?"

Jackson sniffed and smiled. "Yeah. Heard." He laughed and wiped his eye. Felt the scarf around his neck. "This is amazing. Where'd you buy this?"

"Wow, please ask my mom that, she'll shit her fucking pants."

Jackson chuckled and I hugged him. His voice was smothered in my shoulder. "We'll be okay, Phil."

I nodded against the scarf, kissing the skin I could find. "We'll be okay."

I looked up at the nice crystal chandelier sparkling above us in the beautiful Pasternak foyer. Probably cost the price of my apartment building. Dozens of little, ovular reflections of us hanging around the crystal cobweb.

"Jacks?"

"Philip?"

"Can I sleep over?"

"I would love that."

Turning in the air, the melted image of Jackson holding me. Me holding Jackson. Our bodies close and moving. It looked like we were dancing. Jackson and me. Just dancing.

"Jackson?"

"Phil?"

"Will you be my date to the Snow Globe Ball?"

A pause. A moment. The dancing hadn't stopped. But his breath had. And I realized I'd held my own. But the hair on Jackson's cheek scratched my own when he nodded.

"I would love to."

JACKSON

TRACK FIVE
If It Makes You Happy

As far as Pasternak events go, a high school cast party only got about sixty percent of my parents' true party-planning potential, but they were happy I was having friends over. We had music and dancing and a wonderfully themed spread of apps and snacks, all with fun *Hairspray* references. Everyone was wearing their costumes and there were different party games running in every room I passed. Not the flip cups and bag slapping of a DiSario party, we were far more age appropriate, but there was Heads-Up in the living room. Salad Bowl Celebrity in the pool house. A lot of charades. Theater kids were consistent like that.

I was actually having fun. It might have been the first event that calendar year that I was allowed to just attend. Sure, I was hosting, but that was low maintenance compared to my usual endeavors. I could just be. I let myself forget about Cameron Ellis and his posts and next year's student council budget. I let myself just be at the party. Play some charades. Sing some karaoke. And Phil was by my side for every second.

By eleven, we'd entered into the deep conversations portion of the night and every room hosted one-on-one talks about some crush or if they had a future in theater. Chilly heart-to-hearts on my patio about what it all meant or if they'd still be friends after graduation. We'd see the usual suspects weeping over how they didn't want the show to end but no one was particularly messy about it. A bonus of keeping a dry party.

Another bonus was Phil not having to feel the pressure. He never drank and never wanted to which always surprised people. Phil hated that surprise. That he of all people must love getting fucked-up. All those rules he just loved to break, how come drinking never made the list? Phil had his first and last drink at a Fourth of July party down in Tennessee. He was trying to hang with his dad and his rowdy Southern buddies and they all thought it'd be funny to get the kid drunk. Phil spent the night hearing fireworks with his head in a toilet bowl. He was ten. I'm not a big drinker, but I've enjoyed a glass of wine at dinner parties when I'm in the right mood. I never drank around Phil. It wasn't a rule he'd asked for or that we'd discussed, I just didn't want to. The idea of Phil having to take care of another drunk loved one was something I had no interest in and I've never missed the taste.

With more and more people saying their goodbyes and thanking my parents for hosting, I realized I hadn't seen Cameron all night. Phil and I had been doing our rounds and letting ourselves enjoy the party, but we still had our eyes open. Things had been quiet on the Cameron front since the posts, but we refused to be caught off guard again.

We stopped in the kitchen and refilled our cups of Link Larkin Lemonade. Phil leaned on my fridge, scanning the party. "I haven't seen Brynn tonight. Or Augie."

"I asked around, no one's seen them. Not like them to bail on a night like this."

"Unless Cameron told them not to come."

I dropped a cherry in Phil's cup and served him. "You think? Augie's been keeping his distance from Cameron during performances. Brynn too. I don't know if they'd still take orders from the asshole. Especially for a cast party. These things are like the Super Bowl for them."

Phil sipped his lemonade. "Cameron has the list. They could be afraid of him now." I nodded. He killed his cup and popped a stuffed olive in his mouth. "Great party though. They're missing out."

"Yeah? Not too theater kid for you?"

"It's surprisingly not terrible. And I do like you in that costume."

Phil eyed my *Hairspray* getup with interest. Maybe it was the Tennessee in him but Teenage Elvis really worked for Phil. I smirked. "Maybe I'll keep it on. *Later.*"

We laughed and Phil rubbed my back. I sipped my drink and spotted my dad manning the stereo across the room. He looked over at the kitchen so I walked away from Phil's hand on me. It wasn't necessary. It was just what my body did.

"I'm gonna do another round. See if Brynn or Augie are talking out back."

"Oh. Want me to come with?"

"I'll be right back, go talk to Dad." I walked away, looking back. "He's got his cassettes out, you two can geek out over some Alanis—"

Whatever weird, paranoid feeling I was trying to walk away from led me cup first into another person. The lemonade cracked through the plastic and drenched my suit jacket. It felt like I'd smashed into a telephone pole.

"Oh. Sorry." And there was Doug Parson. Standing in my kitchen. Staring at my wet, stained costume. "Wait. Why are you dressed like Elvis?"

Phil was right by my side then, steaming. "Get the fuck out of this house, Parson. Cast and crew only."

I held him back with my arm. Firm. Doug just stared at my hand on Phil. His smile dropped. "…Do you know?"

Phil barked a laugh. "No shit we fucking know! You think you covered your tracks that well, jackass?"

"Phil, easy."

"Oh, right. Right, no, I forgot our buddy Doug here deserves our fucking respect."

Doug looked away. He actually seemed sorry. Anxious. Like a dog who didn't mean to tear up your pillow. "I didn't know. I didn't know this would happen."

"Oh! Oh, okay! Then I guess it's all fine, never mind!"

I pulled Phil back. He was playing this wrong and people were starting to watch. "Philip. Easy."

He huffed and stewed behind me. I got closer to Doug, lowered my voice. "Do you know how bad this could get, Doug? Do you have any concept of how cruel that was?"

"I didn't think—"

"What were you even doing on my laptop? How did you even find my Excel? I hid it. Very well."

Doug just fiddled with his Rutgers hoodie drawstring. "No. You, uh…sort of didn't."

"Excuse me?"

"I was bored, I wanted to watch the Eagles highlights, your shit was just…there. On your desktop. In a folder called *Taxes*, man. You're seventeen, Pasty, what taxes are you doing?"

Now I needed someone to hold me back. Because who was that basic basketball bro to figure me out? Doug Parson broke into my personal laptop and stumbled onto my deepest secrets because he got bored? I guess I'd underestimated Doug. I'd mistaken simple for shallow. I thought I was playing chess against the Skwad but Doug beat me at checkers. How deeply annoying.

He shrugged. "They're just posts, guys. It'll blow over. It's not that big a deal."

I scoffed. Phil backed me up. "Y'know, I used to think you were the lesser of three evils with the Skwad. But you're the worst damn one. At least Augie and Brynn have some fucking shame. *It'll blow over?* I might get fucking ARRESTED."

"Dude—"

"You don't care about what happens to other people! You don't have to! You're a boring, straight asshole, you're gonna be fine either way."

Doug swallowed. I shook my head. "He used you, Doug. Cameron uses you. Ant and Matty and Bolu were your friends, Ronny was your friend, and he humiliated them. And you're helping him? You're still standing by him?"

He couldn't look at me. "Cameron's my best friend. My first friend. You're supposed to stand by your friends."

He said it like some simple truth. A rule he was taught a long time ago and didn't know how to examine.

"Cameron's in your room. He wants you. *Just* you."

Phil snorted. "Oh, you're his bodyguard now? You're gonna stop me?"

"He told me to just get Jackson."

"Yeah, well, that's not gonna fucking happen."

Doug stared down at Phil. Unsure how to proceed. If he wanted to stop Phil, it would just take one clumsy swing. But would Doug really hurt someone for Cameron? What else was he willing to do for his best friend, Cameron?

"It's fine. I'll go. Phil, it's fine."

Phil kept his eyes on Doug but dropped his voice. "You sure? I could be backup."

"I'm sure." I gave his arm a quick squeeze. "I'll be right back. Just keep an eye out, have some cake. Enjoy the party."

Phil's eyes moved to mine. He was serious. "Don't... Don't let him get to you."

"I won't. Don't let my house burn down."

He smiled. I turned to face Cameron's bulldog and let him guide me through my house. We went up the long way and Doug posted up outside my bedroom. I huffed. "Appreciate the security. Excuse me."

I moved around Doug and stepped into my room. I closed the door behind me and locked it. I didn't expect to walk into a blazing fire or all my belongings smashed on the floor, but I did a quick scan for missing items. Everything looked untouched. In place. Except for the boy in the corner. Reading over my high school bucket list. Something I'd been keeping since freshman year. One hundred Post-its, papering my wall.

"Hey, killer. Been a minute."

Cameron leaned close and squinted at one of my missions. *"Learn a fourth language."* He looked at me by my door. "You speak three?"

I let his question linger. Because I'd masterfully avoided talking to Cameron all through Tech Week. Our plan was over and I just couldn't fake it around him after the posts. I wasn't that good of an actor. But I nodded. "Je parle français. And English." I slipped into sign language, "And fuck you."

Cameron smiled. It was earnest. Impressed. "That's so interesting. You're so... You are so interesting, Jackson."

"What's interesting?"

Cameron walked along my wall of goals. *Drive to California. Learn to sail.* "You've got this amazing house. And these amazing parents. Everyone in this neighborhood is so impressed with them and you and your life. It's just...effortless. You make it look so easy. It's impressive. Interesting."

My body was on the defensive. Watching him walk my space. Waiting for his next attack. "You don't know me that well, Cameron."

"I think I've gotten a pretty good read on you, Jackson."

"Then you have some shitty reading comprehension. I am not *effortless*. None of this is *easy*."

Cameron chuckled. "Sure. But you make it look that way. You wear a very good face. Handsome. Easy." He sat on my bed. Felt my quilt. "You didn't have an entry for yourself. On your Excel. I figured it was some sort of diary at first, but people usually talk about themselves in diaries. You're not curious about yourself?"

I wanted to throw him out the window for touching my bed. Our bed. "That wasn't the point of the list. And I don't need to explain that to you."

He smiled up at me. "I think you can tell a lot about a person by how they talk about others. It's why I like keeping my blog. I want people to see that side of me. How I take in my world. But you blew me out of the water, Jackson. You take in so much more than me."

I felt the lemonade sticking to my chest. I just wanted to clean up and change and get Cameron the hell out of my room.

"I think you're fucking disgusting, Cameron." He perked up. "I think you are foul. And bitter. And I think your blog posts are inane. And fake. And really poorly written." I glared at him. "I think you are so fucking empty, Cameron. I listened to you talk at me for months and I couldn't tell you a single thing you said. You have nothing to offer me. You have no depth. You have no taste. I think you are so...fucking...*boring*."

Cameron didn't blink. He just stared at me from my bed. Like he was staring into the sun. "So, you *do* read my blog."

My brows furrowed. "Are… Did you not hear a thing I just said?"

"I did. And I think you're right. You're right about me." Cameron nodded. "I don't know if you're up-to-date but my followers are dying to know about my *mystery man*. And I promised them a reveal soon. They want me to ask him to the Snow Globe Ball. Full circle moment, y'know?"

"Cameron, you need to get out of my—"

"I think we would be a perfect couple, Jackson." I froze. Cameron just continued. In his own little world. "You get it. You understand people, Jackson, you get how they work. You get how I work. I read your entry about me, Jackson, you see right through me." He smiled that winning Cameron Ellis smile. "But you see me. You *really* see me."

It felt like I was being pranked. Like any second now, a trapdoor would open and I'd plunge into a shark tank. Cameron walked over to me. Put his hand on my forearm. "I wouldn't need anyone else but you. I wouldn't need Augie or Doug or the Skwad. I wouldn't need to be mean or bitter or all those things you wrote. If I had you, it would just click. You see that, right? If we were together, people would love us. Everyone would tell us how good we looked together. We would be so good together, Jackson. Don't you get that?"

His smile. His auburn hair and rosy cheeks. The cinnamon coffee on his breath and his nice winter coat. He looked ready for a Christmas card. And it made a certain sense. Cameron and me. More sense than Phil and Cameron, if we asked the world. More sense than Phil and me, if we asked the school. Because Cameron and I were perfect on paper. He was my boy next door. I was his leading man. We would have such a story to tell the world. High school sweethearts. Homecoming kings. The world would be so happy to see us.

Cameron squeezed my arm. "And if you can't come out yet… I can wait. I can make it good for you, Jackson. We can take it slow. Figure out your path. I could make it so easy for you, Jackson."

Some sad part of me had to admit, it was a logical move. A smart play. Being gay was a badge of honor for Cameron and coming out had gone so well for him. No shame. No contradictions. What did he know that I didn't? What had he learned that I couldn't? How could something so complicated for me be so simple for him?

"Cameron. I'm not… I'm not like that."

"What? Gay?"

"I'm not like you."

Cameron smiled, a little coy. "You are, Jackson. You're just like me. You just don't know how to say it yet. And that's okay, I can help you."

I took his hand off my arm. "Like you helped Phil?"

Cameron shook his head. "Phil didn't want to be helped."

"All Phil wanted was your help." I felt myself getting hot. "All Phil wanted was a person to like him. He wanted a boyfriend who respected him. He wanted a friend who didn't treat him like a fucking mistake."

He tried to touch me again and I ripped the hand off me. "Jackson—"

"NO."

Cameron backed away. I followed him down. "You think you're owed this. You think you're owed a boyfriend and friends and a great fucking life. But YOU DIDN'T EARN IT."

Cameron backed into my wall. Post-its fell and I got in his face. "You didn't earn your nice house or your nice life or your nice fucking friends. You didn't earn my respect and you didn't deserve him. You don't deserve Phil. He just wanted someone to love him back, Cameron, and you stomped on his fucking heart. For views. For nothing. You are NOTHING and you deserve EVERYTHING we have done to you."

Cameron was up against my wall but his breathing was steady. His smile was gone. He made his offer and I slapped him in the face with it. He had tried the easy way. "I can delete the list. I can take down the posts and I can say they were lies. An anonymous troll wanted attention. It can all go away. Bolu. The stop sign. All of it." Cameron pushed his hair back. "Phil and Matty can be okay. Veronica DiSario can feel better. You can all win."

I was calming down. I stepped back. "If… If I go out with you?"

Cameron just stared at me. He didn't look so interested anymore. "Jackson. I'm just letting you know what I *can* do. Because I hold all the power here. Was that not clear? I *can* delete the list. I *can* save Phil's ass. I can do whatever the fuck I want, Jackson. Whether you play ball or not."

"Cameron…"

He walked right by me. Straight for my door. "I gave you the good offer, Jackson. A smart person would sleep on it."

"*Cameron.*"

"Let me know about the dance, I want to look into matching—"

I slammed my hand on my desk. "HE COULD GO TO JAIL!"

Cameron stopped at my door. A moment of consideration. "Jackson. Phil won't get in trouble. He won't let himself."

He let that hang. I didn't understand. Cameron gazed up at the shelves of trophies above my door. All my medals and cups. "You really... God, you *really* love Phil, don't you?" Cameron turned around and smiled at me. A little wistful. "Phil thinks he's better than me. *You* think Phil is better than me. I don't want him to go down for the stop sign, Jackson. I just want to prove a point."

Cameron gave the stain on my suit jacket an ugly look. "Phil won't let himself go down for the sign. Because whatever you see in him, whatever you think makes him so much better, you're wrong. Phil is selfish. He's desperate. He might want to be better, but he wants to win more. That's why I didn't name him. I gave Phil an out. And Phil Reyno will always take the out."

I felt my throat pulsing against my skin. "Matty."

Cameron bowed his head. "Matty."

He turned back around and headed for my door. "You can't say he didn't have it coming. All that fighting. All the drugs. Sooner or later, Phil will probably try and tell you the same." He held the knob then scoffed at my *Hairspray* costume. "And dry-clean your suit jacket. Show the costume shop some fucking respect."

The door opened and Cameron was gone. I caught my breath.

That night, Phil fell asleep on my living room couch. We'd spent most of the after-party getting a jump on cleaning, but by two Phil couldn't help himself. I watched him curled up on my couch like he owned it. Like a black cat who wandered in from the cold. And I wondered how much of my life I had loved that boy. When did the feeling find me? Maybe the day we met. Maybe I used to call it something else. Something smaller. The feeling I got when he'd race me to the lake. The feeling I felt the first morning he let me braid his hair. All wet from the water. All sleepy in my lap. I'd liked him right away. I knew that, I knew I liked him the first time I made him laugh. The moment I learned I could make that hard boy cackle. And maybe my like had turned into appreciation. I appreciated his rules against bullying and littering and *No Girls Allowed*. And that appreciation had warmed into respect. His respect for my religion and my respect for his traditions. And somewhere respect had turned to care. Care had turned to want. Want had turned to need and need had turned to love. Love, somewhere down the line. But I knew it. I knew I loved Phil Reyno. And he loved me back. And even if I didn't always understand him, I always understood his love. I could never overthink that.

I pulled his old favorite blanket over him and kissed Phil on the forehead. I smelled his long hair and whispered into his ear.

"We are so fucking loved."

I grabbed my backpack off the table and headed out into the night. The scarf Phil's mom made for me kept the December air from stopping me and I walked down the street until Foxwood became Carter Ave. Carter became Whitman and Whitman became Lakeview. The air became colder the closer I got to Plum. The lake water was black at night and I stopped in the middle of the Lakeview cul-de-sac. The night was silent. I looked across the lake and could see the Clubber side of the Orchard. Ronny and Ant. Brynn and Cameron. Their homes loomed over my lake like a threat. Keep out. Keep off our grass. Even in a neighborhood like ours, with money to burn and homes to remodel, the Clubbers still wanted a name for themselves. The rich side of the rich side of town. I want for nothing, I'm the luckiest kid I know, and those people still need to remind me they have more. Cameron needed to remind me he had more. More moves. More power.

I would not give him the power. I would not give him the move.

I opened my backpack and took out a screwdriver.

I had never, not once, considered putting the blame on Matty. It was the cold, cruel thing to do, even if it would save the boy I love the most. And maybe that said something good about me. That I never considered throwing an angry, blamable, misunderstood kid at our problem and I know Phil never considered it either. No matter what Cameron thought he knew about my best friend, Phil would never fucking do that. Cameron didn't know about Phil and Matty. Their truce. Their connection. Cameron didn't know about Phil and Matty's respect for each other because Cameron never asked. He never cared. Cameron never knew Phil and he never loved him either.

My hands were freezing against the metal and I wondered if Phil would hate me. I wondered if he'd send me away again. Like the last Christmas we'd spent together. I wondered if he'd tell me I never learned my lesson. But I had. This time was different. This Christmas gift wasn't a used Xbox. I wasn't giving Phil this gift to keep him in my life. I was giving this to Phil to keep him in *his* life. Because a kid like Phil's entire world could be knocked over by one bad decision. A kid like Cameron could ruin Phil's life with one bad action. He'd done it time and time again, to no consequence. Everything Phil had done to find his place in this world could be wiped away because Cameron Ellis hit *Send*.

But Phil and I were different. That was the lesson. Our differences mattered and I needed to understand them. If I wanted Phil in my life, I needed to understand what made us different. Phil had been surviving since he was a little boy. I was the luckiest kid I knew. I had been dealt a bigger hand. I had mistakes to spare.

I took the stop sign off its post. It might ruin my life. It might ruin all my plans. My future. Penn. But this mistake wouldn't knock me out of the race. Not like it would to Phil. Because we'd been running this race very differently. I understood that now. Because I'd been given a head start.

I could give him this. I could afford this. I would survive this.

PHIL

TRACK SIX
I'm Just a Kid

The punch was fine. Vague as far as taste goes, could've been anything under the mixed berry umbrella, but it wasn't room temp which put it well ahead of last year's.

"Why not *The Snow Ball*?" Ronny sipped next to me. She had on another one of her grandmother's wedding dresses, but this one was far less ostentatious. Still a terrible thing to wear to a school dance but Ronny had lost our bet.

I nodded. "Yeah. The *Globe* is unnecessary. Cut out the middleman."

Bolu scraped the shredded lettuce off his section of party sub into the trash. "You gotta keep *Globe*. *Snow Globe* sounds way better than *Snow Ball*. More unique. Lose the *Ball* part, save yourself the *Globe-Ball* redundancy."

Ronny considered it. *"The Snow Globe Dance?"*

The three of us stood by the punch bowl and mulled over the name. No one had a better suggestion. Or maybe it just didn't matter. None of our cynical wallflowering seemed all that cool tonight. Our detached superiority rang a little falser, watching our class having fun together. Those shiny happy people. Dancing and laughing and glad they came out. No one in that room knew what happened to their class president that morning. They were too busy enjoying the party he had planned for them.

"I'm gonna walk around."

Ronny rubbed my back. "You okay?"

I looked around the room. The paper snowflakes hanging over a crowd of happy kids. We'd spent a whole week of study halls cutting those out in the art room because no one else could be bothered to help him. I shrugged. "I'm here, aren't I?"

Bolu swallowed a bite of hoagie. "You heard anything? They give him his phone back yet?"

I trashed my cup and put my hands in my pockets. "No."

I left Ronny and Bolu to the punch. Maybe they could have a more cheerful conversation without me. Maybe my rain cloud was keeping them from enjoying the dance. I'd never been a good third wheel and Bolu deserved a nice night back out in the world. So did Ron. They should be allowed to enjoy their date. It wasn't their fault mine couldn't make it.

The DJ was playing a very misguided techno mashup of "Baby Got Back" and "All About That Bass" and I regretted leaving my drumming earplugs at home. I grew up thinking that the music at high school dances would be live. Some student band would get called up to the majors and play rock songs for people to mosh to or love songs for slow dances. Some part of me always wanted to be in that band. I thought that was what high school might be for me. It felt like a good place I could fit. Phil, the drummer. That rebel punk in the school band. It was a tired cliché, something from the mov-

ies, but it sounded nice to me as a kid. I could have my place.
Be understood.

"Bullshit."

I walked along the bleachers and watched some chaperones
mill about the stage. At first glance, I thought Mrs. Stapler
was wearing an ugly Christmas sweater but, in better light,
decided it was just an ugly regular sweater. I wondered if
she'd tell me to leave again. Keep me from ruining everyone's
fun. Or maybe Mrs. Stapler had her fill of drama for the day.
Maybe Jackson had finally worn her out.

Once he was sure his job was done and the Snow Globe Ball
would go off without a hitch, President Pasternak walked right
into the admin office and showed Moorestown's newest guidance counselor a picture. A stop sign. Hanging on his wall. Like
an island in a sea of Post-its. Jackson had bolted a stolen sign in
the middle of all of his plans and goals. A big, red, reflective
sign to **STOP**. Mrs. Stapler didn't believe him. He told her that
didn't matter. She was required to report it and Moorestown
Police was required to take him in. Officer Olowe didn't need
much more. A picture was enough. A picture and a confession. A lie.

I looked over the dance floor of sloppy moves and grinding ass and spotted Ronny and Bolu in the center, showing
our classmates what actual dancing looked like. They moved
well together. They both looked like they were having a real
fun time and they didn't have a problem getting close with
each other. Then I noticed a lonely girl standing by the dance
floor, the only one of the hundred not moving. A statue in
a pink dress stuck beside a thrashing throng. Brynn Forester
was not having a fun night.

My curiosity put me by her side, but it didn't break her
stare. "Hey. Very risqué dance moves."

Brynn looked like she was trying not to get upset. "Can… Can you help me?"

"What?"

"I don't know what to do, Phil. I don't know how to help."

"Brynn, what are you talking about?"

She turned back at the entrance doors. The big Snow Globe Ball banner. The winter-themed backdrop where a photographer was taking pictures of kids with props and snowflakes and those annoying mustache-on-a-stick things. There was a line of students waiting to get their photo op and the current models were taking their time. Trying to get their cute couple pic just right.

I groaned. "Oh, what the fuck now?"

Cameron Ellis needed to get the picture right. Because he had finally done it. The long-awaited reveal of Cameron's secret crush. Someone he'd always known, seen in a new light. Someone he'd grown close to in the *Hairspray* cast. Someone he'd asked to the dance the night of the cast party in hopes to recapture last year's viral moment. But Jackson Pasternak was currently awaiting his fate in a police station. So Cameron would have to settle for Augie Horton.

Cameron held Augie tight and smiled for the camera. Augie gave what looked like a genuine smile in return though he was always a better actor than Cam. But nobody in line looked anything more than impatient toward our school's newest couple. Cameron's newest plan. Augie's newest defense.

Brynn took my arm. "I know you don't owe me anything, Phil. Or the rest of us. But…" She shook her head at the new Golden Gays of Moorestown, just as unsold. "Augie won't talk to me anymore. After what you guys did. I can't stop it, I can't… *Phil.*"

Brynn's eyes went huge. Because Cameron and Augie, her

two former besties, were sharing a very sweet, very still kiss. Lips frozen together. Just for the camera. Augie kept his eyes open and it made my stomach turn. Augie and his defenses. It was a desperate move. But Cameron had promised his fans a boyfriend. His story needed a new love interest and we'd left Augie just desperate enough to play the part. If he couldn't broker a peace, he could at least cover his ass.

The happy couple got their pictures and left out into the hallway. Brynn shook my arm. "He doesn't want this, Phil. He's making a mistake. He's going to get *hurt*."

Brynn was about to cry and I started off. "Phil. W-what—"

I shook my head and walked straight for the hallway door. "I'm gonna wrap this up."

We weren't doing this again. Jackson didn't do what he did for me just so this bullshit could keep going. He didn't risk his entire future, everything he'd worked so hard to put in place, just so Cameron Ellis could drag this story out. I was ending it. Tonight.

I pushed through the double doors and saw them alone down the hall. Augie was staring into space and Cameron was leaning on a locker, going through their pictures.

"No, like, now that it's over, I really believe Corny Collins is sort of the secret lead of *Hairspray*. You know what I mean? Like, it's kind of *his* story if you really think about it."

"I want to go home, Cameron."

"Could you please stop being a wet blanket for one—"

I slammed a passing locker. The noise cracked through the hall. **"HEY."**

Augie stood up. Cameron sighed and put his phone away. "Wow. Philip. Joy. Long time, how's the winter treating you?"

I headed straight for him but Cameron ducked behind

Augie, instantly hiding from a fight. "You put one fucking hand on me, I'll—"

"You'll *WHAT*?" I tried reaching around Augie but Cameron was squirrelly. "Get me arrested? Ruin my life? Make a fucking video about me—Augie, MOVE."

Augie pushed us apart and put a finger in my face. "CUT IT. We are not doing this tonight, Phil, this is not about you."

"Augie, he's fucking—"

Augie bore down on me. "This DOES NOT CONCERN YOU. This is between me and my…him. And I'd appreciate it if you let us be."

"Aug—"

"We will let you be. Leave us alone, Philip, and we will leave you alone." His look was stern. But guiding. "Cameron deleted the list. Jackson's list, it's gone. I watched him do it. Doug did too. It's done. Phil, you need to let it be done."

That was the truce Augie had brokered. No more list. No more posts. The fighting stops and I got left alone. Augie got the guy. Even if he didn't want him. But Augie always appreciated a good deal. A good shield. We could all move on, licking our wounds and pretending we were happy for each other. Finally, peace in the gayborhood. All it took was Augie's dignity.

"You think this'll last, Augie? You think he won't throw you away the second he finds someone more postable?"

Cameron scoffed. Taunting. "Philip. Augie Horton is one of my oldest friends. He was right down the street and I never even noticed. All this time, right in front of my eyes. Why wouldn't that last? I love him, Phil. Maybe I always did."

I just stared at Augie. Then at Cameron. Then back at Augie. Because are you fucking serious? I threw my hands up. "COME

ON! Augie, he doesn't *love* you! He doesn't even care about you!"

Augie closed his eyes. Cameron held his hand. He looked at me smug. Like he'd already had all these discussions with Augie. Like they laid out their agreement nice and clean. Like he'd won.

"And why wouldn't I love him, Phil? What's so unlovable to you about Augles here? I think he's perfect. Everyone in the gym's going bananas for us together, we're perfect together. Sorry if he's not your type, Philip, but Augie's exactly what I want."

Cameron squeezed up against Augie's arm. Augie wouldn't look at me. And I wondered what his terms were. How much of himself was Augie ready to give up for Cameron. The promise of Cameron. The fantasy. That good, easy love. I knew why Augie was doing it. Because I'd done the exact same thing. I could only tell him how that story ended.

"August." He finally looked at me. "You won't deserve it. You won't deserve how he'll make you feel about yourself. Okay? He will make you feel so fucking worthless and he will be...fine."

I turned to Cameron. Not angry. Not crying or mean. I looked at my ex-boyfriend, this person who had hurt me so deeply and often, and I felt steady. Honest. I felt brave. "Cameron will cheapen you."

And Cameron had that cold expression on his face. That look he'd get whenever I got too close. Those blue-green eyes that would shame me for trying to get to know him. For trying to make it real. For being such a fool.

"I don't know, Phil. You were pretty cheap when I found you."

Augie looked away. The hate in my stomach was dripping.

Hot acid was boiling in my gut and I wanted to finally do it. Break his jaw. Tear out his auburn hair. Smash his winning smile like a fist through a window. My brain flooded me with all the terrible things I could say back. A new list of creative ways to spin the word *fuck* and an Excel of my own of all the low blows. I could make fun of his desperate need for attention. I could brag about the boy who'd chosen me over him. I could drag him for his failed stop sign gambit or his off-key *Hairspray* solos or our classmates' obvious disinterest in Cam-Aug. I knew exactly how to throw that boiling hate in his face in a way that would finally hurt him. Finally burn that smug look off his face.

"Enjoy the dance, Philip. I'm sorry your date couldn't make it." Cameron took Augie's arm and led him to the double doors. But I didn't follow. I didn't move.

I didn't have a comeback. I was drawing a blank. Because the hate had never left my stomach. It stayed simmering in my gut, but it never ran up my throat. It didn't burst out of me and I realized I had nothing left for Cameron. I had no hateful comeback or perfect dig worth throwing at Cameron Ellis. Because what was the point? What would it do? Nothing I could say or scream or cuss would change Cameron Ellis. Because Cameron had no interest in changing. He couldn't see his own damage, there was no lesson I could teach him. There was no point trying to hurt him. I was only burning myself.

"What the hell is she doing…" Augie stopped at the window into the gym. Cameron looked just as confused. He opened the double doors and the music was gone. No more bass drops or "Uptown Funk." Just the sounds of our classmates' mutters. The sound of a girl on a mic.

"And I know you probably heard enough from me this year and I know I should probably just shut up but everybody needs to know."

All three of us rushed into the gym, equally concerned. It felt like déjà vu. Like I was right back where I was last January. Only tonight, it was Brynn Forester storming the makeshift stage of the Snow Globe Ball. She had a mic. Tears on her face. She had a hundred eyes on her and Brynn was going off script.

Augie was stuck in place. "Are you *fucking* kidding me?"

Everyone at the front of the dance floor had their phones out, eating up this messy sequel to last year's biggest school scandal. I saw Mrs. Stapler shouting whispers at Brynn from the side of the stage. I caught Ronny in the crowd, covering her mouth and just delighted. Brynn had the school's ear again and she was determined to use it better this time.

"Cameron Ellis posted those things. About our classmates. Cameron created that account and he made up those lies and that's all they are. Lies. He made it all up because he is a liar. Cameron Ellis is a bad, bad person."

I gasped. I actually fucking gasped. Ronny's head whipped around from the front row and found me right away. We both had the same wide-eyed look. *What the fuck? What the actual fuck?*

Cameron was stuck frozen on the dance floor. Catching side eyes and whispers. His knuckles were white and he looked like he'd shit his dress pants. Brynn shook her head, starting to shrink under the sea of flashing phones. "He's hurt a lot of people. And if you don't see that, it's not your fault. If he's lied to you, that's not your fault. He's really believable. But you all deserve to know the truth. Cameron deserves to be seen."

A room of eyes turned to Cameron. His face matched his white dress shirt and he was starting to back out of the room. Brynn burst out crying. "He was my... He said he was my f-fucking *friend*."

Her sobs boomed over the loudspeaker and Brynn was

melting down on stage. "He told me we were fr-friends and he said I was sm-smart and funny and i-interesting and he made me stop talking about h-horses. He's such a f-fucking D-DICK!"

Cameron made a beeline for the doors. Augie hadn't budged. He just watched his bawling best friend make a fool of herself in front of a room of our cringing, laughing peers. And with a dance floor of people making fun of that crying girl, I felt an odd sense of obligation in my stomach. It cooled off all that hate like Pepto and I vehemently despised the decision my brain had already made.

Before I knew it, I was making my way across the dance floor. Because that's what Jackson would do. If he were here, if he weren't facing literal jail time for fixing my mistake, I knew our class president would help his classmate. Especially Brynn Forester. Because Brynn was only spilling her guts to our class because of us. I couldn't fault her for that. I could almost respect her for that. And I unfortunately needed to help her with that.

I passed Ronny and Bolu in the front row and climbed onto the stage. Brynn's confession had turned into a string of stuttering insults about Cameron's acting ability, but she calmed down at my approach.

"Ph-Phil?"

"It's okay. Let me have that. You did good."

"Is Aug-Augie okay?"

"Go check. You're okay. Just…"

I guided her to the steps and she walked offstage. The room booed my interruption and heckled her all the way to the steps. Mrs. Stapler and Augie politely guided Brynn out the side door, both keeping on a good face for the rowdy crowd, and once they were clear, Coach Bianco waved me over from the steps. He wanted the mic back, but I couldn't hear what he was yelling up to me. The boos were just too loud. They might've started because I'd ended the show and ruined their fun, but the noise only grew louder. I saw Ant Lewis flipping me off from the front row. Someone threw a cup at me and I saw a guy from the wrestling team hollering something nasty.

"Really?"

Maybe they were still sore from the stop sign incident. Maybe the news of this morning's confession hadn't reached everyone and I was still in the hot seat for it. Or maybe it was something else. One of the hundreds of crimes I'd apparently committed on this town. Maybe they were still mad I broke Cameron's heart. Maybe they didn't like my attitude or my clothes. Maybe I'd told each and every one of those kids to go fuck themselves this calendar year and they were finally getting their shot to throw it back. Maybe they were homophobic or drunk or bored with their night. Or maybe they didn't need an excuse. Maybe they were just fucking dirtbags.

I raised the mic. "Really? You just heard Cameron Ellis has been lying through his teeth all year and you're booing *me*?!"

A guy who clearly did not go to our school cupped his hands from the front row. "FUCK YOU, BITCH!"

Ronny shoved him and Bolu pushed him out of the crowd. But the shout was contagious and soon enough the whole crowd was popping off.

"GET OFF THE STAGE!"

"TURN ON THE MUSIC!"

"GAAAAAAAAAAAAAY!"

Through the cheers and jeers, I heard a familiar sound start to grow. A chant. Like we were in the middle of a pep rally. The cackling bass of bros having fun.

"FUCK PHIL REYNO!"

Clap clap, clap-clap-clap.

"FUCK PHIL REYNO!"

Dun dun, dun-dun-dun.

The chant echoed over the party. And while it might have felt like I'd inadvertently stepped into a gay kid's waking nightmare, I was surprisingly calm. A calm that kept those boos and chants from filling my stomach with hate. And I wondered if I'd gotten that calm from my father. Spinning a crowd's boos into some sign that he had won. The hate of the world must make him pretty special. Why else would everyone be paying attention?

I saw Ronny pushing and shoving through the crowd. Slapping heads and shutting people up. Like my own bodyguard, trying to protect me. I thought of her wearing my mom's scarf and holding my hand in her Mustang. She told me she was proud of me. Which was something so new to hear. She was proud I stood up for myself in the comedy club. I didn't let my dad run that room or tell me what to do. I didn't let him make me feel bad about myself and I didn't need to scream or boo or be hateful to do it. I could stomach the hate. Not let it burn through my throat. It was so much easier to speak without all that hate in my mouth.

"You know..."

I looked out at the crowd. I had no point to prove. No speech to make. I wasn't Cameron. He made big movie moments. That wasn't me. I didn't need to make some big declaration to get these people on my side. These people who never tried to know me.

"I get why you're booing. I do. I'm no Cameron Ellis. He's nice, I'm mean. I get that."

The booing and laughter never stopped. I doubt most of

the room could actually hear me, even with the loudspeaker. I didn't care. I wasn't saying it for them.

"But I'm not a bad person. Being mean doesn't make you bad. And being nice doesn't make you good. Cameron Ellis is a nice guy. But, believe me, he's a bad person."

I saw Ronny in the crowd. She had just thrown a cup of punch in Ant Lewis's face, but she was smiling at me then. Cheering under all the boos.

I pointed at my chest. "I'm a good person. Have a nice dance and get home safe, faggots."

I dropped the mic on the floor and flipped off the crowd, all smiles. The boos roared loud again and I princess-waved my way off stage. Bianco had given up on trying for the night and Mrs. Stapler was searching the dance floor for the microphone.

Ronny cut through the crowd and caught up to me by the punch. "Tear-jerking, Phil. Very brave. So climactic."

"Really?"

"Maybe. They cut your mic ten seconds in."

"Oh. Well. Oh, well."

"The Electric Slide" blared through the loudspeakers at top volume, the DJ trying to win back the night, and I shouted over the intro. "GONNA BOUNCE. MORE OF A 'MACARENA' GUY."

Ronny nodded and got another cup of punch. "PRISON BREAK?"

I checked my phone. No new news. Stanley Pasternak promised he'd call when they got released from the station. When he wasn't otherwise promising to cut my head off for giving his bleeding heart son the chance to martyr himself.

I looked back at the dance floor. Everyone was back to the bump and grind and the pitchforks had gone as quickly as they'd come. It never really mattered to them. My class could take or leave their beef with me. It was just another school sport for them.

"I THINK I'M DONE HERE."

Ronny toasted her cup and gave me a kiss on the cheek. "DON'T FREEZE! I'M GONNA GO FINGER BOLU IN THE ART ROOM!"

"I CAN BARELY HEAR YOU! WHAT?!"

"NOTHING, BE SAFE! COME OVER LATER!"

She walked me to the double doors and patted my butt on the way out. I made my way down the hall and into the lobby. Past the auditorium. A door to the theater was ajar and I could hear the good acoustics of shouting from within. Odd.

I peeked my head inside and caught the performance, halfway through. On the half-struck set of *Hairspray*, the Skwad was in the middle of their last night as friends. Cameron was screaming at Brynn. Augie was screaming at Cameron. Brynn was getting in Cameron's face and Augie was backing her up and Doug was screaming into a prop pillow. It was ugly. Cameron called Brynn shallow. Augie called Cameron toxic. Cameron called Augie beneath him and Brynn had to be physically held back. But I didn't get involved. I didn't stick around. I headed down to the woodshop, got my spare skateboard, and got my ass out of there. Because it wasn't my fight. The Skwad wasn't my problem anymore. I had found my own friends. I had found my own respect. I had a boy who loved me waiting in a police station and I had better plans for my night.

I dropped my skateboard to the pavement and felt a chirp in my pocket. An old alert, back from Phase One. The Brynn Show Has Gone Live.

My jaw dropped. "No fucking way."

I clicked on the live stream just in time to watch Cameron Ellis call his new boyfriend an ungrateful whale. I could hear Brynn gasp behind the camera. I could see Doug notice they were being recorded. *"Dude..."*

Cameron looked right into camera. Right at me. I watched it dawn on him. I watched his eyes freeze. His nose twitch. I watched Cameron Ellis ruin his own life.

★ ★ ★

Dr. Pasternak held the door open for Jackson. Neither had dressed for the cold, but I suppose neither thought they'd be spending all day in a police station. Jackson had been in the same wrinkled clothes since first period. He looked tired and stale and his hair needed a brush. I'd been freezing to a bus bench for the last two hours and Stan saw me first. Jackson's baggy eyes lit up when he saw me but Dr. Pasternak just rubbed his under his glasses. He gave me a weary pat on the shoulder, barely stopping. "I'll give you *five*. No sleeping over. Very...very tired."

Stan headed to the car, giving us space. We watched him go, unsure how to start. I nodded over to the station and Jackson followed me around the corner. Not too far, just out of sight. I needed Jackson alone. I needed him for me.

Once we were alone, I crossed my arms. I wasn't looking at him. "Are you alright?" Jackson nodded. I did too. "Are... Are you in trouble?" Jackson nodded. I did too. "What kind?"

Jackson took a moment. A cold wind snapped through and he crossed his arms. "We're, uh... We're gonna have to see a judge. That's just how it goes though. Standard next steps. But there will be a fine and—"

"Jackson."

"And I'm not going to tell you how much it is. Not for a

bit. We can talk that out once the dust settles, but it is handleable. It won't kill me."

"Jackson."

"But Mr. Olowe said with my record how it is and some character references around town, it's really just a matter of how much community service they'll want to give me."

I turned back and finally looked at him. "Community…" I couldn't tell if it was the cold or how tired he looked but my eyes were stinging. "No jail? Or juvie or…no arrest?"

Jackson looked up at the flagpole above us. The Moorestown and New Jersey flags whipping in the wind. A sky of clouds covering us. "Well. I'm told it'll be a very serious grounding. Which is all very new to my parents. They are furious with me. And you. Which is also new for them. And we probably won't get to go to France this summer. Oh, I was gonna ask you to go to France with me this summer. And school isn't going to be happy with me and I'll probably have to back away from some of my clubs and I won't be getting that car anytime soon either but…that's what bikes are for."

Jackson wiped the tears off my face. "But no. No arrest. Nothing permanent. I mean, I'm gonna have a record now, but maybe that'll make me stick out come college app season—"

I coughed out a cry and shoved Jackson into the brick wall. He barely flinched, more surprised than anything. "You fucking ASSHOLE."

"Philip."

"How could you fucking do that, Jackson?! How could you—" I pushed him again then fell into him. I hugged him tight and dug my forehead into his sternum. I was trying to kill him and thank him all at once. *"You should have told me."*

"You would have stopped me."

"You should have let me stop you. That was too much. That was

too..." Jackson kissed my head. I pounded my fist on his back. *"I'm never gonna forgive you for this, Jackson."*

"I know. I know, Phil."

I sniffed back a tear. So damn angry. So damn grateful.

"I'm never gonna forget this, Jacks."

"I know."

I brought my head up and kissed him on the lips. We smiled into each other and looked back at the lot.

"We only got two minutes left. Stan's gonna get mad."

"He doesn't know how to be mad at us. It's not in his bones."

"How 'bout your mom?"

"No, she's gonna bury us alive. Me, at least."

The wind was messing up my hair so Jackson held it in place and chuckled at the snowflakes melting across his fingers. We looked up and saw it had begun to snow. I smiled at the white night above us. Snow caught in the wind, looking like a swarm of angry bees.

Jackson took my hand. Held it to his chest. His fingers wrapped around my ear and he looked me in the eye. "You get why I did it, right? You get why I had to?"

He rubbed my piercing. Our piercing. Snow was catching in his hair and his brows and I touched one on his cheek. It melted against my finger and fell down his skin like a tear. It was an easy question to answer. Because even though I'd nearly broken my locker and some blood vessels when I heard what he had done, I never questioned why. It was the smart play. A perfect combination of loving and logical. Pragmatic and passionate. A contradiction to some but not to me. That's just who Jackson was. A beautiful contradiction.

"I understand you, Jackson."

He smiled. Understood. Jackson hugged me close and kissed my cheek. "We're over time. Want a ride home?"

"You think Stan will let me in the car?"

"If you ask nicely. And sit in the trunk."

"Nah, I'm just down the block. I'll survive."

"Okay. I'll call you."

"I'll answer."

Jackson and I walked around the corner and saw the family car idling at the curb. Windshield wipers cutting away at the snow. Jackson yawned. "Long day. I feel like I could sleep till New Year's."

"Police interrogation will do that to a growing boy. You deserve a crash."

"No, I gotta hear about the dance first. I miss anything juicy?"

A grin stretched across my face. And I wondered if I could fit everything that had happened at the Snow Globe Ball into one phone call. "You might want to get some coffee."

"Oh, shoot. That much?"

"There's a lot to catch you up on. Make sure your phone is charged."

We reached the car door and I wished I'd kissed him good-bye before we'd turned the corner. He wouldn't want me doing that in front of his dad, even if the snow was beginning to turn that parking lot into a snow globe. But it was alright. We would have other moments. Jackson might not be ready to give me a kiss in public but I didn't need all that. I didn't need him to rush himself for me. Come out for me. He'd done enough for me and I knew we'd get there eventually. We had time. Jackson had given us time.

The right-hand window cracked. "C'mon, hon, it's started to come down. Need a ride, Philly?"

I waved Stan off. "I'm right down the street, y'all should get going. Beat the snow."

He gave me a thumbs-up but Jackson didn't budge. Stuck on a thought. "Hey, pop the trunk? I have something for Phil."

"Jacks."

"Real quick! I got him something, I forgot to give it to him earlier."

Stan sighed and popped the trunk. He rolled the window up and Jackson dragged me behind the car. I smiled.

"First night of Hanukkah's not till Sunday, pal. What did you—"

Jackson held my face and kissed me deep. The trunk of the car blocked the rearview and we were all alone out there. Kissing in the snow. "Tu ne me laisses pas indifférent, Philip."

Wind whipped around us and flurries stuck to our clothes. Alone in a snow globe. Jackson and me.

"You do not leave me indifferent."

There was snow in my hair and on our faces and I had to laugh. Because it was almost Christmas again. Because I had Jackson in my life again. Because life could be so easy some nights. I was so grateful. I was so grateful for these easy nights.

TAPE FLIP

TAPE TWO, SIDE B

———

HAVE A GREAT SUMMER!

JACKSON

—

OUTRO
Closer to Fine

My backstage pass to the teachers' lounge had been one of many privileges the school silently revoked in the months following my infamous confession. I didn't miss the room in the slightest, but it was a decidedly more comfortable meeting place than Mrs. Stapler's office. The small unventilated box reeked of her lemon vanilla candle and it felt like I was sitting in a pie.

I cleared my throat. "I'd like to make this quick."

Mrs. Stapler looked up from her laptop. It had been some time since she'd called me in for a meeting. I'd become far less useful to her since the winter, and the change in her attitude was obvious. I was no longer her man on the inside. I was no longer class president. We were a month out from summer vacation and I was just another student to her. Simply another problem in her day.

"Well. I'm sorry to keep you, Jackson." She placed a photo in front of me. A locker door. Someone had vandalized it. If

I had to guess, I'd say they used a key. "Would you like to talk about this?"

I just stared at the picture. The locker door. The word so sloppily carved.

F A G

"I think it speaks for itself."

Mrs. Stapler shook her head. "You didn't report it. When it was just Sharpie, you didn't report it either. Why?"

I shrugged. "What's left to say?"

Her nail clicked on the photo. "I think you know who's doing this to you, Jackson. And I think you're covering for them."

"You're allowed to think that."

"Is it the same person you were covering for with the stop sign?"

I cocked my head to the side. Just a little. Because I guess I just didn't understand Mrs. Stapler's dog in this fight. She was more than happy to see me take a step back from every single club I led. She thought it was a good idea that I resign as president and cede my public duties to Bolu. She only ever spoke to me as if I somehow let her down and yet the woman still didn't believe my lie.

"I've said all I'm going to say about the stop sign, Mrs. Stapler. I'm almost done with my community service. If you have any more questions on the matter, you can talk to Officer Olowe."

I had no obligations to her. She had expected so much from me and dropped me as soon as I stepped out of line. At the end of her first year working at our school, I'd decided Mrs. Stapler was my least favorite kind of adult. Always asking for help and giving none in return.

I drummed on my knees. "Super-duper. You have fun out there."

I picked up my backpack, but she stopped me before I could get through the door. "We're having an assembly about the locker, Jackson. Yours isn't the only one getting vandalized and it needs to be addressed."

My nails dug into my backpack straps. I turned. "Sorry. Are you going to sit a class full of teenagers in a room and ask them who thinks Jackson Pasternak is gay? Open it up to the floor?"

Mrs. Stapler was already busying herself for her next meeting. "It will be an informational assembly about the long- and short-term effects of identity-based harassment in schools. Your locker will not be the only one discussed."

"But you do understand how that could be worse, right?"

She just kept sorting and resorting the papers on her desk. "This school year started with some real ugliness, Jackson, and we're still dealing with phone calls about the Cameron Ellis situation. The administration thinks a frank discussion about how you children treat each other will be good for the junior class. We've booked a speaker for it and everything."

I took a step forward. "But you understand how it might make things worse for *me*?"

She nodded, eyes anywhere else. "The administration believes the event will be beneficial to everyone. It's not just about you."

The administration. Delegating responsibility. Never taking a personal stance.

"If *us children* thought we could come talk to you about our problems? If we thought you would do *anything* to help us? Maybe we all could have had a better year. Maybe all of this could have been avoided if I thought you would help me."

Mrs. Stapler finally looked at me. "Maybe you just don't know how to be helped."

I grunted and left her office. I headed for the parking lot and passed my locker on the way out. The school had slapped a black piece of duct tape on the anonymous message, but it didn't help. Even through that thick shiny cover, the rest of the school could still read the word. The accusation. Matty Silva's latest reminder that he would not forget what I did. Even after Phil explained the whole story of the stop sign to him in their laundry room, Matty wouldn't stop. Maybe it was whatever respect he held for Phil, but Matty placed the whole blame on me. It started with Sharpie. **DUMB FUCK. RICH CUNT.** But this morning, I discovered Matty had up-graded to something a little more permanent. **F A G.** Carved into the metal.

I would be allowed to run for president again in the fall. My clubs have been begging me to come back since I took my break and the faculty advisors have always been open to me returning. My reputation has only improved among my peers now that they think I'm more than just a rule-following robot in a polo, by all signs I'm going to have a really great senior year. I'd even gotten some assurances that my Penn prospects aren't totally out the window just because I have a record. I'd been demoted from "shoo-in" but nobody needs to be a shoo-in at an Ivy League school. I wasn't locked out of my future. Not like it could've been for Phil. And maybe that's why Matty did it. Maybe he wanted to make sure I didn't get to walk away from all this so clean.

Phil was furious when he saw Matty's handiwork. Nearly broke his skateboard over his knee. He stormed right into homeroom and got in Matty's face. *"He helped you. He helped us. He fucking saved you."* I almost got between them before any fists could be thrown but Bash Villeda had beaten me to the punch. Always by Matty's side. Matty might have his rules against coming for Phil, but assholes like that would always have their defenses. Their circle of bros. Matty knew how to stay untouchable. But Phil still managed to get the last word. He spit it in Bash's face. *"Great friend you've got there."* Bash the Flash had nothing to say.

I walked into the parking lot and took off my sweatshirt. It had started getting hot this week and we were gearing up for another scorch of a summer. That's Jersey summers though. They begin and end with a heat wave. I was two steps across the hot pavement when I declined yet another call from **SCAM LIKELY**. They were only calling more frequently since the season started and I wondered which fundraiser the robo-voice was calling for this time.

"HONK!"

I jumped and caught my phone before it could smash onto the pavement. The lavender Mustang of Veronica DiSario stopped inches before flattening me. Alone with the top down, Ronny pulled down her giant sunglasses and screamed at me again. *"HONK HONK! RIGHT OF WAY!"*

I took a step back and she pulled up to me. Her radio was blaring "Cherry Lips (Go Baby)" by Garbage and she didn't consider turning it down for a single second. "Amazing coincidence. I was gonna text you, but I don't like texting you."

"Is your horn broken?"

"Half this car is broken." She pushed up her sunglasses. "I need Phil tonight. I know it's your day, but I just got new plates put on his drums and I need to see if he likes them before I throw out the boxes."

I threw on my backpack and nodded. "Okay. That's fine."

"You had him all last weekend, I think I'm being very fair."

"Ronny, I said it was fine. We were only gonna swim today, I'm sure he'll love the new plates."

"Okay. Good."

"...Good."

We stayed there for a moment, listening to her stereo. Usually, Ronny loved to peel off in the middle of conversations to make a point, but she seemed to want to say something more. A rarity as of late. She didn't want to scissors kick my intestines anymore but Ronny never really forgave me for the Excel incident. Brynn might have gotten most of the school thinking that Twitter account was just another cruelty caused by social pariah Cameron Ellis, but Ronny wasn't so quick to forget. She understood the leak wasn't my fault and she knew it was unfair of her, but she just couldn't get over my part in it. That I would keep a log of her secrets like that. That was why we didn't hang out much anymore. And why we had to schedule Phil's weekends like two divorced parents.

She rubbed an ache in her neck. "I have to get to lacrosse."

"Alright. Am I keeping you?"

"Fuck off." Ronny sighed and looked up at me. "I'm sorry about your locker, Jackson. That's not right."

It looked like her civility was taking a lot out of her so I let her off the hook. "Yeah. Well. What's left to say?"

Her sunglasses might've taken up half her face, but I could see Ronny's *What the fuck is wrong with you?* squint from behind a lead wall. "That's a very weird reaction to have to this, Pasternak."

"It's my life, Veronica, I get to have whatever reaction I want."

"Well, fuck my ass for trying to sympathize." She put her car into Drive. "Don't get too hot out here, Mr. President. You'll overheat your CPU."

"Hardy-har—"

The Mustang peeled away, kicking up gravel and cutting

me off. I watched the vintage clunker tear around students and out onto the street. I wiped my face. I was only getting hotter. I got into my dad's car and cranked the AC. I had a food pickup ready for me on the other side of town and Mrs. Stapler had already kept me overtime. Phil was probably already at my house for our swim and Passy's pizza goes cold the second it leaves the oven. But I needed to cool down. Let the sweat dry off my back. Let Mrs. Stapler and Ronny dry off me as I drove over to Passy's and picked up our lake pizza.

Since I started going to therapy again, Dr. DerHagopian had commended me for my progress with the Veronica situation. We'd realized in our first month together that I have a very hard time accepting when people don't like me. And I had to accept that Ronny simply didn't. She doesn't owe me forgiveness. Some ends aren't as tidy as "forgive and forget" and I needed to learn to live with them. Loose threads. Unmet potential. Unsatisfying endings. Ronny didn't want to be my friend and that was alright. I had enough.

My spring of self-care had certainly yielded some nice results. I had a lot more time on my hands and I was crying way less. No more meltdowns. No more jumping out of windows. My life was far steadier than it was this time last and I appreciated that. But while stepping back from my clubs and my presidency had afforded me more space to work on myself, I couldn't ignore that little bitter seed. Because I used to think my clubs and my projects and my school would fall apart without their Jackson-shaped support beam. I thought my impact was vital and necessary. But the transfer of power had been smooth. The dozens of vice presidents across my clubs had stepped up and taken the reins. Bolu stepped in as student body president and nothing caught on fire. Nothing fell apart without me and no one dropped the ball. The hole I left in my social calendar was easily filled and it got me questioning if anything I did ever mattered. Was anything I had going on really all that important? If my role in this world could be replaced by a few underclassmen and the occasional training email, how vital could I have actually been? How special was I? What did I really bring to the table? Who had I helped?

"Crap."

I hadn't even gotten halfway up my driveway, but I needed to stop the car. I closed my eyes and rested my head on the steering wheel. I wasn't cooling down. Because who had I helped? What was my point? Was I ever really there?

"Come on."

I took a long breath and reminded myself what Dr. Der-Hagopian had told me about my detaching. Strategies I could use to tether myself. Reminders I could vocalize and people I could focus on.

"You helped Dani Touscani record her audition for summer stock. She was nervous about her song choice so we rented *The Music Man* and watched it with her parents. You helped Augie Horton rework his college essay. You let him read all your practice ones, even the terrible one you wrote for Brown, and his third draft showed a lot of improvement. That made... He was really proud of himself."

I rubbed my forehead along the leather of the steering wheel. "You helped Sandro Miceli leave a school event he felt trapped in. He was uncomfortable and people were being unfair to him and you helped Sandro get home. He really appreciated it. You really helped him out. You didn't... You didn't need to do that."

I felt myself come back to earth. Back into my seat and back in my life. Easy does it.

I looked out of the window and saw Bolu and Molly by

the lake. Bolu must've taken my advice and bailed on volley-ball practice. They were both in their swimsuits and chucking buckets of water at Phil, still fully clothed on the dock. I smiled. I wanted to join. I wanted to throw Phil into the lake and put him on my shoulders and dry off on the dock together. Tan on the wood and kiss with sun in our eyes.

But I would have to get out of the car to do that. And I would have to ask Molly and Bolu to go inside. We could be best friends all we wanted, but we couldn't be together like that in front of people. I couldn't. And I had no strategies from my therapist on how to work through that. I had no idea how to untangle the contradictions of my want. All my inconsistencies. Did I want Ronny to be my friend or did I need everyone to like me? Did I want a bulletproof résumé of clubs and medals for Penn or did I like everyone to need me? I wanted to stop feeling broken, but I've never told a single therapist about how scared I am of my own brain. How I think. I wanted to show the world how amazing Phil was, but I couldn't even tell Dr. D that I'm in love. I wanted to find the words, but I've never tried to say them. Inconsistencies.

My phone buzzed in my hand and I read the name. **SCAM LIKELY.** I stared at the lake and answered the robocall.

"Hello. This is Amber from the Philadelphia Jewish Community Center. Please listen to this important message about your donation, JACKSON PASTERNAK. Last year, we received a total of—"

"I'm gay." My face twisted. I looked down. "I'm… I'm gay. I'm in love with my friend, Phil. I'm really in love with him. And I'm… I think I'm really gay."

The robocall had paused. I couldn't stop. "I don't know why I can't say it. I don't know what the fuck is wrong with me. I have… I have such a good life. I have such nice parents, I know they love me. I know they'd love me no matter what. I know they probably know."

I started to cry. "And I still... I can't. I can't tell anyone. I can't even tell Phil. He's so patient with me and he knows I'm gonna get there, but what am I waiting for? Why is it so f-fucking hard?" I covered my face. "I want to be in love. I want to love Phil. I want to be fucking happy, but I don't..." It fought through my lips. *"I don't want to be gay. I don't want another thing wrong with me."*

The words calmed me down. Because I finally said them out loud. The ugly, difficult words. I finally cooled down.

"I know... I know I'm not supposed to say that. I know I won't mean it one day. I know I'll probably regret thinking it one day. But..." I wiped my face. "I really... I really just needed to say it. I just needed to fucking tell someone that."

I listened to the other end of the line. **SCAM LIKELY** was leaving me hanging.

"Hello. This is Amber from the Philadelphia Jewish Community Center. Please listen to this important message about your donation—"

I hung up the phone. Dropped it on my stack of pizzas. Felt the air return to me and leaned back in my seat.

"Okay."

My breath was still stuttering. I was still finding myself. My eyes landed on themselves in the rearview mirror. Not bloodshot. Just a little pink. I sniffed.

"Okay."

I nodded for myself. I didn't need to say it again.

"You... You said it. Okay."

I smiled. Because I said it. I finally said it. Out loud.

Was that coming out? Did I just come out?

"You came out to a robot."

Maybe the next one would be easier. Maybe Dr. D. Maybe

Phil tonight. Maybe our Roomba, I don't know. Maybe it got easier each time. Maybe that was as hard as it was ever going to be.

I patted my phone. "Thank you, Amber."

I looked out at the lake. Maman dirty in her garden. My dad drawing her from his chair. Molly sunning on the dock and my friends playing ball in the water. Bolu and Phil. Old and new. All these people. These people waiting for me. Bolu sitting in a floater and Phil trying to flip him. His long black hair clinging to his back. The gym shorts he always preferred to trunks. The shitty stick-and-poke arm tattoo I'd given him last month. A little smiley face. There for anyone to see. The smile I gave Phil Reyno. The smiles he gives me back. My best friend. My blood brother. My Phil.

I was lucky. I was lucky for every part of me. Even the complicated parts. The inconsistent ones. The ones I knew I would figure out. I was smart like that. I was lucky like that. I was lucky for every part of my life. Everything on my list. Every contradiction. Everything.

Phil smiled at me from across the water. And I smiled back. Because I was here. I existed. I mattered. And how lucky that was.

How did I get so lucky?

PHIL

——

OUTRO

I'm Only Happy When It Rains

I turned off my belt sander and slid off my safety goggles. I'd never worn rubber gloves when I used my equipment before, but it had been raining all morning and my storage unit wasn't exactly babyproof. But today was a necessary workday. I had the idea in a dream and couldn't sit still until I made it a reality.

In the dream, I had a band. Ronny and I were getting booked for gigs in the city and ragers in high school basements and we killed every night. Ronny on mic and me on the drums, surrounded by cellos and saxes and anyone we thought could keep up with us. And I had these sticks. These perfect drumsticks, made just for me.

This time last year, I'd broken my bank to buy five slabs of dark wood. A project to distract myself from the hate in my stomach. The loneliness of a summer. That wood became a table. And that table had become scraps. Those scraps became a dream and that dream had become drumsticks. A table, scraps, now drumsticks. All mine. Finally mine.

Ronny's holler howled across the weeds and rain. *"ARE WE DONE?! CAN WE LEAVE?!"*

I stepped out of my unit. Ronny was sitting in her dad's *Big Box of Divorce*, typing away on her laptop. I walked through the rain, wagging my new sticks along the way. "This is a very tough walnut. Couldn't break these if I tried."

"And I do hope you try."

Ronny had her big headphones on, face inches from her screen. With summer break so close, she'd gotten into a big DJ kick. The DiSario Ragers summer series was some of Ronny's best work and she loved to bring a new batch of playlists and mixes to each party.

I straddled Mr. DiSario's stuffed tiger. "I'm surprised I had enough material, honestly."

"It's two drumsticks, how much wood do you need?"

"Well, I was working with the mutilated remains of the Cameron table."

"Mmm. Very practical use of your baggage." She pulled down her headphones. "Hey, how's this sound?"

Ronny pulled the jack and hit Play. A mashup of "Venus" by Lady Gaga and "Venus" by Bananarama crashed out of her speakers. We sat in it for a bit, trying to decide if the marriage worked.

"Is the playlist all songs with the same name?"

"It's for Flop Party. All the songs are off albums that flopped. Justice for Artpop."

"Mmm. I'm not that kind of gay."

Ronny closed her laptop and got packed up to leave. She grabbed a drumstick off the desk and sniffed the wood. "I've gotta get home. Feel free to fashion me a sensible pair of clogs with this desk."

"Do you actually want them? I love a challenge." I played

with the stuffed tiger's ears. "What's going on at home? Your mom around?"

Ron threw up her hood and checked the rain. "She gets back Sunday. Got flown out to Brussels all last-minute. She'll be back for her birthday though, we're gonna cook a big dinner together."

"Does she cook? 'Cause you don't cook."

"Fuck you, I can cook."

"Veronica, I watched you microwave a turkey on Thanksgiving."

"I'm not having this argument again. You can cook bacon in the microwave, why would other meats be different?" I dismounted Tony the Tiger and joined her by the rainy unit edge. She sighed. "But we'll probably just order in. If she shows."

I nodded. Ronny's been telling me more about her home life these past few months. And I do mean months. I am statistically her closest friend in the entire world and I still can't get more details about her family other than *They're fun* and *They travel.* She treated her parents like some secret and I've been obsessed with figuring them out. Because we have been hanging out every other day since the fall and I've still only seen her mom a handful of times. Her dad only once through a car window. They feel like the adults on some old kids' cartoon where you only ever see their legs or hear their voices from the other room.

"Is Bolu invited to the girls' night in?"

Ronny rolled her eyes. "We haven't reached *Meet Each Other's Parents* in the boyfriend rankings just yet. Which is fine. Not exactly sprinting to have dinner with a cop."

"Plus, that would require your parents to stay in one place for a night."

Her rolling eyes landed on me. "I know what you're doing, Philip."

"Me? I'm waiting for the rain to stop."

"Your clumsy attempts at getting to know me have not gone unnoticed, Reyno. You wanna come over later and jam? I just got the keys for the new Hiatus Kaiyote."

I got distracted by my phone. I had missed messages from him. Pictures.

J: *Where are you?!*

J: **Got caught in the rain!!**

J: ***picture attached***

Jackson had taken a picture of himself on his scull. His little one-manned boat was in the middle of Plum Lake and he was shirtless in the mist. The rain must not have hit the Orchard hard that afternoon and Jackson looked happy. Relaxed. Serene.

P: **titties lookin real good**

P: **<3**

I looked up at Ronny. "Right. Fun fact, Brynn Forester is apparently quite good at the guitar. Been playing since she was—"

"NO." Ronny grimaced at the third head I'd apparently grown. "I am not inviting Brynn fucking Forester to my garage, Philip, who are you?"

I shrugged. "Brynn's…alright. And if she was playing the guitar, she wouldn't be talking. We can't just play drums and keyboards at each other forever, Ron."

"So, *you* learn the guitar."

"I play the drums! My skills are way harder to find, *you* learn the guitar!"

"I don't want calluses!"

We peeked out of the unit. The rain was letting up a bit so we buckled down and sprinted across the field.

"Well, so far it's either calloused hands or Brynn Forester!"

"Phil, I would sooner lose my hands!"

We laughed along the wet grass, brainstorming recruitment strategies to get us closer to our newest scheme. It wasn't as deep as revenge on an ex, but we found it got us equally as passionate.

Ronny DiSario and I were going to start a band.

The Mustang was no longer drivable in the rain so we hopped in my mom's car and zoomed across town, windshield wipers at full speed. The downpour eased up around Main Street and we caught the red light. To my right, the dress shop my mom's been working part-time at lately. To my left, Brewster's. I hadn't stepped foot in the place since the fall. Sort of made a rule with myself. Augie tells me I'm not missing much, but Brynn can't seem to let it go. They've invited me out to dinner a few times now to different restaurants with more understandable menu options and I've enjoyed our time together. In doses. With Jackson doing the talking and my meal getting comped. But I had no interest in giving Brewster's a second chance. That wasn't my territory.

Cameron and I hadn't spoken since the night of the Snow Globe Ball and we had no reason to. Even if I wanted to know what his life was like nowadays, it had become a lot harder to find out. He'd deleted his blog. Taken down his videos and deactivated all social media. If the internet's *Fuck Phil Reyno* hate train seemed extreme, the fall of Cameron Ellis was biblical. In a way, Cameron had gotten exactly what he wanted. He had a video bigger than the ***Brave Kid Comes Out at Winter Dance***. Cameron finally had the world's attention again and they saw him at his worst. After the world saw Brynn's video, the wannabe actor having his moment on the theater stage, Cameron had trended for the rest of winter. But calling Brynn Forester a cunt and Augie Horton a whale weren't the straws that broke Cameron's back. No. Cameron only started to apologize when the think pieces and Twitter threads started rolling in. Discourse and commentary and *What this says about the community?* The internet had spoken. Cameron Ellis was bad representation.

I dropped Ronny off in the Orchard with promises to jam later and rolled the quick mile to that front lawn. I parked where I always did and found him out on the dock. The rain had seemed to stop the second I crossed Orchard lines. Like the weather just couldn't afford the rent. The shirtless rower had his single-man scull docked and was checking his knot, sitting on the edge with his bare feet in the water.

I pulled my waistband down and whistled at him. "Hey! Brought you a post-row snack!"

Jackson perked up and looked my way. He saw me wagging my pubes at him and sighed. "Bushing is very last year, Phil."

I waved him off and dropped my CVS bag next to him. Kicked off my boots and joined him in the water. I scratched his big, bare back. "I finished the drumsticks. And Veronica says hi."

"I don't believe you."

"They're in the car, they're my perfect babies."

"No, I don't believe Ronny said hi."

I snorted. His hands tightened around the ropes, fingers covered in Band-Aids. The rowing season had only begun a few weeks ago, but Jackson was already mostly all calloused up. It was going to take some getting used to, my favorite hands in the world going through their annual metamorphosis. Every spring into summer, watching those soft, beautiful things get hard and cracked, all in the name of gripping an oar.

"Did you get the stuff? My parents are in Philly till late."

"Molly around?"

"Yeah, but she doesn't give a shit."

We rooted through my shopping bag. "Went to the CVS in Cinnaminson, they had more selection. I could only find one of those weird long lighters but everything— Oh, that's for you."

Jackson gasped and immediately cracked into the can of Diet Ginger Ale. I pulled out the travel sewing kit I'd found in aisle five. Jackson paused his chug and burped. "Finally sewing all your sleeves back on?"

I chucked the spools back into the bag and pulled out the tiny needle. Inspected it closely. "This will do nicely."

Jackson popped open the rubbing alcohol and started rubbing some on his right ear. I was surprised. "Oh. Oh, shit, now? Here?"

"No time like the present."

"Well, damn. I thought I'd be talking you into it till three in the morning. Like last time."

Jackson put the bottle back in the bag and opened our new lighter. "Dr. D said I should work on trusting my decisions. Not double- and quadruple-checking myself as much. So, next session, when he sees I have committed to the decision of piercing my ear, he will say *Well done, Jackson, you are very good at therapy.*"

"Wow. You've got it all figured out, Pasternak." I giggled and kissed his shoulder.

Jackson took my needle and started heating it under the flame. I sipped on his ginger ale and looked across the lake. The cool weather softening the afternoon. Jackson singing a song I didn't know. Me humming along to his melody, keeping up where I could. I watched a goose trot around the lake edge, tapping its feet along the mud.

"Does your therapist like me?"

Jackson snorted. "I'm sure he thinks you're a fine boy, Philip."

"Not looking to breach confidentiality, man, I'm just curious."

"Do you need my therapist to like you, Phil?"

I laughed and played with his hair. Got a curly lock around my finger. "How does he *refer* to me?"

"What do you mean?"

I didn't really know what I meant. You don't ask a guy what he talks about in therapy, I'm pretty sure it's a rule. But Jackson had always been very open about their discussions and what he was working on and how he was learning about himself. I guess I just got curious. "He knows we're friends?"

"Of course."

"And…he knows we *weren't*?"

Jackson nodded, done with the lighter, and handed the hot needle back to me. "Do you wanna know if Dr. D knows what we are?"

I laughed and pulled my feet out of the water. Crossed my legs and inspected his ear closer. "I just wonder how he'd define it. Professionally."

I was sure, no matter how much or how little Jackson had told him, Dr. D must've had some clue there was something more happening between his client and his friend. It was as clear as it must be for Ronny. For Stanley and Marion. My mom and Charmaine. Everyone who saw us together had to know there was more. We might keep things nice and platonic at school, but best friends just don't look at each other that way. They don't talk about each other that way. They don't

say each other's names like we do. They don't. I've checked.
Maybe people were just being polite. Letting us pretend we're
fooling anyone. But I was okay with that. Jackson's glass closet
was his and his alone. I had no right or interest in rushing him.
We had time. I would give him as much time as he needed.

I rubbed Jackson's wet earlobe. Made a little dot with my
Sharpie. My hands were busy and my focus was set, but Jacks
had his hand moving around my side. Feeling up and down
my T-shirt.

"How do *you* define it?"

I shrugged, readying the needle. "You're my...you know."

"I know."

"I love you. You know that. You're my best friend. I love
your ass."

Jackson smiled. "Sure. But...do you love me like you love
Ronny? Or like you love Charmaine? Or a good chair? Boba?"

"I love you a whole bunch of ways, Jackson. I don't got a
better word for it."

"Sure. But what if you had to? Gun to your head."

I moved my attention from his ear to his face. Because I
wasn't the one between us who had trouble with labels. Jackson
Pasternak despised defining his connections with the world.

I smirked, holding up the needle. "...You're *stalling*."

"No, I am incredibly curious to hear you speak on our relationship, Philip."

"You're fucking stalling me, you little bitch baby!"

"I am not! I was simply picking up *your* line of questioning, you could pierce me whenever you wanted to. I just—"

"Fine."

I stuck the needle in his ear, sure not to stab myself in the
process. Jackson's yelp echoed across the lake. "AGH. Oh. Oh,

that's not so bad. The babies at that mall kiosk were being very dramatic."

I took the needle out and held the new hole tight. Jackson inspected the bloody needle while I cleaned up the war zone. "I'm gonna look so good."

"You will."

"Maman's gonna kill you."

"She'll have to catch me first."

I pulled out the temporary earring we'd picked up at the mall and clicked it into his earlobe. I leaned back and took in my effort. Jackson smiled big for me. "How'm I looking?"

I realized I was fighting the urge. And I realized I didn't need to do that anymore. I pulled Jackson close and kissed him. I put his hand in my hair and mine on his bare chest. I kissed his lips and his neck and a quickie on his ear.

"It looks sick, Jacksy."

"Sick."

He hugged me and I hugged him back. I smiled into his neck and we pulled apart. I put my feet back in the water and so did he. I laughed.

"That's the gay ear, you know. Not to get too middle school on you."

Jackson laughed back. It was softer though. "Oh. I forgot about that."

He watched his feet in the water. Tried to catch his reflection. The ripples would come and go but every few seconds, Jackson could get a good look of himself. The whole picture. A calm face looking back.

"I think it looks good. Like that." He nodded to himself. For himself. I nodded too. It was a small thing to say but an important one too. Another step down a path. A path I'd walked down years ago. An ending that got rushed for me. Jackson would not get rushed.

"I think so too, Jacks." And I would walk with him. I held his hand. "If I had to define it?" Jackson smiled at my face in the lake. Our hands, hanging off that dock. Our reflections, always moving. I smiled back. "Best friends. Best friends... with benefits."

Jackson snorted up a laugh and shoved me with his shoulder. "Don't you quote Alanis to me."

I laughed and shoved him back. "Sorry. I couldn't help it."

Jackson put his head on my shoulder, sure to not get any blood on my T-shirt. "It's all your fault."

Meeting Jackson Pasternak had been a series of definitions. The first morning I saw him, he was waiting in his foyer. His big eyes on me, bobbling around a bigger head. He was wearing these huge socks that ran up to his knees and he had on his old *Jurassic Park* tee. When I couldn't be bothered to come inside, he met me out on the swing. I was ready for comments about my hair or my clothes or all the reasons I felt like I didn't belong on a lawn so green. In a neighborhood so perfect. On a swing made for two. But Jackson said he was supposed to keep me entertained. I asked him if that meant he was funny and Jackson told me he had never told a joke his entire life. And I laughed. I laughed so fucking hard.

I never meant to laugh. I never meant to make a friend that day, I never meant to show him I could. But Jackson laughed with me. Sat with me. He asked me my name and he liked my Tennessee accent and I asked if he wanted some candy corn. And I never shared my candy corn. And when we finished my bag, he asked if I liked Xbox. One game turned into another and Jackson didn't need to ask if I could stay for dinner. We kept our first conversation going from the swing to his bedroom floor and we never took a moment to wonder if it made sense. How easy those hours had been. How much we had in common. I'd never been invited to a sleepover. But Jackson never asked. We just couldn't stop talking.

And when I woke up that night, in our fort on the floor and my hand on his face, I wondered what we'd talk about in the morning. I wondered what kind of toothpaste he smelled like and why he drooled so much. I wondered what his middle name was and if he rode a nice bike and where he liked to sit on the bus. I wanted to know. I wanted to know everything about that boy on the carpet with me. Did he know my tricks to stop crying? Did his parents look him in the eye when he messed up? Did he feel silly and ugly and small when he tried to act like the other boys and did he ever make rules with himself? Had we made the same rules? Had he been looking for someone like me? Maybe he could be friends with someone like me. I didn't know. I didn't know if Jackson would even like me when he woke up. I just knew he was like me. The second I saw him there. Standing in his lawn. I knew Jackson and I would be friends for a very long time.

I looked at the picture of us in that lake. His smiling face on the water. A piercing he never would have gotten if he hadn't met me. If we hadn't shared our secrets. If we never had that first sleepover. If we weren't the same. If we weren't so different.

I put my fingers on his piercing. A hug on his ear. Just to let him know. If he was ever unsure, if he was ever scared, I knew. I knew him.

"We are so loved."

I knew Jackson Pasternak.

★ ★ ★ ★ ★

ACKNOWLEDGMENTS

Thank you to everyone who got me to this exact moment.

Thank you to Bess, Brittany, and the fine folks at Inkyard Press for believing I could do this and taking care of me during these last few years.

Thank you, Carlie. You found me and you took me seriously. I'll spend the rest of my life making that up to you.

Thank you, Claire. I spent years getting my boys ready for school, but you made sure they were ready for the world.

And thank you to Jackson Pasternak. Philip Reyno. Sandro Miceli. Bash Villeda. You helped me say things I thought would always stay inside.

How did we get so lucky?